ONLY YOU

He pulled the jersey up and over her head. It flew across the room as she tumbled forward, giving him full access as she hovered above him, her hands planted firmly on his shoulders.

His mouth instantly opened, drawing her breast into the warmth therein. Her breath caught, held by the quickness of the physical intimacy. She shivered with delight. His tongue licked and savored the sweetness drawn by her passion. Her hips began to move, and her hands roamed freely over his chest. They delved deep into the abyss of their desire. Surging and riding the swell of their passion, he sucked, kissed, and caressed her, sending a shockwave of nerve endings dancing on edge.

OTHER BOOKS BY CELESTE O. NORFLEET

Only You

Celeste O. Norfleet

BET Publications, LLC
http://www.bet.com
http://www.arabesquebooks.com

ARABESQUE BOOKS are published by

BET Publications, LLC
c/o BET BOOKS
One BET Plaza
1900 W Place NE
Washington, DC 20018-1211

All Kensington Titles, Imprints, and Distributed Lines are available at special quantity discounts for bulk purchases for sales promotions, premiums, fund-raising, and educational or institutional use. Special book excerpts or customized printings can also be created to fit specific needs. For details, write or phone the office of the Kensington special sales manager: Kensington Publishing Corp., 850 Third Avenue, New York, NY 10022, attn: Special Sales Department, Phone: 1-800-221-2647.

First Printing: March 2005
10 9 8 7 6 5 4 3 2 1

Printed in the United States of America

To Fate and Fortune

ACKNOWLEDGMENTS

To Otis Johnson, my father, who first instilled the love of football; and to Andrew Stephenson and Charles "China" Smith, who took the time to answer dozens of my questions on sports, I thank you. Your patience and detailing helped me tremendously. To William "Butch" Mitchell, you're the best. And to Charles, for always pointing me in the right direction, for keeping me centered and focused, and for always being there when I needed it.

Chapter 1

It was a glorious day.

Oh my God, fire.

At the first faint smell of smoke, Prudence Washington ran.

Within seconds she burst through the large, cumbersome wooden doors into the enormous smoke-filled kitchen. Her dark brown eyes immediately widened in shock, then closed slightly, squinting from the sting of lingering fumes. The room was empty. "Where is everybody?" she called out loudly. No one was around to answer her.

Earsplitting buzzers resonated as she ran to open the industrial ovens and turn off the alarms. She grabbed the oven mitts and flung open the heavy glass doors. A blast of thick dark smoke blew into her face as she reached into the darkness and pulled out several trays of burnt rolls. Moving quickly, she dropped the trays onto the counter, then turned the exhaust fans on full blast. She opened the side windows and began fanning the remaining smoke from the room.

Then, with a broom handle, she frantically waved at the smoke detector mounted on the fifteen-foot ceilings. After three minutes of constant fanning, the blaring noise of the alarm finally stopped. The smoky air slowly dissipated, but the pungent scent of burnt rolls persisted. Prudence looked down at the four trays of charred bread that now resembled rows of charcoal briquettes. Angrily she threw the towels and oven mitts onto the countertop and with exasperation raked her fingers through her short curly locks. The room was empty, not a soul in sight. A frown of complete annoyance quickly furrowed her brow. "Where is everybody?" she said aloud to the empty room.

Prudence was completely confounded. Just forty-five minutes earlier the room had been bustling with activity. Twenty or so jubilant volunteers joked, laughed, and toiled diligently making last-minute preparations for the First Baptist Church Thanksgiving celebration.

This was the church's biggest holiday undertaking to date. Three hundred and seventy-five homeless people were expected to enjoy Thanksgiving dinner tomorrow afternoon. Although everything was on schedule and under control, Prudence didn't need any last-minute surprises.

She scanned the deserted area again, completing a full circle as she turned around. She spotted the only exit and the only logical explanation. Grumbling loudly, she threw her holiday apron down on top of the trays of burnt rolls and hurried to the rear door. As she pushed through the open pantry doors a loud boisterous din rose from outside. "Now what?" she muttered as she stepped out into the daylight.

As soon as she opened the heavy steel doors she stopped, stunned in disbelief. There, seated on the church's back steps, leaning across the iron handrail and scattered in the parking lot, were most of the volunteers along with a few hundred more people. "What in the world?" she began as the crowd roared again.

With the door wide open, she stood staring at the massive assembly. "Where did all these people come from?" she asked. The growing crowd cheered again. Then, as if it just suddenly appeared out of thin air, she spotted it, a shiny, ebony double-decker bus parked right in the center of the boisterous maelstrom.

How could she not have immediately noticed something that big and monstrous? Painted inkwell black, the bus glimmered and sparkled as if it had just been driven off the assembly line. A gleaming silver knight donning full metal armor, including a ten-foot lance, charged across the side surface of the bus on a massive steam-snorting steed. Twelve-inch letters in extra-bold type paraded across the top section proclaiming its equally massive inhabitants, the Philadelphia Knights.

The crowd roared again as Prudence slowly stepped out onto the cement steps and watched as one by one, huge men came out of the bus. She stood stunned for the next few moments, her mouth agape. She couldn't believe her eyes. The men were enormous. They were mountains with heads sitting on top of twenty-inch columnlike necks with chests exceeding forty-five inches. Their massive arms and legs, which resembled wooden barrels, were neatly pack-aged in business suits and casual slacks, silk shirts and expensive ties. "Oh Lord, professional athletes," Prudence groaned aloud. "Perfect, that's all I need today."

After a sleepless night and another disturbing crank call at work the day before, she was stressed to the point of screaming. On top of everything else her telephone had rung at two o'clock that morning. When she picked the receiver up, no one answered. But the eerie sound of someone breathing on the other end of the line got her out of bed double-checking and securing her condo's door and window locks. She'd crawled back into bed, turned off the telephone ringer, and stared up at the arched ceiling until she fell asleep just before dawn.

With all the attention, a loud roar from the crowd erupted as another name was announced and another mountainous man stepped out of the bus. He looked around at the large crowd in childlike awe, then care-fully descended and stood next to his teammates. Their fierce gladiatorlike prowess on the field belied their boy-ish grins and friendly smiles as the crowd favored them with more cheers and applause. Each man smiled easily and waved as the next in line descended the bus steps.

They strutted and pranced like peacocks to the loud music. The crowd clapped at the familiar tune, which was obviously played regularly at the football games. Prudence scoffed at the sideshow. *This is so not what I need right now.*

Reluctantly, she turned her attention to the anxious gathering. She recognized several television and radio station vans parked haphazardly along the side of the church building. An array of news and sports anchors talked animatedly into microphones, while jockeying for better positioning. Each reporter gained just a few feet at most. But every inch was precious as they impatiently waited for the bus's final passenger.

As if anticipating some miraculous arrival, everyone instinctively surged forward to get a better look at the bus's last occupant. The newsmen maneuvered as cameramen aimed their lenses at a single figure that appeared at the bus door. A collective silent gasp rolled over the eager crowd.

As soon as he stepped down into the doorway the crowded parking lot went wild. Screams, cheers, and whistles deafened everything within a fifty-foot radius. Prudence's young male volunteers whooped loudly while the young women volunteers giggled, pointed, and squealed with delight. The older men and women in the crowd applauded wildly as the chanting began. "Speed. Speed. Speed."

Prudence stood dumbfounded. This was the most outrageous spectacle she'd ever witnessed. It was as if the greatest man in history was about to descend to earth, here right before their eyes. The crowd's behavior was unprecedented yet oddly contagious. She stepped closer out of curiosity, unable to fathom the crowd's exuberance. Just how impressive could one man possibly be? she wondered. After all, he was just a man, wasn't he?

She held her breath as he stepped out from the shadows of the bus's interior. Unwittingly, a slow, satisfied sigh escaped her full lips. *Oh my God.* He wasn't just good looking. He was sledgehammer, toe-curling, knee-buckling gorgeous. He had the kind of face that made women ache and men extremely nervous. Without exaggeration, he was sheer magnificence in motion.

His smile was bright and charismatic as it lit up his perfectly chiseled face. No, she decided thoughtfully, he didn't just smile, he radiated. She returned the smile along with countless others. It was impossible not to. He grasped at the collar of the stylish black leather jacket that cloaked his broad shoulders and accentuated the intense richness of his honey-tanned complexion. Then, with the grace of a gazelle, he eased his lean muscular body away from the bus. Everything after that was a blur as the crowd surged forward and engulfed him.

Prudence leaned over to one of her female volunteers who was propped up on the side rail. "Who are all these people? And who is he?"

The young girl turned slowly, unwilling or unable to tear her eyes away from the man in the center of the storm of reporters and admirers. "Prudence Washington," she protested, stunned by the ridiculousness of the question. "You mean to tell me you have no idea who he is?" She pointed to the man in the center of the storm. "Where have you been for the past five months?"

The answer *hiding* came to mind, but she decided to just remain silent. Prudence bit her lower lip and looked away. The last thing she needed to hear was a lecture from a teenage football groupie. "I gather he's a football player along with the others," Prudence responded facetiously as the swarm of reporters began shouting questions at the men. The main question, as far as she was concerned, was, what were they doing here? And how soon would they be leaving?

By the time she said anything, the young volunteer had apparently lost interest. Prudence studied the girl's profile. Her eyes were glazed over in starstruck adoration. Prudence shook her head and eased farther down the steps, her eyes still riveted on the celebrity at the center of attention, who was apparently enjoying every minute of it.

A small opening appeared and Prudence took the opportunity to get another quick glance at the man surrounded by the media and fans. His smile, though easy and gracious, seemed more guarded than genuine. His voice was inaudible over the female shrieks and spirited cheers. Whatever his answers were made the crowd laugh enthusiastically several times. The few volunteers who were perched on the church's back steps moved closer to hear more clearly and to get a better look, as did the area home owners and bystanders. The steadily growing crowd laughed again.

"What's the big deal about this guy?" Prudence asked as she walked up beside another one of her women volunteers.

"The big deal is, that's Speed Hunter," she proclaimed breathlessly, sighing. Prudence remained unimpressed, so the young woman continued. "*The* Speed Hunter," she reiterated, "as in Michael 'The Speed' Hunter. He's unarguably the fastest man alive. He's been on the front page of every newspaper, sports, and men's magazine since he signed with the Philadelphia Knights this past March. They say he's going to single-handedly lead the team to the play-offs this season."

"I find that hard to believe," Prudence scoffed, unimpressed. "I'm sure it's a team effort."

"You obviously haven't seen him play," the woman replied.

Prudence shrugged, completely bewildered by the remark. No, she hadn't seen him play. As a matter of fact she hadn't seen much of anything. Lately she had avoided the newspapers and television news broadcasts like the plague. Being the lead story for weeks and largely responsible for the possible demise of her father's political career and her family's reputation had a tendency to do that. After the horrendous few months she'd had, the last thing she cared about was sports.

Gorgeous as he might be, she didn't need this, not today. This was the last day before the big dinner. The last thing she needed was a distraction, particularly one of this magnitude. She'd been in charge of planning the church's Thanksgiving dinner for a year now. This was the home stretch and the last thing she needed was a busload of NFL publicity hounds messing up her schedule.

She marched over to those assembled around the team. "I hate to break this up, guys, but we still have a lot of work to do." There was a collective "aw" as the volunteers began to move back toward the church's back doors. As soon as they stepped away, others from the neighborhood readily took their places.

Spotting several more volunteers, Prudence moved closer to the large gathering. One by one she tapped the shoulders of her helpers, encouraging them to return to their duties. Another round of laughter turned her attention to the central figure again.

His eyes, though hidden behind dark sunglasses, seemed to be focused in her direction. She grimaced in the bright sunlight at the odd feeling of being observed and scrutinized, then shrugged it off to her imagination, apparently on overdrive. Why in the world would this man be looking at her?

The rapid-fire questions continued. "So, Speed, what brings the team here, the day before the big game?" a female reporter asked, batting her lashes wildly. This time Prudence was close enough to hear his quick humble response.

"As a team leader and members of the community, we've come to help with this important event. Homelessness can happen to any one of us at any time. No one is immune." The crowd gave the appropriate deep sigh of compassion.

"Oh, brother," Prudence moaned as she cast her eyes to the heavens and tapped another shoulder and nodded to the church's back door. "This guy can really shovel it."

Moments later a second reporter yelled out, "Not you, Speed, at least not after that multimillion-dollar contract you signed in March, not to mention your three new endorsement deals and your new sneaker line." The crowd snickered and nodded in agreement.

Speed nodded his head and smiled appropriately with equal parts boyish charm and sincere modesty. "True, but all it takes is just one bad investment and one devastating hit and my football career is over." The crowd instantly switched sides and nodded in agreement.

He continued. "Yes, I've been extremely lucky and blessed with my career choices. But that doesn't mean I can turn my back on those less fortunate. Giving money is one thing, but giving of your time is quite another. Yes, even before the big game tomorrow."

Prudence continued winding through the crowd, then tapped the shoulder of another volunteer. He nodded knowingly and moved back toward the church steps. Another question was asked and answered with the same characteristic earnestness and self-assurance. *This guy is so full of it, he could use a great big slice of give-me-a-break cream pie,* Prudence thought as she eased farther into the crowd of fawning Speed-worshipers.

Unexpectedly, a bubbling giggle took her by surprise as a naughty stray thought entered her mind. The image of Speed Hunter's face covered with cream pie made her smile. Maybe this wasn't going to be such a bad day after all.

Chapter 2

Speed smiled. It was impossible not to. He'd been taken completely off guard, yet was utterly thankful for whatever it was that changed the frown into a smile worthy of an angel.

He'd noticed her as soon as he stepped through the door of the bus. She was impossible to miss as she burst through the back door of the church. She looked like an angel backlit by her halo of curls as she stormed through. Hellfire blazed in her eyes. She stood staring, frowning, clearly not impressed by his celebrity or the spectacle that surrounded him. But it was the cynical gleam in her eye that intrigued him.

Through darkened sunglasses, his eyes, catlike and quarterback quick, watched her every move. Each time she spoke to someone, tapped a shoulder, or nodded toward the church, he saw. Weaving in and out of the crowd, she continued her task as he watched.

When the press began directing questions to him and the crowd thickened, he'd lost her among the adoring faces. Then he spotted her again. She had weaved her way toward the bus, then begun heading back to the church's back door. He smiled, genuinely impressed. She was definitely more beautiful as she got closer.

After asking the last volunteer to return to the church, Prudence looked around one last time. The crowd had

gotten thicker since she'd been outside. Area residents
and neighborhood kids had begun coming over to the
parking lot. Delighted to finally have some semblance of
control again, Prudence started back toward the church.
She opted to skirt the perimeter instead of maneuvering
directly through the madness. Muffled, but distinct, she
stopped, hearing her name called.

The frightening thought of reporters harassing her
again sent a chill down her spine. After weeks of intru-
sions and invasive questions into her personal life, she
had finally found some measure of peace and the media
had found someone else on whom to focus their ardent
interest.

She froze and then looked around timidly. Seeing all
eyes directed toward the center of the impromptu press
conference, she turned and continued walking away,
only to be halted a second time by her name being
called again. "Ms. Washington?" She turned, frowned,
and then watched a tall, thin, wiry man in a jumbled in-
expensive suit and cheap shoes jog toward her.

"Ms. Washington?" he asked, removing his team cap.
She nodded silently, leery of his presence. "Ms. Washington, my name is Luther Phillips," he began,
extending his hand to shake.

She hesitated for a split second, eyeing his extended
hand suspiciously. He had the appearance of a sleazy used-
car salesman about to sell her a lemon of a deal. The
overzealous grin was a dead giveaway. Nobody was ever
that happy to meet or see someone for any reason. Instinctively she knew that whatever he wanted or needed
would take longer than she had time or patience for.

"How do you do, Mr. Phillips?" Prudence said automatically as she shook his hand. "How can I help you?"

"Actually, I've come to help you." He smiled with a familiar grin that made her immediately question her
sanity for stopping when he first called her name. "I'm
with the Philadelphia Knights public relations department. My office spoke to Pastor Rawlins yesterday

afternoon. He said it would be all right for the team to do a little volunteer work today."

Prudence's attention was momentarily distracted by riotous laughter and frenzied applause. She tilted her head, still amazed. The man and his teammates had the entire neighborhood captivated. Then, to her surprise, another fleeting feeling gripped her. She frowned and looked away with jaded astonishment. She could have sworn that the man in the center of the storm was actually smiling and looking in her direction. She shook her head and discounted the thought immediately. It was too ridiculously absurd to be true.

Luther Phillips was still staring and smiling like a proud parent when she turned back to their conversation. "That's our Speed," Luther stated proudly to her lack of expression. Suddenly taken aback by her severe grimace, Luther stammered to regain his composure. "Uh . . . as I was saying, the team would like to volunteer to help with today's proceedings. You know, help out in the kitchen, move boxes, things like that. I hope that's okay with you."

Prudence smiled graciously while inside she seethed and churned in anger. Living a large portion of her life in the spotlight of politics, she'd learned long ago to mask her true feelings behind a polite smile. All she needed was a useless group of spoiled, pampered professional athletes getting in the way.

"This is quite a surprise, Mr. Phillips," she said. "Of course we can always use every available hand to help prepare for tomorrow's dinner. I thank you for the offer, but as you can see—"

"Great!" His loud shout of delight was startling as he cut her off before she finished her statement. "Pastor Rawlins said you would be very receptive to our coming out this morning," Luther added, but failed to mention to Prudence that the pastor also suggested that he call first and speak to her before bringing the team on a bus and alerting the media.

"Really, is that what he said?" Prudence asked skeptically.

"Oh yes, definitely," Luther said as Prudence only half listened, making a mental note to speak with Pastor Rawlins. But she knew it would be a waste of time.

The Reverend Dr. Mark T. Rawlins, a product of the sixties Civil Rights Movement, believed in the power of the media. He was incorrigible when it came to publicity. Even if she did take him to task about not consulting her about the Knights' arrival, he'd have her eating out of his hand while reminding her that publicity was always the answer when it came to getting public support for a worthy cause.

Excluding her father and brothers, Pastor Rawlins was the most persistent and persuasive man she knew. He could talk a leopard into tithing his spots, the devil into singing solo in the church choir on Easter Sunday morning. She still couldn't believe the ease with which he'd persuaded her to chair the Thanksgiving dinner this year.

In the rectory study, sitting in an overstuffed red velvet chair, sipping peach peppermint tea, and eating homemade sugar cookies, Pastor Rawlins had begun. "Sister Washington," he said in his best South Carolina drawl, "God has answered my prayers. He has shown me the light, and that light"—he smiled brightly—"has fallen upon you."

Prudence had choked and coughed, sending sugar cookie crumbs flying into the air and down the front of her sweater. "What light?" she stammered, and asked after sipping hot tea and regaining control of her voice, "Exactly what light are you referring to, Pastor Rawlins?"

He looked heavenward. "The light that has told me that you, Sister Washington, will supervise next year's Thanksgiving dinner for the masses."

"I can't. I don't know how and I don't have time."

Closing his eyes in reverence, he nodded, adding, "Have faith and good courage." When he opened his eyes and looked at her, she actually believed that she could do it. He smiled in that fatherly way that made it pointless to resist. "Don't worry about the budget, don't worry about the money, don't worry about the extra mouths to feed. God will make a way. He's our rock and our salvation. He fed a multitude with just a few fish and loaves of bread. Have faith, child. He will see us through."

Three months later he cut her budget by 20 percent, invited two more shelters, and changed the menu to add a personal childhood favorite food. And if that weren't bad enough, now he'd approved this mass hysteria without even warning her.

Luther Phillips smiled brightly after finally finishing his long-winded monologue. ". . . Pastor Rawlins is a wonderful man, and on behalf of the entire Philadelphia Knights organization, we thank him, the congregation, and the church officers for giving us the opportunity to serve in any capacity you see fit." The ever-timely—and as far as he was concerned, extremely moving—speech was a stroke of genius. Luther beamed at his own brilliance.

Bored by the mindless speech that she only half listened to, Prudence just stood staring in utter disbelief. Luther immediately began walking, prompting her to follow, as he moved toward the church's back door.

"Wonderful, wonderful. Now, I was thinking," he began as he pulled out his small computerized schedule. "I'd like to get a photo of the team posing inside the church and milling around in the kitchen. Then, next, maybe a shot of Speed standing at a large pot stirring something, gravy or soup, whatever you have readily available, I'm not choosey."

Prudence stopped walking as Luther scrolled down his Palm list checking off his notes. "Oh, before I forget, if you can scare up one of those big white chef's hats, you know, the kind with the tall puff at the top, that would be fabulous."

Prudence began laughing at the audacity and absurdity of his requests.

"Let's see, what else?" Luther muttered to himself, continuing to click buttons with his stylus. "Here it is, I also need a photo of Speed passing a loaf of bread to one of the receivers across the room, sort of a Hail Mary type of thing. Then maybe a shot of him setting the dining tables with a homeless person looking on thankful, or a young kid would be better if you can spare one. After that, I'd like—"

Prudence was no longer amused. "Whoa, whoa, whoa, wait a minute. So that we completely understand each other, let me get this straight, you want to take posed photographs today, right now?" Luther nodded, giving her the *what's the problem?* innocent look she had always detested. "I thought you said that the team was here to volunteer to help with the dinner, not to have photo ops and interviews all day."

"Yes, oh yes, of course we fully intend to lend a helping hand. But the press can't stay all afternoon. So I thought we'd just get a few snapshots in before they left," he insisted as Prudence nodded skeptically. "I promise we'll do anything you say. Whatever you need done, just let us know. But first we'll just get the photos out of the way. It should take no more than an hour, maybe two at the most."

"You've got to be kidding." She threw her hands up in disgust. "That's it." Prudence's temper, simmering for the past twenty minutes, finally blew. She knew Luther Phillips's type—long on ideas and short on actually helping out, constantly blowing smoke and trying to pull the wool over everyone's eyes. After spending most of her life in the muddied political waters and working ten years in the retail fashion industry, she knew a con artist when she saw one.

"I have a better idea, Mr. Phillips. Why don't you take your bus and your players and go find someone else to help? There's too much to do to have . . ." She paused to consider the best diplomatic wording. "Your team and the press mingling around getting in the way."

A deep masculine voice boomed from behind her, "Are we to understand that you'd rather not accept our assistance?"

Prudence spun around and gazed up. His sunglasses were dark and his smile was perfectly practiced. Overwhelmed by the sheer power of his presence, she took a step back, then suddenly caught herself. She refused to be intimidated by an athlete. She turned back to Luther Phillips, completely ignoring the unwelcome intruder.

"If you and your team wish to help out, fine, that would be great. But don't use us as a photo opportunity. If that's the best you can do, then yes," she threw over her shoulder at the brawny figure she knew stood behind her, "I'd prefer you leave now. There's too much to do and we don't need our serious volunteers distracted by this media circus."

Stunned by the impertinence of her dismissal and refusing to be ignored, he moved in closer. "And how do you know we're not serious volunteers?" Speed asked. His smile had faded into a smirk behind the dark sunglasses. His stance was relaxed and easy as his thumbs were casually hooked on the belt loops of his jeans.

Prudence's temper grew shorter and shorter. She turned to Speed. "Let's just say I know the type."

Luther Phillips stepped back and slyly nodded to the team's cameraman, who began filming the couple immediately.

"And what type is that? We came here in good faith, intending to lend a hand and volunteer our valuable time, Ms. . . ."

Prudence winced at his implication. "Washington. Prudence Washington. And we are so grateful that you stepped down from your lofty perch to grace us with your presence," she added sarcastically. "But be assured, our time is just as valuable as yours, Mr. . . ."

"Hunter. Michael Hunter."

"Well, Mr. Hunter," she continued, "for your information, the majority of these volunteers have been here since six o'clock this morning. Others arrived at four or five o'clock. Not to mention, we've been working on this project for over eleven months. We, unlike some people, don't need the media around to do a job. We do it willingly, not for the glory or the thanks or to profit from the media attention. We do it because we care and it's the right thing to do. You"—she stepped closer and pointed her finger into his massive chest—"on the other hand, as evidenced by your flamboyant entrance and the ensuing media circus, seemingly volunteered for other purely selfish reasons." She rolled her head for emphasis.

"So as you can see, we don't have the luxury of indulging your publicity whims. Over 375 homeless people are invited here tomorrow afternoon, and they're expecting a pleasant Thanksgiving dinner. I, for one, do not intend to disappoint them. Now, if you'll excuse me, I have work to do." She turned on her heels and marched away.

By then several members of the media wandered over to where Speed and Prudence had openly sparred. Speed smiled his signature smirk as he watched the slow sexy sway of Prudence's hips as she took the cement steps two at a time.

The press immediately started in. "Speed, is Prudence Washington one of your new female friends?"

"Is Prudence Washington the new lady in your life, Speed?"

"A lovers' quarrel, Speed?"

"Speed, are you dating the mayor's daughter?"

"How long have the two of you been together?"

"Does your relationship have anything to do with the mayor's and McGee's stalled stadium talks?"

"Is your relationship with the mayor's daughter a publicity stunt for the reelection campaign?"

Speed ignored their remarks and watched Prudence disappear back into the church. The woman had fire, he concluded. He was furious with her boldness at first. But now he found himself more curious than angry.

Prudence Washington was the embodiment of contradiction. She had the divine face of an angel, the beguiling smile of a sprite, the intelligence of a Rhodes scholar, and a body designed for mortal sin. She was a paradox, and that fascinated him, often a difficult task. He smiled. Unyielding, and devouring everything in its path, her temper, once lit, could spark into a raging inferno. She definitely had fire.

It had been a long time since someone blessed him out so thoroughly. He didn't like it, and he definitely didn't like being dismissed.

Being relatively new to the city and spending most of his free time back home in Texas, he didn't know much about the city's politics, the mayor, or his family, but he decided that it was high time he learned more.

Chapter 3

Luther, as usual, was stuck between a rock and a hard place. A week ago he had been called into the owner's office and given explicit instructions to raise attendance to overflowing, or update his resume. He had no idea how he was even going to attempt that feat. The only thing he could think of was bringing the team to the people and garnering as much publicity as he could. So he had contacted every source he knew, and nothing big and publicity-friendly was going on in the city the day before the holiday except for the First Baptist Church's Thanksgiving dinner preparations.

So he'd made arrangement with the pastor to bring a few team members to help out. As he looked around at the crowd and the media, he knew that this wasn't nearly enough publicity. He needed something big, something that the whole city could be fascinated with. But what?

Now he was stuck putting a positive spin on this latest fiasco. He could just see the headlines: SPEED HUNTER GETS DUMPED ON BY MAYOR'S DAUGHTER. Then it hit him like a bolt of lightning. The mayor's daughter, Prudence Washington, had just gone through a very public breakup with Garrett Marshall. What if he spun a love triangle into the scenario?

Everybody knew that there had been some kind of cover-up that led to Garrett leaving town so suddenly. Everything about the situation had been just too perfect, and the big promised exposé on corruption in the mayor's office turned out to be just another political publicity stunt with the mayor coming out looking like a saint.

The question and possibility that both Speed Hunter and Garrett Marshall might have been involved with Prudence Washington was perfect. The potential was endless. Luther smiled, noting the interaction between the two. Did they know each other? He thought about it, then shook his head dismissively. It didn't matter. By the time he was finished, they would be walking down the aisle and he would have pulled off the public relations coup of the century.

He relaxed his stance and began to spin the situation to the media as only he could. If McGee wanted that stadium full, he'd have it. After all, they didn't call him "Skins" for nothing.

Rick Renault, accompanied by a few teammates, sauntered up next to Speed as Luther began answering more of the reporter's questions. His slow Louisiana drawl was unmistakable. "Looks like that sexy little spitfire really chewed you out, my brotha."

As expected, the remark drew chuckles from the others. Speed was still smiling behind the dark glasses.

"How's your chest, man?" Rick asked as he watched Speed gently rub at the spot where Prudence had just repeatedly poked. Speed's smile never faded.

Michael turned and eyed Rick suspiciously. He'd always been leery of his presumed offer of friendship, though Rick never gave him reason to mistrust him. The obvious situation that the two men were thrown into had to offer Rick some measure of jealousy.

Once touted as the greatest quarterback of his time, Rick now stood waiting in the wings as a second-string behind Speed. He was past his prime and spent just as much time on the injured reserve list as he did as backup quarterback.

"Forget her, man," Rick advised. "You don't have to take crap like that from some holier-than-thou churchgoing goodie-goodie. She's not worth it." Rick leaned in closer. "Now, what you need to do is hang out with me and my crew tonight. We'll introduce you to some real lovelies, ones who appreciate us, if you know what I mean."

"Sure," Michael said absently while glancing at the church's rear door. "One of these days I'm gonna take you up on that offer."

Rick began to walk away. "Come on, man. Let's blow this place. If they don't want us here, I say we leave." Several other players began to slowly drift toward Rick.

"You guys go ahead if you want," Michael said. "I'm staying. I came to do a job and I intend to do it. This isn't about Ms. Washington. It's about the people who need us." Michael began walking toward the back door of the church. Several players turned and followed his lead.

Rick stood with his beefy hands on his narrow hips. His eyes blazed, revealing the volatile temper that always seethed just below the surface of his cool, calm facade. Then, just as quickly, he smiled, shook his head, and followed the rest of the players into the church.

"Ms. Prudence Washington, I am appalled." Prudence kept walking as her childhood friend Whitney Barnes hurried to catch up and walk beside her. "I can't believe you just did that," she said as she followed Prudence back into the kitchen. "You actually pointed your pushy little finger into that man's chest and laid him out. Are you nuts? Half the single women in this country, let alone the city, are dying to get next to him and here you go kicking him out of here. I repeat, are you nuts?"

"Not now, Whitney," Prudence said as she continued walking.

Whitney sucked her teeth and followed. "I have a feeling that kicking the Philadelphia Knights football team to the curb on live television wasn't exactly a good idea,"

Whitney said, ignoring her friend's dismissal. "I don't know, girl, what would Pastor Rawlins say about you kicking out free publicity?"

Prudence slowed her pace as she arrived in the bustling kitchen, which was now completely cleared of any remnants of the earlier smoke-filled disaster.

Prudence shot Whitney a stern look that she completely ignored. Whitney, an on-air television personality, did a morning talk show on women's issues called *Foresight*.

"For that matter," Whitney continued, "what would your parents say?"

Prudence froze. She hadn't thought of that.

Still too angry to respond, Prudence glared at her friend before stomping over to the side table. "If they hadn't made me so mad," she reasoned aloud, "none of this would ever have happened."

She picked up an Idaho potato from the huge mound and began peeling frantically. Good old-fashioned hard work always cured her desire to punch something or somebody, in this case, Michael Hunter. "How dare that overgrown juvenile come here and just disregard everything we've done for a few photos?" she mumbled to herself as Whitney glanced at the man slowly walking up behind her. "Like his time is more valuable than everybody else's. Who does he think he is?" She continued mumbling and complaining.

"Michael J. Hunter," he said, now standing just behind her.

Prudence stiffened and held her breath. She was completely surprised when she instantly recognized the very distinctive voice behind her. She never expected him to come inside. A smooth, honey-toned arm leaned around her and across the table toward the large pile of potatoes. She watched as his hand gently grasped the spud, then pulled back. She stiffened again as he moved closer and reached around the other side of her waist and picked up a peeler. "You don't mind if I peel a few pota-

toes, do you?" he whispered into her ear while already
putting peeler to potato.

His deep, penetrating voice and rich spicy cologne
shot right through her. Prudence closed her eyes, leaned
to the side, and swallowed hard. Her suddenly parched
throat felt as dry as the Mojave Desert. "By all means,
help yourself," she managed to answer stiffly, then slowly
moved toward the other side of the room.

Within a few minutes a number of volunteers worked
their way over to the table to begin peeling potatoes
alongside Speed. Brief introductions were made and the
work continued amid talking and laughter.

It wasn't until Prudence looked up from her overstuffed clipboard that she realized she was surrounded
by mountainous men all peeling miniature potatoes in
their enormous hands. She had to admit, these men
were dedicated and dutiful. Although she purposely
averted her attention from Michael, it was nearly impossible to keep up the pretense. Everywhere he went,
excitement followed.

The women volunteers attached themselves to Speed
like glue, eagerly offering single daughters, grand-
daughters, and nieces, while the men volunteers talked
football and sports. The kitchen and dining rooms were
abuzz with laughter and chatter, and as usual, Michael
Hunter was at the center of it all.

He, on the other hand, ignored most of it. He was too
busy. He couldn't take his eyes off of Prudence. He
watched closely, careful not to be too obvious. When she
moved across the kitchen to the other side of the room,
his eyes followed with interest. He nearly peeled his fingers along with the potato in his hand. Her body, slim,
womanly, but firm, gave him a number of ideas, all re-
quiring adult consent. When she walked, she swayed in
a hypnotic dreamlike way that had his mind whirling
with possibilities. Hips made for holding, legs long and
luscious for caressing, and her tight bottom firmly fitted
into jeans made his smile widen with inspired potential.

The sexy way she unconsciously twirled the curly hair at the nape of her neck sent a hot chill through his chest that then surged southward. She had style, a remarkable quality rarely seen in his opinion. Her subtle sexuality and mischievous glint held him captivated.

She moved around the room with authority, dispensing orders and offering suggestions like a seasoned professional. She was practiced, proficient, and calm amid frayed nerves and impossible expectations. With cool, even-tempered reserve, she smiled and nodded appropriately. Yet just beneath her reserved exterior, he sensed something more. There, just beneath the surface of her all too cool demeanor, he picked up on a heat, a fire, a seething blaze of passion bubbling very close to the surface.

It was in her eyes when she glanced in his direction. With a glimmer of awareness, his eyes met hers from across the room. Their eyes held, and a seductive promise was confirmed. It wasn't just him, she felt it too. And he knew that it scared her.

Prudence's heart pounded like a jackhammer on a rough patch of hard cement. She looked around nervously, wondering if anyone else realized what was happening. She knew that he sensed it too. The same inner turmoil that had gripped her was there in his eyes and in his cocky smile.

Feeling the sudden flush of heat spreading down, through, and across her body, she spun around quickly. It was getting too hot in here. So, she did what any mature female adult would do in this situation. She went shopping.

An hour later she returned with twenty-five packages of brown-and-serve rolls. She looked around, surprised that the past hour had been remarkably productive given the celebrity of some of the volunteers. True to their word, the players worked hard and took instructions well. Hours passed as a few players left and others came to take their place. Speed stayed the entire time, much to Prudence's unease and the other women's immense pleasure. He was cooperative, agreeable, and extremely helpful with his suggestions and comments. Although most of the players yielded to his lead, in most situations he conceded to Prudence.

When all of the players finally left, Prudence breathed easier for the first time since early that morning; having Speed in such close proximity was unsettling. She brushed this off as just anxiety, but Whitney noticed their quick intimate glances and told her so.

Distant but in close quarters, the two danced around each other like sparring partners. Speaking only when necessary, they tried miserably to ignore each other.

It was a long productive day and well worth it. Just after nine-thirty Prudence locked the church doors and stepped into the chilly night air. She looked around the empty parking lot. Her bright yellow antique 1965 Volkswagen Bug shone brightly under the many street and security lights. Driving home, her mind on automatic, she tuned the radio to her favorite music station.

After a few minutes Prudence found she wasn't in the mood for the usual symphony classics. She quickly surfed through country, hip-hop, R&B, easy listening, all-news, all-talk, sports, and adult contemporary. She finally settled on a smooth jazz station, letting the sexy soulful melodies of a rich tenor saxophone fill the night air.

Her mind wandered aimlessly, thinking through the events of the day, namely, the arrival of Michael Hunter. As the mellow sounds drifted, so did images of him in the kitchen peeling potatoes, slicing bread, and taking out trash. With all his arrogance and conceit, why did he have to be so good looking and so damned agreeable.

At the top of the hour, local news and weather headlined the late night updates before a series of commercials interrupted the night sounds. One ad after another of mindless babble promised a flavorful soda guaranteed to quench the mightiest thirst, or the latest sneaker that was guaranteed to make you jump higher and run faster. The last ad, a particularly rancid political commercial, drew her attention.

She knew the political game well enough. Nothing was ever personal. The attacks on family, friends, and associates came with the territory. No one and nothing was off-limits as far as some politicians were concerned. This, her father's mayoral reelection campaign, had gotten particularly ugly. Aside from the usual name-calling and mudslinging, the opponent had decided a direct attack was the best strategy to assure himself of victory at the polls.

Prudence listened, ashamed to be part of a system that condoned such vicious lies. The opponent, desperate and panicky, had been floundering miserably in recent polls, and had no doubt decided to pull out all the stops and ride roughshod over the truth. Prudence shook her head with a mixture of disgust and pity. Honor and integrity meant very little to some people.

Moments later the disk jockey's deep sultry voice introduced a series of upcoming songs for the late night lovers' hour. Prudence sighed absently as an old favorite began to play softly. As the first tune began to spin its web of romance, the announcer noted his well-wishes to the Philadelphia Knights football team and particularly to Speed Hunter. He jokingly talked about Speed's most recent female encounter that afternoon. Apparently the whole city was talking about it. Prudence immediately changed the station. She'd had quite enough of Michael Hunter for one day.

Five minutes later she arrived at her condo. After a nice hot shower, exhausted, she poured herself into bed by eleven o'clock in hopes of getting a few hours of sleep before the big day. But much to her dismay, she lay in her bed watching the darkened shadows and thinking about the one man everyone seemed to be talking about, Michael "Speed" Hunter.

Frustrated by her wayward thoughts, she punched the

pillow several times, rolled over, and finally slipped into a sound, comfortable sleep. Michael Hunter appeared in every dream.

Chapter 4

The red blinking message light caught her attention as she sat down at the vanity. She pushed the button and listened while fluffing her halo of tiny curls with the small brush and blow-dryer. There were two hang-ups and then her friend's voice blasted through the speaker. "Quick, turn on channel six news, you're not going to believe this."

Prudence stopped midbrush, switched off the dryer, and looked down at the machine. As usual she'd forgotten to turn the ringer back on. She frowned; the LCD showed twenty-seven messages. "That can't be right," she muttered. Assuming there was a malfunction, she erased the messages and prepared for the busy day ahead.

Dressed in comfortable jeans, a colorful loose-knit sweater, and a thick leather jacket, she stepped out into the darkness of predawn morning. The usual crisp chill of late November was in the morning air. She pulled the heavy knit cap down around her ears, her usually futile efforts to ward off a chill. Breathing wispy puffs of cold air, she felt happily invigorated. After a quick look around she hopped into her car and headed back to the church. Humming several popular tunes, she was ready for action. Today was the big day. And even the past few days of insanity couldn't dampen her mood.

She arrived just as the sun peeked out over the landscape of the church's trimmed front lawn. The sun's vibrance promised a beautiful day. She parked her car and hurried across the empty parking lot. The note on the church's back door instructed her to come to the rectory. Prudence pulled it off, and with dread headed down the steps toward the small garden path that led to the pastor's home.

On the path lined with colorful leaves from a century-old oak tree that shaded the rectory's wraparound porch, Prudence trod over the last remnants of summer's bloom. Winter was arriving with a vengeance. She shivered at the thought of snow, ice, and subfreezing temperatures. She was definitely not a cold-weather girl.

Having rung the bell, she stood at the rectory door, her mind awash with last-minute details. Then the reality of being summoned to the pastor's home hit her like a blast of arctic air. Before she could come up with a plausible excuse to avoid chairing next year's Thanksgiving dinner, the door swung open.

"Good morning, good morning." Pastor Rawlins beamed with his usual spark and liveliness. At the age of eighty-something, Pastor Rawlins was the epitome of good health and good cheer. His mind was as sharp as ever and just as quick. Dressed in a tattered old cardigan sweater, neatly pressed trousers, and a crisp white shirt and tie, he had all the trappings of a stately old grandfather. A beloved and cherished leader, he had recently buried his wife of sixty years and now lived in the church rectory with his youngest daughter and her family.

"Prudence," he said brightly. "Happy Thanksgiving. Come on in out of the cold," he instructed her.

"Good morning, Pastor, happy Thanksgiving." She smiled and kissed his leathery cheek as she passed into the warmth of the foyer. After taking off her jacket, Pastor Rawlins announced to his daughter that Prudence had arrived and that they were ready for coffee and biscuits in his office. Just then, the telephone rang in the pastor's study. Pastor Rawlins excused himself and hurried to answer it as Rachel Rawlins-Coleman walked into the living room to greet Prudence.

Rachel, seventeen years Prudence's senior, had her mother's smile and her father's good sense. She was pleasingly plump with a sense of humor that rivaled most stand-up comedians, and she had a pure rich soprano voice that could bring a Sunday morning congregation to its feet. She reached out and hugged Prudence warmly. "Good morning, Prudence, happy Thanksgiving," she greeted her dear friend.

"Good morning, Rachel, happy Thanksgiving." The two kissed each other's cheeks, their usual greeting.

"I know you're not looking forward to this weather changing. I hear it's gonna be a blast of winter coming any day now."

Prudence smiled and chuckled. "You know me, if I had my way, I'd live on the equator."

"I know that's right," Rachel said. "I hope all that's happened recently isn't driving you too crazy."

Prudence, presuming that Rachel was referring to the Thanksgiving dinner, shook her head. "Nothing I can't handle. It'll be over with by this evening, so I'll be fine."

"I presume that the press has been all over you as usual."

"Of course, you know I'm always their favorite target."

"I know. Ever since that Garrett Marshall thing." Rachel sucked her teeth and shook her head in disgust. "Who would have guessed that a man seemingly that nice was actually a bald-faced liar and conniving parasite?" Rachel looked at Prudence, frowned, and then sighed. "Oh, honey, I'm sorry. I just get so mad every time I think about that lowlife and what he tried to do to you and your family."

Prudence smiled weakly. "I know, and I'm okay with all that now. And you're right, ever since Garrett, the media can't wait to find something new so that they can get on my case."

"I still can't get over how that man used you just to further his career. But let's not get into all that again. It's over, he's gone, and I say good riddance to filthy trash."

She turned on hearing the teakettle whistle. "Go on into Daddy's office. I'll be right in with coffee, tea, and scones."

Prudence nodded and watched Rachel walk back to the kitchen. She tried to focus her thoughts, but it was futile. The bitter memory of Garrett Marshall sent an icy chill through her. She hadn't thought about Garrett in months. His betrayal of her affection still ran too deep.

The man she thought she'd be married to by now turned out to be the worst mistake of her life. He had almost cost her everything, her family's trust, her heart, and most importantly her self-confidence. There was no way she was going to open her heart up to another man like she did with Garrett. One mistake was enough as far as she was concerned. She had learned her lesson well.

She took her time walking over to the pastor's study. She looked around the comfortable home. The love and warmth that radiated from the surroundings were evident. This was a place of love, God's love. She felt cherished and sheltered just standing there. The living room, with its heavy-shaded lamps, was dark and cozy and boasted a beautiful old Steinway just beneath the staircase leading upstairs. Rachel, being the music director, could play the piano like a jazz musician, but had chosen to follow her mother's footsteps and play for the church choir.

Prudence knocked gently on the pastor's door, which was ajar. He'd just hung up the phone as she peeked inside. "Come in, come in, have a seat." He beckoned her inside as he sat down behind his well-organized desk.

Pastor Rawlins was a purist. No computers, no Palm Pilots, no television or DVD; not a single electronic gadget for him. No, he was a man of God and insisted that a sermon should always come from the Bible and not a Cracker Jack box. Hence, the bookcases lining the walls were filled with Bibles of every imaginable shape, size, and denomination.

"Pastor Rawlins," Prudence began, still standing,

afraid that this was going to turn into one of his hour-long chats. "I don't have a lot of time. I have several last-minute details to see to."

He leaned over to gently pat her hand while wiggling his finger at her with his other hand. "You have plenty of time for tea with an old friend. Now sit yourself down and be at ease."

Prudence moaned inwardly as she was swallowed up in the big comfy chair across from his desk. *Here it comes,* she warned herself, steeling her resolve to decline his request for her to head the committee again for next Thanksgiving Day dinner.

"Bet you think I'm gonna ask you to head the committee for next year's Thanksgiving dinner," he said with complete self-assurance.

Her face said it all. Her mouth dropped open as she feared he'd just read her mind.

He chuckled loudly, then pulled a crisp white handkerchief from his pocket and wiped his damp eyes. "Well, I'm not," he finally added, ending the suspense. "Calling you here this morning is just my way of thanking you for your wonderful devotion and enthusiasm. I've heard many wonderful reports about you, young lady."

The small tapping drew both their attentions to the direction of the study door. Beaming from ear to ear, with the face of her mother, Rachel stepped into the room carrying a tray piled high with breakfast treats.

Rachel set the tray down on the coffee table, then turned to retrieve a smaller tray carried by her youngest son, Jamal, a preteen, who at nearly six feet already towered over his mother. Jamal smiled slyly, then disappeared back into the living room. Rachel shook her head and remarked on the joy of motherhood and teenage boys. After setting the table just right she disappeared into the main house, closing the door behind her.

Prudence poured tea while Pastor Rawlins helped himself to a plate of biscuits, jam, and clotted cream. His white linen napkin tucked neatly into his shirt collar made her smile as usual, particularly since a small glob of cream adorned his chin. As soon as he sat down he went to work fussing and picking out the small currants baked into the scones. "That girl will drive me to the crazy house if she doesn't stop putting these things in my morning biscuits."

Prudence smiled. "I think that they're scones with currants."

"Same thing," he assured her. "Biscuits should be flour, yeast, and water, that's all. Just like my Hazel made them, God rest her soul. None of this fancy stuff," he said as he piled the last of the tiny raisins on the side of his plate. After a huge bite, he chewed with satisfaction, then looked up and began his talk.

Their chats, as he was fond of calling them, were pleasantly relaxing. Forgetting the time, Prudence laughed and delighted in the pastor's tale of his childhood, the turbulent sixties, and his courtship with his wife, Hazel. It wasn't until the chime rang out six times that she realized the lateness of the hour.

On her way out she hugged the dear older man, grateful for their time together. The anxious feeling she had had when she arrived at the church an hour earlier had completely vanished, replaced instead by a feeling of calm and joy.

The parking lot was by now partially filled with familiar cars. Prudence was late, but she didn't care. Her morning chat with Pastor Rawlins was just what she needed to be certain that everything would be perfect. He assured her that she'd done her best and the rest was in God's hands. A wonderful sense of calm made the smile on her face widen.

As soon as she stepped into the kitchen a joyous round of applause greeted her. Her mother, father, and three brothers had all showed up, joining the other volunteers to lend a last-minute helping hand. After a short pep talk, and words of encouragement, she assembled her troops and they continued the final preparations for the Thanksgiving dinner.

Delivery trucks arrived nonstop, dropping off donated food from catering companies and restaurants. Prudence stood at the back door checking off the many representatives and handing out charitable receipts.

Whitney eased by her side wearing a Cheshire cat smile. "Good morning, Ms. Prudence."

Prudence turned around. "Hey, you made it." She hugged her friend. "Thanks for coming. We can always use another pair of hands." She looked behind Whitney. "Where's Valerie?"

"With your brothers, where else? She nearly broke her neck trying to get out of the car as soon as she saw their cars parked in the lot."

"That sounds about right," Prudence added, knowing her friend as she did. Valerie Hall had had a crush on her brothers since the sixth grade. Deciding which one she wanted to be with had always been her biggest problem.

Prudence and Whitney watched as another large van backed up to the double doors. "Did you get my message last night?" Whitney asked.

"No, I got in late last night, but I heard it this morning. I think I'm going to have to buy a new answering machine. Mine has suddenly started going nuts. I had a few dozen messages this morning."

"Are you sure it's the machine?"

Prudence looked at her friend questioningly. "What was I supposed to see last night?" she asked.

Valerie smiled knowingly and began laughing. "You'll see. I e-mailed you a copy, download it," she said.

The van driver got out and opened the rear doors. Dozens of boxes of mouthwatering pumpkin pies greeted them. Valerie held her stomach as she peeked into the top box. "Umm, they look delicious. I knew I should have taken time to eat breakfast this morning." She grabbed a stack of boxed plastic-covered pies and disappeared into the back of the church. Soon an assembly line formed, passing pies down the line until reaching the dessert table in the dining hall.

By ten o'clock Thanksgiving morning everything was ready. The mouthwatering aroma of sliced roasted turkey and all the trimmings filled the dining hall. Prudence took one last look at her clipboard as she marched along surveying the kitchen countertops and tables, looking over the many foil-covered dishes. Everything was ready.

Industrial-sized pots held gallons of gravy, green beans, and sweet corn. Mounds of sliced turkey and ham rested on heavy trays. Mashed potatoes, cranberry sauce, and golden brown dinner rolls completed the massive meal.

By noon the serving team readied themselves as hordes of guests began arriving. Transportation provided by several city services brought men, women, and children to the church. Pastor Rawlins arrived just in time to say the blessing and be the first in line for a platter of food. After everyone was served firsts, seconds, and thirds, Prudence sat down to eat with her family and volunteers.

The Thanksgiving celebration was a complete success. By seven-thirty the cleanup committee shifted into full gear, making quick work of the few leftovers and mounds of trash. The local waste and disposal company, having volunteered its services, arrived just as the last trash bags were filled and hauled out to the parking lot dumpster.

When the last good-byes were sounded, Prudence looked around the cleared and empty kitchen. After months and months of planning, days of preparation, and hundreds of hours of hard work, the church's annual Thanksgiving dinner celebration was a resounding success. Elated with the day's outcome, a weary Prudence got into her antique yellow Bug with the vanity license plates and headed home.

The vivid fall foliage of the Benjamin Franklin Parkway added to her cheerful mood as she easily navigated the curves of Kelly Drive. She was invigorated when she rounded the Philadelphia Museum of Art and headed down Boat House Row. Painted treetops of yellow, red, and gold spread out before her as she maneuvered down the tight lanes along the Schuylkill River. Dusk had fallen. The sky was tinted a brilliant glowing red with purple and gold streaks for added glamour. Prudence smiled to herself greedily. All was right with the world.

She exited at Girard Avenue toward the Philadelphia Zoo, detoured by the late night traffic. As she glanced at the Lemon Hill basketball courts, she smiled warmly, seeing the familiar, lone player on the court under the overhead lights, cheered on by several spectators.

North Philadelphia had once been her grandparents' home, and the familiar streets welcomed her like an old friend. Driving through Fairmount Park, seeing the old homes, which were once nearly decayed ruins, now restored to their original grandeur, gave her a sense of renewed joy.

Seeing her father's revitalization plan in motion made her heart soar. For years the area had fallen on hard times, but now it was coming back in full bloom and she was proud that her family was part of that.

The steep hills of Manayunk were treacherous in winter, but in late fall they afforded her the perfect view of the splendor that was downtown Philadelphia and the city's Main Line. As the yellow Bug zipped along the streets with ease, Prudence felt a surge of energy.

She reached over and flipped on the radio to listen to her favorite sounds, but instead was stunned to hear her name bandied about by a caller.

"Well, I think Prudence Washington should apologize to Speed. Girlfriend or not, he came there to lend a hand, not to be harassed," a young female voice admonished strongly.

Prudence's mouth dropped open as she nearly ran

a stop sign. "What?" Just then the on-air DJ took another call.

"No way, girlfriend. I think Prudence should have read him the riot act. Some of these big-name athletes forget where they came from after they make it big. As his girlfriend, she had every right to be angry with him," another woman added.

Completely stunned, she slammed on the brakes, nearly missing the turn into her condominium's security gate. "What in the world is going on?" she said when she pulled into the garage parking. As soon as she reached home she grabbed the cordless, and phoned her mother and father.

"Dad, I just heard my name mentioned on the radio. What's going on?"

"Yes, we heard it too," her father said, failing to keep the disapproving tone out of his voice. "It's all over the local news tonight."

"What's on the local news?"

"Your behavior has drawn a number of questions," he said.

"What behavior? I haven't done anything," Prudence said defensively at hearing the disappointment and disapproval in his voice.

Blake Washington had always been the perfect father in the eyes of the media and the city-at-large. But at times his single-minded dedication to his career and the city overshadowed his own daughter.

As much as she loved and adored him, he had always seemed saddened that she hadn't become an attorney, and that she hadn't attached herself with the right families and hadn't dated or married the right man.

She, the only Washington daughter, was held to a different standard than her brothers. She had to walk an impossible line, to be a prim and proper young lady who was at all times placid and even-tempered. But it just wasn't her.

"Hold on, here's your mother," he finally said, exasperated.

Marian Washington was slightly more understanding. "Prudence, we know you're not one to publicly embarrass your father. But, dear, in the shadow of this particular campaign and on the heels of the Garrett Marshall situation, your timing couldn't have been worse."

"My timing for what? What's going on, what am I supposed to have done this time?"

Her mother continued. "I'm sure you did what you had to do and what you thought was right at the time."

"Mother, what are you talking about?" Prudence questioned, completely confused. But before Marian could reply, the other phone line interrupted. "Hold on, Mother, the other line is ringing." She clicked over. "Hello?"

"Ms. Washington?"

"Speaking," Prudence answered hurriedly.

"Ms. Washington, my name is Peter Hall. I'm with the *Philadelphia Sports Voice*. I'd like to set up a time to interview you about your relationship with Speed Hunter."

"My what?" The request caught her off guard.

"I'd like to interview you about your relationship with Speed Hunter. If you'd feel more comfortable having him there with you, that would be perfectly all right as well."

"I have no idea what you're talking about and I have a call on the other line. Good-bye."

She was prepared to hang up when Peter Hall quickly added, "Ms. Washington, just one more thing. In Speed's post-game interview this afternoon, he alluded to the fact that the two of you were involved romantically. Is there any truth to the rumor that you're the reason Speed accepted the offer to play in Philadelphia in the first place?"

"Look, Mr. Hall, I have no influence whatsoever on what Michael Hunter does and doesn't do, and for that matter I . . ." She paused briefly, thinking better of her next statement. "Good-bye, Mr. Hall."

"One more question, Ms. Washington," he insisted. "Did your father's position as mayor and your relationship with Speed Hunter influence Graham McGee's request for a tax-free stadium in any way? Were there any promises made, Ms. Washington?"

"Good-bye, Mr. Hall," she said firmly and clicked back over to her mother.

"That was some sports reporter. He wanted to do an interview with me about my relationship with Michael Hunter. Can you believe this madness? He even implied that Dad and Graham McGee have some kind of tax-free stadium deal going on."

"I'm not the least bit surprised," Marian offered. "Your father has been bombarded with calls since we got home an hour ago."

"Mom, I'm sorry. I had no idea," she said, exhausted, as she walked into her bedroom. "I just can't believe this mess. To tell you the truth I still don't know exactly what's going on."

"Prudence, what precisely happened between you and Mr. Hunter?"

"Nothing happened," Prudence promised. She relayed the events leading up to yesterday's misunderstanding, including the altercation she had with Speed Hunter. Her mother accepted the explanation silently. The other line beeped again. "Mother, I'm going to let you go. I'll talk to you tomorrow after work. I think I'm just going to take a long hot bath and crawl into bed. Good night." Prudence clicked over to the second line, not knowing what to expect. "Hello?"

"Hey, girl, you're a celebrity," Whitney's buoyant voice beamed through the receiver. "How's your love life?"

"Don't start with me, Whitney, this isn't funny. Mother and Dad are furious." The second line beeped.

"Is that your other line?"

"Ignore it." She kicked her shoes off and rubbed her throbbing feet as she sat down on the side of the bed.

"I don't know why you're getting all upset. At least you finally have a love life."

"Whitney, I don't have a love life. Remember me, too busy to be bothered? I don't have time to deal with the pressures of a relationship. But if I did, I certainly wouldn't choose another arrogant, selfish, conceited, knuckle-dragging Neanderthal like Michael Hunter." She systematically tossed the pillows that decorated her bed, while making her point.

Whitney chuckled during her friend's tirade. "Well, my dear, it looks like that's exactly what you have. Whether you like it or not, you and Speed Hunter are an item."

"Please. You know good and darn well I'm not seeing that pigheaded man."

"Well, apparently it doesn't matter what I think. Hell, it doesn't even matter what you think. The media say you're seeing Speed Hunter, so face it, doll, you're seeing Speed Hunter."

"That's the most ridiculous thing I've ever heard."

"Be that as it may, you'd better get used to it. You of all people know the power of the press. As far as the majority of Philadelphia is now concerned, Speed Hunter's the flavor of the month. And right now, my dear, you are his number-one topping."

"Thanks, Whitney, you have no idea how happy you've made me," Prudence said sarcastically.

"Hey, don't kill the messenger. I'm only saying what you know to be true. Think of it this way, with the recent nastiness on the political front, you should be lucky that's all the press is saying."

Prudence smirked sarcastically. "I guess you've got a point there. But somehow I don't consider myself lucky."

Her second line beeped through again. "Hold on, it's the other line again. It might be important." Without thinking, she automatically clicked over.

"Girl," Valerie drawled out in an extended tone, "you'd better hook a sister up."

"Don't you start," Prudence warned her friend. "I'm still in shock. I can't believe this mess."

"Who cares about your shock? You'd better hook your friend up."

"With what?"

Valerie blew at her wet nail polish. "Let's see, the defensive line. The offensive line. Special teams. Hell, I'll even take the second-string kicker at this point."

"I have to go, Val. Whitney's on the other line."

"Okay. Call me right back," Valerie said, just as Prudence disconnected.

"I'm back," she said, returning to Whitney. "That was Valerie."

"Have you downloaded the file yet?" Whitney asked.

"What file?"

"The file I sent you last night. I told you about it this morning, remember?"

"I forgot all about it. Hold on. I'll download it now." Prudence padded barefoot back into the living room to retrieve her laptop. She plugged it into the phone jack and the system sparked to life. After it filtered through, she found Whitney's e-mail and began downloading.

As soon as she picked up the phone the download was complete. "I'm back." She pushed the download icon. "It's about to begin, what's on it?"

"While you were gone, your second line beeped again."

"Ignore it. Okay, here it is." A blur of images appeared for the first few seconds; then suddenly she saw her face. She was glaring up at Speed Hunter with a deep frown etched on her face and her finger pointed at his chest. "Oh no!" she uttered, after a long humiliating sigh. She fell back onto the bed.

"Oh yeah." Whitney chuckled.

Although the camera seemed far away, there was no doubt that there was a heated disagreement taking place. The sports anchorman laughingly joked about witnessing a lovers' quarrel. The second line beeped again.

"I can't believe this. How can they say this was a lovers' quarrel? It doesn't even make sense."

"Girl, you know that it doesn't have to. As long as it sells newspapers and ups the ratings, that's all that matters. Listen, I've got to go. I'll talk to you tomorrow. Don't worry about all this, Pru. It'll all go away sooner or later."

"I'd prefer sooner than later. Bye." As Prudence hung up, the phone rang before she removed her hand. "Hello?"

"Ms. Washington, this is Bryce Howard from News Channel Six Sports. I'd like to ask you a few questions about Speed Hunter."

Prudence gathered her composure quickly and answered with the standard "no comment at this time." As soon as she replaced the receiver the phone rang again. It was another news personality asking for an interview. Again, she declined politely. The phone rang six more times before she decided to just let the machine get it. Unfortunately, when she looked over to the answering machine the message light showed forty-six messages. She erased them all, took a long hot shower, crawled into bed, and pulled the covers up over her head.

Chapter 5

Black Friday was by far the busiest retail-shopping day of the entire year. Department managers and store executives waited 365 days for the day after Thanksgiving, the traditional beginning of the holiday season. The shelves were packed, the merchandise was available, and the staff was ready.

Prudence knew she'd be busy when she arrived at five-thirty A.M. for the six o'clock store opening. As the head buyer for the women's fine-fashion department, she was also a floor manager and was expected to assist with signing credit slips, approving costly bank checks, and generally keeping order in her department and on her floor. Usually these tasks were annoying and time-consuming. But for the first time in ten years she didn't mind being on the floor and away from her office. Her desk was laden with messages and requests for interviews, flowers, cards, and much to her surprise, several marriage proposals.

The store security team's futile attempt to request that all media personnel refrain from disturbing their customers and staff was useless. By one o'clock the media circus became unbearable even after Prudence insisted she'd only respond if there were purchases made. Her department practically sold all the merchandise with pricey expense account purchases. An hour later, Prudence was called into the executive store manager's office.

"Business was even brisker than we expected," he announced, almost salivating with delight. "I have a feeling that's due mainly to interest in you and Speed Hunter." Gene Reynolds, the store's executive manager, was openly ecstatic. Prudence had never seen him so animated. As soon as she appeared, he had jumped up and made a mad dash toward her with his arms open wide.

"Prudence, thanks for stopping by. I know you're swamped, particularly today, but I need to get some information. First of all, is it true that Speed Hunter is picking you up from the store this evening? Because if he is, I need to make a few added security arrangements."

"Gene, of course it's not true, I barely even know the man."

Prudence walked into the office and sat where he motioned. He sat in the opposite chair, both facing his big oak desk. "Gene, believe me, there's nothing between me and Speed Hunter. The whole thing is one big misunderstanding."

Gene continued smiling. "Well, this misunderstanding is bringing ten times, no, twenty times more business than we expected. I just looked at the preliminary numbers." He gestured to the numerous spreadsheets littering his desk. "If business keeps up at this rate we're going to have to either close the front doors or start selling the wallpaper and carpeting off of the floor." He giddily laughed at his rare attempt at humor.

Prudence wasn't amused. "This whole thing has gotten way out of hand." She stood and began pacing, her arms locked tightly around her body. "I can't believe they're swarming around the store like this. You'd think they'd have a little consideration."

Gene shook his head sympathetically as he watched her pace his office floor. "I'll tell you what. Why don't you call it a day? You look exhausted. I'll sign you out myself." He stood and walked over to her. "Take the weekend. By Monday morning I'm sure all this will have been replaced by another news story and you'll be old news. No offense."

"None taken. Believe me, Gene, I just want this whole mess behind me."

Gene grasped her hand. "Monday morning, you'll see. It will be as if all this never happened."

Slightly comforted by his words, Prudence nodded and began moving to the door. "I really hope you're right, Gene."

"I am, you'll see. Are you scheduled to come in Saturday and Sunday?"

"No."

"Good, you'll have a nice long weekend. Take advantage of the time and get some rest."

"Thanks, Gene. I really appreciate this."

"Are you kidding? It's my pleasure," he said, practically beaming. It's the least I could do. We've never had this much free publicity. You're a godsend. Our fourth-quarter totals are going to be phenomenal."

Prudence walked out of Gene's office shaking her head. The expression on his face was positively giddy. The man was unbelievable. She was almost certain that she heard him dance a jig and kick up his heels as soon as she closed the door behind her.

Gene Reynolds was by no means a sympathetic man. He ate, slept, and drank retail. If company policy would allow it, Prudence was sure he'd have a bar code tattooed on his forehead. He'd do practically anything to keep the store profits in the black. But he was right about one thing, she could definitely use some rest after the hectic day yesterday and today's madness.

She went back to her office, straightened up her desk, packed her laptop, then slipped out the side door and headed home.

By the time the yellow Bug pulled up at her condominium building the place was swarming with reporters. Thankful that her car windows were rolled

up tightly, she skirted them easily by keeping her head
down and repeatedly mouthing, "No comment."

Prudence hurried to the safe refuge of her home and
secured the door behind her. For a while she just stood
there leaning against the wooden door, stunned by the
unexpected homecoming reception. She held her hand
over her still-racing heart as her mind spun. "Maybe if I
stay out of sight the rest of the weekend, this mess will
blow over quicker," she reasoned aloud. One thing she
knew for sure, there was no way she was going to risk
going back outside until this ridiculous misunderstanding was old news. Unfortunately, that meant missing an
important fund-raiser tonight and the mayor's fraternity
reception tomorrow night.

Thinking quickly, Prudence walked over to the living
room's picture window and closed the drapes, shield-
ing her from the media still clambering below. As soon
as she stepped in front of the window, she could see the
flashbulbs of reporters' cameras until the drapes were
completely closed. There was no other alternative. She
picked up the phone to make the call.

All she had to do was persuade her parents that in
light of the current predicament her presence tonight
and tomorrow night would not be beneficial to the campaign. It sounded plausible enough. But she knew her
parents too well. They'd never go for the coward's way
out. Still, she decided to give it a try.

Marian Washington was adamant. "Hiding from a
problem is not our family's way, Prudence. We do not
avoid conflict. We rise above it."

Her mother always had a way of making the worst
situations sound noble. "Mother, there are over a dozen
reporters in front of my building. There's no way to
rise above this mess except to stay in the rest of the
weekend. Hopefully by Monday morning all of this will
have blown over."

"Prudence, your father is expecting you to be there
tonight, and so am I. How will it look if the mayor's only

daughter doesn't show up? It is imperative that the whole family be in attendance. This is a very important event."

Prudence exhaled an exasperated breath. She knew this was a hopeless cause. There was no denying her mother once she got started. "Fine, Mother. I'll be there." She sat up and looked at the large walk-in closet and spotted the bright yellow evening dress she had bought just for tonight. "I'll be a little late, but I'll be there."

"Not too late, dear. We wouldn't want you to miss your father's speech. He's worked so hard on it."

"Yes, Mother. I'll see you there."

Four hours later Prudence sat in the midst of a political campaign fund-raiser. Speeches, promises, and praises were what the devoted supporters received for their 250-dollar-a-plate contribution. Everyone smiled for the cameras, posed with their favorite celebrity and politician, while delighting in the evening's atmosphere.

Prudence looked around the immense hotel ballroom. Sparkling holiday lights twinkled from the ceiling surrounded by balloons, crepe paper, and red, white, and blue bunting. Everyone looked to be having a wonderful time. The meal, of tasteless cardboard chicken, had been cleared away, the obligatory speeches were over, and the standard band had begun its opening number, a rendition of Tina Turner's "Proud Mary." Afterward they slipped into a medley of Barry Manilow tunes from the seventies.

Prudence found herself dancing several dances with her father's assistant, James Pruet, a tall, thin man with delusions of romance. He made a point of dancing with her at every available opportunity. His lisp made him comical, not because of his speech defect, but because he was prone to malapropisms that made the impediment even worse.

Having gotten the position through Prudence's and her mother's influence, he began as a lowly campaign envelope stuffer, then worked his way up to become virtually indispensable to her father's political campaign. Realizing his own limitations early on, he was completely satisfied to be behind the scenes and enjoy the lofty post of chief political adviser to the mayor's office.

Now holding her closer, James leaned in to whisper into her ear, "Have I told you how beautiful you look this evening?" His breath was scented with scotch and spearmint.

Prudence, in her high heels, easily stood equal to his five-foot-eight frame. She smiled politely, adding a thank-you while maneuvering several inches away from his grasp. With arms like tentacles, he was either innocently brushing against the side of her breast or fanning his fingers inappropriately down her lower back.

"So, James, how's my father's campaign going?" she asked, changing the subject to a less personal one.

"Fine, I predict he'll be reelected easily."

"I hope so. He's a wonderful mayor. The city has really prospered under his leadership. But I guess I don't have to sell you on my father and his success in running this city."

"You realize of course that your father has help. He doesn't do this alone. I play a crucial rule in this city's prosperity."

"Of course you do, James. And I know that my father is grateful and appreciative for everything you've done. He speaks very highly of you and considers you like another son." James smiled happily as Prudence patted herself on the back for her fawning insincerity.

At times James could be a live wire. His eagerness to succeed and his overly ambitious zeal to accomplish something had always been disproportionate to his talent. He wanted to own the world, but had no idea how.

"Have I told you how lovely you look this evening?"

"Yes, you have, and thank you again," she said.

"I hate to repeat myself, but you look beautiful this evening." He held her closer as his hand drifted down again. "I remember when we went out the last time and we—"

"I appreciate the compliment," Prudence said, cutting him off, fearing his next remark.

"That's not what I was going to say," he started.

"I think the evening turned out well, don't you?" She looked around and smiled pleasantly at the other guests on the dance floor.

"Prudence, we need to talk about us."

"James, there is no us. We're friends, and I hope we'll be friends for a long time. That's all, just friends."

"You know I want more than just friendship. You and I—"

"Have known each other for a long time," Prudence began in an attempt to dissuade him. "We've been through a lot together. Our families are close. As I said before, I don't want a personal relationship to ruin that closeness." She instantly felt his body tighten.

"I suppose he's more than a friend?"

"Who?" she asked.

James's lips tightened to a thin line at her feigned innocence. "You don't have to play the coy one with me. I've seen the reports. What does he have that I don't?"

"If I knew who you were talking about . . ."

James looked away in anger. "If this is about my problem, I assure you I'm over it. That's in the past."

"James, this has nothing to do with your . . ." She paused as another couple danced close, then smiled and moved away. "With your problem. And I'm delighted to hear that you've done something about it. The fact that I just don't feel what you want me to feel for you is the problem."

"I think you need to get your priorities straight. He's just another pretty boy with a bank account, same as your precious Garrett. And we all know how that turned out. Only this time you can get yourself out of trouble."

Her anger immediately began to boil to the surface. The fact that she was at a political function with her family did little to stem her anger. James was asking for it as far as she was concerned, and she intended to give him both barrels.

She opened her mouth to lash back at him when she noticed one of her father's biggest supporters smiling and waving to her as she danced nearby. Prudence returned the gesture, biting her tongue in the process. After what she'd done to her father's career recently, she refused to do more damage. *Patience*, she reminded herself, *patience*. She'd have another opportunity to rebuke James.

Relieved to finally hear the bandleader announce their first break, she quickly slipped from James's grip and headed toward the family table.

She had no idea what James was talking about. His annoyance with her was completely unfounded. They'd gone out a few times, but nothing ever developed other than a better understanding of his shortcomings. James had problems that he needed to resolve. She just hoped he could resolve them before he got himself into trouble again.

Seated at a round banquet table, three attractive men were discussing the soundness of investments in a fluctuating market and the consequences of investment banking online and day-trading strategies. Prudence joined in the discussion, disagreeing with any- and everything her brothers said.

Keith Washington, Prudence's oldest brother, had watched with great interest as a meticulously dressed man entered and carefully scanned the room. Eventually his eyes had settled on Prudence, who was still on the dance floor with James. The envious gleam in his eye was unmistakable.

Keith recognized Michael Hunter immediately, as did a number of other attendees. He was instantly surrounded. With curious interest Keith cocked his head, speculating about Speed's presence, and his very obvious attention toward his sister. The latest gossip implied that the two were more intimately acquainted, and not simply casual friends as was first reported. Keith grimaced. By the look on Speed's face upon seeing Prudence dancing with James, he was inclined to believe that the reports were, at least in some respects, true.

For fifteen minutes Michael Hunter mingled among the large crowd watching Prudence, as Keith, in turn, watched him. In typical big brother fashion he sized up the athlete quickly, as was his nature. He saw that Michael Hunter's interest in Prudence was anything but casual. Speed looked single-mindedly determined. Why, Keith hadn't a clue. But he would most assuredly find out.

Eventually Prudence sashayed over to her eldest brother and elbowed his ribs teasingly. "What's with you tonight, Grumpy? You're not your usual charming self," she quipped sarcastically. She chuckled at his expression when she used her childhood nickname for him.

One of three names she'd given to her brothers when, as a child, she'd seen and fallen in love with the Disney classic *Snow White and the Seven Dwarfs*. Drew, the second eldest, was Doc because he was seldom in a bad mood and was by far the most levelheaded of the Washington brothers. Jeremy was Bashful, because as the youngest he was always the quietest.

Keith leaned down purposely and lovingly kissed Prudence on the cheek. She smiled brightly and hugged him, returning his surprising and rare public show of affection. Keith's eyes intentionally drifted to the intense reaction of Michael Hunter. Jealously? Keith surmised and chuckled at the expected and questionable response.

"What was that for?" Prudence asked.

"For being my baby sister," he answered, still chuckling, knowing the word "baby" would spark her temper. She opened her mouth just as another of her brothers grabbed her around the waist and skillfully guided her onto the dance floor. The two moved with grace and

style until Keith cut in a few minutes later. He got right
to the point.

"Tell me about Speed Hunter?" he asked.

"Who?"

"Who?" Keith repeated, looking at her oddly. "According to news reports, the man with whom you're
having a tumultuous love affair." Prudence sucked her
teeth and rolled her eyes childishly. "Also," Keith continued with a nod toward the side of the bandstand, "the
man who's been glaring at you since the moment he
walked into the room."

Prudence quickly glanced in the direction that Keith
had nodded to. There, standing by the bandstand,
speaking to several guests was Michael Hunter. He
looked up as she spotted him. Their eyes met and held
for a few seconds, and then she hurriedly looked away.
"There's nothing to tell. We met when he came to help
out with the Thanksgiving dinner two days ago."

"Is that all?"

"Yes," she answered. Keith looked down at her skeptically. "And you can skip the big brother cross-examining
routine. I've said all I'm going to on the subject. If you
have more questions you can speak with my attorney."

"I am your attorney," he responded firmly. Prudence
looked up at him, her eyes narrowed. Keith nodded patiently. "And as your attorney, the question still remains,
why do you suppose he's here, other than the obvious
opportunity to frown at you all evening?"

She casually glanced toward the bandstand again.
Michael was looking straight at her. "I don't know, counselor. If it bothers you so much, why don't you go ask
him?" she remarked flippantly, seconds before Keith
spun her to the upbeat rhythm.

Keith immediately stopped dancing. "Good idea." He
released her and stepped back.

Prudence quickly grabbed her brother's tuxedo jacket
and pulled him back. He lost his balance momentarily
and slammed into her. The two started laughing at her

feeble attempt to stifle him. "Are you nuts?" she chastised in an urgent whisper. "Leave that man alone. He's here minding his own business, so I suggest you do the same. So behave yourself."

"I will if he will."

"What's that supposed to mean?"

"Exactly that." They continued dancing until the band took another break. Prudence glanced around the room, spotting and avoiding Michael the remainder of the evening. Keith was right. He had been staring at her all evening. Unfortunately, to make matters worse, she'd now begun glaring at him.

Marian came up to stand beside her daughter. "That color looks great on you, Prudence."

"Thank you, Mother."

Marian paused a moment to glance around at the festivities. "I'm happy you decided to come."

"You didn't give me a lot of choice in the matter," she muttered as she casually looked away.

"I heard that," Marian said, smiling as she continued gazing around the room. "What a wonderful turnout this evening. I see your father's aides have invited a few new faces."

"Yes, Mother, I saw him too."

Marian smiled and nodded. "Your father and I will be leaving shortly. I'll see you tomorrow evening," she said pointedly, just as Blake Washington walked up and stood beside his wife, taking her hand in his.

Prudence smiled and air-kissed her parents' cheeks. "Good night, Mother, good night, Daddy." Prudence stole one last look across the room. Michael Hunter was nowhere in sight.

"He left," Keith said as he came up to stand beside her. Prudence rolled her eyes, then followed her parents out.

Michael had no idea what made him attend the last-minute affair. It certainly wasn't his cup of tea. He'd long ago had his fill of staunchly boring, black-tie affairs, solely designed to stoke the ego of some loudmouthed, do-nothing politician. Yet, there he was, nonetheless.

He smiled to himself as he sauntered to the side of the band after taking another slow stroll around the room. Sometimes fame was annoying. Having dozens of fans come up to you, as if they actually knew you, and begin dissecting your life, was sometimes irritating.

Tonight was one of those times. Tonight, he just wanted to be Michael Hunter, not Speed. After years of being in the limelight, he'd finally grown accustomed to its bright lights and the glare of the spotlight. But on this occasion, this evening, he simply wanted to observe and not be on display.

The deep golden-colored dress was perfect on Prudence—streamlined, sexy, and inviting—and her slim curvy body filled it flawlessly. If her intention was to catch every man's eye in the room, then she certainly succeeded. No matter where she went or what she did, eyes followed. His hazel eyes in particular.

She dazzled. With just a touch of shimmer on her cinnamon shoulders and the sheen of the close-cropped halo of curls, she sparkled. He had been instantly hypnotized by the soft sway of her hips and ease of her stride as she moved. She laughed happily and worked the room like a professional. She danced with several men, much to his annoyance, and joked continuously with several men in particular.

If her intentions were to taunt and tease him, she'd succeeded masterfully. Usually strong-willed and detached, Michael found himself physically yearning for this sexy minx. She had aroused a primal need in him the instant he'd seen her, and his insatiable appetite demanded to be satisfied. And Ms. Prudence Washington was the only one who could do it. She had started this blaze burning inside him, and she would damn sure quench it. After all, he was Speed Hunter. What woman in her right mind wouldn't want him?

Chapter 6

Prudence sighed heavily. Saturday evening came too quickly. For the second night in a row she had endured the usual fund-raiser fare. She couldn't wait until this campaign was over and her life could get back to normal.

Normal. What was normal? The question rested on her mind like a weighed anchor on a still lake. Being hounded by the press wasn't normal. Being photographed without her permission or her knowledge certainly wasn't normal, and being attracted to a pig-headed, sexy football player definitely wasn't normal, at least not for her.

After her less than passionate two-date relationship with James Pruet, and her whirlwind disaster with Garrett Marshall, she'd held back on anything more than hanging with close friends. But her confusion persisted. Strait-laced, wing-tipped, pin-striped men with lapel hankies and wire-framed glasses were for her, not a Neanderthal football player with a gladiator complex, whose sexy body kept a constant heat burning in the pit of her stomach and lower body.

Prudence smiled a cockeyed grin that crinkled her nose as the last stray thought lingered. Admittedly her attraction to Michael was real; doing something about it would prove tempting but would be totally out of the question. She knew she'd never act on her newly admitted attraction, the risk was too great and the cost much more than she was willing to pay.

She'd never been attracted to motorcycle-driving, leather-wearing bad boys before, and in her eyes that's exactly what Michael was. The security and steadfast dedication of a boardroom executive far outweighed the complicated, problematical life a playboy would offer. Still, the excitement and adventure of stepping out on the wild side did appeal to her. She bit at her lower lip, intrigued by the fantasy. Her smile broadened. "Tempting, very tempting," she admitted easily.

Prudence looked around the crowded room, embarrassed by the tint of added blush to her warm cheeks and startled by the exuberance around her. She stood up, along with the others assigned to her table, and applauded, for what, she had no idea.

This time the event was an honor bestowed by her father's fraternity on worthy recipients in the community. The room was packed with professional associates, local celebrities, and old family friends. For some reason, all three of her brothers had wormed their way out of attending at the last minute. She made a mental note to render paybacks when she next saw them.

Prudence was stuck with another dance partner with drifting hands. She smiled graciously, reached behind her, and raised the roaming hand. Her partner smiled, chuckled, and made some veiled attempt at an excuse.

With eyes locked, he approached, interrupted only by stops to shake hands, make quick remarks, and accept pats on the back. With bulletlike precision and defined determination, he refused to be deterred from his target.

She wore red this time, and just as the night before, the sight of her enticing movements scorched a heated path straight through his body. The dress, the color of a Caribbean sunset, was just as mesmerizing, just as dangerous, and just as alluring, promising to singe all who dared to touch. His fingers ached to feel the burn of her body. Memories of a twisted, tangled, sleepless night goaded him. He needed to purge this siren from his mind once and for all.

Prudence yawned openly. This was ridiculous. Surely she could make her excuses and go home by now. She'd made the required appearance, listened to the boring speeches, and danced the appropriate number of dances. She looked around for her parents in anticipation of her departure.

Then, just as she was about to excuse herself, her dance partner stepped back and was replaced by a tall man with shoulders as wide as Texas and a grimace as determined as its most feared desperado. Michael Hunter. Her heart thundered in her chest and her stomach quivered. Last night could have been a coincidence, but seeing him two nights in a row was definitely not an accident.

He stepped closer, completely dismissing her previous partner. He slipped his hand around her waist and pulled her close to the firmness of his body. They danced wordlessly for a few moments until Prudence broke the awkward silence. "I suppose I should apologize for my part in what happened the other day," she began, then paused for his obligatory response and admission of equal guilt.

He leaned back and looked down into her dark brown eyes. A smirking grimace crossed his brow. "Go ahead, apologize," he said, lacking less compassion than a lion devouring a lamb.

"What?" she said, surprised and taken aback by his blatant conceit. She stopped dancing and instinctively took a step back, her mouth still open in amazement. He grasped her closer, making her more than a little aware of the muscular solidness of his body. Recovering quickly, she continued the dance. Yet she was still angry and equally unnerved by his audacity and the close proximity of his body against hers.

"Go ahead, I'm waiting, apologize," he prompted.

Prudence frowned, causing tiny ridges to crease her smooth forehead. His audacity was unbelievable. "I believe

I just did," she responded in the barest whisper. She looked around at the polite smiles and interested glances of those dancing around them. There were too many eyes on her. She knew that for her parents' sake she had to keep her temper down.

"No, you didn't. I believe you said that you *supposed* you should apologize. I don't consider that an actual admission of guilt."

She glared up at him. "If I'm supposed to find your arrogance charming, you're wasting your time. I don't."

Michael smiled openly. "Actually, Ms. Washington, I'd say you found my arrogance more arousing than charming, and it seems to scare the hell out of you. You're shaking."

"You mistake anger for arousal."

"Or possibly lust."

"Why, you pompous, egotistical, conceited cretin, I thought your kind went extinct after the Jurassic age, but apparently I was mistaken."

"Apparently." He smirked. She scowled. "I'm still waiting, Ms. Washington."

Prudence looked around and smiled at the couple nearest them on the dance floor. "You like provoking me, don't you?" Squaring her expression, she stared directly into his dreamy eyes.

"The questions you'd really like answered are, why are you so attracted to me?" He knew exactly what buttons to push. Prudence looked away and his voice softened to a mere whisper. "Why can't you stop thinking about me? And why is there a slow burn of attraction inside you even now?" He suddenly found that he enjoyed watching her obvious anger rise. The blush of her ire and the fire in her eyes excited him.

Appalled, Prudence gasped and then her jaw dropped. "Are you implying that I get some kind of perverse pleasure in these childish altercations?"

"Don't you?" he baited her further.

Prudence pushed her full lips together and glared up at him.

She was furious. Thoughts of stomping on his foot came to mind just as she glanced around to see a good number of guests still watching them, including her mother and father, now on the dance floor. Damn, that's all she needed. Her mother would never let her live down embarrassing her father in public. Her only recourse was to offer an apology and get the dance over with as soon as possible.

Michael continued to look down at her. His eyes centered on her mouth. Curved to perfection, and covered with the palest coral hue, her lips glistened and begged to be ravished. He leaned to dip his mouth to hers, and then stopped himself. This was neither the time nor the place. He was sure that there would certainly be other opportunities to taste her.

Michael watched closely, knowing he'd backed her into a corner. He could see her contemplating alternative options. He smiled openly, innocently. She was right, he did enjoy provoking her.

Her tongue slipped delicately between her lips and his pulse quickened. *Steady,* his mind warned. *This is supposed to be no big deal. Just put the little minx in her place, grab a little fun, and then get back to your life.*

That was his original plan, but then he had shocked Luther and at the last minute accepted the invitation from the mayor's office for the event last night and again tonight. Both receptions were sponsored by the mayor, so he was sure that his family would certainly be attending, particularly his daughter. He was right.

As soon as Michael arrived last evening, he had spotted her bright yellow dress on the dance floor. She danced with a beady-eyed pest with roaming hands. Afterward she was surrounded by a number of tuxedoed men. They stayed with her the remainder of the evening. But tonight she was alone. There was no one to run interference.

She looked up at him. His smile was automatic. She was too attractive, he decided absently when he allowed himself to become aware of her. Her body felt womanly, curvy, not like his usual model-thin, borderline anorexic girlfriends. He found he enjoyed holding her against his body. Instinctively his grip tightened, drawing her thoughts to her present dilemma.

Without missing a beat Prudence took a deep breath and began. "I'd like to offer my sincere apologies for my part in last Wednesday's incident. It was not my intention to embarrass you, your teammates, or your organization in any way. I offer no excuse for my behavior. I humbly ask your forgiveness." She lowered her head and looked away.

The smug triumphant sneer quickly left Michael's face, replaced by a serious solemn expression. He had expected far less than this long, drawn-out formal statement. He reached up and turned her bowed chin upward with his forefinger and smiled at her hooded eyes. With his lips just inches from her mouth he whispered, "Accepted." The music stopped. "Thank you for the dance," he added.

She stepped back and nodded curtly. "Good night." She turned and left him standing alone on the dance floor. Within seconds several women joined him, all clambering to be his next dance partner.

"What's going on?" James asked as Prudence walked toward him on her way to the coatroom. Having closely watched Prudence and Michael on the dance floor and the interaction between them, he took the opportunity to voice his objections.

"Nothing," she said.

"So what was that all about?"

"Nothing," she repeated more firmly as she passed by him.

"Well, it looked like something to me," he said with equal firmness, taking her arm to halt her as she passed him.

Prudence looked down at his hand on her arm, then

glanced back up at him. James removed his hand. "I've gotta go," she said. "Tell my mother and father that I had a headache or something." She hurried to the small booth, waited in line to retrieve her coat, then headed to the hotel's main entrance.

As soon as the automatic glass doors swung open, Prudence regretted her decision not to drive her own car. A horde of reporters mobbed her. Microphones, bright video lights, and flashing cameras nearly blinded her. "No comment!" she yelled to no avail while searching through the madness for the hotel doorman or an available cab.

Spotting a line of available taxicabs, she maneuvered herself closer to the curb. As soon as she raised her arm to hail a cab a sleek late-model black Mercedes Benz sedan blocked her path. The passenger-side window slid down silently. "Get in," the disembodied voice commanded.

Michael instantly got out of the car and headed around to the passenger side of the car. The smile he flashed was typical Speed. The reporters immediately swarmed all over him.

"Gentlemen, ladies," he said as he smoothly opened the door for Prudence, "Ms. Washington and I have no comment at this time."

Prudence stood still, stunned by his sudden appearance. As the car door opened she looked down into the comfortable leather surroundings as if she'd been invited into a lion's den. She looked back up at Michael. He handled the media mob with the finesse of a jackal and the wiliness of a fox. Within seconds he had their attention completely diverted from her and onto him. Taking advantage of the subterfuge, she hurriedly slid into the car.

The questions continued to fire at him. He answered most dealing with the team and the upcoming game. But to those of a more personal nature, he smiled and just shook his head innocently: "Ms. Washington and I have no comment at this time." By then Prudence was safely tucked into the dark-windowed car.

"Come on, Speed, give us something for the eleven o'clock news," a reporter yelled out.

Michael smiled and winked. "Not this time. Catch me after the game on Sunday. Ya'll have a good evening." A collective "aw" resounded and several reporters turned away while others continued taking photos of the dark-tinted car windows.

As Speed returned to the driver's seat, he looked over to Prudence. She leaned her elbow on the side armrest and held her head. "Don't expect my undying grati-tude," she snapped immediately.

He chuckled. "I wouldn't dream of it."

"Good, 'cause you're not getting it. It's your fault I have to deal with this mess in the first place. I can't believe this."

"Believe it. It's the price you pay for fame."

"I'm not famous and I don't want to be."

"Well, let's say you're just along for the ride right now." He pulled smoothly into traffic. "They'll let up in a few days."

"You actually enjoy all this attention, don't you?"

Grinning to himself in the darkness, Michael shrugged his broad shoulders. "It comes with the terri-tory. After a while you just learn to deal with it." He spared a quick glance in her direction. His voice soft-ened to a kitten's purr. "I'm sure there's some small part of you that likes the attention."

"Save it."

"Excuse me?"

"Your charms, they won't work on me. So save it."

"Ah, that's right; you're immune to my charms," he said, smirking easily.

Lying had never come easy with Prudence. The truth was, she was affected by Michael Hunter, very affected. He had a way of looking at her that turned her stomach to Jell-O and sent her heart on a treadmill race nonstop to nowhere. She looked out the side window, stubbornly refusing to respond. She was well aware of Michael's knowing smirk, his cocky smile.

The car went silent for a few blocks as Michael pulled onto the expressway. Prudence looked at the side-view mirror. The glittering lights of Center City, Philadelphia shone brightly in the distance. It was beautiful compared to the madness she'd just witnessed. "How do you live like this?"

"I don't usually. It seems you've added a new dimension to my notoriety. As I understand it, you've brought a new stability and maturity to my reckless bachelor life."

"Well, you've brought nothing but grief and aggravation to my life."

"All of this added attention must be just a little exciting?" he asked optimistically.

"Not in the least. I try my best to stay out of the public eye."

"How is that possible when your father is the mayor of one of the largest cities in the United States?"

"My father's political position has nothing to do with me. Unfortunately the press doesn't always agree. Believe me, I've had my fifteen minutes of fame already and I'd rather not have any more, thank you very much."

"It sounds like you've had difficulty with the media."

"Yes, I've had my difficulties with them in the past." She looked away.

"What kind of problems?" he asked.

She looked at his profile in the darkness. "You're kidding me, right?" she asked, knowing that everyone in the City of Brotherly Love had witnessed her very public breakup with Garrett and the ensuing political storm that nearly swallowed her up.

"What do you mean?"

"Have you been on Mars or something?" she asked sarcastically, thinking that his ignorance was some kind of ploy.

"Mars? I don't get it," he said, completely confused.

"You really don't know, do you?"

"I would if you'd just tell me. What kind of problems with the media?"

She ignored his question again and decided to give him the benefit of the doubt. His ignorance of her past seemed just too convincing. "Until recently, we've had a very cordial understanding. I left them alone, and they left me alone. Simple."

"What happened?"

"You happened."

"No, what happened in the past?"

The car went silent until Michael broached a sensitive subject. It was obvious that she had no intention of answering his question. "So tell me, what do you have against football players, other than the obvious?"

"Do you want it alphabetically, numerically, chronologically, or a mixture of all of the above?"

"Come on, we're not all that bad." He stole a glance at her stoic profile. "Are we?"

Prudence turned away to look out of the window. This conversation was going where she didn't want to go. The last thing she wanted was to relive a past relationship with an egotistical jerk. "Why don't we change the subject?"

"How many have you actually gotten to know?" he persisted.

Lost in her own troubled thoughts, Prudence went silent for a few moments, then sighed heavily with purpose. "I'm too old to babysit someone's bruised ego."

"Do you want to elaborate?"

"Arrogant, cocky, conceited, childish, stubborn—and that's just the short list. Then there's moody, temperamental, and volatile. Shall I stop there or continue?"

Michael smiled and then began to chuckle, drawing Prudence's stern expression. "Childish," he said.

"Yes, childish, what about it?"

"It's out of order." He glanced in her direction. Their eyes met in the dimmed outside overhead lights. Her quizzical expression delighted him. "Alphabetically,

childish comes before cocky and after arrogant."
Michael smiled at his own astute perception.

Prudence rolled her eyes and looked out the side window again.

He backed off quickly. "All right, you made your point. I get it. You obviously have had a bad experience in the past and you think that we're all alike. I can't argue with what I don't know. Yes, I'll admit, some of my comrades are less than honorable, but don't condemn us all for one man's actions. We're not all bad."

Prudence refused to answer, more because he was right than because she didn't want to rehash her personal life with a virtual stranger. She was prejudging all because of one man. She grimaced, refusing to relive the past. What was done was done. And if she condemned an entire gender because of one man, so be it. What possible difference could it mean to anyone what she thought?

Michael realized that Prudence had no intention of answering his question. He surmised that he must have gotten very close to the truth. So, if he wanted to be with this woman, and at this point he did, he'd better stay on his toes or she'd mash them along with what was left of his dwindling ego.

Suddenly the possibility and realization of wanting to be with Prudence Washington hit him again. Why would he want to be around a woman who apparently couldn't care less about his money, career, or athletic prowess? Michael smiled in the darkness of the car. She honestly detested him and he could not have been more delighted. "So, Ms. Washington, where am I taking you this evening?"

Prudence looked out of the window, gaining her bearings. They were on the expressway headed west toward the city limits and nearing the exit to City Avenue. "Exit here."

The car eased effortlessly from the expressway and pulled smoothly to the first traffic light. "You can drop me off anywhere over there." She pointed to a large hotel with a number of cabs waiting in line. "I'll catch a cab home."

"I'll take you to your front door."

"I'd prefer to catch a cab."

"I don't think so."

"When I left this evening, there were several reporters camped outside my building. I'd rather not give them anything more to write about if you don't mind."

"Sorry, no can do. My mom would skin me alive if she heard I dropped a woman off to catch a cab home. You see, that's not how we do things in San Antonio, Texas."

The Texas accent she had barely noticed before eased into the inflection of his voice more and more until it sounded like he should be sitting on a horse out on the open plains, rather than cruising the city in a stylish Mercedes-Benz.

"We're not in Texas," she informed him needlessly. He shrugged his shoulders apologetically. "I'll tell you what, I won't tell your mother if you don't."

"I can't lie to my mother," he proclaimed innocently.

"You wouldn't be lying, you just wouldn't be telling her everything."

"Same thing." The light changed and he continued driving down the wide avenue.

"I'm supposed to believe that you tell your mother everything."

"Yes, ma'am, I sure do." He exaggerated the southern drawl again.

"Liar." She smirked and looked away into the darkness of the streets.

He looked at her with a stunned expression. "I can't believe you just called me a liar."

"You are," she informed him in no uncertain terms.

"What makes you think I don't tell my mother everything?" He was enjoying this conversation too much. Her brash honesty was so refreshing after the pointless chatter from women he'd been used to most of his adult life.

"Do you sleep with women?"

"What?"

"Just answer the question, do you sleep with women?"

A smooth smile crossed his lips. "Yes."

"And of course, you tell your mother everything that goes on between you and these women, I presume."

"That's different."

"No, you said you tell your mother everything. Everything means everything. I'm only going by what you yourself testified."

"Very good. Smooth. You did that very well." He smiled brightly in the darkness. "If I didn't know any better, I'd ask to speak with my attorney. I think I just got nailed." He chuckled at her quick strategic legal maneuvering. "So, counselor, what should I say when my mother asks me about you?"

Prudence's expression changed. "Why would your mother ask about me?"

"Because, as per the media, you are now the woman in my life, remember? You and I are having a hot and heavy affair according to most reports. Of course, there is one way I wouldn't have to lie to her." The lecherous leer in his voice was evident.

"Tell her the truth."

"Which is?" he asked innocently.

"You know what the truth is."

"Truth is a relative term. There's the media truth. They just saw us leaving a hotel together tonight after a slow romantic turn around the dance floor."

"You and I know differently. There were dozens of others on the dance floor with us."

"Yes, but abridged truth for gain can still be the truth."

"Tell your mother whatever you'd like."

"I'd like to tell her that I met a woman who interests me. She drives me crazy with her temper, her sharp tongue, her addictive smile, and her mesmerizing eyes.

I'd also like to get to know her better, without all the media drama."

Prudence sighed, then went silent. She was touched by Michael's honest and heartfelt declaration. She smiled in the darkness as the car eased around a smooth turn.

Michael pulled into a well-lit driveway and stopped the car but left the engine running and the headlights dimmed. Prudence looked at the fabulous home in front of them. "Would you like to come in and have hot sweaty sex with me?" he asked jokingly.

Prudence smiled, then laughed, taken completely off guard by his absurd request. "You're good, Michael Hunter." She chuckled again. "But not good enough. I was actually this close to buying into that good-ole-boy Texas-gentry line. I even half expected that you were serious." She looked away, staying her heart from wishing that he had really meant what he'd just said earlier about getting to know her.

Likewise, Michael's heart sank with choked sincerity. The irony was that he was telling the truth about his feelings. He really did want to get to know her better. But the roguish reputation he'd allowed to develop through the years had worked against him for the first time. "So, is that a no?" he asked jokingly.

"Yes, that was a no," she said, still smiling.

"I tried," he said, shrugging back his disappointment. In actuality he would have been more disappointed if she had agreed to have sex with him tonight. That he wanted her was a fact. That he would have her was a foregone conclusion, as far as he was concerned. But he was prepared to bide his time and be patient. He turned to look out the back window. He spared a quick glance at Prudence's profile. If only . . .

He shifted the car back into gear and pulled back out of the driveway. Within moments he was back on City Avenue, headed away from his rented house. For the next fifteen minutes the two talked generally about growing up in Texas versus Philadelphia, his travels and job with the team and hers for the flagship department store, and their family differences and similarities.

"So tell me about your family."

"What about them?"

"I know the basics, your father is the mayor and your mother is a family court judge. What about other brothers and sisters, do you have any?"

"I have three brothers, two older and one younger."

"I assume that the gentlemen with you last night were your brothers."

"Yes."

"Are they lawyers also?"

"Yes, Keith, my oldest brother, is a corporate attorney, Drew is a computer technology attorney, and Jeremy, the youngest, is in law school at the University of Pennsylvania."

"And you're not an attorney."

"No."

Michael nodded as the conversation drifted into an easy silence interrupted only by her brief directions. When he finally pulled up in front of her building, there wasn't a reporter in sight. He parked the car and helped her out of the passenger side. They walked together to her condo, where he waited patiently as she nervously fumbled with the door keys.

"I'll be glad when all this is over and we can get back to our lives," Prudence admitted nonchalantly. Then she realized she didn't mean it as offhandedly as it sounded. She actually had had a good time this evening. And she had to admit, Michael wasn't the total dumb, arrogant jock she first assumed he was.

A little disappointed by her remark, Michael nodded. He too was actually beginning to enjoy the circumstances with Prudence. She was beautiful, intelligent, funny as hell, and he really enjoyed her company. "I know this has been trying for you, Prudence, but it'll be all over within a few days. You'll see, by Monday morning all this will probably be just a memory. Just fifteen minutes of fame, and as you said, we can each get back to our lives."

Saddened by the implication of possibly not seeing or being with Michael again, Prudence turned away pensively. This was the first time in a long while she'd had such a good time with a man. Granted, the reporters and the media were bothersome, but nothing was perfect. "Thanks again for the ride home. I really appreciate the rescue. I had no idea that being a Philadelphia Knight was actually also an occupation."

"My pleasure," he said, only half smiling at her attempted humor. In actuality the tenseness and awkwardness of the strained moment were annoying to him. He felt like a teenager out on his first date. Should he kiss her? Should he wait for a signal? Should he just walk off gentlemanly?

Prudence smiled and took the decision out of his hands. She opened her front door, turned, reached up, and kissed his lips briefly. The kiss was a gentle connecting, but in that instant something began to stir inside her. She stopped, stepped back, stunned by her impulsive action and its equally troubling effect.

They stood there for a moment, lost in wondering eyes. Apparently he'd felt the attraction also. In the coolness of the night, a sudden flush of heat gripped them. The shy awkward moment had faded and was replaced with a strong magnetizing pull.

He lowered his head, and she met him halfway. They connected again. The naturalness of the kiss, filled with passion and desire, took both of them by surprise. This one was anything but chaste.

Playfully, their tongues intertwined in a passionate dance of arousal. Pulsating with thrusts of wanton need, they clung to each other, melding closer. Michael wrapped his strong arms around her and she gripped his neck, pulling him toward the fire that now burned inside. Then just as suddenly the haze of passion cleared and the reality of the moment returned. She pulled back, turned, and went inside.

Michael smiled at the closed door. He was right about Prudence Washington. She wasn't at all what she appeared to be. The smart-mouthed, temper-flaring minx was actually a sexy siren with enough class to rival all of the women he'd known. He turned and walked away. It had been a good night.

The automatic shutter clicked several times.

Chapter 7

By Monday morning, Prudence's fifteen minutes of fame had extended into the fifth day and was showing no sign of letting up. Thanks to the constant media surveillance, she hadn't left her condo all day Sunday. Her one attempt to go out ended in her retreating ten minutes later with a reporter hot on her trail. She was not happy.

Apparently Speed had played exceptionally well. Then when asked what he had attributed his performance to, he'd jokingly admitted that it was his ongoing relationship with Prudence. At that point, the media's passing curiosity had instantly turned into a feeding frenzy. The headline had been splashed across every major newspaper in the city, and was the lead story on many of the news and sports programs. Prudence was definitely not happy.

She tossed the daily fashion journals onto her cluttered office desk. The style and fashion sections, which regularly gave her a quick dose of pleasure, inspired her purchases, and kept her current with the fashion trends, also boasted two all too familiar photos. One was a photo of her and Michael in an intimate embrace on a dance floor, the other was with her kissing him passionately in the dimly lit hallway of her condo.

Both showed him holding her tightly and her body pressed close to his in an exaggerated romantic setting. The headline stated that the lovers had reconciled at the awards dinner for Prudence's father, Mayor Blake Washington, and that their fairy-tale romance was back on track.

Prudence removed and hung up her coat, then dropped her purse into the lower drawer of her desk. Already her day was shaping up to be a stressful one, and showing no sign of getting back to normal. Several of her coworkers had requested advance playoff tickets, autographed footballs, and personal introductions. She'd even received a message from Gene telling her to feel free to invite Speed to the company holiday party.

Prudence sighed wistfully and looked down at the newspaper headline. This was getting out of hand. She wasn't sure how much longer she could take this constant attention, all this because of one man and his high school locker-room, overgrown ego. All he had to do was clarify their relationship and all of this would go away. She knew that she just needed to get him to make a statement to the media disclaiming everything. Then finally she'd have her life back.

Prudence sat down and buried her face in her hands. She was on a Speed Hunter merry-go-round and there was no stopping in sight. The dizzying feel of being swept away on a nonstop ride with Michael sent an arousing tingle flowing through her. Then, without warning, a sly, easy smile brightened her face as thoughts of her last kiss with Speed drifted in. Admittedly, he was a charmer.

She remembered the feel of his body enticingly pressed to hers as they danced. The security and comfort she felt being held in his strong embrace were unmistakable. And even though she would never admit it to him, the truth was, she did find him arousing and charming, and that did scare the hell out of her. That now familiar feeling began to sweep through her again as the idea of a more intimate relationship with Michael piqued her interest.

A quiver shot through her, reminiscent of the feel of

his arms wrapped around her as his body pressed against her. Being caressed by his touch and the gentle tenderness of his lips had touched her, sending a burning warmth through her body. She shuddered even now, hours later.

Without realizing it, her thoughts drifted to the last time she and Speed were together. She'd kissed him. It was impulsive and impetuous, but she was glad she did it. The tender feel of his lips was still implanted on her mouth and she hated to admit that she'd thought about and nearly obsessed about that kiss all day Sunday. Michael's dynamic presence and style were just too addictively seductive.

"All right, I admit it, I'm attracted to him," she confessed openly to the empty office. "It's no big deal." She shrugged nonchalantly. "I'm allowed, I'm a healthy single woman with urges and desires, and he's, he's . . ." She sighed. Although their brief kiss lasted only seconds, the electric spark still remained. Even now she reached up and touched her lips, still feeling the warmth of his mouth. The dazed expression shadowed her face as the excitement of Speed swept through her. ". . . He's too sexy for words, and can kiss a woman to madness."

The same wistful smile that had been on her face when she closed the door after their first kiss crossed her face again. The memory of their good night kiss at her front door appeared in a haze of passion. She'd kissed him. With ardor and wanton need, she had reached up and taken the kiss she'd unconsciously fantasized about all evening.

Afterward she had leaned back against her front door with weakened knees waiting for her racing heart to still. But it didn't and it still hadn't. All day Sunday she stayed in, secluded from the rest of the world with only the memory of Michael's kiss to keep her company.

The phone rang instantly, sending the memory into a fading puff of whimsical wishful thinking.

Since she had her home phone off the hook all weekend and her cell phone turned off, she knew that it was only a matter of time before her mother would be calling, particularly given the black and white photo in the newspaper. She picked up the newspaper again and stared at the grainy photos. The photo of them on the dance floor was easy enough to account for, but the one with her kissing him outside her condo would take a bit more explaining.

A sly smile curled her lips again as she ran her finger over Michael's profile. "Too, too sexy."

"Prudence," her assistant, Tanya Stewart, called out after peeking her head around the side of her office door. Prudence glanced up briefly from the pile of papers, fabric swatches, and design sketches. "Good morning, are you in here talking to yourself?"

Prudence instantly flushed. "No," she lied.

Tanya nodded and shrugged. "Your mom's on line one."

"Thanks, Tanya." As soon as Tanya pulled the door to, Prudence cleared her throat and ran her fingers through her perfectly trimmed hair. She removed the newspapers from her desk as if to hide them from the telephone call, then picked up the receiver. "Good morning, Mother."

"Good morning, dear," Marian said firmly. "I presume you saw your photo gracing this morning's style section."

"Yes, I saw it."

"Looks pretty convincing."

"I know, but even you can attest to the fact that there were hundreds of people at the banquet Saturday night. This photo makes it look like we were the only two people in the room."

"True, there were others in attendance, but obviously not in the *other* photo." Prudence rolled her eyes to the open-vaulted ceiling. She knew her mother would eventually bring up that photo. Prudence had to admit, it was pretty damaging to the *there's nothing going on between us* theory she kept spouting.

"There's a logical explanation for that photo," she assured her mother ardently. Prudence opened her mouth, yet, in retrospect, the only explanation was that she wanted to kiss him.

"No need to explain to me, dear," Marian began. "You're well over twenty-one, a grown woman, and I'm sure the photo was innocent enough. But keep in mind . . ."

Prudence rolled her eyes to the ceiling again as her mother's lecture began. It was the "but" that always got her started. However, today Prudence wasn't in the mood to hear the "you represent the Washington family" speech. She'd been confined all weekend, her desk was stacked to the rafters with work, and she had a new designer and three manufacturing reps coming in this morning. So she listened halfheartedly, and then just as she opened her mouth to interrupt, her mother wrapped up the sermon with her usual "a woman's reputation is all she has" speech.

"You know of course that a woman's reputation is all she has in the end. And men do not respect women with loose morals. Your father and I have raised you to be mindful of all you do. After all, you represent not only your father and me, but the entire Washington family." Following the eloquent dissertation, Marian waited patiently for Prudence's explanation.

"It was just a good-bye kiss. Well, actually it was more like a good night and thank-you kiss." Prudence swore that she'd actually heard her mother's neatly trimmed eyebrow raise.

"A thank-you kiss? Really? By that I assume he did something for you?"

"Yes, Mother, he did."

Marian waited quietly again. Patience was one of her stronger qualities. Patience, combined with intelligence, tenacity, and ingenuity, made her a formidable adversary. When she had practiced family law at her father's law firm years ago, her opponents dreaded the sight of her entering the courtroom. They knew without a doubt that they were in for a challenge. Yet her search for truth never outweighed her passion for justice.

"I thanked him for seeing me home safely after I was set upon by some very persistent reporters outside the hotel lobby."

"I see. Well, that certainly explains it, doesn't it? Speaking of Saturday night, your father and I are very appreciative that you decided to attend. We know how difficult it was for you given the current media climate. As a matter of fact I was just speaking to Emily Pruet. She said James was also delighted to see you there."

"I hope she's not starting her matchmaking again. I will never be called Mrs. Prudence Pruet."

"I'm sure she was only being gracious. She's very proud of James. He's come a long way and she wants the best for him."

"Fine, as long as the best doesn't include me."

"James is extremely competent as your father's administrative aide and political assistant," Marian defended.

"As Dad's assistant, fine, swell, I'm happy for him, but as a husband and mate for life, no, thank you. Competence isn't exactly the description I'd put in a personal ad when looking for Mr. Right."

Marian reacted instantly. "A personal ad?"

Prudence smiled openly, knowing that her mother's brow must have just arched again. "It was just a figure of speech, Mother. Rest assured that I haven't placed any ads in the personals. Somehow I doubt very seriously that I'd find my future husband in the newspaper." Prudence reached down and picked up the paper she had dropped on the floor earlier. The photo of her and Speed was right on the top. A split second's thought of her and Speed married sent a tingle through her.

"Who mentioned anything about marriage? I just said that James was happy to see you."

Tanya poked her head into the office doorway again and clicked her tongue to get Prudence's attention.

Prudence looked up from the papers she'd been reviewing while on the phone. "New York and Houston offices on conference call, line two," Tanya whispered quietly.

"Thank you," Prudence mouthed. "Mother, I gotta go. I have a conference call that I have to take. But you and Dad can definitely be assured, there'll be no more photos or articles in the newspaper about me and Michael Hunter. There's no way he and I will ever be in the same place at the same time. I'm sure I'll never see him again other than on the television on Sunday mornings." As soon as she said the words, a knot tightened in her stomach.

"There's nothing wrong with publicity, dear, we just don't want the wrong kind of publicity, do we?"

"I'll talk to you later, Mother." After Prudence hung up she shook her head and fell back against the highback leather chair. She was always exhausted after a conversation with her mother. But now that it was over, it was time to get some work done, and hopefully, with any luck, Michael wouldn't intrude in her thoughts as much as he'd done the past four days. She picked up the phone and went back to work.

The morning's practice was long and frustrating. Every pass Speed threw was either too short, too long, or just plain wrong. While in the huddle he'd call a play only to have the team set up on the line of scrimmage, and then he'd execute a completely different play.

The offensive line was baffled, the defensive line was perplexed, and the sideline coaches were totally bewildered. Dave Hawkins, the head coach, paced up and down the sidelines shaking his head wordlessly. Nicknamed the Quiet Tyrant, and usually a calm and subdued man, he fought hard to control the frustration building inside him. He eventually called the team back in, cut practice to half a day, and sent the men to the showers.

Speed was the last to leave the field. The day's disappointing frustration had reached its limit. He slammed his helmet against the stadium's brick wall, cracking the shiny silver surface and sending splinters of acrylic shards onto the concrete floor. He knew that his mind wasn't on practice, it was on Prudence. For the last two days that's all he could think about. How he'd gotten through, let alone won, yesterday's game was a complete mystery. Then, when the reporter asked him about his motivation, he said the first thing that came to his mind, Prudence Washington.

Surprisingly it was true. Thinking about Prudence during yesterday's game had given him a single-minded vision of what he wanted. He wanted to win the game and he wanted to be with Prudence. One out of two had been successful. Having gotten her phone number from Luther, and although he'd tried, he wasn't able to get in touch with her all day.

He stripped and stepped into a hot shower. Prudence slipped into his mind. The memory of her body enticingly pressed to his on the dance floor was overwhelming. He turned the cold water on full force. Still the brush of her lips and the small of her back sent urges through him. Michael dipped his head directly under the flow of cold water in an attempt to erase Prudence Washington from his thoughts. It didn't work.

What was it about her feisty spirit that drove him to distraction? Her vivacious daring and her unlimited flow of energy had caught and kept his ardent attention. Their first strained impression had quickly turned into relaxed conversation and comfortable joking. There was no pretense about her. What you saw was exactly what you got, and that was his problem, he wanted what he saw.

Later, after most of the team had departed, Speed knocked on the door of his coach's office. Coach Hawkins looked up from his television monitor showing the day's review tape. "Come on in, Speed." Using the pause button on his remote, he stopped action just as the video image of Speed overtossing a receiver by a good ten yards froze on the screen.

Michael looked at his image and shook his head. "I'm sorry about that, Coach. I don't know what's with me today. I can't seem to get my head into the game and concentrate."

"Don't worry about it, Speed, we all have off days. Why don't you grab the tapes of yesterday's game and call it a day? We'll meet back here tomorrow evening for the team meeting. Hopefully by then whatever or whoever's been on your mind will have been taken care of." The implication in Hawkins's voice was unmistakable. Everyone knew about Michael and Prudence.

Michael nodded, grabbed the stack of waiting tapes, then closed the door behind him. He decided to take the long way around the arena to the reserved parking lot. He walked through a short tunnel and exited on the fifty-yard line. He took the steep steps downward two at a time until he reached the green field.

Several of the stadium workers who'd been resurfacing the turf waved as he passed. Speed smiled and returned their greeting. He walked to the center field, stopped, turned, and looked at the upright field goals at either end. On a perfect day he could set a ball soaring through the uprights with the force of a rocket. But today, he doubted he had the focus to even hit the sidelines.

He walked through the long dark tunnel to the exit. Mr. Henry, the security guard, stood menacingly at the last gate. "Rough day?" Mr. Henry asked, already knowing the answer.

"Yeah," Michael admitted, "something like that." He lowered his head and kept walking. "See you later, Mr. Henry."

"Best get that gal off your mind and into your life or you'll be in for a mess of trouble come another Sunday afternoon kickoff."

Michael stopped and looked up. Old Mr. Henry was an enduring staple at the stadium's rear door. Every player, reporter, and front office staffer for the past fifty years knew and respected him. When he held his wrinkled hand up and said, "Sorry, no admittance without a pass," that's exactly what he meant. No one dared argue or debate the issue.

Except once, some time ago, a fast-talking, wet-behind-the-ears rookie reporter tried to talk his way into the stadium. Mr. Henry held up his shaking hand, but the reporter brushed right by him. Unfortunately for the reporter, there were several huge guards at the next post, and when they found out what he'd done to Mr. Henry he was literally tossed out on his rear. Rumor had it that the young reporter tried to sue the franchise for damages but settled out of court in exchange for keeping his job and getting his press pass back. Needless to say, he never tried that again.

Michael smiled down at Mr. Henry. He had to be all of five feet four and nearly ninety-five pounds. He always wore a clean, perfectly starched official stadium guard's uniform, thick trifocal eyeglasses with flip-down sunshields, and kept his hat cocked slightly to the side. He walked slowly with a noticeable limp, but faithfully showed up for work every day, come rain, shine, or snow, without fail.

Michael thought for a moment. Mr. Henry's simplistic solution to his current predicament was so obvious. In fact, it was so blatantly clear, he wondered why he hadn't seen it himself. Prudence Washington was the answer. She was both the core and the cure of his problems. He had thought about her the whole way home Saturday evening, he dreamt about her both nights, then woke up this morning with her still on his mind.

Michael mumbled to himself, "Of course." Then aloud, he added, "You're right, Mr. Henry. You're absolutely right."

"Always am, young man, I always am," Mr. Henry confirmed, brimming with self-assurance. He watched as the last few players waved and drove out of the parking lot. Mr. Henry looked back to Michael. "What, you still standing here jawing with me, go do something about that young lady."

"Yes, sir, Mr. Henry." Michael nodded his head and smiled. "I'm on my way."

Luther Phillips had been summoned up to the main office fifteen minutes ago, then told to have a seat and cool his heels. He was perched on the secretary's desk and beginning to discuss her refusal to have dinner with him when he observed Coach Hawkins leaving the owner's office. He got up and sauntered over to the open door and looked in. He knocked and stepped into the office. "Sir, you wanted to see me?"

"Phillips, yeah, just the man I want to see. Come in, have a seat."

A half hour later, Luther left the office and strolled along the corridors of the empty stadium heading back to the team's public relations office. He even whistled along with the bland elevator music on the way down to his office. He was blissfully content and extremely proud of himself. He had pulled it off.

Drumming his fingers noisily on the desk, he picked up his new favorite file of photos and shuffled through. Choosing a particularly interesting one, he picked up the phone and dialed the number of his friend Peter Hall at the *Sports Voice* newspaper.

The phone was quickly snatched up. "Yeah." Peter's brash voice bellowed through the receiver with annoyed impatience.

"Peter, it's Skins. How are you?"

"Busy." He reached up and stopped the recorder but continued typing from the notebook of notes set beside his keyboard. The deadline was looming and he was almost finished and well on his way to meeting it.

"Want to be busier?" Luther asked.

Peter immediately stopped what he was doing and casually leaned back in his chair. He smiled knowingly. Luther was one of his best sources of inside information when it came to the Philadelphia Knights organization. "So tell me, Luther, what's going on that I should know about?"

"You tell me. How did the little story I gave you go over?"

"Like a dream," Peter said. "Seems like your friend Mr. Hunter and Ms. Washington have become a hot little item. They're the city's very own real-life Romeo and Juliet. My wife is actually asking me about my work. Can you believe that?" He paused to puff on the last remains of his cigarette, then stamped it out. "My phone's been ringing off the hook. Everybody and their brother wants to know what's going to happen next. It's like a damn soap opera over here."

"Tell me about it." Luther smiled smugly as he looked at the enormous stack of interview requests and phone messages sitting on his desk. Now, *this* was the public relations business he'd signed on for. This was what he lived for, when a chance occurrence blew up into a media frenzy. The idea was to ride the wave while getting as much free print space and airtime as possible.

"So tell me, Skins," Peter asked, "are they really together or is this another one of your lead-into-gold publicity spinning wheels?"

Luther smiled. His nickname, Skins, or the more representative Rumpelstiltskin, had followed him through much of high school and all through college. He often amazed even himself. The talent he possessed to turn the negative into the positive and his much-deserved reputation for bending the truth and delivering near impossible results had been his claim to fame and had instantly gotten McGee's attention.

"They're together all right and we're loving it over here." Luther smiled broadly as he savored his conversation with McGee. "I was just in a meeting with McGee. It seems that the interest in Speed and Prudence has sent revenues through the roof. McGee wants to keep this going as long as possible."

Apparently the budding romance between Speed and Prudence Washington had been just the ticket the team needed to reenter negotiations for a new football stadium. And since Blake Washington had a vested interest either way, the Knights franchise would come out on top no matter what.

After all, who wouldn't want Speed as a potential son-in-law? So, even though his PR job had turned to Cupid, he didn't mind as long as the results were the same and he would garner all the credit.

"Of course he does," Peter said. "He'd be nuts not to, particularly if the Knights go to the play-offs. It'll give him more leverage when it comes to that stadium he wants so badly. Speaking of which, what do you have good for me?" Peter probed. "Any talk on that new stadium deal between McGee, Washington, and the city council, or is McGee still threatening to take the team someplace else?"

"Sorry, no comment," Luther said in his standard PR voice.

"You've got to be kidding me. You can't *no comment* me. I need a scoop on this stadium deal. Who's McGee going with?"

"To tell you the truth, I have no idea yet. As far as I know the deal's still in the air. It'll probably come down to whoever wins the election. If Washington wins, then the team stays; if he loses, then the team moves," Luther said, then paused, knowing that he was giving his friend just enough to appease his readers but not enough to cause serious concern for his job. "But don't quote me on that."

Peter began jotting down notes, then stopped and tossed his pencil on the desk. "That's it, that's all you got?"

"Well, my friend." Luther reared back in his chair casually. "There is something interesting that just recently occurred. It looks like Ms. Prudence has really gotten under our fearless leader's skin. Today's practice was just called off early because of technical difficulties. Seems Speed had a hard time concentrating on throwing the football more than ten yards. One guess as to what's on his mind?"

"Interesting, but not exactly earth-shattering," Peter said. "I'm talking real news, Luther, none of the PR frill stuff that you feed the gossip pages."

"That's all I have, honest," Luther lied easily.

"I can get a better lead over the wire," Peter said as he blew out the lit match and puffed another cigarette.

"I'm not exactly in the inner circle around here," Luther noted. "Besides, I'm not the newspaper guru, you are. Why don't you go find out the answers to your questions? All I have for you so far is the Speed-being-distracted thing. Use it or not." Luther paused for added drama. "But remember this, if you don't, believe me, somebody else will. So, Guru, you have your lead for tomorrow's headline, run with it."

Luther hung up as Peter laughed at the long-forgotten nickname. Luther had given him the nickname Guru after his first big scoop hit the front page of their college newspaper. The scandal rocked the student body, the faculty, and the board members. Peter smiled as he stamped out another cigarette. Those where the days.

He looked down at his byline and article in tomorrow's sports section. It was a good story, pungent and informative, but not earth shattering. If he ever wanted his career to jump-start, he needed a big story, something like the undercover exposé that Garrett Marshall had done on Prudence Washington a few months back.

Garrett had very nearly brought down the Washington family and the sitting mayor of Philadelphia in one story. Using Prudence was the key for Garrett, and Peter was sure that she'd be the key for him as well.

He typed in the final paragraph, entered the send code, then printed it out for himself. He still preferred flipping the pages to holding down an arrow key.

As the article printed he considered the question that he had asked Luther about McGee and the mayor's office. If he could get an exclusive on dealings between the two men, he'd score the ultimate sports and political upset. A slow, beguiling smile eased across his face as thoughts of Garrett's career surge came to mind.

Garrett's story wasn't nearly as pungent as it could have been. Peter was sure that Garrett had lost focus somewhere along the way, letting his emotions and feelings for Prudence Washington cloud his writing. But that wouldn't happen to him. He was too focused and vigilant when it came to his career goals. He grabbed the printed pages, his jacket and camera, then headed out the door. It was time to get started.

Prudence stepped down from the high platform and took a step back to admire the display she'd just put together. The new-style mannequins were perfect for the new designs she'd ordered. She just hoped that the merchandise would sell as well as she'd forecasted. Tilting her head from side to side, she picked up some accessories and returned to the platform. She applied the jewelry and hats, then reached up and readjusted the scarf to a more asymmetrical slant around the hips. She nodded, smiled, and took a step back. She teetered, then began to fall backward.

A split second later she found herself wrapped in Michael Hunter's arms. Her heart beat rapidly as she scrambled to her feet, but she was firmly held in place.

Click.

"What are you doing here?" she asked, completely stunned.

"Preventing you from falling, rescuing you again, obviously."

Prudence was mortified. Why was it that every time this man was around she was at her worst? "You can put me down now."

Michael smiled. "I kind of like you where you are."

Several customers walked by and openly stared at the embracing couple. They pointed and smiled, while others moved in closer to get a better look at the city's now famous couple.

"Put me down," Prudence gritted through clenched teeth. She looked around at seeing a crowd beginning to form.

Michael obeyed instantly, then removed his sunglasses and graced her with his famous knee-melting smile. From behind his back he produced a dozen long-stem yellow roses. "These are for you."

Prudence looked around nervously. It was starting all over again. In a few minutes this whole thing would be out of control. So if she didn't want a repeat of the media crush from the hotel, she'd better get them out of sight quickly.

"Come on," she instructed, grabbed her samples, his large hand, and made a quick dash to her office through the women's designer boutique department. As soon as Michael entered, she closed the door behind them, walked across the large crowded space, and dumped her samples on the already full countertop. Short of breath and her heart pounding full force, she turned to face him.

"I asked you a question, what are you doing here?"

"I came to rescue you." He looked around the cramped claustrophobic office filled with racks of hanging clothes, unopened boxes, and naked mannequins. It wasn't at all what he expected when he found that she was a designer clothing buyer for an East Coast flagship department store. He walked over to her desk and placed the roses on top of a pile of fabric swatches. "Come on, grab your coat, let's get out of here. I know this great little restaurant in Cape May."

"Cape May? New Jersey? You are joking?" she asked rather than stated.

"No," he said innocently. "Come on, let's go."

Prudence's quick temper began to surge. "This is my

job; I can't just up and leave at the drop of a hat, or better yet at one of your whims. I have work to do." Prudence moved back to her cluttered desk. "You see, this is what the real folks do for a living, we work. We sit in cramped, hot little offices and work all day while you get to play outside in the yard with your friends."

"What is your problem? I asked you out for the afternoon, no big deal. It's dinner and a few laughs."

"No, you want me to just drop everything and hang with you right now. I can't do that. You see, if I don't work, I don't get paid. I enjoy having food to eat and a roof over my head. So I have to work for a living, unlike you who can play all day and still pull down a million dollars a game."

"Actually, it's more like two million 5.5 with endorsements, but fine, if money's the problem, I'll pay you for the day." He reached into his pocket and pulled out a wad of cash that could choke an Arab sheik. He peeled off ten one-hundred-dollar bills and handed them to her.

Shocked, Prudence stared at the cash in his hand. Her temper immediately blew. "What did you just say?" He opened his mouth to speak but closed it just as quickly as she picked up the roses, shoved them into his chest, and pushed at his unyielding body. He took a step back. "What do you take me for? Do I look like I exchange favors for cash? How dare you imply that you can buy me, or my time for that matter?"

"What?" he asked innocently.

"Get out!" She pushed at him again. This time he didn't budge.

"What did I do?" He actually had no idea what he'd just implied. "Prudence, wait, listen." She succeeded in turning him around and steering him toward the door only because he didn't want her to hurt herself trying to push him.

"Leave, Mr. Hunter." She opened the door as he swaggered out with crushed flowers in one hand and cash in the other. He turned with a pleading, questioning expression. "Good-bye, Mr. Hunter." The door soundly closed in his face.

Michael shook his head and walked away.

The shutter clicked.

Chapter 8

"He said what?" Valerie repeated, barely able to keep the humor out of her voice.

"I still can't believe his nerve," Prudence said, still shaking with anger. After closing the door and pacing the office for several miles she picked up the telephone and dialed her friend's extension in the D.A.'s office. "Can you believe him, like I'm supposed to drop everything and go with him just because he snaps his fingers?"

"To tell you the truth, Prudence, I bet the average woman would have done just that."

"No way."

"Oh yeah, definitely. Pru, look at who we're talking about. Speed Hunter is the catch of the decade. He's drop-dead handsome, deep-pocket rich, comes from a great family, intelligent, and God knows what else. Damn, girl, give me his number, I'll go out with him." Valerie laughed and Prudence reluctantly joined in.

"Don't even try it; you're worse than me when it comes to men. Do I have to remind you of the last man you dated, the New York runway model? Handsome, built, successful, and had a master's degree in psychology in his back pocket. You dropped him like a bad habit."

"Actually, his bad habits were why I dropped him. Particularly that little habit of constantly giving me orders."

"See? That's what I'm talking about. It's the same thing with Michael."

"No, it's not. Girl, the man brought you roses and asked you to join him in Cape May. How is that the same? But what I want to know is why you're still so angry. You said there was nothing between the two of you, so what difference does it make? You could have just said no, thank you and let it go at that."

"That's not the point, Valerie. The point is I thought, after we spent that time together last Saturday night, that maybe I was wrong about him. Maybe he wasn't like the rest of them, spoiled, selfish, and arrogant." Her voice lowered to an almost whisper. "I actually thought he might be different."

"Why don't you just give the man a chance and stop prejudging him, Prudence? You have the poor man tried, sentenced, and executed before he even opens his mouth. You always talk about how you wish you could be like your dad. All right, here's your chance, Blake Washington is legendary for giving everybody a chance."

"I am not my father," she said bitterly.

"True, Blake is a lot more tolerant."

"With everyone but his daughter," Prudence interjected.

"Prudence," Valerie said in warning.

The conversation fell silent as Prudence absorbed her friend's words. She hated to admit it but Valerie was right. Her father always said that people deserved as many chances as they needed. Nobody's perfect.

"I'll think about it," Prudence finally promised.

"Good. Now get off of the phone, I have a nut ball that needs to be locked up for dumping his four kids at an amusement park all day."

"He did what?"

"Girl, don't get me started. This fool actually dropped the kids off at the front gate with no money and hung out with his girlfriend all day while the mother was at work."

"How old were the kids?"

"The oldest was fourteen."

"Convict him."

"I wish I could. Unfortunately, that part's up to the judge. But you better believe that once I'm finished with him he'll have a lifelong phobia of amusement parks. I can't wait to get his butt on the stand."

"Go get him, girl. I'll talk to you later."

Prudence sat for a long time thinking about what Valerie had said. Valerie was right. She had jumped to conclusions. Michael did seem like a nice guy after you scraped off the macho exterior. She decided to stop by the stadium and leave him a message. But for now, she had a ton of paperwork to complete, some samples to look at, and a buying trip to New York and Houston to finalize.

Michael ranted and raged for forty minutes, the entire time it took for him to go from Center City, Philadelphia to get to his comfortable suburban home off the Main Line, a suburb of Philadelphia. He was furious. Here he was offering an olive branch and Prudence shoved it in his face and pushed him out.

He slammed the front door and headed for the kitchen. After tossing the football tapes onto the counter, he went into the refrigerator and grabbed a cold soda. He pulled the tab and took a long swig. As he turned, he spotted his reflection in the refrigerator's chrome surface. The man who looked back at him was a stranger. He shook his head in disgust. The reflection was a man in serious trouble and headed for even more.

On an average day he received at least three marriage proposals and any number of less honorable illicit propositions. What was so special about this one woman?

That they were attracted to each other was blatantly obvious, even though she emphatically denied it. No one kissed like that without some pull of attraction. Michael reached up and touched his lips, remembering the feel of Prudence's mouth pressed to his. The now familiar slow burn, ignited the first moment he saw her, began to simmer again. She had him on fire for the last three days and it didn't look like he'd be cooling off any time soon.

How could one innocent encounter six days ago escalate into the preamble to war? Prudence Washington was a live grenade, and he had had just about enough of her going off on him. He reasoned that his best bet was to walk away now while he could still distance himself. What was wrong with him? Why did he put up with this, with her?

He couldn't believe it when the answer came almost immediately. The alluring pull of his attraction to Prudence was too strong. It was too late and he knew it.

His attention was drawn downward to the cat at his feet. He reached down and picked her up and stroked the soft fur. His anger began to fade. Then suddenly, the cat leaped from his arms, shook her fur, licked her paw, and strolled out of the kitchen. Michael shook his head in exasperation. "Females." He picked up the tapes and went into the study.

After fifteen minutes of mindlessly watching game and practice tapes and not listening to play strategies, he picked up the remote and turned the television off. He hadn't heard a thing the coach said and hadn't remembered a single play called. His total lack of concentration was beginning to become a habit. But what could he do?

The telephone rang just as he propped his feet onto the sofa. He recognized the number and picked it up on the second ring. "Hi, Mom, how are you?" The cat leaped onto Michael's lap, circled twice, then purred and relaxed comfortably.

"Hi, sweetie, I was just thinking about you and thought I'd give you all a call." Michael smiled. Her comforting voice was never so welcome. "I'm doing just fine. How are you doing up there?"

"All right, I guess." The moping tone in his voice was evident. Michael absently stroked the cat's soft fur again.

"Oh dear, is it that bad?"

"What do you mean?" He tried to perk his voice up.

"Why don't you start from the beginning and we'll see if the two of us can make sense of it?"

The woman was amazing. Elizabeth Hunter had a double dose of intuition and a triple dose of compassion. Had she not married his father in their last year of college, Michael was sure his mother would have been a fantastic psychiatrist. But she gave it all up for her husband. All her dreams and hopes were laid aside to be the best mother and wife she could be. She had succeeded tenfold.

"I presume this has something to do with a very attractive young woman by the name of Prudence Washington."

"How did you know about that?"

"Obviously you haven't seen the sweet little article in this week's edition of *Sports Wrap-up*."

"Don't tell me I made the cover again."

"No, nothing that drastic. But there was a nice little photograph of you and a certain young lady battling it out behind a church, of all places. From the look of the expression on your face, I'd say she won."

Michael propped a second pillow behind his neck. "Then you'd be right."

Elizabeth laughed. "Knocked you down a few pegs, did she?"

"What do you mean? I do not walk around with some kind of chip on my shoulder and my nose up in the air."

"No, I didn't say you did. But I know my boys, and you all have a manner of confidence that has to be taken down every now and then and shaken out. I was just about to do it myself, but it looks like Ms. Washington got to you first. Thank her for me."

"I can't believe what I'm hearing. My own mother's feeding me to the wolves." The sound of purring drew his attention. He began stroking the cat's fur again.

"Nonsense, how do you think I've dealt with your father all these years? Where do you think you get it from?

He was exactly the same way as you boys. It took me a few swings, but I finally dropped him a few pegs lower."

Michael began laughing as Elizabeth continued, "Listen, there's nothing wrong with being confident, especially when you have the ability to back it up, and make no mistake, you do. But every now and then, if we're lucky, we come across someone who's got that certain something. I'm not talking about playing football or basketball. I'm talking about life, real life. That person will be able to see right through you. All the charm and poise in the world won't hide your true self."

"So you're saying that she's that person."

"No, I'm saying that not everybody's going to buy what you're selling. And those that don't are sometimes worth a second glance. Don't take the easy way out, Michael. Sometimes easy isn't always what we want even if we think it is at the time. It's the challenges that make life interesting. Be patient. Whatever you truly want will come to you in time."

"I hear you, Mom."

"Good, now hold on, your father wants to say hello."

As Michael waited for his father to pick up the receiver, he considered what his mother had said. She was right about one thing at least. Prudence was a challenge and she sure as hell made his life interesting.

After Michael spoke with his father he showered, dressed, and met up with a few of his teammates at a local club. The music was hot, and the women were lively, so Michael did what any red-blooded man would do. He sat all night trying to figure out what he did to anger Prudence and then took equal time to decipher his mother's cryptic advice.

Rick Renault slid into the seat next to him. "So what's up with you, man? You gonna sit around like that all night or what? You got the honeys all over you and you're just sitting here brooding."

"I don't brood." Michael took a sip of his soda. "I'm just not in the mood to listen to your honeys babble about my career, my life, my looks, and my money. Can't they talk about anything else?"

"Man, you must be crazy," Rick drawled out in his very distinctive Creole dialect. "Your problem is, that woman in the newspaper has got you whipped already. You don't need a woman mouthing off like that." He looked around and spotted a skintight bright red dress moving seductively on the dance floor. Rick watched hypnotically as the woman gestured to him while gyrating her hips seductively. He smiled and nodded his ardent attention. "Forget her. Now, these honeys act like women are supposed to act. You talk, and they listen. Other than that, they got nothing I want to hear except *yes, baby.*"

"See, that's the difference between you and me, Rick. I want more. I want a woman who can think and reason and yes, talk back and argue if need be. You see, an intelligent woman comes with a price and I don't mind paying it."

"That's you, man, you got that." Rick stood up and held out his fist. Michael pounded the top, as an indication of brotherhood. They'd come to an unspoken agreement. Rick preferred his type and Michael preferred his. To each his own.

As soon as Rick strolled over to the bright red dress, a woman dressed in skintight pants and a sparkling bra top took his place next to Michael. She inched closer, smiled brightly, and slid a folded piece of paper across to him. Michael looked at the paper questioningly. "It's my cell phone number, my measurements, and the number of ways I can please you," she said seductively.

Michael slid the folded paper back to her without even opening it. "You might want to give this to someone who's in a better mood."

She placed her long-nailed fingers on the folded paper and slid it to him again.

"It's not your mood I'm interested in, baby." She licked her ruby-red lips slowly and smiled.

Michael smiled back, then shook his head at the obvious attempt at seduction. "All the same." He slid the paper back to her. She took it and pushed it into the sparkling bra top.

She stood and turned around slowly, giving him the full view of her perfectly formed body. "Are you sure you want to pass this up?" She placed her palms on the table and leaned over to him. Her piercing green eyes glared into his.

He smiled at the performance. "Some other time."

She nodded and walked on, leaving him alone at the table again. Several more women sat down periodically, but soon moved on after surmising his disinterested and withdrawn demeanor.

The remainder of the night was a complete waste of time. Michael took time to sign several autographs and pose for a few snapshots before deciding to call it a night, much to the dread of most of the women in the club. A number of overly zealous women who had attached themselves to him and his teammates were nearly enraged when he announced his early departure. Several even followed him to his car to offer their services for the evening free of charge.

He declined, much to their dismay. Then, while he was driving home, it suddenly dawned on him. In retrospect, he realized that he had insulted Prudence by offering her money for her time. "Damn." He hit the steering wheel with the flat of his palm. "Damn."

Chapter 9

"You're gonna love these." The Knights' PR photographer opened up a manila envelope and dropped a number of photos on Luther's desk. "I got them last night at the End Field, Rick Renault's club. I thought it was just gonna be another one of his party nights, a waste of time, but who do you suppose showed up?"

"Speed Hunter." Luther picked the photos up one by one, laughing at each in turn. "Oh man, these are priceless." He picked up the last two. "Oh, these are interesting." He stood and reviewed the photos again. "You, sir, will notice a little something extra in your check this week."

The staff photographer beamed. "Thanks, Luther, I appreciate it." He moved to the door, then as an afterthought offered, "Hey, any time you need me to get more photos, no problem, any time of day or night. I'll be available."

Luther grinned and nodded as he walked over to the photographer and shook his hand. "That's exactly what I wanted to hear." The photographer left, closing the door behind him. Luther went back to his desk and shuffled through the black-and-white photos again. He laughed loudly as he picked up the phone and dialed.

Prudence dumped her things on the desk and plopped down in her chair. She had a ton of things to do today and she hadn't gotten a wink of sleep last night. All she kept thinking about was how awful she had been to Michael Hunter the day before. Valerie was right. Everybody deserved another chance. She decided to stop by the stadium that afternoon.

The ringing phone interrupted her thoughts. "Prudence Washington."

"Hey, Pru. It's Whitney."

"Hey, girl," she responded with a silent yawn.

"I talked to Val last night," Whitney began.

"I figured she'd call you. Did she tell you about my visitor yesterday?"

"Yes, and she told me about your very interesting proposition."

"And?" Prudence prompted, knowing that Whitney was primed to say more.

"And I'm gonna have to agree with Valerie on this one. I don't think Speed necessarily meant anything by stopping by like that. And as for his invitation, sounds to me like he just wanted some alone time with you, that's all. It's kind of sweet when you think about it."

"And the payment for my time?"

"I'm sure he didn't mean it like that."

"Well, that's what he said."

"Have you heard anything from him lately?"

"No," Prudence said, turning on her laptop computer.

"Have you seen this morning's style section yet?" Whitney asked.

"No, why? It can't be another picture of Michael and me." She frowned. "Can it? Hold on, I have the newspaper right here." She quickly flipped through the paper, then stopped. There, for all to see, was a photo of Michael leaving her office and then later that evening him out with another woman. A prolonged silence followed.

"Pru?" Whitney questioned.

"Wow, that was quick. I guess I'm old news."

The slow disheartened sound in Prudence's voice piqued Whitney's concern.

"That's what you wanted, right?" Whitney asked.

Prudence went silent again. Whitney had known Prudence for over fifteen years. They'd been friends, sisters, and comrades through thick and thin. Together, they'd been through it all, from the painful divorce of Whitney's parents, to the hurt and heartbreak of a broken engagement. Each time Prudence had been by her side.

"Pru, that's what you wanted, right?"

"Yeah, definitely," she barely whispered.

"Are you going to be okay?"

"Yeah, sure, of course I am," Prudence lied as she tried to brighten and add more spark to her voice. "Why wouldn't I be? It means that this nightmare is finally over for me."

"You sound a little upset."

"Me? Upset? No way. I'm just looking at this desk. The store will be open in a half hour and it's already a mess. I had floor duty yesterday, so my desk is still covered with yesterday's work. I've gotta go, I'll talk to you later."

After hanging up, Prudence sat at her desk and stared at the photo of a smiling Michael and an unknown woman in a sequin bra top. She was too late.

Any delusions she might have had about getting to know Michael better were totally out of the question now. Apparently he moved on quicker than he scrambled on the field. She shook her head. To think she had actually been considering going to the stadium and apologizing for kicking him out of her office. No way. She closed the newspaper and started her morning.

The day dragged on endlessly with one annoyance after another as she drifted mindlessly through the daily business of department management. Several reporters showed up asking about Michael and the photo. She declined comment. Eventually, Prudence stayed in her office, leaving only to handle a problem in the shipping and receiving of several special items.

Buried under the usual mound of paperwork, Prudence read a fashion report on a new line for the coming spring. Tanya, her assistant, poked her head into her office. "Prudence, you have a call on line one."

"Who is it?"

"I don't know, he didn't say."

The first thing that ran through her mind was the latest surge of reporters who had called earlier to get her reaction to the photo of Michael sitting in a nightclub with another woman. "I hope it's not another reporter."

Tanya crinkled her nose. "I don't think so. The person actually sounded somewhat human, although not by much." She giggled at her male-bashing humor. She was still smarting from an ugly breakup with her boyfriend, who worked in the store's shipping department.

"Be nice, Tanya, they're not all bad," Prudence warned, surprising even herself with the reply. She picked up the first line as Tanya closed her office door. "This is Prudence Washington, how may I help you?" There was a slight hesitation before the person on the other end spoke.

"You can have dinner with me for starters."

The unfamiliar deep male voice puzzled her. "Excuse me?"

"I said, you can have dinner with me," the man repeated, slightly louder and clearer.

"Who is this?" Prudence stopped writing and put her pen down. It was him, the man who had been calling her for the past two months.

"You mean to tell me that you don't recognize my voice, sweet thing? Have you forgotten me already?"

"Maybe if you told me who this is it would help."

"Ah, Prudy baby, you wound me. After all we've gone through together, you still don't recognize my voice." An array of men's names and faces began flashing before her as she tried to mentally identify the stranger. Her father and brothers were definitely out of the question, and even though she hadn't known Michael Hunter for long, she was certain that this wasn't him. The only other person might be . . .

"Pruet, James Pruet, is this you?"

"Do you want it to be?"

"This isn't funny, James."

The man's voice turned dark. "Is James Pruet your lover or do you want him to be?" The vengeful tone of his voice startled her.

"Look, whoever this is, I'm not in the mood for games. So if you'd rather not identify yourself, then I'd rather not play." Her tone was stern and adamant.

"Oh, you'll play, baby, and you'll love every minute of it."

Prudence immediately hung up. The man's voice had turned from annoying to venomous. Prudence gathered her hands around her arms as a cold chill ran up her spine. Instinctively she looked around the cluttered space, feeling trapped and closed in. File cabinets, rolling displays of merchandise, and huge shipping boxes surrounded her at every turn.

She shuddered again. The chilling sensation wouldn't leave. She felt violated, as if the stranger knew more about her than he'd said. Quickly she gathered her coat and purse and walked out of the office.

Tanya was just clearing her desk for the day. She looked up. "Don't tell me you're leaving so early. I don't think I've ever actually seen you walk out of the building. I just assumed you slept in the bedding department all night."

Prudence stopped at Tanya's desk and waited as she gathered her belongings. "Very funny. Come on, it's late. Let's get out of here."

The two women walked to the employees' exit while talking about new fashion trends and the upcoming buying trips. As soon as they stepped out of the building a cold blast of wintry air blew into their faces. Prudence quickly pulled on her gloves and tucked her head deeper into the thick coat collar. "It got really cold out here," Prudence complained through chattering teeth.

"Are you kidding? It feels great. It's invigorating. I can't wait until it starts snowing. I love winter."

Prudence looked at Tanya in disbelief. "How can you walk around in this weather with your coat wide open, no gloves or scarf or hat?"

"This is nothing. When I was growing up in Minneapolis we used to go swimming in the public pool in this kind of weather. Look at you; I can't believe you're so bundled up. It's not that cold."

"Believe it! I'm not just cold, I'm freezing," Prudence said, still bundling herself up. Tanya began laughing at the comical way Prudence shivered under the thick bulky coat. "I just hope the weather warms up a little before we leave for New York next week."

Tanya beamed. "I still can't believe you're taking me with you next week," she said as they walked to their cars. They arrived at Prudence's bright yellow Bug first since she had arrived at work earlier. They paused and continued talking.

"Come on, Tanya, you've been to New York before."

"Yeah, sure, but not as an assistant buyer."

Prudence smiled and continued. She was happy to be able to take Tanya with her this trip. It would be fun to have someone with her since she usually went on the buying trips alone. "Now, don't think it's going to be all fashion shows and fun. There's a lot of hard work to do and a lot of tough decisions to make."

Tanya's expression changed to serious. "I know and I'm fully prepared to do whatever it takes, long hours, paperwork, anything, I don't care. I'm ready."

"Good, because the work is stressful and you'll have to hold your own and keep up. I'm going to need you one hundred percent in New York." Tanya nodded her agreement and dedication as Prudence continued. "Some of those designer fashion shows, boutique shopping excursions, and late-night cocktail parties can be horrendous."

Prudence smiled as Tanya realized that the trip would be more fun than she'd originally let on. "Handsome models, manufacturers begging you to take their clothing, free samples, it's positively brutal." They both laughed as Prudence got into her car and blasted the heat.

"See you tomorrow, Prudence," Tanya said as Prudence shut the door and waved from the car's closed window.

Before shifting into gear Prudence glanced around the store's parking lot. A few scattered employees hurried out of the store carrying shopping bags, but no one seemed to look in her direction. Maybe she was just being overly cautious, but her intuition told her to be careful, so she listened. She locked the car doors and pulled slowly out of her parking spot. After another quick look around, she blended into traffic and continued home.

Tiny wisps of smoke dissipated into the bitter air through the slightly open car window. Grabbing the expensive camera from the dashboard, he tossed it on the passenger seat along with the shopping bag filled with purchases he'd just made. He fingered the soft, frilly, sexy negligees, then watched as Prudence nervously looked around the parking lot and drove off. Smiling contentedly, he tossed the thin cigar butt from the open window and followed her home.

Chapter 10

Nearly a week had passed and Prudence was still edgy and nervous. She sat in her parents' living room surrounded by familiarity. There was no place safer than home and she was undoubtedly glad to be back.

The four-day excursion to New York was grueling and exhausting, but it was definitely worth it. Prudence and Tanya tried to shop at, or visit, just about every upscale boutique in Manhattan. They met the haute couture designers of the fashion industry. They saw the chic, classic elegance of various Paris collections and Milan designs that were breathtaking and they loved every minute.

They ordered merchandise for the spring and summer seasons, along with a number of new designs from several up-and-coming designers. They found a little shop in Soho that boasted a number of fascinating accessories. Elegant jeweled pieces were ordered along with silk scarves, straw hats, gloves, and belts.

By the time they had returned to Philadelphia, the storm of controversy around Prudence had thankfully dwindled, having all but faded into oblivion. The only thing that remained was her strong, inexplicable desire to see Michael. As her days returned to relative normalcy, the apprehensive feeling also subsided.

She had been a nervous wreck ever since that nutcase called over a week ago. The first call, a couple of months earlier, had stunned her. It happened just after Garrett left town. When she told her two friends, both Whitney and Valerie were obstinate that she contact the police. They had even insisted that they go with her. Valerie, an assistant district attorney and officer of the court, had been particularly insistent. But Prudence adamantly refused.

She knew that a report of harassment would surely be leaked to the media, and now that her life and her family's life were getting back to normal, she didn't want to rock the boat by causing more undo attention. Then when the calls stopped she was relieved and glad that she had decided not to call the police.

Now, after months of silence, the caller was back. Although he hadn't called in a few days, she kept having the strange feeling that she was being watched. She rearranged her work pattern in hopes of always arriving and leaving with a number of store employees, and stayed indoors most evenings.

"So tell me about your trip to New York," Marian said.

Distracted by thoughts of her bizarre telephone calls, Prudence nearly jumped out of her seat when her mother returned to the living room with the tray of tea and cookies.

"What on earth is the matter with you?" Marian said after seeing Prudence's jittery reaction. She placed the tray on the coffee table and sat down next to her daughter.

"I don't know. I'm just jumpy lately. I guess all of this public attention has finally taken its toll on me. I've been on edge for days. I even have the weird feeling that I'm being watched." Prudence stood, walked over to the window, and glanced out, something she'd been doing a lot lately.

Marian poured two cups of steaming hot peppermint lemon tea. "Prudence, come, sit down and drink your tea." The concern on her face was evident and Prudence did as her mother requested. "Are the reporters still taking photos of you and this football player?"

"No. Well, actually, I really don't know. I haven't seen

any photographers around lately and there haven't been any new photos in the newspapers, so probably not."

"Well, maybe that's the feeling you sensed, when the photographers took the picture before they were candid and unposed. That means that someone was indeed following either you or *this football player*. How else could they take such intimate photos without your knowledge?"

The stern legal tone in her voice made Prudence feel as if she'd been sitting on the witness stand.

"Mother, I wish you wouldn't refer to him as *this football player*. He has a name, you know. It's Michael, Michael Hunter."

"Yes, dear, I am well aware of the man's name. I am also well aware of his reputation. Are you?"

"What do you mean?"

"Prudence, if you intend to get involved with this . . ." Marian paused and corrected herself. "With Michael Hunter, you ought to know who you're getting intimate with."

"Meaning?"

"Meaning Mr. Hunter has quite a reputation with the ladies."

"Mom, he's a man, he's got money, he's famous and handsome. Of course he has a reputation with the ladies. You should hear the reputation your three sons have with the ladies."

"That's not important now."

Prudence shook her head. Her mother's blinded belief that her sons were saints never ceased to amaze her.

"The Washington men have always had woman falling over them; it's their charm. Mr. Hunter, on the other hand, seems to enjoy the adulation."

"And my brothers don't." She started laughing at the absurdity of that statement.

"Prudence, I'm not going to sit here and debate the issue of Michael Hunter's alleged reputation versus your brothers'. I am, however, going to caution you on becoming another one of his many, many conquests. His reputation is one thing; the public expects and even condones a certain amount of cavalier behavior from men, particularly athletes. You, dear, on the other hand, are still expected to be a paragon of virtue. Whether you are or not doesn't matter, what matters is the perception."

"I know, Mother, and you're right. There is a double standard. And I have no intention of becoming another notch on *this football player's* jockstrap."

Marian smiled at Prudence's choice of words.

A pregnant pause stilled the room as each woman sipped tea from the delicate porcelain cups. Marian glanced over to her daughter. "Do you see something developing between the two of you?" she continued softly.

"No," Prudence said, then paused, to think and possibly reconsider.

Marian waited patiently for her to search and realize her feelings.

"I don't know, maybe. I guess I just wanted to get to know him without all the opinions."

"Do you still want something to develop?"

Prudence looked at the veiled worry in her mother's eyes. "I know we've had this conversation before, and the thought of another Garrett situation is always in the back of my mind too. I nearly destroyed this family when I brought him in. I'm so sorry. I still feel so ashamed of what happened."

The sadness in Prudence's voice tore at Marian's heart. She reached out and took her daughter's hands. "No, you will not be ashamed for having honest feelings and for falling in love. Love is a gift and Garrett sacrificed that gift when he took your love and betrayed you. You did nothing wrong and you have nothing to apologize or be ashamed for. You followed your heart and were misled. Garrett is a self-serving liar who used you and this family to further his career, not you."

"But you knew, even from the start, you knew that there

was something about him that wasn't right. I remember
we used to argue about why you didn't like him. You told
me even then that you didn't trust him."

"Yes, it's true, I didn't trust him."

"But I was closest to him and I didn't sense anything.
How did you know?"

"A mother's instinct, a feeling, I don't know. He was
your first real serious relationship. Maybe I just didn't
want my little girl to leave me, so I wouldn't have trusted
or cared for any man you brought home."

Prudence smiled at her mother's use of the words *my
little girl.*

"Maybe I was jealous that you were becoming a woman
and pretty soon I'd no longer have you as my darling
child."

"And Michael, what about him?"

"Every man isn't a potential Garrett," she warned.

"Aren't they?" Prudence said, firmly meeting her
mother's gaze.

"No, sweetie, believe me, they aren't." Marian recognized the seed of possibility in Prudence as the rebirth
of hope overshadowing despondency. "There are good
men out there. Whether Michael is or isn't is for you to
find out. You do that by trusting your heart."

"How can I ever trust my heart again after Garrett?"

"You will. You have to decide what you want and not
be afraid to take a chance on love."

"To tell you the truth, I don't know what I want. One
minute I'm lost in some fantasy dreamworld thinking
about him and then the next minute I'm kicking him
out of my office."

"I presume you saw the photo of him at that club last
week."

"Yes, I saw it." Prudence stood and walked back over
to the bay window overlooking the large front lawn.
"That's the same day I kicked him out of my office. I
know he was furious with me."

"I gather now you don't particularly feel great about discouraging him."

Prudence shrugged her shoulders. "He hasn't tried to contact me since that day."

Marian stood and walked over behind her daughter. "Sometimes men need to make a fool of themselves before they realize what they really want. Be patient, give it time, Prudence. Then if you find that you still want to, contact him. There's nothing wrong with a woman picking up a phone and calling a man. Somehow I doubt he'll turn you down. After all, you are your mother's daughter. No man could possibly resist."

"Is that firsthand knowledge talking?"

"Are you kidding? Definitely firsthand knowledge. After four uncles, three brothers, three sons, your grandfather, and your father, I'd say I was an expert on the ways of men." Marian glanced at the huge mound of overstuffed shopping bags and packages still sitting in the foyer after her day of shopping. "Why did you let me buy all these Christmas gifts? It's going to take until next Easter just to wrap them all." She smiled at her daughter slyly and arched her brow.

"Really subtle, Mother. All right, I'll give you a hand with the wrapping, but no criticizing because I'm taking too long on one package. I prefer the outside wrapping to look just as special as the gift inside."

Marian rolled her eyes to the ceiling. "It's not rocket science, Prudence. Wrap the thing up and then move on. Honestly, I don't know where you get your perfectionist streak from."

"Yeah, I wonder." Prudence slowly scanned the room. Every pillow, every magazine, and every knickknack was perfectly in place, even the Persian rug's fringe beneath the sofa was neatly aligned over the polished wooden floors. Prudence knelt down and picked up a roll of brightly colored holiday paper. "Come on, let's get started, maybe we can get this done by Groundhog Day."

* * *

It was late Sunday night when Michael dropped his two travel bags on the spotless marble floor of his leased Philadelphia home. He walked over to the small table and picked up a week's worth of mail from the foyer table. After two successful weeks on the road and a quick visit to Texas, he was delighted to finally be in one place for a while. He went into the den and pressed the button on his phone.

In anticipation, he listened to the various messages. Most were sales, investment, and management companies all offering him a deal he couldn't possibly live without. As each call played, a part of him hoped that by some chance one message would be from Prudence. After the final message played, he pressed the button and erased them all. She hadn't called, so he went upstairs to bed.

As usual for the past few weeks, sound sleep had eluded him. Restless nights filled with images of Prudence drifted through his subconscious as readily as through his consciousness. In seductive clarity, his dreams were arousing and detailed in every way.

Prudence would come to him, ready and willing to give herself to their pleasure, and he would accept her offering. Taking her in his arms, he'd love her until their bodies burned with the release of pleasure. Then they would join in the ancient dance of life. But, just as his moment would come, he'd awaken to an empty bed and an empty life.

The following day the team had the day off, but Michael was too edgy from restless nights. He decided to go to the stadium to get in some extra work. He spent several hours in the weight room and then did some practice plays with his trainer.

Sweaty and breathless, he continued, driven like a madman. He needed the distraction, and physical exertion was the best way to forget anything. Unfortunately, this time it wasn't working. Prudence Washington was always there in his thoughts, dreams, and fantasies.

Michael stood at the fifty-yard line, set in position. He faked left, then right, then tossed the ball into the air. The brown orb soared, spinning endlessly until it finally descended and hit the circular target directly under the goalposts. He picked up a second football and repeated the action. This time he hit the right target. After hitting the left and final target he reached down for the last ball. But, instead of tossing it downfield, he spun it on the flat of his index finger and watched the dizzying rotation.

He felt exactly like the spinning ball. The more he tried to clear his mind of Prudence, the more he thought about her. Like the ball, she had him constantly spinning in circles. He stopped the rotation and held the ball still, then walked toward the locker rooms. He'd had enough.

Three figures stood in the owner's box and watched the Philadelphia Knights' star quarterback practice. "Damn, did you see that ball hit the target?" the team's owner, Graham McGee, questioned excitedly.

Coach Hawkins nodded. "Speed's arm is getting stronger and stronger and his snap is right on the mark, but he needs to buckle down and work on his release. We still have a number of games ahead of us, but barring distractions and injuries we'll be looking pretty good in postseason play."

"Postseason play? Are you joking? His arm has Super Bowl MVP written all over it."

Coach Hawkins tipped his cap back and scratched at his balding head, frustrated by Speed's erratic performance. He'd won the last three games, yes, but his concentration was scattered to the wind. There was no way Speed could continue to perform at that level without getting himself injured.

"The Super Bowl is months away," he warned his boss. "First we have to get through the regular season and the play-offs."

McGee didn't care about the particulars of the day-to-day routine of the game. He was a businessman plain and simple. As far as he was concerned, the team was on a winning track headed straight for a Super Bowl win and a new stadium with multimillion-dollar corporate skyboxes.

McGee slapped Dave on the back affectionately. "Yes, yes, always the voice of reason and logic." He chuckled, prompting Luther to join in as if on cue. McGee was, as usual, blinded by the excitement of winning. He saw play-offs, the Super Bowl, and a new stadium with his name on it. "Phillips?"

Luther, who'd been on the cell phone, hung up immediately and jumped to attention. "Yes, sir," he shouted and stepped forward. Coach Hawkins shook his head and moved toward the door. The only thing missing from Luther's appearance was clicking heels and a salute.

"Order those hats, T-shirts, and banners we talked about. I want this place hot with Super Bowl fever by next week. The way Speed's been playing and throwing lately he could very well win the play-off games single-handedly."

Coach Hawkins excused himself. Having been an athlete, he was superstitious by nature, and talking about a win before playing a game was the surest way to lose. But he had to admit, Speed had been unstoppable on the field. He'd almost doubled his game stats and had already broken several of the team's longstanding regular-season records. But he also noted that for some reason Speed's heart wasn't in the game, and that was dangerous. He had been easily distracted and needed to raise his concentration level. But all that could be worked on. It was the lack of enthusiasm that bothered him.

* * *

An hour later Michael walked down the security tunnel exit toward the parking lot. "Good night, Mr. Henry," he said.

"Looks like you have a visitor." Henry nodded his head toward the parking lot. Michael glanced around the empty lot until he spotted the glaring yellow Bug. A smile crept across his full lips. "Well, son, you going, or do I have to carry you over there?" Mr. Henry asked.

"No, I think I can handle it from here," Michael said and casually walked over to the waiting car.

Prudence looked up from her magazine. In the rearview mirror she watched every step he took as he came closer. She had to admit the man had style. Dressed in black slacks and a black turtleneck sweater, he could easily pass for one of the models she hired every year for the store's spring fashion show.

Prudence shook her head in wonder, admiring him as he approached. Every ounce of his body was toned, firm, and fine. His legs were long and powerful and bowed just right. His hips were narrow and his stomach was strong, flat, and hard. Over one broad shoulder he'd slung his carry-all bag and on his head he wore a backward team Kangol cap that matched his expensive black leather coat, which was open and billowing casually as he walked. Prudence smiled lustfully as she got out of the car. *Lord have mercy, this man is too fine.*

Michael observed the long legs swing from the car's yellow frame. Her charcoal-gray coat made the short teal business suit pop out. The floral-print chiffon scarf around her neck whipped seductively in the gentle breeze. Three-inch teal heels and a gray tam topped the classic ensemble.

"Hello, Michael," she said as he approached.

"Hello, Prudence." His tone was formal and questioning. He wasn't quite sure what she was doing here, particularly after their last encounter. The scarf she wore blew restlessly in the wind.

Prudence took a deep breath and forged ahead. "Looks like I'm starting to make a habit of this." His expression never changed. He looked solemn and intense. Prudence licked her dry lips and continued. "I came to apologize for my behavior the last time. It was unfair of me to treat you like that and I'm sorry."

"That's it? What, no patiently rehearsed speech like last time?"

"No, not this time." She looked around the empty lot nervously as Michael stepped closer.

"You came all the way down here just to say that?" She half smiled and nodded. "Well, Ms. Washington, you're gonna have to do better than that." Her smile faded. "I don't think that just a verbal apology is gonna do it this time." He reached out and caught the chiffon scarf as it blew across her face. She turned away. He pulled at the silky softness as it gently flowed through his fingers. "Plus," he added as she looked up into his heavenly eyes, "I think there's more that you want from me."

"Really?" Her brow arched with interest and blatant denial.

"Really." He smiled broadly as he slowly pulled the scarf from around her neck. "I think you came down here for another reason."

"I don't think so," she stated firmly.

"I do," he replied with assurance.

The standoff began as they stood staring at each other.

"Tell me what you want, Prudence." His enticing statement was explicit enough for a deaf person to hear the seduction implied.

"Nothing. I came to ease my conscience and correct an injustice, that's all. Apparently you've mistaken me for one of your *other women.*" His brow rose with interest as she continued. "I don't want, need, or expect anything from you." She turned and yanked open the car door.

Speed, named appropriately, intercepted her before she stepped inside. "My *other women*, is that why you're so upset? You saw the picture of me and some hootchy-mama in the newspaper. You can't possibly think that that photo is anything more than a meager attempt at raising circulation."

"I don't think anything about it. I have no concern and nothing at all to do with what you do or with whom you do it."

"On the contrary." He dropped his bag, spun her around, and captured her mouth before she could react. The stolen kiss surprised both of them. When she finally did respond she impulsively pulled back and glared at him. Seconds later she threw her arms around his neck and gathered him closer.

Click.

As his head moved from side to side to get as close as possible to the sweetness of her nectar, she dug her nails into his leather coat. Neither one was concerned about anything except the feel and pleasure of the embrace. When the kiss eventually ended, Prudence stood breathless as Michael stroked the length of her back with his hands.

She looked around nervously.

"We've gotta stop doing that," she said, still winded.

Michael chuckled and smiled. "We haven't even begun."

She looked at him, then looked away, completely understanding what he'd implied. He tipped her chin back to face him. "You are so beautiful," he proclaimed. Prudence blushed at the compliment. "Let's get out of here, go some place less public."

Prudence bit at her lower lip. "I can't," she whispered, grimacing as his euphoric expression collapsed briefly. "I have to get back to work."

"When do you get off?" he asked as he kissed her forehead and then the palms of her gloved hands.

"Whenever I finish," she said vaguely, truthfully.

Michael frowned at the cryptic remark, then pursued yet another direction. "We can meet later or I can pick you up or you can come over to my home. Whatever you want to do, we'll do."

"I wish I could tonight but I can't."

He immediately stepped back. "What's going on here, Prudence? Do you get a kick out of being a tease? You come here looking like that, kiss me like that, and then you just go cold as ice. If you don't want to get together, fine, just tell me. I'll back off."

"I didn't say that. I just have other plans tonight. I didn't expect for this to happen between us. I have responsibilities that I have to take care of."

"I see." He nodded and looked away. "Look, when you have time in your schedule for me, let me know. Maybe I will too." He walked away.

"Good-bye, Michael," she called out. He threw his hand up, waving without turning around.

Prudence kicked herself after returning to the store. She was into her second hour of restocking, displaying new merchandise, and paperwork when the telephone rang. She picked it up abruptly. "Prudence Washington."

"I have a message for you."

"James, if this is you I'm not amused, and this little game of yours is getting boring." Silence answered her. "James?"

"Is in the hospital."

"What?"

"A dislocated shoulder and a few cracked ribs."

"Who is this? What are you talking about?"

"You'll find out soon enough."

Prudence hung up the phone. Her hands were shaking and her heart was beating wildly. She stood, grabbed her coat and purse, and ran to the door. When the phone rang again she froze. She slowly turned and walked back to her desk and picked up the receiver. "Yes?"

"Prudence, is that you?" her mother asked.

"Mother." Relief flowed from the single comforting word.

"Prudence, what's wrong? You sound scared to death."

"Have you spoken with Emily Pruet lately?"

"What a coincidence. I just spoke with her a few minutes ago. It seems something terrible has happened to James."

Prudence sat down slowly. "What happened?"

"He's in the hospital. They said that he was mugged."

"I know." She began crying. "He told me."

"Dear, James couldn't have told you. Emily said that he's pretty bad off. I doubt that he'd call you from the hospital."

"I'm not sure who he is."

"Prudence, what are you talking about? You're not making any sense. Who's he?"

"The man on the phone," she began. "The one who did it, I think. He told me that James had a dislocated shoulder and cracked ribs."

"Oh my God." Marian looked over to her husband. "Blake," she called out across the room, "pick up the phone."

"Marian?" Blake immediately picked up the extension. "Prudy, what is it? What's wrong with your mother?"

"Daddy," she cried. "Daddy, he did it. Oh my God, he really did it."

"Who, Prudy? Calm down, now tell me slowly. Who did what?"

"James, the man on the phone, he knew about James. I think he did it."

"Where are you, Prudy?"

"I'm still at work."

"Stay there, I'm on my way."

"No, Dad, the store has already closed and I don't want to wait in the parking lot alone. I'll meet you there."

"Let me call someone to pick you up."

"No, Dad," she said calmly, wiping her tears and taking a deep breath. "I'm fine now, really. I'll be there in half an hour."

Chapter 11

Four stoic men stood in the living room of the Washington family home. Marian sat in the antique Queen Anne chair and Prudence stood at the bay window staring out into the darkness. The festive nine-foot Christmas tree reflected in the window. Prudence pensively watched the sparkling lights. Keith broke the silence. "Where are they? What's taking them so long?"

Drew, the calmest of the three brothers, walked up behind Prudence and put his hand on her shoulder. "You all right, Prudy?"

She nodded, watching Keith continue to pace and rant in the window's reflection.

"Calm down, Keith, we just called. It's only been five minutes," Marian said just as the front doorbell rang.

Three uniformed police officers and two detectives walked into the large sitting room and Prudence retold her story. They asked questions that continued for thirty-five minutes with no real lead or resolution.

"Is this the first time this man has contacted you?"

"Yes," Blake said.

"No," Prudence answered. Eyes turned to her from all over the room. "What!" reverberated in her ears like a chiming gong as the room immediately went into an uproar. Prudence looked from face to face of the people she loved the most in the world. Their shock, disappointment, and anger were evident and reminded her of her confession about Garrett just months earlier. She knew this was

only the beginning when she saw Keith throw his hands in
the air and turn away.

The lead detective, much to his credit, gained a semblance of control and resumed the interview. "When did
the phone calls first begin, Ms. Washington?"

"Two months ago," she said. Marian grasped Blake's
arm and her two brothers sitting beside her gripped her
tighter.

"What!" Keith said again. "Two months ago! Exactly
when were you going to tell anyone about it, never?"

"I handled it," Prudence shot back.

"Apparently not."

"Keith, let the detective handle this, please," Marian
insisted."

Keith immediately walked away mumbling, "Two
months, two months, and she never bothered to tell anyone. I can't believe this."

"Please continue, Ms. Washington," the detective said.

Prudence started from the beginning. She told about
the first call and ended with the call earlier that evening.

"Has this man threatened you in any way, Ms. Washington?"

"No. Not really. He just sort of makes innuendos."

"What kind of innuendos?"

Prudence lowered her head, embarrassed by the new
line of questioning. Her brothers Drew and Jeremy,
sitting on either side of her, put their arms around her
shoulders and waist. "He, uh, he promised that he
would make sure that we would be together and he'd
take care of me."

"And what makes you think he assaulted James
Pruet?"

"I object," Keith instantly responded. "That's not important at the moment."

With five lawyers in the room, it was hard not to smile
at the remark. "Sir," the lead detective said to Keith, "I'm
going to have to ask you to please refrain from objecting
at this point. I need to be clear as to exactly what Ms.

Washington knows." Keith frowned and nodded his head, obligingly consenting to the request.

"All right, Ms. Washington, is there anything else you can remember about the man's voice?" Prudence shook her head no.

"Maybe you recognized any background sounds, trains, planes, car noises, music, talking, anything like that."

"No, I could hear him clearly. There were no other noises. But he kept talking like we already knew each other. Like maybe I should have recognized his voice or something. But I didn't."

The detective nodded and wrote in his booklet. "I'm sorry, Ms. Washington, but I have to ask this question." He paused and looked pointedly at her brother. Keith waved his indulgence. "Ms. Washington, might your past relationship with Garrett Marshall or your recent association with Speed Hunter have something to do with the phone calls?"

"I don't see how it could. Garrett and I are ancient history, and Michael and I are just barely acquaintances. The press has built the relationship up to something it really isn't."

The detective turned to Blake. "Sir, might this be politically motivated with the election coming up?"

"I've already thought about that. As I'm sure you are aware, lately we've had a few office break-ins and some trouble with inner-office leaks about campaign strategy. But apparently this man speaking with Prudence has made no reference to the election. I don't see how it can be related at this point."

The detective nodded and wrote more notes, then closed the book. "Well, Ms. Washington, I think we have everything we need." He pulled out a card and handed it to her. "If you think of anything else that might be of help, just give me a call. My cell and pager number is on the back. We'll contact the security at your job and at your condo. I can have a patrol car outside your home this evening and tomorrow at the store. It's merely a precaution. I'm sure it's just some crackpot who happened to hear about Mr. Pruet's condition and decided to try and scare you. I wouldn't worry about any more calls. But if by some chance he does contact you, let us know."

She nodded. "Thank you."

"Good night, ma'am." The detective nodded to Prudence and Marian, then turned to Blake. "Sir, if I could speak to you in the foyer." Blake, Keith, Drew, and Jeremy all followed the detective, his partner, and the three officers out.

"I could use a cup of tea, how about you?" Marian asked.

"I could use a drink," Prudence replied.

Marian laughed nervously. "That's actually a better idea."

She walked over to the small bar in the corner of the room. "What will it be, scotch, bourbon, or something a tad milder?"

"I think I'll just have a glass of wine."

"All right, one wine coming up." The four Washington men returned to the room and joined Marian at the bar. "What will it be, gents?" she asked.

"Scotch, neat," Blake said, rubbing his forehead in helpless frustration.

"Ditto." Keith sat on a stool.

"Make it three," Drew chimed in.

"Four," Jeremy said, at just twenty-four years old. Everyone looked over to him. "Hey, I'm legal, remember?" Blake and Drew nodded and smiled while Keith grimaced as usual.

Marian set up five small tumblers and two long-stemmed wine goblets. She distributed the drinks around in silence. Prudence walked over to the fireplace and fiddled with the fresh pine branch decoration. She adjusted the shiny gold ribbon, then turned several glass ball ornaments. Her small distorted reflection stared back at her. She took a timid sip of her wine, then turned. "It's getting late, I think I'd better get home."

The room erupted. Objections were hurled at her from every direction.

"Don't be ridiculous," Keith said, "you can't go home."

"That's absolutely absurd. I will not permit you to stay at the apartment alone. It's out of the question," Blake said.

"Dad, the man calls me at work, not at home. Anyone can call the job. It's a public store, for goodness sake . . ."

Keith cut her off. "That's another thing, you're not going back there until some measure of security has been implemented."

"What? Keith, it's a huge flagship department store. At any one time there are at least fifteen to twenty thousand people mingling around. It's the safest place I could possibly be."

Drew added his opinion. "You're right, Prudence, hundreds of nuts, crazies, lunatics, you name it." She looked at him and glared. "Prudy, I agree with Dad and Keith, you can't go home, at least not tonight. And you can't go back to the office. You'll be a sitting duck in that boxed-in office of yours."

"Who asked you?" she snapped, annoyed by his betrayal.

Jeremy started to say something when Prudence threw up her hand in warning. "Don't even think about it. Not one word out of you. It's bad enough the rest of you are trying to lock me away for the rest of my life, I don't need to hear it from you too." She walked over to the bar and set the half-empty glass on the counter.

"Now listen, everybody, I will not hide in my old upstairs bedroom for the rest of my life because some nutcase feels like growing a brain stem. I'm going back to my home tonight and every other night and I'm going to get up tomorrow morning and go to work."

She grabbed her things and stomped to the door, then stopped and returned to the living room. "Mother, Dad, guys, I know you love me and are concerned about my safety and welfare. I just can't live like you want me

to. Just like I couldn't be a lawyer like you wanted me to."
She looked at her father pointedly.

"Prudence," Marian said, moving to her side, "your father and I never wanted you to be an attorney if you didn't want to be. Between me and your father, your grandfather, Keith, Drew, and now Jeremy, I think we have quite enough attorneys in this family." The room smiled in unison. "The point is, dear, we're not trying to control your life, we just want you to be safe."

"I know, Mother, I know. But I'm beat and I really need to go home. I promise to be extremely careful and not take any stupid or unnecessary chances. Okay?"

Marian nodded her approval. "Is that okay with everyone here?" Everyone approved with the exception of Keith and Blake, who insisted on adding an amendment. "Yes, Dad, I will call home every night without fail, no matter what, cross my heart."

As soon as Prudence returned home she kicked off her shoes, put water on for tea, then went into her bedroom and collapsed onto her bed. She lay there for a few minutes delighted to finally be home. The day's events and the evening's had drained her more than she thought. She sat up on hearing the teakettle whistle.

After making her tea she went back into her bedroom and pushed the button to listen to her messages. Five minutes later she was still listening.

"I suppose now it's my turn to apologize. I overreacted this afternoon. Sorry. I thought we . . . uh . . . I thought maybe we . . . it doesn't matter. I . . . uh . . . Call sometime, anytime, I'll make time for you." Prudence smiled as she listened to the phone message a sixth time. God, he was so sexy. Even his voice was sexy. She pushed the replay button again and gently traced her fingers across her lips. The memory of the kiss they shared made her blush as the phone rang. "Hello?"

"Prudence."

"Hey, Whitney, what's up, girl?"

"What's up? What are you talking about? You blew me

off. We were supposed to have dinner and catch a movie tonight, remember?"

"Oh, Whitney, I'm so sorry, I completely forgot all about you."

"Some best friend you are, you completely dissed me. I hope at least you dumped me for a gorgeous hunk of man."

"Sorry to disappoint you."

"So, what happened? Don't tell me you blew me off for work again."

"Actually I did go back to work after I saw Michael. Then all hell broke loose when I went back to work and things got even crazier."

"Whoa, whoa, whoa, hold it. Go back. What do you mean after you saw Michael? Are you referring to Michael as in Speed Hunter?"

"Why does everybody call him Speed? Is that his middle name or something?"

"You're asking the wrong person. You should be asking him that question, not me. Now, getting back to you seeing him earlier, since I already know the who, give me the what, where, when, and how." The on-air investigative reporter in her instantly surfaced.

"Late this afternoon, instead of my dinner break, I drove over to the stadium."

"So what happened?"

"We talked, we kissed, and then as usual we argued. He got mad, called me a tease, and walked away without a word."

"He'll cool off, then he'll call you. Wait a minute, did you say you kissed him? Again?"

"Again." Prudence sighed heavily. "At twenty-eight I thought I knew a thing or two about kissing, but this man sure 'nuff is the master. He does things with his tongue that I never even dreamed of. I still can't believe we kissed in the middle of an empty parking lot in broad open daylight. Thank God there were no photographers around."

"Get out of here, really?" Whitney began to laugh. "I

can't even imagine that you, Prudy-Prudence, were necking in a parking lot in the middle of the afternoon." She laughed again. "I can't believe you did that."

"Tell me about it, I just hope I don't see another photo plastered across the newspapers tomorrow morning."

"So, if you two were sucking face, what's with the argument?"

"He wanted us to get together tonight. I told him that I had to get back to work and that I had a previous engagement."

"You realize of course that you two deserve each other," Whitney said.

"No way, the man is like my own personal purgatory."

"Don't be so dramatic. You two are perfect together. Believe me, any two people who argue as much as you two belong together. If for no other reason than to save the rest of us from your drama."

"Thanks, but no thanks. Opposites don't always attract."

"Opposites—are you kidding? You two are exactly alike. You're both nuts. But I wouldn't worry too much, he'll call, you'll see."

"He already did."

"When?"

"Tonight, he left a message on my machine and asked me to call him whenever I had some free time. He apologized."

"What did I just say? Exactly alike. You deserve each other."

"Yeah, yeah, whatever."

"So you blew me off, you blew Speed off. What did you do tonight?"

Prudence sighed and relayed the entire evening to her friend. Beginning with the phone call about James and ending with the discussion at her parents' home.

"This has been going on for too long. It's ridiculous. Valerie and I were just talking about this the other day. We knew that we should have just dragged your butt to the police station two months ago. Prudence, I just did an on-air report about this last week."

"I thought it would just blow over."

"Things like this don't just blow over—we told you that."

"I know."

"Valerie and I have seen it too many times to just presume that this idiot will suddenly grow a brain and smarten up. These men are usually troubled and in need of serious help. Ignoring them isn't the answer."

"I know," Prudence repeated.

"I know you were told about all of your legal options."

"Get real, Whitney. There were five and a half lawyers present. They cited every harassment case from the 1960s until those being brought before the Supreme Court in the next few years. Believe me, I've heard it all."

"I assume that the attending officers spoke to you about security, and what to do if there are any future annoyance calls."

"Yes."

"Good. How's James doing?"

"His mother said that the doctors are very encouraged. He's bruised and sore, but there was no serious or permanent damage, and he should be back to his old self in a few days."

"Good. You sound tired."

Prudence yawned. "I am. I'm totally beat. I'm gonna let you go. I'll call you tomorrow."

Surprisingly, Prudence slept soundly and peacefully that night. All thoughts of the mysterious stranger on the other end of the phone disappeared as soon as she played Michael's message one last time.

Chapter 12

"Did you see it?" Peter bragged as he stamped out a spent cigarette in the already overflowing ashtray.

"How could I miss it? It's great," Luther said, spinning his chair around joyously. "How'd you come up with the caption?"

"Hey, you're talking to the *guru reporter,* remember? Words are my game."

"This is great, I love it. McGee's gonna love it too; looks like we're back on top."

"What do you mean?"

"The gates are moving like crazy. We're sold out for the season, and next season's presale tickets are up ninety-five percent. *Sports Wrap-Up* just called, they want to do a feature on Speed and Prudence, the romance angle, something about the new wave of how star athletes are settling down. I also got a call from *Sports Illustrated*; they want the same basic thing."

"This Speed thing could have you opening up your own PR business sooner than you expected."

"Not just me, buddy, you too. Before I sign Speed and Prudence over to do the *Wrap-Up* and *Sports Illustrated* thing, I'll set them up with an exclusive with you. I'm sure your getting the first shot will be a major accomplishment in the eyes of the top brass over there. Hey, maybe you'll make senior editor after this thing is all over."

Peter lit another cigarette and took a deep drag. "Let's do it."

"It's a done deal, Speed's out on the field right now. I left a message in his locker. He'll stop by right after practice."

"That's it, buddy, we're on our way. Later."

"Later."

Three hours after that conversation Michael knocked on Luther's office door. Luther looked up. "Speed, come on in." Michael walked in and sat down and rested his duffel bag in the seat next to him. "I've got fantastic news."

"Really, what?" Speed said dryly.

"Just wait until you hear this," Luther promised excitedly.

"Make it quick, I have an offensive line meeting to attend in fifteen minutes and another two hours on the field."

"I just set up the coup of the century." He paused for dramatic effect. "An interview with Peter Hall from the *Philadelphia Sports Voice.* Everything's all set. I just need a time that's good for you and we're there."

"Luther, you know I don't like doing these one-on-one interviews. They all ask the same stupid questions. Get someone else, I pass."

Luther's eyes bulged. "No, Speed, you're kidding, right? This is free press for the whole franchise, the team, Speed. Think of the team. With us going on to the play-offs next month, all eyes will be right here. Everyone benefits, from the third roster all the way up the ladder to the owner's box."

"Luther, you know I don't talk about certain things, my personal life being one of them."

"Okay, yeah, that's good." Luther grabbed a pen and began writing notes. "We can work from there. I'll make a list of taboo topics, how's that sound?"

Michael cocked his head. After four practice hours on the field, two in the weight room, and an hour-and-a-half players' meeting, the last thing he needed was to sit here and listen to Luther blow smoke. With Luther, there was always some catch or bottom line to every deal. Michael grabbed his bag and stood. "I'll tell you what, I'll think about it and get back to you."

"Wait, wait, wait." Luther stood and came around his desk. "There's more. After the *Sports Voice* interview I have *Wrap-Up* and *Sports Illustrated* already in line drooling for you and Prudence."

Michael stopped. "Me and Prudence? You said this was a team thing."

"It is, it is. It's just that the whole town, hell, the whole country's rooting for you two kids to get together. It's like some Romeo and Juliet or Cleopatra and Mark Antony thing. You know, fate, love, and romance. Everybody wants the live-happily-ever-after ending with you two."

"Well, the best I can do is tell them the ending."

Luther half smiled. "What do you mean?"

"It's over."

Seldom taken by surprise, Luther froze. "What? It can't be." He scrambled for the newspaper still open on his desk. "What about this? It says here it was taken just yesterday. What the hell happened between yesterday afternoon and today?"

Michael took the paper and glanced at the clear photo of the kiss he and Prudence shared in the parking lot. "Now, those are the kinds of personal questions I don't answer. Later." He nodded, tossed the newspaper back on the desk, opened the door, and walked out.

Luther stood openmouthed, staring at the closed door.

James Pruet rolled over in the hospital bed and held the bandage wrapped around his ribs. He'd never been so sore in his life. He leaned up gingerly and pumped the switch on the pain-relief drip. His cell phone rang just as he released the button and eased back onto the pillow. He winced as he leaned over to pick up his phone from the side table.

He knew that he wasn't supposed to use a cell phone in the hospital room, but he didn't care. He needed to talk to Truman as soon as possible. He'd already left six messages. The last thing he needed was to have Truman or one of his associates after him again. "Yeah," he said as he picked up, assuming that it was his mother again.

"Pruet."

"Yeah," he grunted in anguish.

"Sorry to hear of your recent misfortune. The streets can be very dangerous when you're out of your league. Seems like even someone as well connected as you can have an accident."

James remained silent and held his ribs tighter. Truman was the worst kind of thug. He had no sympathy, no remorse, and no conscience. Publicly he was a real estate broker, but in actuality, the bulk of his resources came from illegal gains and gambling. "I'd say that in the future it would be in your best interests to pay your bills when they come due."

"I need more time, Truman. Please, I swear I'll get the money to you. I just need a few more weeks," he pleaded earnestly.

Truman snapped the end of a thin cigar, then rolled it between his fat fingers. He nodded to the woman sitting on a stool across the room. She immediately sashayed over and sat down on his large lap and lit his cigar. "Why should I give you more time?"

"I can get you things." James looked around the hospital room in a panic. "I have influence in City Hall. The mayor listens to me. I'm as good as his son-in-law."

Truman's loud laughter took James by surprise. "Fool, what, you think I can't read? Everybody knows that the mayor's daughter is with Speed Hunter."

James fumed. He'd never get from under Truman if he didn't get back together with Prudence. He needed pull in City Hall, and just being Blake's assistant wasn't enough for him anymore. "I can make sure that you have total access to whatever you want, whenever you want it."

Truman laughed again. "I already got that. Just get my money, you've got one week."

"I need more time," he said as the line went dead on the other end. James closed his cell phone and placed it back on the side table. He looked to each side of him at the two large bouquets of flowers. One was from the mayor and his wife and the other from Truman. He was exactly as they say, between a rock and a hard place.

Truman, known only by the one name, was a parasite that had come out of the rich suburbs of Camden, New Jersey. He was a menace that had grown out of control and was now almost completely untouchable. The D.A. had been after him for years, but each time the witness had changed his testimony and Truman remained a free man.

James held his ribs tightly. He should never have gotten involved with Truman. He'd sworn to himself that he'd stop gambling but he didn't, he couldn't. Ever since high school he'd found that he had an attraction to the excitement of gambling. Casinos, cards, and horses were his weakness. But dice had always been his game. That's why he did it. He'd gone to Truman's private club and made bets that he couldn't cover. Now he needed fast cash to cover the interest and payments.

He buzzed the nurse, got up, and took his clothing from the closet. An hour later, after dire warnings from the doctor, James stepped into a cab and headed home. He needed to get his life back on the fast track.

"Gene wants to see you in his office," Tanya announced as she walked up to the rolling cart of newly hung clothing.

"Right now?" Prudence asked, still hanging the new merchandise.

Tanya shrugged and nodded. "Yep, right now."

"All right." Prudence closed the box she'd been emptying and rolled the cart to the rear of her office.

"I'll finish hanging those. Don't you have a dinner break coming up?" Tanya asked.

Prudence looked at her watch. It was far later than she'd thought. "I'll go to dinner after I see Gene. I'll catch up with you at the meeting tonight. She gathered her coat and purse, then took the escalator to the top floor. Gene's office door was already open, so she tapped lightly on the frame and walked in.

"Prudence, come in, have a seat." She did. "I'll get right to the point. As of this closing today, you will be escorted to and from your car by security. In addition, I'd like you to hire another assistant and delegate some of the workload so that your in-store hours are more reasonable. Also, your departmental phone will now have caller ID. Lastly, the door to the storage space behind your office will be locked at all times. Ah, let's see." He peeked at a yellow legal pad filled with writing. "It looks like that's it for now. Any questions?"

"Which one of my brothers called you, or was it my parents?" The innocent look he gave was pathetic. "Come on, Gene, who was it, Keith? Dad?"

"No, as a matter of fact I didn't hear from anyone in your family until after the arrangements had already been made."

"So who got you to do all this?"

"Prudence, it doesn't matter how we found out, what matters is you should have informed us that this was going on. Harassment of an employee over store phones is intolerable. We will not have our employees tormented like this."

"I appreciate your concern, Gene, really I do. Who called you?"

"It is in our best interests to protect you."

"Gene, answer the question, who called you?"

"I received a call from the Philadelphia Knights organization."

"What?"

The blur of anger stung her eyes. She was so tired of people usurping her life she could scream. She vaguely muttered something to Gene that she was going on break, then grabbed her coat and purse, left his office, and headed for the Knights stadium.

Prudence was beyond furious but she promised herself she wouldn't go ballistic, at least not right off the bat. She'd give him a chance to open his mouth and explain, and then she planned to stuff a football down his throat. She marched up to the back door of the stadium.

"I know you, young lady. You're that gal who takes pictures with Speed Hunter," the old man said as she approached the rear door.

"Yes, I am. My name is Prudence Washington and I'd like to speak with Michael Hunter if I may." She was brisk and curt.

"A pretty thing like you shouldn't look so angry. You look like you're fit to be tied."

Prudence grimaced at his remark. She'd been ranting and raving and verbally battling in the car for the last fifteen minutes and apparently her anger showed. But there was no need to take out her frustration on this gentleman. So she relented. "You're absolutely right."

He nodded and smiled. "The name's Mr. Henry."

"Thank you, Mr. Henry."

"Now just a minute and I'll get you all straightened out." Mr. Henry picked up his clipboard and scanned the list of names with his bony finger. Prudence rolled her eyes. She knew she was taking a chance by just coming here unannounced. Being overly impulsive had always been her downfall. Her brother Jeremy had always warned her about it. He was right. An icy chill streaked through her. The last time she attempted to surprise someone had ended in a devastating outcome for both of them.

But, not having any other way to contact him, she had no choice. "Here we go, Prudence Washington. You're on the list." Mr. Henry pointed down the dimmed tunnel. "Go on in; just follow the tunnel to the signs on the walls directing you to the practice field." He looked at his watch. "I believe they ought to be just about finishing up for the day."

She didn't move. Why on earth would her name be on a back-gate stadium list? "Go on in; best get moving before they start filing out of there. Don't want to get crushed in that stampede of bulls when they leave the field."

"Yes, no, of course, thank you, sir." She turned to begin walking, following in the general direction that he had pointed.

"Henry."

She stopped and turned back to him.

"Folks around here call me Mr. Henry." He looked up at the darkening blue sky. "You know, I once knew a young gal named Prudence back in 1942. She lived in Biloxi, Mississippi. I was stationed down there in forty-six. Mighty pretty gal she was, sweet disposition, smiled just like her mama. Any relation to you?" he asked.

"I don't think so," she said, then, seeing the dejection in his eyes, she softened her response. "But hey, you never know. Your Prudence could have been my long-lost great-aunt or something."

Mr. Henry beamed. Prudence couldn't help but smile. The old man oozed enough charm to fill the stadium he guarded.

"My sentiments exactly. Go on in, gal, he's been waiting a long time for the likes of you."

"Thank you, Mr. Henry." Prudence was amazed. He knew just what to say to soften her mood.

"Next time you come by here, don't sit out there in that big yellow ball in the parking lot. You come on up and talk to me. I won't bite you."

"Definitely. If by some chance I find myself here again, I sure will."

"You'll be back." He winked through his thick glasses

and then flipped the shaded covering down. "You see, I know these things."

"Mr. Henry, I believe you do at that." Prudence smiled happily as she continued down the tunnel. Then she caught herself. Wait, this wasn't how it was supposed to go. She was furious. She wasn't supposed to be humming while on her way to rip someone's head off. As directed, she watched for the practice field sign and followed the arrow's direction.

The dark tunnel made a deep turn and she found herself standing in the bright stadium light surrounded by tens of thousands of empty stadium seats. She walked down a narrow row of steps and sat down watching the several groups of players huddled together. She couldn't tell which one was Michael. They all looked alike, big, padded, and mean. After ten minutes the players began heading to the locker rooms. Several removed their helmets and waved. She returned the gesture. She'd recognized them from the Thanksgiving dinner.

"Well, hello, are you here to see me?"

She turned, squinted at first, then forced a smile. "Mr. Phillips."

"That's right, but please, it's Luther. I'm pleased you remembered me."

"Of course, how could I forget you?" The dry tone of her voice didn't match the plastered smile on her face. "Thank you again for all your help with the Thanksgiving dinner preparations. The dinner was a great success and everyone had a wonderful time."

He nodded, smiling broadly as if he'd single-handedly done it all. "Yes, I received your note. You're quite welcome. If there's ever anything we can do, please don't hesitate to call my office." He handed her a business card.

"That's very generous of you. I'll certainly keep that in mind and pass it along to the head of the children's and youth ministries at the church."

"Splendid."

A brief silence drifted in as Prudence turned again to the men leaving the field. Luther followed her line of vision. "The team's looking really good for the play-offs this year. That certainly makes my job that much more rewarding."

"I can imagine it would."

"Do you follow the game?"

"Not really, not anymore."

Prudence feigned interest as Luther embarked on a rehearsed speech on the merits of football and competition and the Philadelphia Knights. "The public relations business for the Philadelphia Knights is a twenty-four-hour job . . ." he continued.

She nodded, then looked down as the last of the players straggled from the field.

She interrupted another one of Luther's long-winded speeches. "Mr. Phillips, do you know where I can find Michael Hunter?"

"Right here."

Both turned around. Michael stood right behind them, leaning against the railing. Their eyes connected, then fixed. The sly seductive charm of his wicked smile took her breath away. "Hello, Prudence," he said invitingly. "I see you've found some time."

Prudence opened her mouth but didn't speak for a second. Her breath still caught in her throat and her mouth went Sahara Desert dry. She was stunned. A crisp, pleasing smile crossed her face as her eyes slowly traveled his body. She definitely liked what she saw.

Michael, uniformed from the waist down, was breathtaking. But it was his arms, chest, and stomach that she couldn't turn away from. He wore a cropped red jersey that exposed his arms and stomach. Thick, braided triceps and biceps formed his upper arms. His broad chest covered by the midriff jersey left the tightly packed abs to peek out. She knew he looked good in his clothes and, left to her wayward fantasies, she imagined he looked incredible without them. The sight of him now left little doubt in her mind. She definitely wanted to see more.

Michael looked at Luther. Luther nodded, having gotten the hint. "All right, I guess I'll leave you two alone." He turned to Prudence. "It was nice seeing you again, Ms. Washington, Speed." He immediately turned and walked down into the darkness of the stadium tunnel.

Prudence looked at Michael. Michael looked at Prudence. "Yes," was the only thing she could rasp out.

He walked over to where she stood and placed his helmet on the nearest stadium seat. "Yes? Is that the answer to anything in particular?" He arched his brow for added interest. "Or should I take my pick?"

Prudence cleared her throat. "Yes, I found time," she clarified, then looked down at him again. "Aren't you freezing?"

Michael, following her eyes, looked down at his attire. "No, not at all." He smiled, seeing her eyes linger longer than intended. "So to what do I owe this visit?"

Prudence stepped back, getting her bearings and mentally distancing her thundering heart. She took a deep grounding breath. "I think you know the answer to that." Her crisp tone told him that this wasn't the social call he'd hoped for.

"Are we back to hostilities again?" He picked up his helmet and sat down on the seat's armrest.

Prudence took another deep breath and exhaled slowly. "Not at all." She paused calmly. "I just don't appreciate your office calling my manager and discussing my personal business. This is my problem; it has nothing to do with you."

"We've had this conversation before, haven't we?"

"This isn't some jockstrap gridiron game we're playing. This is my privacy, my life. I have enough trouble controlling issues with my brothers."

Michael rolled his neck, stretching in a circular motion. "I told you before the publicity will eventually blow over." The tedium in his tone was evident.

"I'm not talking about the publicity."

"Then what are you talking about?"

"I'm talking about the phone calls, the harassing calls."

"What harassing calls? You mean the reporters are harassing you now?"

"Oh, come on, don't pretend like you have no idea what I'm talking about. The phone calls, Michael. The calls from whoever assaulted my father's assistant last night."

"What assault? Who was assaulted? What are you talking about?" Michael sat up with more interest.

"Michael, don't play innocent with me. You know damn well what assault I'm talking about."

He stood and walked over to her. "Start from the beginning, Prudence. What happened?"

"Wait a minute." She looked at him suspiciously. He looked too shocked and too stunned. "Gene, the general manager at the store, told me that the front office of the Philadelphia Knights called him."

"My front office? Here? Come on." He grabbed his helmet. "We're going to clear this up right now." He took hold of her hand and pulled her along as he headed for the team's executive offices on the upper levels.

Luther was already there along with Coach Hawkins and the vice president of player affairs. The instant Michael mentioned Gene Reynolds, Luther owned up to calling him. He said that he'd received a tip from the precinct that Prudence had had a problem at the store. Then, as the team's publicity manager, he had acted in the best interests of Michael and the team.

Fifteen minutes of quick talking, then a deluge of apologies flowed from the executive offices like Niagara Falls. Luther was sweating bullets by the time he was finally excused, and slithered back to his office. Prudence made clear that no matter what the media printed regarding their relationship, her professional and private life were off-limits.

"I just assumed it was you," Prudence said as they walked down the stadium's empty corridor back toward the main level.

"Am I really that bad?"

She didn't reply, so he stopped walking and waited. After a few steps she realized that he had stopped, so she turned to him. "No, not at all," she said. "You're . . ." She sighed. "Not bad at all."

He smiled. "Was that an actual compliment?"

Prudence smirked. "Yes."

He smiled more broadly. "I'm glad to hear that."

"I guess I just jumped to the wrong conclusions. It's getting to be a habit. I have a tendency to do that when it comes to reporters and my privacy," Prudence continued. "I've always had a distant relationship with the local media, so all this, between you and me, has broken our unspoken truce."

Michael looked at her curiously. There had obviously been something between Prudence and the local media. Having no idea exactly what it was, he decided to make it a point of finding out.

They continued walking. "I guess if Luther knows, then the media and everybody else also know about the calls."

"Luther was only trying to protect me, and the team."

"So, not only does Luther do public relations for the team, he's also responsible for protecting your moral reputation."

"Something like that."

"Sounds like quite a job; that must keep him very busy."

Michael looked at her oddly. "If you're referring to my alleged reputation, I have no delusions or excuses regarding my conduct. But, in my defense, you of all people understand how things are blown out of proportion in the press, particularly when it comes to my romantic interests."

"Is that what I'm considered to you now, your romantic interest?"

He stopped walking again and took her hand and held her still. He looked into her softened eyes. "Some people seem to think so."

"What do you think, Speed?" she asked shyly.

His smile weakened her knees. "That's the first time you called me that name."

"What, Speed? Really?"

"Yes, really, and I kind of like it." He moved closer.

"Ditto. I kind of like it too." She moved closer. "But you didn't answer my question."

"Yes, I did." She looked at him questioningly. "Yes, and I kind of like it," he repeated. "And your feelings?"

"Ditto."

"So, what should we do about all this liking going on, Ms. Washington?" He moved closer still, raising his brow for added interest. She began laughing, her nose crinkled, and she turned away. "What? What's so funny?" he asked. The rich cinnamon tone of her face flushed a crimson red. He tipped her chin up to meet his face. "What?"

Still smiling, she bit at her lower lip and said, "Please don't take this the wrong way."

Michael immediately stepped back. "You have to get back to work, right?"

"Well, yeah, eventually I do, I have a buyers' meeting after closing tonight. But that's not it. Promise you won't get too upset."

"Just tell me."

She reached up and pinched her nose. "You stink."

His mouth dropped open when he realized he was still wearing his practice sweats, and after a full day on the field and in the weight room he knew she was right. A glint sparked in his eye as she watched him carefully for a reaction. He came closer and she backed up. But her three-inch heels and his long legs didn't give her much of an advantage.

"I stink, huh?" The look in his eye gave her pause. She stepped back farther just as he wrapped his arms around her body and held her tight. She began squirming to get away. The dam broke and loud spontaneous laughter echoed throughout the empty stadium corridor. He picked her up in his arms and swung her around.

When he stopped she slowly slid down the length of his body, every inch igniting a sensual flame of desire. The intimacy of their bodies touching caused their eyes to lock. The feast of rapture gripped them as their lips met in an explosion of passion. When the kiss ended she smiled up at him.

"Consider yourself a branded woman," he said, his voice husky with desire. Prudence smiled shamelessly as he pulled her back into his arms, keeping her close. "You're mine now."

Chapter 13

After calling Tanya and telling her that she had been detained and would meet her later that evening at the buyers' meeting, Prudence sat and waited in the players' family lounge while Michael showered and dressed. She flipped through recent sports magazines, wandered around the room reading the various wall plaques and certificates, and stared out of the huge plate-glass window overlooking the stadium grounds.

Michael walked into the room unannounced. He observed Prudence for a few minutes before saying anything. He had to admit, the woman was totally audacious. She had spunk, intelligence, and the ability to weaken his knees with just a glance.

Her short, curly, pixie-styled hair gave her a free-spirited persona that contrasted drastically with her always sleek, always professionally styled demeanor. He smiled to himself. She had a hair-trigger temper and the courage and fortitude to fight what she deemed injustice. And she didn't mind saying what she thought and holding her ground, especially when it came to him.

Of all the women he'd been involved with in his thirty-two years, she was by far the most remarkable. She could see right through him. And with her, his emotions ran the gamut. One kiss and he saw stars, and then the next minute she had him so crazy he wanted to scream. She was delicate and strong with a will as solid and flawless as a diamond, and worth every ounce.

She turned to see him standing in the doorway be-hind her. "So, what would you like to do this evening?" he asked.

"I have to go back to the store for a buyers' meeting. After that, whatever you're up for, I'm game." She smiled seductively.

"That's very enticing, Ms. Washington." He walked over to her. "I like the way you think." He glanced at his watch, then took her in his arms and snuggled close. "Why don't I follow you home now? You can leave your car, and then I'll drop you off at the store and pick you up when you get off."

"But you're probably beat from your practice today. You go home and rest, I'll call you later, we can meet some place."

"I don't think so. You and I, Ms. Washington, will def-initely need to have a long talk later about this need of yours to be so independent, but for right now, don't argue with me. I need to make sure you're safe. I don't like the idea that there's some nut out there who enjoys upsetting you."

She opened her mouth to speak but he placed a fin-ger across her lips. "Before you say anything, I'm not trying to run your life or crowd you; I just want the op-portunity to get to know you. Is that all right with you?"

"Yes."

"Good, so can we do things my way this one time?" Michael braced for another battle.

"Yes."

He smiled with a mixture of relief and delight. "Good, let's go."

An hour and a half later Prudence and Tanya walked back into her office after the buyers' meeting had ended. They talked about concerns and ideas discussed in the meeting as Tanya gathered her belongings to leave for the night.

"I was surprised to see you walk into the meeting," Tanya said as she shot Prudence a side glance and smiled knowing that she had gone to the stadium earlier. "I really didn't expect to see you until tomorrow morning. Gene said you'd probably be out the remainder of the day."

"I know, but I wanted to finish up some paperwork. These past few weeks have had me playing catch-up all day long. I'm just about ahead of the game and I don't intend to slip behind again." She walked into her office and stood at her desk. "What are these?" she called out to Tanya, who had stopped at her desk.

Tanya, looking over her notes from the meeting, stopped and came into Prudence's office. "Offhand, I'd say that they were flowers." She smiled at her observant remark.

"Very funny, Tanya, when did they come?" Prudence leaned in and smelled the bouquet of bright yellow roses.

"Just a few minutes before I left for the meeting. The guard's receipt with the time stamped is on the desk."

Prudence picked out the envelope and read the card. She smiled. The note simply read, *Compliments of the Philadelphia Knights.*

"Speaking of guards," Tanya continued, "Gene came down and told me about the new security changes around here."

Prudence smiled helplessly. "I was going to talk to you about all that tomorrow morning. Sorry about all the unnecessary distractions."

"Are you kidding? We could always use some beefed-up security around here. I'm just sorry it took something so serious for management to make a move. We already have our new phones with the caller ID features. They were installed a little while after you left earlier. The plainclothes security team began making both scheduled and unscheduled stops by here late this afternoon. To tell you the truth, I feel safer already."

"I'm glad. I'm surprised it all happened so quickly.

Usually it takes weeks to implement changes. What's this?" Prudence asked, referring to a large white box sitting on her chair. She picked up the package and placed it on her desk.

"I don't know, it wasn't there when I came back from shipping earlier or when we left for the meeting. Security must have dropped if off just before closing. Is there a card?"

Prudence looked on and around her desk. "I don't see one."

She pulled the bow's ribbon and took the lid off of the package. She peeled away the white tissue paper. A sickening feeling formed in the pit of her stomach. A slinky black lace negligee, leather-strapped handcuffs, a short cattail whip, and freely scattered extra-large-ribbed condoms were inside. "What the—" Prudence exclaimed.

Tanya walked over and peeked into the box. "Okay, that's something you don't see every day." Prudence picked up a pen and started gingerly poking at the sleazy items. Tanya grimaced. "Who would send you something like that?"

Prudence sighed heavily and looked away as the bile of disgust rose in her throat. "I think it's from my new telephone pal."

"Ah man, not again. That means he must have been in here to deliver it." Tanya looked around nervously.

"The store's been closed for over an hour. I don't think anyone's here now, Tanya, we're safe enough."

Tanya took Prudence's hand and squeezed it in a show of solidarity. "It's not me I'm worried about. This guy has some warped ideas about you. I'm calling security." Tanya picked up the receiver as Prudence touched her hand before she dialed.

"It's too late for that, Tanya. I'm sure he's long gone. I'll notify security on the way out tonight."

"Come on, Prudence, let's get out of here. We can have security walk us to our cars." Tanya gathered her jacket and purse, then turned to Prudence just as she settled herself behind the desk. "Wait a minute, you're not still staying late, are you?"

Prudence nodded and pulled out several folders. "Yes, I am." She grabbed some samples and her leather folder of notes.

"Prudence, are you sure?" Tanya asked.

"Yes, I'm sure. I'll be fine. Go home, I won't be here long."

"Okay," Tanya said reluctantly. "Good night."

After Tanya left, Prudence found it hard to concentrate on her paperwork. The white box still sitting on her desk gave her a nervous feeling that made her angry and uneasy. She looked around the dimly lit office. Mannequins and merchandise-filled boxes surrounded her at every turn. A sudden claustrophobic feeling washed over her. She reached over to pick up the telephone just as it began to ring. "Hello?"

"Hey, beautiful, I'm about ten minutes away, but if you're not ready to leave, I'll wait for you in the parking lot."

"Michael?"

"Yeah."

She sighed heavily. "I forgot all about you."

"That doesn't sound very promising." When she didn't respond, Michael frowned. "Prudence?"

The nervousness in her anxious voice was evident. "I'll be downstairs waiting."

"Is something wrong?"

She looked over to the white box, but didn't speak.

"Prudence, what's wrong?"

"I'll meet you downstairs at the security office."

She hung up, quickly gathered her coat and purse, and hurried through the empty store. She headed for the elevators, then changed direction and took the stilled escalators. By the time she arrived at the security office she was near panic.

She went and dropped off the box. Fortunately, the head of store security hadn't left and took personal charge of the situation. He opened and examined the contents of the box, then took several pictures of the items and helped her fill out a report. Michael arrived and was directed to the security office.

"Prudence?" She looked up and he glared at the man behind the desk. "What's going on?"

The security chief explained the situation and showed him the items. Michael insisted on phoning the police. They came and filed another report. They took the items at Michael's insistence for fingerprints and evidence.

Half an hour later Prudence sat in Michael's car as he pulled out of the store's dark parking lot. "I'm glad that's over with; I've never been so humiliated in my life. All those men staring at those things made me so angry. I'm glad you were there with me. You seem to be in the right place to rescue me again."

Michael was still too furious to speak. The package was the last straw. "Why didn't you tell me everything that was going on?"

"I did."

"No, you said the store's front office added unnecessary sanctions on your life because of our relationship, that you had received a few crank calls, and that a friend of yours had been assaulted. You never said anything about knowing this guy. Who is he, an old boyfriend or something?"

Prudence rested her head back on the comfortable headrest. "I don't know. He's not an old boyfriend, but he seems to think that I should know him."

"What does that mean? Either you know him or you don't."

"Michael, please, I don't want to discuss it. Let's talk about this later, please."

With great difficulty he held his tongue for the remainder of the ride to her condo.

Michael parked his car in the available space next to Prudence's yellow Bug. He got out and walked around

to the passenger-side door. Prudence was already halfway
out. "In the future, allow me to open the door for you."

"I'm perfectly capable of—"

He interrupted her firmly. "Prudence."

"Fine."

They walked in silence to her apartment. When they
approached the front door Prudence pulled the key
from her purse. Without bothering to ask, Michael took
the key from her hand and unlocked the door. He entered first and felt around for a light switch. After the
room was illuminated he looked around, then stepped
back and allowed her to enter. She did, and then anxiously looked around. "Stay here," he said as he began to
walk around the apartment opening and closing doors
and checking windows.

When he disappeared to the rear of the apartment,
Prudence looked around cautiously. Everything seemed
to be as she'd left it earlier. With her coat still on, she
wrapped her hands around her arms. She hated the feeling of not being in control. She hated the fact that
someone was dictating her life and there was nothing
she could do about it. She gathered her strength and followed Michael to the back of the apartment.

She found him in her bedroom securing the window
lock. She walked over to him.

"There's no one here and no sign that anyone's broken in. You shouldn't have any problems tonight."

She nodded as she removed her coat and suit jacket.
"Thank you . . ." Michael took her coat and laid it on the
chair at the vanity, then came to her. They stood toe to toe
beside her bed. ". . . for everything." Her voice softened.
The look she gave him left little to the imagination. She
took his hand and guided it to her cheek. "I don't know
what I would have done if you hadn't been there with me
tonight."

Michael turned his hand and cupped her smooth, soft
skin. "We'll get to the bottom of this." A solitary tear fell

to his hand. He watched as it slowly crawled along his thumb.

"Prudence."

"Hold me." The urgency in her stressed voice was heart-wrenching. She looked up into his soft, velvety eyes. "Please."

He instantly took her into his arms and soothed her with his gentleness. They stood serenely united for several minutes. Prudence let herself wallow in the feel of his strength. This was how love should be, not forced or bargained, but easy and comforting. Suddenly the impulse gripped her. She kissed his neck, then nuzzled into the arch of his chest. She felt his tense body give slowly.

She looked up at him. The intensity of the moment left its mark irrevocably on both of them. He could either walk away now or not. The truth was, he wanted to stay as much as he wanted her. Ever since the first time he'd seen her burst through those church doors, a deep longing had burned inside him. But now, at this moment, he had the opportunity to step up and go beyond his physical need and desire for her.

She was vulnerable; she was exposed and susceptible to the slightest tender provocation. He'd never been known as a man to use an advantageous situation to his benefit except on the field, and he wasn't about to start now.

Michael chose. "Prudence." He stepped back, an arm's distance away from her. He didn't know Prudence Washington well, but he knew that she wasn't some hot-in-the-bottom football groupie who just wanted to hang his numbered jersey on her bedpost. She was a woman who would want more, who needed more and deserved more. Unfortunately, more wasn't what he could offer her, not now. He turned and walked away.

"Kiss me," she said. He stopped dead in his tracks, as if cemented in place. She walked up behind him and let her hand trace a searing burn down his back. Hearing his sharp intake of breath, she moved around to face him. If he was going to reject her, it would be to her face.

"Prudence," he began again.

"Kiss me," she repeated in earnest. When he didn't reply she stepped closer to him. "Please."

Before the words tumbled from her lips she was wrapped up into his arms with his mouth firmly sealed to hers. The kiss sent a burning hunger seething through her. This was more than a kiss of comfort. It was a kiss of passion, of wanton promises, and of desire yet untouched.

She molded her body to his, feeling the urgency of his arousal. She pressed even closer, feeling his response in needful earnestness. He had something she wanted, and tonight she planned to get it. Since the entire city thought that they were lovers, it was high time she partook in the luxury of that notion.

She inched her leg up and wrapped it around his body. Without breaking the connection, he gripped her bottom and pulled her upward to wrap both legs around his waist. Holding her firmly, he ravished her mouth, leaving her breathless, weak, and glad that he held her so firmly, lest she fall right there at his feet.

Then he gently released her, letting her body slowly slide down the length of him. There was little doubt that he wanted her. His eyes and his body affirmed that fact, but still he hesitated.

"Make love to me," she requested.

"Prudence."

"I want to feel you inside me, Michael, tonight, now."

"You don't know what you're asking." He held her away as his libido was held by the barest thread of honor. If he did what he wanted to do, he could never look at himself in the mirror. She was too vulnerable and he was too aroused.

"I do. I know what I want, Michael. I want you."

"Prudence, don't tempt me like this."

She captured his eyes and kept them with methodical

intensity. Without thinking, she began unbuttoning her blouse. When she'd finished she let it drop to the floor. Her ample breasts were barely covered by a satiny lace material. She immediately unzipped her skirt, letting it follow the blouse to the floor.

Michael watched, dry-mouthed and stunned. The erotic sight of her stripping in front of him sent his body on overdrive. He took a sharp breath and opened his mouth to speak, but the words singed, burned away by the smoldering heat of his desire. She gripped the waistband of his slacks and unfastened his belt, then slowly pulled it from the loops.

Michael watched hypnotically while inwardly fighting the battle of a gentleman's honor versus wanton lust.

Prudence gradually tugged his knit sweater from his pants, then pulled it up and over his head, exposing the firm masculine splendor of his torso. Her sure hands instantly went to the solid hardness of his chest, taking pleasure in feeling the tight muscles. She let her fingers dance a pirouette around his taut nipples. Then she leaned in and let her tongue taste the sweet-as-dark-chocolate kisses of his body. The sensation caused a quaking shiver to go through him, shaking him to the core. Prudence smiled and delved deeper, feeling his dwindling hold over self-control.

His moan, guttural and primal, fanned the already scorching flame that opened a flood of wanton abandonment. She ravaged his body as he'd done her mouth, giving him pleasure and sending him teetering on the edge of yielding to her whim.

After she'd had her fill she lowered her hands to his waistband and unsnapped and unzipped his slacks. His need for her bulged through the fabric and stood ready to join with her and receive what she so eagerly offered. Just as she reached inside, Michael clamped his hands on her wrists. The quickness of the action made her gasp.

"Prudence." His voice was hoarse and husky. "Listen

to me. You're vulnerable now, and tomorrow morning you're gonna regret this. You don't know what you're asking." He removed her hands from his waistband, then dropped his hold on her wrists.

"I know what I'm doing and I know what I'm asking. I just have one request." He dipped his head closer to listen and look deeper into her eyes. She looked up at him and smiled. "Please don't break my heart. I don't want to be hurt again, not again."

"What?" He stopped, completely stunned by her request. "Hurt you? Prudence, I would never—"

"Then touch me now, Michael, I'm asking you to touch me. I need to be with you tonight."

Her earnest plea slashed through him like a knife on fire. His heart opened to her and poured out a feeling of giving that he'd never experienced. No one had ever opened herself to him like this before.

She inched her body closer to his, feeling the engorged firmness of his desire. "Touch me," she said. He froze solid, so she took his hand and placed it on her breast. "Here." Slowly she rubbed his hand against the pert orbs of her breasts, feeling the heavenly awareness of his hand on her. An instant later his hand found its own will as his other hand snapped the front clasp, freeing her from confinement. He took her breast in the palm of his hand and weighed the last reasons for hesitation.

"You want me to touch you?" he asked.

"Yes, now, touch me, feel me."

The dam of restraint broke. In an instant she was whisked upward into his arms and then held against the wall. As she'd done before, she wrapped her legs around his waist and held as his body relinquished all notions of honor and principle. Like a starved man, he fed from her mouth while his skillful hands sent sparks of pleasure dancing through her body.

He broke from the wall and walked her to the bed. Laying her down gently, he stood over her waiting for the last rational bit of control to stop him. Prudence

reached up and pulled his zipper down. His pants fell.
She pulled him down to her side and he willingly joined
her there on the sweet coverlet of prim flowers and delicate ribbons.

She rolled over, pushed him back onto the bed, and
climbed on top. He instantly grabbed her waist and
aimed her body down to his. Her breasts, positioned
inches from his mouth, were immediately covered. His
tongue licking and suckling her nipple sent her over the
edge of ecstasy. Then he sandwiched each breast with his
hands and gently rubbed both with his thumbs. Going
from nipple to nipple like a man famished with hunger,
he ravished her with such intensity she begged for their
joining.

He slowly rolled her over, pinning her beneath his
muscled weight. She reached down and took the shaft of
her pending pleasure. "Fill me now," she commanded
with ease.

He moved her hand away, making it obvious that he
wasn't finished touching her yet. "Do you still want me
to touch you?" he asked, nuzzling closer and lower.

She nodded, her mouth too dry to answer.

He leaned in and kissed her long, hard, and lovingly,
then burned a path down her neck and shoulder hot
enough to rival the sun. She gasped when his kisses
delved even lower along the thin elastic of her satin and
lace panties and garter. He bit at the elastic and unsnapped the garter ribbons with his teeth. A tiny hiss of
desire escaped from her lips. "Do you still want me to
touch you?"

"Yes." Her breath came in gasps of anticipation.

"Here?" He fanned his hands along the sides of her
body, then gently raked his neatly trimmed nails downward, pulling her scant panties and garter belt along.

"Yes."

"Here?" He fanned his hands down her inner thighs,
then placed one of her legs on his shoulder. He kissed
and stroked her knees, her legs, her thigh. "Here?"

An Important Message From The ARABESQUE Publisher

Dear Arabesque Reader,

I invite you to join the club! The Arabesque book club delivers four novels each month right to your front door! It's easy, and you will never miss a romance by one of our award-winning authors!

With upcoming novels featuring strong, sexy women, and African-American heroes that are charming, loving and true… you won't want to miss a single release. Our authors fill each page with exceptional dialogue, exciting plot twists, and enough sizzling romance to keep you riveted until the satisfying end! To receive novels by bestselling authors such as Gwynne Forster, Janice Sims, Angela Winters and others, I encourage you to join now!

Read about the men we love… in the pages of Arabesque!

Linda Gill
PUBLISHER, ARABESQUE ROMANCE NOVELS

*P.S. Watch out for the next Summer Series **"Ports Of Call"** that will take you to the exotic locales of Venice, Fiji, the Caribbean and Ghana! You won't need a passport to travel, just collect all four novels to enjoy romance around the world! For more details, visit us at www.BET.com.*

SPECIAL OFFER! 4 BOOKS FREE!

BET BOOKS

www.BET.com

A SPECIAL "THANK YOU" FROM ARABESQUE JUST FOR YOU!

Send this card back and you'll receive 4 FREE Arabesque Novels—a $25.96 value—absolutely FREE!

The introductory 4 Arabesque Romance books are yours FREE (plus $1.99 shipping & handling). If you wish to continue to receive 4 books every month, do nothing. Each month, we will send you 4 New Arabesque Romance Novels for your free examination. If you wish to keep them, pay just $18* (plus, $1.99 shipping & handling). If you decide not to continue, you owe nothing!

- Send no money now.
- Never an obligation.
- Books delivered to your door!

We hope that after receiving your FREE books you'll want to remain an Arabesque subscriber, but the choice is yours! So why not take advantage of this Arabesque offer, with no risk of any kind. You'll be glad you did!

In fact, we're so sure you will love your Arabesque novels, that we will send you an Arabesque Tote Bag FREE with your first paid shipment.

* PRICES SUBJECT TO CHANGE.

YOU'LL GET 4 SELECT ROMANCES PLUS THIS FABULOUS TOTE BAG!

**Visit us at:
www.BET.com**

THE "THANK YOU" GIFT INCLUDES:

- 4 books absolutely FREE (plus $1.99 for shipping and handling).
- A FREE newsletter, *Arabesque Romance News*, filled with author interviews, book previews, special offers, and more!
- No risks or obligations. You're free to cancel whenever you wish with no questions asked.

INTRODUCTORY OFFER CERTIFICATE

Yes! Please send me 4 FREE Arabesque novels (plus $1.99 for shipping & handling). I am under no obligation to purchase any books, as explained on the back of this card. Send my free tote bag after my first regular paid shipment.

NAME

ADDRESS _____ APT.

CITY _____ STATE _____ ZIP

TELEPHONE (   )

E-MAIL

SIGNATURE

Offer limited to one per household and not valid to current subscribers. All orders subject to approval. Terms, offer, & price subject to change. Tote bags available while supplies last.

AN035A

Thank You!

Accepting the four introductory books for FREE (plus $1.99 to offset the cost of shipping & handling) places you under no obligation to buy anything. You may keep the books and return the shipping statement marked "cancelled". If you do not cancel, about a month later we will send 4 additional Arabesque novels, and you will be billed the preferred subscriber's price of just $4.50 per title. That's $18.00* for all 4 books for a savings of almost 30% off the cover price (Plus $1.99 for shipping and handling). You may cancel at any time, but if you choose to continue, every month we'll send you 4 more books, which you may either purchase at the preferred discount price. . . or return to us and cancel your subscription.

* PRICES SUBJECT TO CHANGE

THE ARABESQUE ROMANCE BOOK CLUB
P.O. BOX 5214
CLIFTON NJ 07015-5214

PLACE
STAMP
HERE

Prudence closed her eyes and bit her lower lip as she moaned her answer. The sensation of his hands on her was thrilling. The sensation of his mouth on her was maddening. "Yes." She held out her arms, beckoning to him. "Michael, now, now."

Michael reached down and gently pulled at the tangle of delicate hairs at the core of her desire. He heard the soft sound of her all too familiar sigh and smiled. His jaw tightened, but he needed to hold back. This was about her comfort, her need, her pleasure. For the first time in a long while he refused to be selfish.

Women had thrown themselves at him all of his life— high school, college, the pros, the groupies, the fans, and the fanatics. They'd offered themselves and he'd taken, willingly. But this time, with this woman, in this place, something had changed. This wasn't about his selfish desires. The moral quandary of his sudden un-selfishness had stopped him.

He leaned over and looked into her sparkling eyes. They were hooded and sexy. He stroked the softness of her stomach, watching a smile widen across her face. The feeling struck him: this was more than a one-night stand.

Prudence tilted her head to the side. Something had changed. He had changed. "Are you okay?" she asked. When he didn't answer she feared the worst and draped her arm across her breasts.

"No, don't," he said, taking her hand and kissing it while looking into her eyes. "I'm fine."

"You're distracted. Is there somewhere you need to be?"

He didn't know what to say. An unfamiliar emotion had overwhelmed him, yet the clarity of the feeling made him smile. "Yes, here, with you." He leaned down and kissed her gently, causing a slow, steady burn to flood their bodies again.

She reached over and pulled a small plastic packet from her top drawer and opened it. She fingered the latex as she pulled it out. "Shall I?" His kiss was his answer. She did the honors.

Then, when they were ready, he entered and together they began the ancient rhythmic dance of lovers. He rocked his hips as she raised her legs to encircle him. Deeper and deeper he thrust, joining their bodies again and again.

In wave after wave, rocking in, out, up, down, they moved in unison, feeling the crescendo of passion inch higher and higher. In a frantic pace they pinnacled to ecstasy, sailing over the edge of the world. Then slowly they drifted back down to earth and in a warm comforting embrace they held each other. Neither spoke as they lay there breathless.

Michael rolled over and looked up at the ceiling, then closed his eyes. This was the point where he usually got up, grabbed his clothing, and left. But instead he lay there, surrounded by the frilly pillows and delicate lace, in serene peace. This was completely out of character for him. He opened his eyes and reached over and touched Prudence's arm. The sweet softness tugged at his heart.

He looked over to her. Her eyes were closed and a contented expression graced her face as her body relaxed and her breathing eased. He reached out and pulled her closer to the side of his body. She came willingly and cuddled against him and tucked beneath his arm. The calming, at-home feeling was foreign to him. But he liked it.

The feel of her body curved against him drew a heavy sigh of contentment. Prudence comfortably nuzzled her cheek against his chest as she closed her eyes again. "Are you okay?" she asked.

Michael smiled, gathering her closer, and closed his eyes in blissful peace. "Perfect," he muttered. Together, they drifted off to a calming, restful sleep.

* * *

James was led through the club to the private offices in the rear. He saw Truman as soon as the door was open. At nearly three hundred pounds and wearing a bright orange and blue track suit, he was impossible to miss.

"Damn, man, you look like hell. What happened to you?" The room, filled with lackeys and flunkies, broke into riotous laughter. Everyone knew that Truman had ordered James to be taught a lesson.

James ignored the remark and glared at the two men responsible for his current physical condition. "Look, I came here because I need more time. I can't come up with that kind of money in a week."

"That's not my problem. I don't make stupid bets I can't afford to cover." Laughter rose around him again. "Okay, I'll tell you what, I'll let you make a down payment."

"How much?" James asked eagerly.

Truman smiled broadly and nodded his head. The room instantly cleared out except for a woman at the bar, Truman, and James. "You're gonna do me a little favor."

James was suspicious. "Sure, what is it?"

"You say you're in with the mayor's daughter."

"Yes, we dated awhile until recently."

"Good, get her new boyfriend to miss a few passes."

"What?"

"You heard me."

"How am I supposed to get him to do that?"

"That's not my problem. I'm offering you a way out for the time being. I suggest you take it or pay what you owe in full."

"How about I get you some more information from Blake's office? Your friend was able to use it before. I know I can find something else useful."

"Look, this ain't no *Let's Make a Deal*. I'm in the business of influencing outcomes. I manipulate the odds, from football and basketball, to the mayor's office. I control the outcome. That's what I do. So, either get me the money you owe me or talk to your girl about fixing the games."

The woman at the bar walked over to the door and opened it. James turned around to see Truman's flunkies enter and take their seats again. The two men that had attacked him walked over and stood on either side of him. Truman nodded and they each took one of James's arms and escorted him out. The meeting was apparently over.

Chapter 14

A stupendous dawn barely peeked over the top of the century-old trees in bright colors of yellow, red, and orange, but Keith Washington was oblivious to it. "She didn't call at all last night?" Keith asked as he accelerated to the right and exited the expressway off-ramp.

"No, and she's not answering her phone either," his mother answered, using the wired cell phone through the car's speakers. She looked to her focused husband as he maneuvered the late-model car around several slow-moving vehicles in front of him.

"I knew we should have insisted that she move back in with you and Dad." Keith slammed his fist against the steering wheel when the traffic light turned red.

"Keith, Prudence is a grown woman. We have to trust her decision," Blake said. "We don't like it any more than you do, but it's her life."

"You're her parents, do something, overrule her."

"This isn't a courtroom, Keith, it's Prudence's life. Have you talked to your brothers?"

"Yeah, they're on their way."

"Good," Blake said as he exited the expressway.

"I'm turning into her place now. Her car's here." Keith waved to the security guard, then maneuvered his SUV to park next to the yellow Bug but stopped when he spotted a black Mercedes with the tag that read SPEED. His temper instantly flared. "That son of a . . ."

"We're right behind you," Marian said as they turned

into the main entrance and saw two of her sons following right behind them.

"Better hurry," Keith warned, "and I hope you brought bail money."

"Keith? Keith!" Marian called out as she watched him run into the building.

Prudence stayed in the bedroom far too long. She'd been showering and getting dressed for nearly forty minutes. In actuality, she'd been hiding out like a coward. She sat at her vanity and looked over to the closed door as the soft music drifted through. Michael was out there.

She smiled when her thoughts turned to their night together. It was like a dream. They had fit perfectly and each movement, each gesture, each action was met with a perfect reply. It was as if they were made for each other. And that's what scared her. They were too perfect together.

As far as she was concerned, as opposites go, they were as opposite as it got. He was a super-jock media addict with a fleet of women waiting in line for his attention. She, on the other hand, was a commitment-phobic clothes junkie with serious anger and privacy issues. But when they came together it was if the heavens shined a radiant warmth down on them that erased everything, their uncertainties, their doubts and fears. How could they fit so perfectly and still be miles apart?

Last night was just about last night, she resolved for herself with bolstered assurance. "Last night was just a physical thing," she reiterated firmly to her mirror image, "a release of pent-up emotion over the events of the day, a physical act by two people in need of mutual comfort and a sexual outlet. It was nothing, unimportant, meaningless." She nodded approvingly at her reflection. "So, why are you hiding in your bedroom for forty-five minutes?" Frustrated, she buried her face in her hands and parked her elbows on the vanity.

A multitude of mixed feelings went through her

mind. This wasn't the first time she'd been with a man, but it was the first time that she'd awakened with the sense that something had changed. She looked back up at her reflection. She tilted her chin from side to side. She looked exactly the same, but there it was nonetheless. Something was different, her eyes, her lips, her heart, something had changed, and that something was because of the man in the next room. *Coward.*

Michael looked back at the bedroom door as he sat comfortably on the sofa and listened to the music. Prudence had been in there for over half an hour. He didn't mind. He needed the time to think. Things were flying through his mind at supersonic speed. He needed to take a few minutes to regroup. But one thing was sure, she'd gotten to him.

Prudence was everything any man could ask for, smart, attractive, salacious, and sexy as hell. Even now, the thought of their time together sent an instant longing swirling through him. The first time was brazenly erotic; the second time was playful and scintillating. The third time, earlier that morning, was heaven on earth.

The smile she put on his face was endless. She was a remarkable woman, that much he already knew. The fact that she had touched a part of him that he had long forgotten was a complete and welcome surprise. He rested his head back and reveled in the beauty of Prudence as soft jazz played on the CD player.

He looked around. Everything reflected her style and good taste. From the antique spinning wheel in the corner to the Tiffany lamp hanging above the Queen Anne armchair by the fireplace.

Her home was tasteful and comfortably decorated with soft pastels and artistic accents. He browsed through a fashion magazine, then flipped through an open art book on the coffee table. After several restless moments he stood and walked over to the live

Christmas tree in the corner of the living room. The numerous white twinkling lights sparkled and he smiled at the unique hanging ornaments.

Anger rose when he thought about the sick mind of the man who had called and sent perverted gifts to her. He vowed right then that if he ever had the opportunity to face the man who was terrorizing her, he'd tear him apart with his bare hands.

Suddenly Michael heard the jingle of keys in the front door lock. As quick as his nickname suggested, he vaulted over the sofa and sprang behind the front door. As soon as the man entered and his hand released the doorknob, Michael pounced.

Grunts, groans, and shouts blasted in the living room, prompting Prudence to run from her bedroom still half dressed. "Oh my God, no! Michael, Michael stop!" The opening punch was heard throughout the room.

Fists flew threw the air with ease as the two men wreaked havoc on her furniture and each other's faces and bodies. Marian and Blake arrived and stood at the open door witnessing the spectacle of their son and an unidentified assailant rolling around on the carpet punching each other out. Jeremy and Drew quickly brushed past Marian and shoved Blake back, then joined the ruckus on the floor.

The three men grabbed Michael and threw him back and began punching his midsection. Barely fazed, Michael lunged forward, knocking the two down on the floor and pulling Keith back down with a thud. Prudence continued screaming. She pulled at Michael's arm and finally got his attention. "Michael, stop it, stop it. They're my brothers."

Completely winded, Drew staggered back against the wall. Jeremy made himself comfortable on the floor where he'd been knocked down. Keith staggered to his feet and glared at Michael and Prudence. "What the hell are you doing in my sister's apartment at this hour?" Keith rasped out, chest heaving.

Michael glared at Keith, refusing to even acknowledge his question, as Prudence blushed bright red.

Blake closed the door, removed his wife's coat, and gave it to his daughter to cover her lace bra. "Here, dear, you might want to go finish dressing."

Prudence looked down at herself. She'd raced from the bedroom with only her jeans, socks, and bra on. She quickly turned and left the room.

"Well, gentlemen," Marian began, "now that we have the general introductions out of the way, shall we be seated?" She held her arm out for Blake, who promptly took it and guided her over the broken coffee table, end table, and shattered antique curio cabinet.

Michael followed, scarcely fazed by the onslaught of three angry brothers. Each man glared as he strolled past, barely scathed, behind the courtly pair.

As Drew, Jeremy, and Michael began to clear and set aside the broken furniture, Keith continued to glare at Michael. "I still want to know what he's doing here this time of morning," he grumbled, loud enough for everyone in the room to hear.

"It's none of your business," Michael shot back instantly. "What's between Prudence and me is just that, between us."

With that remark, an argument immediately began. This time Keith and Michael stood across the room from each other as Blake tried to calm them. After a few minutes of open hostilities, Marian finally got the two men to calm down and stop arguing.

The room went silent except for the sound of Jeremy piling the broken furniture by the front door.

"Mr. Hunter," Marian began.

Michael looked to her and smiled openly. She looked older than Prudence but just as striking, her face firm and smooth and accepting. He could see where Prudence got her attractiveness from. Prudence and Marian could almost pass as sisters. "Yes, ma'am, please call me Michael," he said, adding a more pronounced Texas accent to his dialect. Keith, still annoyed by his presence, rolled his eyes to the ceiling and turned away.

"Michael," Marian continued, "I presume you know about the recent phone calls." He nodded. "Prudence was supposed to call us last night. She didn't. Has something happened that we should know about?"

"Yes, ma'am, there was an occurrence at the store last night."

Keith turned back around and walked closer to the center of the room.

"What were you doing at the store?" Drew asked.

"I had a date," Michael said, and then he turned to Keith. "With Prudence. Unfortunately it had to be canceled." Keith was just about to open his mouth when Michael pulled out the photos taken in the security office. He passed them around and told of the events from the night before, omitting of course his intimacy with Prudence. By the time Prudence returned to the living room, a stilled hush hung in the air.

Blake and Marian were stunned silent. Jeremy cussed as Drew, uncharacteristically angry, vowed to kill. Keith and Michael, now standing side by side, had formed a strange bond as they stood fuming over the situation. Prudence tilted her head in curious interest as she smiled nervously. It seemed that her older brother had finally found a formidable ally.

"We've been discussing these photos, dear," Marian began, and Blake continued.

"Michael was kind enough to brief us on last evening's events. This has obviously gotten more serious than we originally presumed. I think—"

"Dad," she interrupted, "before you start, I want to say something." With everyone's attention she began. "I know that you all love and care for me, and I love you all too, but this is something that's just out of your hands."

She turned to Marian and Blake. "Mother, Dad, you

taught me never to run from a fight and always to rely on my inner strength. That's what I'm doing. You can't take that away from me by expecting me to run away and hide until this nut goes away. I'd be hiding all my life and that wouldn't be right. I'd be letting you down and myself too."

She moved to where her brothers were assembled. "Guys, you've been my protectors all my life. You've showed me how to stand up for myself and protect myself both mentally and physically. I'm not saying that I can take on a big strong man physically, but thanks to you and a black belt, I definitely know how to hurt him and run fast."

She stood in front of Michael. "Michael, you and I have gone through a lifetime of troubles before we even got a chance to get to know each other. I don't know where this thing between us is going or if it's going anywhere. We'll have to wait and see. But if you're looking for a damsel in distress, I'm not her. I know you want to be my knight in shining armor, but some things I have to do my way. Can you understand that?" He nodded reluctantly.

"So with that said, I've been thinking. One thing about this guy keeps sticking out in my mind." Everyone inched closer with interest. "He keeps calling me Prudy, not Prudence or Pru but Prudy."

Her brothers all looked at each other and said in unison, "Prudy?" That had always been their nickname for her. No one else called her that except the man on the phone. If someone ever did casually refer to her as her Prudy, she'd immediately correct them.

Keith walked to the center of the room and scratched at his bruised jaw. "So, whoever we're looking for is the only one outside of the family that calls you that?"

"Apparently."

Drew added, "And you still didn't recognize his voice?"

"I've been thinking about that too. There's something about the way he talks that sounds . . ." She stopped and thought about the best word to describe her feeling. "Familiar."

"What do you mean?" Blake asked.

"His voice is kind of familiar, but I can't place it. He keeps changing it somehow. As soon as I think that I have a handle on it, he changes the accent again. I know for sure he's not using his real voice. At first I thought it was James."

"James Pruet?" both Marian and Blake asked simultaneously.

"Yes," Prudence confirmed.

"What made you think that?" Drew asked.

"The caller kind of sounded like him at first."

"I never trusted him," Keith mumbled.

"You don't trust anyone," Drew, Jeremy, and Prudence all said in unison, then chuckled at the coincidence as Keith glared at each sibling one at a time.

"Getting back to the caller's voice," Blake injected.

"Well, it would make sense," Marian said. "If he has met you before and he's not ready to reveal himself, he would have to disguise his voice." Everyone nodded in agreement.

"Since all of this started up again soon after those newspaper photos, could it be that he's a reporter you once spoke with, particularly after the Garrett thing?" Drew asked.

"Garrett thing?" Michael asked. But no one replied.

"That's a possibility. But I'm just not sure," Prudence said.

"So what kind of accent did you hear?" Michael asked.

Prudence shook her head slowly. "I'm not sure. It's vague. I only hear it when he's really angry."

"Midwest, southern, New England?" Drew asked.

"Texan?" Keith asked Michael directly. Everyone looked at Keith as he spoke up for the first time since the fight had ended.

Michael chimed in, ignoring the direct hit. "The security chief told me that he'd install a tape device on your office phone. The next time he calls, try to tape the conversation."

"Good idea, Michael," Blake said. "We'll all listen to his voice. Maybe one of us will recognize something. If he does call again, keep him talking as long as possible." Prudence nodded.

The conversation eventually drifted to more general topics, including Michael's family in Texas and his thoughts on the upcoming play-off season. After a half hour of lively conversation Marian stood up. "Well, dear, it's getting late and your father and I have a busy schedule today."

"Mother, did you want something when you came over here this morning? I mean before all this started." She gestured to the pile of broken tables and chairs lying by the front door.

"You said you'd call every night. When you didn't call and your father couldn't reach you either here or at the office, we called your brothers and came right over. I'm just glad that Keith arrived first. I'd hate to have my husband tossed around the room with that guy." She nodded her head in Michael's direction as everyone laughed.

After her parents left, Drew and Jeremy stood and moved toward the front door. Prudence hugged and kissed each in turn and again promised to call nightly and be extremely cautious in the future. Michael leaned against the wall watching the touching family scene. The two picked up the broken furniture and left.

Keith was the last to leave. He whispered a few words to Prudence, then kissed her forehead. After the final good-bye he gave one last warning scowl in Michael's direction. Michael ignored him and moved back to the sofa and sat down. A few moments later Prudence came back to the sofa. "Are you hungry?"

"No," Michael said as he watched Prudence nervously fidget with her buttons. She shifted from foot to foot, then moved to lean against the back of a chair. "Prudence, why don't you sit down and relax?" She moved to sit on the chair across from him. "Here." He patted the sofa cushion. "Next to me. I promise I won't bite you."

Prudence smiled at her silliness, then plopped down on the sofa next to him. "So," he began, "that was the Washington family legal team."

"Most of it. My grandfather is the only other attorney in the family, but he's away on business for a few days."

"So, why didn't you become a lawyer?"

Prudence laughed. "I think there are quite enough attorneys in the family, don't you?"

"Yeah, maybe you're right about that."

She glanced nervously around the room. "I think my poor tree could use a little help." Her Christmas tree had been knocked askew during the fight and now leaned haphazardly against the wall. She stood and began picking up the fallen ornaments that had scattered beneath the tree.

Michael walked over to straighten it and began helping her replace the trimmings. "Anything broken?" he asked. She looked over to the missing furniture. He followed her line of vision. "I mean besides the obvious."

"Just this one." She held up a glass ornament of an African-American angel dressed in delicate white and silver crystal beading. The head was cracked and the crystal gown had been shattered into several pieces. Michael took the broken ornament and pieced it back together, but it was useless.

"This was beautiful," he said sorrowfully. "I'm sorry. Where did you find it? I'll get you another one."

She took it from his hands. "Don't worry about it. I've had it forever. I don't even remember where I got it."

Michael nodded but he could see the veiled disappointment behind her unconcerned facade. "Still, I want to compensate you for the broken furniture."

"It wasn't all your fault, Michael, so don't worry about it. My brothers will take care of all this later." She adjusted the tiny white lights and nervously rearranged another ornament.

He moved behind her and inhaled the fresh, delicate scent of her perfume. She relaxed against him. "That doesn't sound quite fair. It was my fault too. I heard the key in the lock and just reacted. I thought it might be . . ." He paused, not wanting to bring up the caller again.

"I think they liked you," Prudence said as she moved back to the sofa and sat down. He followed and sat next to her.

"Your family, really?" He turned his body to face her. "Enough to approve of my being in their daughter's and sister's life for a while?"

Prudence took a deep nervous breath and exhaled slowly. "I don't know." She leaned back comfortably and smirked wryly. "How long is a while?" she asked jokingly.

"I'd say eighty or ninety years ought to get us started," Michael said with complete sincerity.

Chapter 15

Prudence smiled broadly, humored by Michael's remark, and then seconds later she tensed as her breath caught in her throat. She stared at Michael's serious expression. She read what she saw as easily as if she had read a book. "You're not joking, are you?"

"No, I'm not, I'm very serious," Michael said, realizing and voicing the truth of his feelings.

Prudence moved to stand, but Michael caught her arm and eased her back down beside him. She turned and gazed into his soft hazel eyes. They were filled with raw honest emotion. She knew he wanted more, but she wasn't sure that she had it to give. The last time she had opened her heart it was crushed. How could she trust herself again?

"Michael," she began, swallowing hard, in an attempt to distract the conversation she knew was coming. There was no way she was ready to discuss her feelings for him. But she had to say something. "Michael, the truth is," she continued, then paused again.

He tenderly ran his fingers through her curls. "I love your hair short and curly like this," he confessed as he gently rubbed her temples to relax her.

"Michael," she began again, "the truth is—"

"The truth is, Prudence," he interrupted, "there's more to this than just one night of passion." She went silent. "How long are we going to dance around this thing?" He spoke in barely a whisper. She looked away. Michael turned her body around and gently laid her back against his chest as he wrapped his arms around her.

Prudence sighed and floated on the dream that they'd created together. "Prudence, what happened between us last night wasn't just a physical attraction or sexual release. You know it and I know it. Pretending won't change that fact," he said, speaking even softer. "We connected."

"I know," she mouthed quietly.

He began rubbing her neck. She swayed with the arousing sensation of his hands on her body again. "Something happened between us. We both felt it and it's been happening since the day we met." Prudence remained silent. "Am I wrong?"

"Michael, our lives are as far apart as east is from west. You live in the public eye, and I, well . . ." She shrugged. "I don't. The only connection, the only thing we have in common is right in there." She nodded her head toward the bedroom.

"You're wrong, it's more than just a physical attraction."

"How do you know?" She pulled away from him and sat up straight. "How can you be so sure?"

"Because I do know and I am sure. I trust in us," he rasped huskily.

"Really?"

"Yes, really." He kissed her gently for assurance.

"I don't think I'm ready for this, for you, for us."

"Maybe we moved too fast last night," he said, then paused. "I'll tell you what, we'll slow it down. Your pace, you lead and I'll follow."

"It's not that simple, Michael."

"Of course it is. It's whatever we want it to be."

Prudence shook her head adamantly. The idea of trusting another man was too much to ask. "I've been down this road before, Michael. It didn't end well. I don't want to go through that pain again."

"Prudence, you can't speculate on a relationship before it even begins."

"Michael—"

178 *Celeste O. Norfleet*

"No, if you're gonna refuse me, let it be because of *me*, Michael Hunter, not because of another man and a past relationship. At least give me a chance, give us a chance. We'll take it slow, one day at a time."

Prudence looked into Michael's eyes, the honesty of his feelings sweeping through her. She nudged closer and laid her head back down on his shoulder. "No matter how long it takes?" she asked.

"Yes, no matter how long it takes," he promised.

The promise of his steadfast patience was more intoxicating than she imagined. Prudence began kissing the soft smooth planes of his neck. Michael moaned when she nibbled at his earlobe, causing pangs of pleasure to erupt inside. Before she knew it his arm had encircled her and she was again tucked against his strong chest. Her hand drifted to the muscled ridges of his flattened stomach. She could feel the hard firmness of his arms through his viselike embrace.

"Prudence," he said, "wait, we still need to talk."

"We just did," she muttered and continued kissing.

"No, there's more." Michael leaned his head away from her and held her roaming hands still. "I'm no innocent, Prudence. I get propositions and keys thrown at me all day long. I know this sounds arrogant and conceited, but it's the truth and that's just the way it is in professional sports."

"I know that."

He continued, "A man in my position, making millions of dollars, has a tendency to draw that type of woman like moths to an open flame."

She withdrew her hand slowly. "What are you saying, Michael? If you think that I intend to follow you from city to city, waiting in line outside locker rooms after the games for my turn to service you, it's not gonna happen."

"All I'm saying is that I have always been extremely careful when it comes to getting emotionally involved. There are a lot of women out there with questionable motives."

Her anger began to spike. "Do you think that what

we did last night was some kind of attempt on my part to trap you?"

"No, of course not." He reached to take her hand, but she quickly pulled away. "Prudence, that's not what I think and that's not what I said."

She ignored him and stood with her hand firmly planted on her hip. "But that's what you meant, isn't it? Just because I invite you to my bed doesn't make me some kind of sports groupie, or worse—"

"Stop it. Stop fighting this, stop fighting us." He stood in front of her. "That's not what I said and not what I meant, and you know it." He grabbed her hand before she moved away.

"So what are you saying?" she asked.

"I'm saying that"—he pulled her reluctant body forward—"last night, we didn't just have sex, we made love."

Prudence looked up into his eyes. The feeling of connection deepened, and no matter how hard she tried not to, her heart opened up to him.

"No." She shook her head.

"Yes." He nodded in barely a whisper. "I want you now. You can't imagine how much I want to bury myself inside you, right now, more than ever. I want to lay you back down on that bed and taste every part of your body."

Her stomach fluttered when he licked his lips for emphasis.

"But I want it to be the right way." He tipped her chin up with his finger. "Can you understand that?"

They stood silently for a few moments and then she hesitantly nodded her understanding. "So, what's the right way, Michael?"

"I don't know," he admitted. "But I know falling into bed again isn't. Why don't we start at the beginning, the old-fashioned way?"

She looked over to him curiously.

"Would you do me the honor of having dinner with me tonight?"

"You're asking me out on a date?"

"Yes."

She smiled wide and bright. A warm blush spread across her cheeks.

"Well?" he prompted.

"Okay. Yes, I'd love to."

Michael smiled. "Good. I'll pick you up tonight at eight."

"Better make it later; I have to work till closing tonight."

"Even better, I'm supposed to attend a team thing, so I'll pick you up after that. How about ten o'clock?"

She nodded, biting her lower lip shyly. He stroked the side of her face. Together they walked to the front door.

"See you later." She kissed his cheek.

"Yes, tonight at ten." He winked, kissed her forehead, and closed the door behind him.

"Anything interesting?" Marian asked as she noticed her husband reading.

"Not really, just a transcript from a telephone conversation with Graham McGee."

"How are the negotiations going?"

"Slow, very slow. Four hundred million dollars is a lot of money. The city can't afford that right now. The schools need books, the roads need repairing. Where does he expect me to get the money? I will not raise taxes for a football stadium."

"I know, dear."

"He's going to leave and take his team with him."

"Not necessarily."

Blake looked to Marian. She smiled easily. "What, you have a thought?" he asked.

"A possibility. Perhaps there is a way to have your cake and eat it too."

Marian pulled out an outline that she'd been working on. The idea was new and had merit and possibilities.

Blake added a few thoughts, adding depth to her pro-
posal, giving the idea dimension and weight. Fifteen
minutes later the two had hashed out an intriguing con-
cept that might just solve his immediate problem. Blake
looked at the notes again. "It looks good." He nodded
agreeably.

"If McGee goes for it . . ." she said.

"He will. Despite his threats and blustering, he wants
to stay in this city as much as we want him here. He can't
afford to leave, and to tell you the truth, I doubt very
much that the other team owners will go for it. This
might just work for all parties involved."

"Good," Marian said. "By the way, I received your
e-mail."

"And?"

"Interesting idea," she responded, smiling. "We
haven't done that in quite a while."

"Will you be able to clear your docket?"

"I think that can be arranged."

Blake smiled. The passion he had for his wife would
never be diminished. He couldn't imagine living a single day without her.

"So, what did you think of our daughter's new friend?"
Marian asked as she sat at her vanity brushing her hair.

Blake, sitting at his desk, looked up from his reading,
then over his half bifocal glasses, toward his wife. "The
jury's still out," he grunted.

Marian stopped brushing her hair and turned around
to face him. "Really? I found him rather charming."
Blake scowled and huffed at her remark. "Oh, come
now, Blake, Prudence is a grown woman. It's high time
you and the boys stop treating her like she's still twelve."

Blake closed the file he'd been reading, pushed his
chair back, and stood. "I object to that remark, counselor. His alleged notoriety with the ladies speaks for
itself." He crossed the room to where his wife sat.

"Sustained." She turned back to face the mirror and
smiled seductively. "But you know I'm right."

"I know no such thing," he said, looking down at the beautiful enchantress's reflection in the mirror. Her cocoa-brown skin glowed against the silky material of her blouse. He took the brush from her hand and set it on the glass table, then glided her to her feet. "I'd like to request a sidebar, Your Honor." Once she was in his arms, he swayed their bodies to a melody he hummed.

Marian immediately fell into step. "If I didn't know any better, I'd say you were trying to sway the judge."

"If the court allows, I'd like to submit exhibit A." Blake kissed her neck softly. "And exhibit B." He smoothly began to nibble her ear while caressing the small of her back.

"I'll allow it this time," she moaned. "But I must warn you, counselor, you're violating several criminal codes. I'll have to ask for your conclusions."

"You haven't even heard my opening statement yet," he whispered.

"I think I've heard enough." She sighed deeply. "How do you plead?"

"I plead guilty." He stopped dancing and spun his partner around. "And I throw myself on the mercy of the court." He spun her again, then finished with a dip. "I'm ready to be sentenced."

Marian chuckled. "Taking into consideration your long-standing service, your commitment and dedication to your family, I sentence you to life without the possibility of parole."

"I find that sentence a little harsh, Your Honor. You leave me no choice but to file an appeal." Blake kissed her passionately, then picked her up in his arms and crossed the room.

"I have a feeling we're gonna be late for work this morning," Marian muttered between kisses.

"That's okay, I'm the boss and you're not due in court until noon. That ought to give us just enough time."

Marian smiled. "In that case, counselor, sentence suspended and reduced to time served."

Blake smiled at his adoring wife as they sat down together. He held her tightly and reached for the lamp on the bed stand. "I think you need to reexamine the evidence more closely."

Marian beamed. "I completely agree."

Chapter 16

For the next five days the rumor mills churned out tasty morsels of romance fed by the frequent sightings of Prudence and Michael around town. Their cuddling, holding hands, and huddling close added fire to the flame of speculation. Was Michael Speed Hunter finally hanging up his bad-boy football image for the mayor's daughter?

Brunch at the Philadelphia Museum of Art, lunch at the Four Seasons on the Parkway, and late-night dinners all over Center City kept their smiling faces alternating between the sports pages and the society pages. But thankfully the flashbulb frenzy had subsided and, much to the Washington family's relief, the only pictures of late were tastefully posed.

Marian sat in her husband's office and listened to him read the latest report from his public relations image specialist, speculating on the recent poll trends. "Thanks to your daughter's relationship with the Knights' quarterback, Michael Hunter, your numbers have skyrocketed. Each time she is seen with Speed, your numbers take a substantial hit upward. My recommendation: encourage the relationship and get as much positive press coverage as you can."

Marian and Blake looked at each other with steadfast awareness. He'd always won on merit, but this time the race had been ugly, inundated with mudslinging and reckless, malicious charges aimed at discrediting his reputation.

"Encourage the relationship and get as much positive press coverage as you can," Blake reread as he stood at the office window looking out at the mass of traffic circling the building.

"Prudence is happy and the polls are encouraging, no one's being hurt. Maybe it's a blessing," Marian said.

"Maybe," Blake said.

Marian stood and walked to his side. "So why do you look so disturbed?"

Blake turned and took Marian's hands. "You know why."

"Integrity."

Blake stiffened his jaw and half smiled. "Without that, a man has nothing." He walked away and tossed the letter on the desk. "I refuse to use my daughter to stay in office."

"Blake, you're not using Prudence. What happened, how they met, the current relationship, none of it was intentional on your part, or anyone else's for that matter. You had nothing to do with it. As a matter of fact, in the beginning we went as far as to even discourage the relationship as soon as we saw what was happening."

Blake shook his head. "It doesn't matter. I will not use my daughter to win a race."

"So the alternative is what, insist that Prudence stop seeing him just so the polls can equal out again? Does that make any sense?"

"But not this way, it would be a hollow victory."

"You've dedicated your life to this city. You've done tremendous work here. Maybe we should talk to Prudence. See what she says, let her be the judge. After all, it concerns her too."

It was five days before Christmas and the store was packed with holiday shoppers. The seasonal decorations had been up since before Black Friday and the place looked especially festive with added touches. Prudence spent the entire day reviewing tapes of the European and New York fashion shows and choosing fabric swatches and fashion designs for the coming summer season. She sketched out a floor plan for the summer displays and ordered the necessary mannequins and risers.

She had stayed late the night before, come in early that morning, and had even worked through her lunch break. At two o'clock she cleared her desk for the day and gathered her belongings to leave.

"Are you all set for tonight?" Tanya asked as she looked up from the computer monitor. Prudence stopped at her desk wearing her heavy coat and carrying her briefcase and dress bag.

"Yes, I think so; I still have a few last-minute things to pick up for the birthday celebration."

"Are you still gonna stop by City Hall to see your dad?"

Prudence nodded. "Yeah, I told him I'd be by tomorrow morning, but I'm gonna try and see him today."

Tanya noted the dress bag. "That dress is gonna knock Speed's socks off."

"That's exactly what I'm hoping."

"Does he have any idea what you're planning?"

"Nope." Prudence smiled brightly. "He doesn't have a clue."

Tanya shook her head from side to side. "Surprise parties are tricky. What happens if his family suddenly shows up in town to celebrate his birthday?"

"Not a problem. I already asked about them having something for him tonight. He told me that they usually celebrate his birthday when he goes to Texas during the Christmas holiday. He told me that he has absolutely no plans except a quick stop at a friend's house earlier this evening."

"Good," Tanya said, "so basically all you have to do

is sit back, relax, and have a wonderfully romantic evening."

"I can't wait." Prudence nodded her assurance with confidence as she placed several material swatches and a file on Tanya's desk. "These are the fabric samples I told you about earlier." Tanya nodded and flipped through the file and swatches. "I need you to go through these when you get a chance. Oh, and remember, there are new shipments coming in tomorrow and I won't be here."

"Prudence, relax, I know what needs to be done. Go have a good time tonight and enjoy your day off tomorrow," Tanya said, shooing her away from her desk.

Prudence smiled as she walked to the escalators. Tanya was right; she had been her assistant for over a year. She knew the job as well as Prudence did.

Tanya finished entering the orders into the computer, then began flipping through the fabric samples Prudence had given her. She marked off several favorites and checked off her choices. Afterward she cross-referenced the availability of the merchandise with the preordered items and double-checked the shipping dates. She was so engrossed with the computer files and stock orders that she didn't see the man walk up until he had already passed her desk. She looked up suddenly. "Uh, excuse me, sir, can I help you?"

"No," he said dismissively as he continued walking toward Prudence's closed office door.

Tanya, surprised by his short tense answer, said, "Sir, you can't just walk in there. This area isn't part of the department store." She picked up the phone and called for security, then followed him into Prudence's office. "Sir, can I help you?"

The man looked around the empty office. "Where's Prudence?"

"Excuse me?"

"Prudence," he snapped firmly. "Prudence Washington, they told me at the information desk downstairs that this was her office. Where is she?"

"She's away from her desk."

He looked around, noting that she had simply stated the obvious. "I can see that," he snapped.

"Do you have an appointment?" Tanya asked.

He completely ignored her question. "When will she be back?"

"Later," Tanya said evasively.

The man ignored her and walked away. Tanya followed him out of the office. "Sir, if you'll tell me your name and phone number, I'll leave them for Ms. Washington. She can get in touch with you as soon as she returns." Tanya eyed him suspiciously. His single-minded focus on finding Prudence was unsettling. She watched as he turned at the next department and headed to the escalators. As he disappeared into the rush of customers, store security walked up next to her.

"What's up, Tanya?"

She blew out her breath, exasperated. "Never mind, you just missed him."

"Missed who? Who was it?" The security men looked around.

Tanya shook her head and waved them off. "Just some guy looking for Prudence." She described him, then watched as the two undercover security officers walked away in the same direction the man went. Afterward, Tanya went back to her desk with the nagging feeling that the man was the sender of Prudence's gift box.

"Hello there, is Prudence Washington around?"

Exasperated by another interruption, Tanya looked up with annoyance into the most gorgeous eyes she'd ever seen. "Hi," she barely rasped out.

"Hi there." He smiled again, wider this time, prompting the golden flecking in his eyes to twinkle and spark. "Is Prudence Washington around?"

"No, she's out at the moment. I know who you are. You play on the Knights football team, don't you?"

He smiled. "That's right, I do. Rick Renault." He reached out and shook her hand. Tanya nearly swooned. "I came by about Speed's birthday party tonight."

"I know, Prudence told me about it. It sounds incredible."

"It will be, guaranteed." He turned to walk off.

"Any message for Prudence?" Tanya asked.

"Nope, I'll evidently see her later."

The timid knock prompted James Pruet to quickly lower his feet from the desktop. But before he could say, "Come in," the door had already begun to open.

Prudence peeked around the side of the door as James sat up straighter and his feet hit the floor with a thud. Prudence stepped into the room and looked at him oddly. She didn't expect to see her father's assistant sitting at his desk with his feet up, reading a racing form. "Hi, stranger," she said with open curiosity.

James reddened, knowing she'd just witnessed his casually unprofessional display. "Prudence," he breathed out with hurried exhaustion. He stood and walked toward her. He tried to appear casual, but his gait was tight and forced. "I didn't know you were coming to visit this afternoon."

"Apparently."

He ignored the remark. "What a coincidence, I just stopped by your office earlier. I must have just missed you."

"Really? I had a few errands to run. What did you want?"

"I was picking up a few things and decided to just stop by to see how you were doing after everything that's going on."

"I'm fine, thanks."

"Have a seat; you just missed your mother and father. They didn't mention you'd be stopping by."

Prudence noted that he was way too nervous and talking way too fast. The first thing that occurred to her was the recent inner-office leaks. But she instantly brushed the thought aside. James was a trusted and valued member of her father's staff, and if he was here sitting at her father's desk reading a racing form, there had to be a very good reason. "It was an impulse. I just wanted to stop by to say hello. So how are you feeling?"

"Much better, thanks for asking."

"Did the police ever catch the men who attacked you?"

"No, not yet," he said, finally relaxing and leaning back against the front of the large desk.

An awkward pause hung in the air until Prudence spoke. "So I hear you've moved back in with your mom."

He laughed. "Who told you that?"

"Your mom told my mother a few days ago."

"Yeah, well, she was nervous after the attack, you know."

Prudence nodded. "Yeah, of course, I can imagine she was."

"What about your town house?"

"I sold it."

"Really? That was quick."

"What can I say? My mother's a great realtor. But it was a cash thing, you know. I needed to get a flow going. I had some investments to see through."

Prudence nodded. "Sure, I understand."

"I've noticed that you've been busy lately. Speed Hunter, quarterback, big shot, lots of publicity. I didn't know that you went in for all that, guess I was wrong." Each word dripped with animosity, bitterness, and resentment. "Obviously I was never your type, but it seems Michael Hunter is."

The uncomfortable way he blazed Michael's name made Prudence frown with concern. "James, you and I go way back. We're friends, always will be, I hope. When we dated in college and then . . ." She shrugged. "Like I said before, I think it's best for us to just remain friends."

"Of course, sure, I understand. I was just remarking on how you've moved on, that's all."

"College was a long time ago, James."

"I realize that," he said, snapping at her more than he intended. "Prudence," he began, softening his tone, but a knock on the door drew their attention from the awkward hostilities that had muddied the room. "Come in," James called out with ease. A petite young woman stepped into the room. She smiled at James and he winked, not seeming to care that Prudence observed the interaction.

"James," she purred easily, then noticed Prudence in the room. "Excuse me, Mr. Pruet, you have a call on your cell phone. You left it in my, uh . . ." She looked at Prudence uncomfortably. "Uh, at my desk."

"Thanks, Pam," James said. Then, seeing that she hadn't budged, he continued. "Is that all?"

"I, uh, I answered it."

"You answered my cell phone?" he said tightly.

"Yes, I thought that it might be important," she added hastily. "So I answered it."

Prudence stood to leave, but James, seeming uncomfortably anxious about his cell phone, stopped her. "No, Prudence, you don't have to leave, everything's cool." He glanced back to the waiting assistant. "Tell whoever it is that I'll call them back."

"I think it's important," she said. "The caller ID said that his name was Truman, and it noted 911."

James immediately stood away from the desk. "Mr. Truman, good, I've been waiting for his call," he lied easily. "We've been playing phone tag for the last few days." He held his hand out for the phone as Pam approached the desk. "This won't take long," he mouthed as he took the phone and covered the mouthpiece.

"Actually," Pam began, "he's not on the cell phone any longer."

"Okay." James nodded tensely, turning his attention back to Prudence.

"Uh, he called on your office line and I put him through in here, line six."

The panic in James's voice thickened. "You put him on hold in here?"

"Yeah, line six," she affirmed.

James looked behind him onto Blake's desk. Line six was indeed blinking.

Prudence watched James's reaction. "Truman again?" she questioned. "Haven't you had enough of that world?"

James turned back to her. "I know what you're thinking, but the answer is no, I'm not gambling again. I stopped, remember?"

"Yeah, I remember." She glanced at her father's desk, seeing the racing form still lying there. "I also remember that you said that same thing twice before, and that Truman openly associates with my father's opponent."

"He does and this is strictly a professional call. We're discussing debate questions for an upcoming televised session in a few weeks."

She nodded, only half believing him.

"Don't look so skeptical, it's not like I'm sleeping with the enemy."

"Sure looks that way," Prudence said.

The implication hit home, and hard. "Looks can be deceiving."

"Okay, fine, whatever; actually I have to go. I have a birthday party to get ready for. If you don't mind, tell my father that I'll catch up with him later. You take care of yourself," she said as she crossed the room to the office door.

"See you later. Yeah, I'll tell Blake that you stopped by." James nodded and smiled as the assistant looked at him questioningly. He dismissed her and she followed Prudence out the door.

"Yeah?" he answered nervously as he moved back to sit behind the desk.

"Got any news for me?" Truman asked through his speakerphone.

"Truman, what the hell are you doing calling me on my office phone? I told you that I'm through with gambling. I sold my house and gave you your money. Our business association is finished."

"Really? Got a receipt?" The air was sucked out of James's lungs as the ash-gray shadow of fear darkened his face. His heart pounded wildly as he tried to regain his composure. Then laughter broke through like a crack of thunder. James heard the added laughter in the background.

"Nah, man," Truman said, "I'm just messing with you. Listen, that information you gave me a few months ago worked out well for my friend and I'm brokering another very lucrative deal on his behalf."

"What kind of deal?" James asked.

"Profitable, for all of us. Is there any other kind?"

"I'm not with that anymore. It nearly cost me my job last time. Besides, Blake has the whole office on information lockdown. He probably has his phones and office wired." James looked around the room nervously.

"But you're the man, you can do it. My friend is in need of some juicy bits to add a little more interest to the campaign. Surely you can handle that."

"I can't help you," James said emphatically.

"I'll tell you what, why don't you think about it? Bring me what you can get, and I'll pass it on. My friend can be very generous. He's willing to pay you considerably more than before, minus a small broker's fee for my troubles, of course."

James grimaced. *Of course,* he thought, picking up the racing form he'd been reading earlier. His attention was drawn to the circled item. The horse Jimmy's Back on Top in the fifth race looked like a sign from heaven. All he needed was one big score and he'd be back on top, just like the horse's name suggested. But with his being short on funds and having sold his house, there wasn't much he could do, unless . . . "I might be able to get a little something going."

"Good," Truman said, knowing that of course he'd do it.

"I . . . uh . . . think we can work out a little arrangement."

"What do you have in mind?"

"I need today's fifth race, Jimmy's Back on Top, to win."

"How much?" Truman said as he took the racing form handed to him by his associate.

"A nickel," James said without flinching.

"Bold move, my man, five thousand at seven to one odds."

"Yeah, only I don't have that kind of cash right now." James could almost hear Truman's menacing smile through the phone wire. But he didn't care, this was a sure thing as far as he was concerned. It was his turn and Jimmy, as his mother often called him, would be on top again.

"I'll front you the nickel at twenty-five percent."

"In exchange for what?" James asked, knowing that Truman never did anything for nothing.

"The first play-off game odds are running too close. Take care of it."

"What, how am I supposed to do that?"

"That's you're problem, you want the deal or not?"

James paused for a moment; this was getting out of hand quickly. First he had to get information out of Blake's office again and now he had to somehow manipulate the point spread of a play-off football game. He closed his eyes and answered weakly, "Fine, do it."

"That's thirty-five thousand minus my quarter if you win and sixty-two fifty if you don't, with another quarter on the back every week until it's paid in full."

James took a deep assuring breath. "What exactly do you need from the office?"

"Surprise me; just make it worth my while."

The phone went dead. James immediately began shuffling through the papers on Blake's desk, looking for something to toss Truman. It was always a good idea to have Truman asking him for favors. He opened the center drawer and picked up a letter from Blake's public relations consultant. He read it, then smiled. *Encourage the relationship and get as much positive press coverage as you can.* Perfect. One little bet wouldn't hurt. After all, the horse was named Jimmy's Back on Top.

Dressed and ready, Michael was on his way out the door when the telephone rang. He wanted to leave early to give himself plenty of time to get to Prudence's house. "Hello?" The blaring music and loud talking made it difficult to hear.

"Speed, my man, where are you?"

"Rick?"

"Yeah, man, get over here. The party's already started."

Michael remembered the small gathering that his teammates had planned to celebrate his birthday. "Rick, I'm gonna have to pass tonight. I made other plans."

"Ah, man. How can you do that to your teammates? These men save your neck every Sunday morning. They just want to wish you a happy birthday."

Michael looked at his watch. It was still early by over half an hour, so he decided to make a quick stop at Rick's place and then pick up Prudence and have a nice quiet birthday dinner in town. "All right, Rick. I'm on my way. But I can't stay long."

Michael hopped into the car and headed toward Rick's place. The last thing he needed was a loud, obnoxious party with his teammates and Rick's out-of-control friends, but he knew that Rick was right about one thing: they were teammates and he had to make an appearance.

So, the quiet romantic evening he had planned with Prudence would have to be put on hold for a few minutes longer, but he knew she'd understand.

Michael smiled, recalling the unparalleled change in Prudence after their first real date. A relaxed, comfortable feeling now surrounded them as they talked and joked for hours on the phone, over meals, and just out enjoying the city. Even though they were constantly set upon by photographers and fans, she didn't seem to mind anymore. As a matter of fact she actually seemed to enjoy joking with the fans at times. He realized that she was truly a phenomenal woman.

He opened his cell phone to call just in case he would be late but decided against it. There was no way he was going to stay at Rick's any longer than half an hour. A few handshakes and a couple of old-age jokes and he'd be back on the road to Prudence.

The loud music blasted as Michael turned into the driveway fifteen minutes later. There were expensive cars haphazardly parked everywhere, on the street, in the drive, and on the front and side lawns. It looked as if the entire team had showed up.

Michael walked up the short bricked path to the front door and rang the bell. Seconds later Rick, dressed in a paisley silk pajama set that would make Hugh Heffner green with envy, swung open both double-hung large wooden doors. He had the cord and mic of a small cell phone ear set to his ear and mouth and donned the familiar crooked smile while beckoning Michael inside.

"Speed, my man, happy birthday, welcome to my abode," he exclaimed theatrically as they hugged briefly. Michael shook his head and laughed at Rick's dramatics as he stepped inside.

Rick, with his pajama top completely unbuttoned, exposing his mulatto complexion, was even more flamboyant than usual. A five-inch gold and diamond football medallion on a heavy gold chain hung around his neck, and all fingers were covered with large gold and diamond rings. He spoke softly on the phone as Michael followed him through the elaborate labyrinth he called his home.

The immense residence was just as Michael had imagined it to be, ostentatious on every level. The structure, the rooms, and the furniture were all big, bold, and extravagant and matched Rick's gregarious personality perfectly. Michael smiled as he entered the huge recreation room that connected to the oversized indoor pool area. It was crammed with every imaginable adult toy: a pool table, a wall covered by an entertainment center, pinball and video machines, a jukebox, and a wall-to-wall bar.

The two rooms, connected by a wall of open French doors, were already packed with exuberant revelers. The place looked more like Rick's nightclub than his residence. Michael, shaking his head at the spectacle, walked in and greeted a number of teammates and front office staff. Rick introduced him to a few of his hanging buddies as he placed a bottle of beer in his hand.

The room, shaking with the base vibration of the enormous speakers at either end, took on a surreal atmosphere of ancient Roman proportions as the decadence of overindulgence surrounded him at every turn. Several players danced with scantily dressed women, while others played a blindfold tag game with topless women perched on their backs. Michael shook his head at the outrageous spectacle around him. The quiet dinner alone with Prudence was looking better and better every second.

Michael walked out through the connecting door to the pool area. Several players had stripped down to their briefs and shorts and played water football as bare-breasted women cheered them on from the sidelines.

Rick passed by, taking Michael's untouched beer bottle, and replaced it with a neat scotch in a crystal goblet. As he placed it in his hand, two women came to his side and each dropped an ice cube in the glass.

"Drink up, Speed," Rick yelled above the speakers as he waved his arms wide. "This is all for you."

Michael looked at his watch, then shook his head as he hollered above the music and laughter, "I gotta go. I already made plans with Prudence."

"Prudence, yeah, I thought your girl was coming." Rick looked around as if he had misplaced her.

"Prudence?"

"Yeah."

Michael chuckled, shaking his head no. There was no way he'd bring Prudence to a Rick Renault–sponsored bash.

"Don't worry, these ladies will take good care of you, won't you, ladies?" As if on cue, the women dropped their bikini tops, exposing several thousand dollars' worth of plastic surgery. Michael instantly broke into laughter and shook his head at the bizarre sight. Only Rick could find triple-D twins.

"I gotta go," Michael still insisted.

"Yo, yo, yo, Speed, man. You can't leave before the entertainment begins. That would be just plain rude."

"I'm already late, man. I told you I made other plans."

Rick wrapped his arm around Michael's shoulder. "Hey, at least stay until we cut the cake. It's an old favorite family recipe."

Michael reluctantly agreed, then took a sip of the drink. The taste of scotch warmed his throat while the pungent spark of the vodka ice cubes snapped his tongue. He frowned. "Interesting drink."

"It's the house specialty. I thought you'd like it," Rick said as he turned back to the recreation room and nodded to one of his friends across the room. The music instantly lowered.

"Gentlemen, ladies," Rick began, "thank you all for coming this evening. Tonight we celebrate Michael Speed Hunter as he gets closer and closer to retirement." The crowd roared with cheers and laughter as Rick turned to Michael and smiled. "Happy birthday, buddy." They shook hands and a round of deafening applause filled the room. Finally Rick held his empty champagne glass up and toasted. "To Speed," he proclaimed.

Everyone followed suit. "To Speed," echoed throughout the room.

"Let the festivities begin," Rick shouted. At that cue, the twins escorted Michael to the center of the room where a seat of honor was placed. As soon as Michael sat down, a familiar buxom silhouette in a blond wig appeared in the doorway. She began to sing. Slow sultry crooning surrounded the room. Michael frowned; he recognized that voice. With the seductive ease of a siren, Michael's ex-girlfriend/model-turned-nightclub entertainer, Deidre Marks, sashayed over to him.

Dressed as a duplicate of Marilyn Monroe, she sang the infamous "Happy Birthday, Mr. President" as "Happy Birthday, Mr. Quarterback." The assembled guests laughed hysterically as Michael turned bright red and buried his face in his hands.

Deidre ended the tribute as a huge seven-foot white-and-green-frosted cake was wheeled in by two members of the defensive line. On cue, the entire room sang "Happy Birthday." When the song was finished the lights dimmed and a simple ceiling light illuminated the huge cake.

With the enticing agility of an acrobat, a woman began slithering out of the cake. Her leather-clad and glitter-covered body oozed and pulsated to the rhythmic beat played over the speakers.

The place went silent as her enticing dance hypnotized everyone in the room. When she finally emerged from her iced tomb the men went wild as she crept through the audience in four-inch spiked heels and lace garters. Her performance was a mixture of Middle East belly dancing and hip-hop exotic.

Rick stood to the rear of the room, smiling, overseeing the spectacle of carnal lust he'd so astutely orchestrated. He looked at his watch. This was only the beginning of many more surprises that he had planned for their evening. He watched as Michael stood and reluctantly walked over to cut his cake, prompted by the twin double-Ds. At the first slice the guests cheered and the partying began all over again.

* * *

Michael knocked at Prudence's front door four hours late. There was no answer, so he knocked again and then rang the doorbell. Just as his concern began to elevate she flung the door open. She laughed when she saw him standing there, but her anger was evident. "You have got to be kidding."

"Prudence, please, I know I'm late," he began as the partially cracked door began to close in his face. He put his hand up to block her wooden shield. "I can explain." The glare in her eyes showed she didn't particularly care to hear what he had to say. "Prudence, I know I'm late."

"You're damn right you're late. You know, you've got a lot of nerve showing up looking like that."

"Excuse me?"

"Do you expect me to just greet you with open arms?"

"I don't expect anything, but the least you can do is listen."

"Listen to what? Listen to how you've got three different shades of lipstick smeared all over the side of your face, or how about the fact that you reek of perfume? Which would you like me to listen to first?"

Michael lowered his head. This had started out as such a promising evening. "If you'd just be quiet and listen for half a minute, I can explain."

"You can explain to someone else, or better yet, why don't you go back to where you came from? I guarantee, you'll have more fun."

"Prudence."

"Good night, Michael." She attempted to close the door again.

Michael held the door open with his forehead, in complete exasperation. "You, woman, are the most aggravating, hardheaded, hot-tempered, frustrating woman I have ever met."

"And you, man, are the most arrogant, conceited, self-centered, inconsiderate, spoiled child I have ever met. When you decide to grow up, give me a call." She slammed the door in his face.

Chapter 17

Three days had gone by without a single word from Michael. Prudence adamantly refused to think about him, call him, or even watch him play the last regular-season football game. But curiosity got the better of her and she caught the late-night sports. The team had won. She watched highlights as Michael was sacked by a huge linebacker and thrown headfirst into the turf. She held her breath until she saw him get up and trot over to the sidelines. The sportscaster reported that he was fine as he went back into the game on the following play.

When he stood topless at his locker with several microphones pointed at him, her heart began to flutter wildly. The reporters asked him questions about the game, the ending season, and the upcoming play-offs. He answered them as if cued by a script. One reporter asked about his relationship with Ms. Washington. Prudence held her breath and watched as he stopped smiling and said, "No comment."

Two nights before Christmas, Prudence sat alone in her condo watching the muted old holiday black-and-white standard *It's a Wonderful Life* and listening to Nat King Cole Christmas carols. She sipped her eggnog, not particularly feeling merry or jolly, but continued to wrap the last of her gifts anyway. She just wanted the whole holiday season over with as quickly as possible. Work was stressful and her social life was nil.

The night before, she'd gone to the department store's

holiday party after having her arm twisted by Tanya. She stayed all of thirty minutes before making her excuses and leaving. She just wasn't in a partying mood.

Both Whitney and Valerie had invited her over to each of their houses for the evening, but she declined saying she just wanted to relax and finish wrapping her Christmas gifts. When the last gift was finally wrapped she sat back on the sofa and stared at the muted television as the black-and-white movie faded to a Speed Hunter sports drink commercial. She hated to admit it, but she missed Michael.

Raising his fist, he paused a moment before he knocked on the door. He could hear Nat King Cole singing "The Christmas Song." He waited, then knocked again. When the door opened, they just stood for a second and stared at each other.

The soft glow of candlelight illuminated the living room. The effect was soft and comforting. Prudence's off-white angora sweater, matching wool skirt, and mop of tiny curls made her look almost angelic. His first instinct was to reach up to stroke her short pixy ringlets, but he resisted. "Hello, Prudence," Michael said as he quickly took in every inch of her face and body.

Prudence's heart leaped, overwhelmed as she was by the sight of him standing there, hoping that this wasn't an eggnog-induced vision she'd conjured up. "Hello, Michael."

Silence drifted between them again as they just stood there staring at each other a few seconds more.

"I wanted to stop by and drop this off before I left." He held out a beautifully wrapped box. "Merry Christmas."

She looked down at the small gift and accepted it. "Thank you." She stepped back, opening the door wider. "Do you want to come in for a minute?"

"Sure, just for a minute." He walked in and stood in the center of the room and looked around. Everything was exactly as he remembered, including replaced furniture and the sparkling Christmas tree. "I see you finally have all the furniture back in place." She nodded. "It looks good." She nodded again.

She closed the door and followed him into the living area. "Thank you," she finally said. "Take your coat off and have a seat. Can I get you a glass of wine or eggnog or something?"

"Sure, a glass of eggnog would be great." He removed his tailored cashmere coat and laid it across the back of the armchair. She went into the kitchen and poured a cup of holiday cheer. After sprinkling the top with spices she returned and gave him the cup.

Michael was standing in front of the Christmas tree when she entered. He turned and walked to meet her halfway. Their hands brushed as he took the cup. "You look beautiful as usual."

"Thank you." She blushed slightly. "So do you." Nervously, she began gathering several of the gifts spread around the room. She collected the wrapping paper and ribbon from the sofa and chairs and placed them on the coffee table out of the way.

"So how've you been?" he asked after sipping the smooth milky drink.

"Fine, busy, working hard."

"Of course, I guess this is your busiest time of year."

"It is," she droned out, mindlessly annoyed by the trivial small talk. A slight pause hung in the air. "I'll be in your home state in a few days," she blurted out.

"Texas?" he exclaimed. She nodded. "That's great. I'm on my way there now, tonight. Maybe we can get together while you're there." He hesitated. "I'd love to show you around. San Antonio is fabulous this time of year."

"That sounds nice, but I don't think I'll have that much time. I'm actually going to Houston and I'll only be there for a few days before the new year. It's the annual buyers' meeting at the main office."

He nodded his understanding. "Maybe next time." His nod led to another awkward silence.

He motioned toward the silent television and the coffee table covered with ribbon, tissue wrap, and gifts. "I see you've gotten into the holiday spirit."

"No, not really, I just finished wrapping the last of my gifts. I guess the season hasn't hit me yet."

The stiff awkwardness of the conversation was pathetic.

"Open your gift," he finally requested.

She picked up the small box and tore at the wrapping. She removed the tissue paper and exposed a white square velvet box. She opened the silver clasp and gasped in wonder. "Oh, Michael, it's beautiful. Where did you find it?"

He smiled at her surprise and delight. "I had an artist friend in San Antonio design and make it. I hope it's all right. I know it won't replace the one that broke, but maybe . . ."

"It's beautiful, thank you so much. I can't believe you went through so much trouble to replace my angel." She reached up and kissed his cheek lovingly.

He held on to her, locking their eyes. A myriad of emotions passed between them in an instant. She lowered her chin and looked away. He leaned down and kissed her forehead.

"I've missed you," she confessed quietly.

"I've missed you too," he said as she melted into his strong embrace. "I want to apologize and explain about the other night."

"No, that's not necessary; there's nothing to apologize or explain about. You're free to do whatever and see whomever you wish. It's just that I had this wonderful evening planned and then when you were late and then when you showed up and looked . . . I guess I assumed—"

"We had plans, I know," Michael said, finally interrupting her.

"I overreacted. It was really none of my business—"

"Prudence," he interrupted again.

"This is just a friendship, right?" The words tumbled out of her mouth before she could stop them.

"Friendship?" Michael stepped closer. "Prudence." She stepped back just out of his reach. "This, us, what we started is more than just a friendship." He stepped forward again and took the sides of her arms, drawing her close. "We both know that." He lowered his head to look into her eyes. "I was wrong, I should have called and told you about the surprise party as soon as I found out."

"I have to go," she mumbled.

"Where?" Michael frowned. "To work, this late?"

She took a deep breath. "No, to church, there's a holiday cantata this evening."

"May I join you?"

"Aren't you leaving for San Antonio tonight?"

"I can always change it for another flight tonight or tomorrow morning. May I join you?"

"Sure, I'd like that."

Michael smiled. "Let's go."

An hour and a half later Prudence and Michael stood in the church vestibule watching the gentle snow fall.

Click.

A host of parishioners walked past, shaking his hand and wishing him well in the upcoming play-off season. Prudence's parents came out of the sanctuary and smiled at the young couple. Blake looked up at the darkened sky. "Looks like it's going to be a white Christmas after all." Everyone nodded in agreement.

"Are you going home for the holidays, Michael?" Marian asked.

"Yes, for the week. I have to get back for practice by the first of the year. I have an early flight tomorrow morning."

"I don't know if you'll be catching that flight out tomorrow if the snow keeps coming down like this," Blake said.

Keith walked up, followed by Drew and Jeremy. "I saw

your brother play a few nights ago. He looked pretty good out on the court," Jeremy said.

Michael turned to him. "Yes, he did. I saw the game too. Looks like it's going to be a good season."

The conversation drifted to the NBA and Michael's brother and his father, who was an NBA general manager.

"Are they with the same team?" Marian asked.

"No, but they do face each other at times. As a matter of fact, they'll face each other in San Antonio on Christmas Day."

Prudence gathered her collar closer and shivered as the icy wind blew inside the vestibule. Instinctively Michael stepped closer to her to block the wind's path. Marian smiled and Blake's brow rose.

Marian chuckled. "That ought to make for interesting dinner conversation at the holiday table. How does your poor mother put up with it all?"

"She has had a firm rule ever since I can remember, *no shoptalk at the table.* And what she says goes." Everyone laughed at the remark.

"I'm freezing!" Prudence proclaimed as she shivered again. Michael placed his arm around her shoulder and pulled her closer to his body. Keith frowned, Drew smiled, while Jeremy hoped they wouldn't have to fight again.

"Shall we go, my dear?" Blake held his arm out and Marian tucked her gloved hand under it. "Good night, all," he said. Marian chimed in, "Don't forget, Christmas Eve dinner is at five. Good night. Drive carefully."

Michael kept his arm wrapped around Prudence. "We'd better get going too." She nodded. They said their good-byes, then slowly walked toward Michael's car.

Click.

Prudence sat in the car as it warmed while Michael dusted the big fluffy snowflakes from the black enamel of the hood and the frosted windows. He looked through the windshield and smiled. Prudence looked back out at him and waved. At that moment she realized just how much she really cared for him. The surprising revelation seeped through as the warmth of the heat surrounded her.

"I really enjoyed tonight," Michael said as he drove through the emptying streets. "Your pastor reminds me of my minister back home in San Antonio."

"Really? You don't seem like the churchgoing type."

He laughed. "Why is that?"

"I don't know, I guess the life you lead isn't exactly conducive to a fire-an-brimstone sermon on Sunday morning, particularly when you are in uniform and preparing to go out on the field and rip somebody's head off."

"Quarterbacks don't rip heads off."

"Whatever. You get the idea."

"You have a pretty low opinion of me, don't you?"

"No, of course not. It's just that you do have a reputation for living the wild life."

"*Did* have a reputation. But you know, even my wild nights couldn't compare to what the media wrote. If I did half the things they wrote about me I'd be out of the league."

"So, what, you're saying that they fabricated a lot of things written about you?"

"You of all people should know that. Just look at the way we met and how the whole thing was blown out of proportion."

She nodded her agreement.

He pulled into a snow-covered parking space and they got out and walked to her front door. "I really enjoyed the service and the sermon tonight. Thank you for inviting me. I'd like to visit again, if you'd go with me."

"Sure, anytime. Pastor Rawlins is a huge fan. I'm sure he'd be delighted to have you in church again."

"And what about you?"

"What about me?"

He reached up and brushed the wet flakes from her hair. "I've been wanting to touch your hair all night."

She didn't know what to say, so she just lowered her head.

"The other night when I was late—" he began.

"I don't want to talk about that. It's in the past." She turned, unlocked the door, and walked inside. She took off her coat and moved to the living room. Michael stayed at the door and watched as she turned the gas fireplace on, bathing the room in a soft glow of smoldering embers.

"We need to talk about it to clear the air," he said. She stood still with her back to him. "That night the guys decided to throw me a birthday party, a surprise birthday party. I stopped by and stayed longer than I intended. Yes, there were women there, there always are, but not exactly the kind of women your mother would invite to afternoon tea."

"I see."

"There's more," he said, then paused and walked farther into the room. "Deidre Marks was at the party."

She turned, looking confused. Of course she'd heard of Deidre Marks, everyone had. She was a high-priced fashion model who had done several well-received films, but now concentrated her talent on singing.

"Deidre Marks?"

"Yes, she and I dated a while back."

Prudence held her breath. She knew what was coming next. She raised her hands up to halt any further confessions. "You don't have to say anything more. I understand. You and Deidre—"

"No, there's more. Deidre and I were over months ago. I didn't even know she was going to be there. We talked. I found out that—"

"Michael, I understand," Prudence said as she turned away again, assuming the worst. "You don't have to say anything else, I get it." There was no way she could look into his eyes now. She couldn't stand for him to tell her that he and Deidre were getting back together. But she had no one to blame but herself. She closed her eyes, summoning her inner strength to get her through the next few moments of dejection.

"She's getting married," he continued anyway. "The wedding is early next year."

Prudence's mouth formed a perfect O. Apparently she didn't understand. She opened her eyes and looked down on the table and spotted the small gold-wrapped present she'd purchased.

Relieved, she sighed loudly and then turned to face him as she leaned back against the sofa table and picked up the gift. "I guess that would explain the perfume and lipstick," she said.

He nodded in agreement. Still holding the wrapped present, she cupped her hands behind her and walked toward him as he stood near the front doors. "So, I suppose this is the part where I apologize again."

He flashed the famous Speed Hunter smile.

"You know, Speed." She poked him in the center of his chest with her finger. "I'm really getting tired of apologizing to you for my temper."

He took her hand and kissed the poking finger. "You should be." He reached around to take her other hand and felt a wrapped package. He took it from her. "What's this?"

"What's it look like? It's a present. Merry Christmas."

"You didn't have to do this." He began to pull at the ribbon, but she stopped him.

"No, you can't open it now. You have to wait and open it on Christmas morning."

"I don't think I can wait that long."

"It's worth the wait," she said with a hint of mischief in her eyes.

"Why do I have the feeling we're not talking about this gift anymore?" He enveloped her in his arms. Neither said a word as they just stood holding on to each other. "Ah, woman, what you do to me."

She grinned. "And what might that be?"

He took a deep breath, then whispered in her ear, "I

think you already know that." He pressed against the small of her back and kissed her neck. "I have to get home to finish packing."

"That's right, Texas awaits," she said, then stepped back as he turned and opened the front door. "Have a safe trip."

Michael turned back to face her. He touched the curly ringlets around her face. "I love you, Prudence Washington." He leaned in and kissed her tenderly.

Prudence's heart stopped and her mouth dropped open as he stepped back, turned, and walked away.

For the next five minutes she stood there in the open doorway staring down the hall, still hearing Michael's voice in her ears. *I love you, Prudence Washington.* Her heart lurched again. At first she'd thought that she had misunderstood what he said. But the clarity of his words and the sincerity in his eyes assured her that he said what she heard. *I love you, Prudence Washington.*

Prudence finally closed the door and went back into her apartment. She walked over to the open present and gently pulled the angel from the wrapping. She held it up by the thin golden chain. *I love you, Prudence Washington.* Her heart lurched again. She placed the angel on the tree, then stepped back to watch it sparkle in the dimmed lighting.

In a trance, she showered, dressed, and lay in her bed. All night long Michael's last words reverberated in her mind and in her heart. She couldn't imagine being any happier. *I love you, Prudence Washington.*

Chapter 18

"Happy holidays."

"Hey, Whitney," Prudence said, juggling the office phone while distracted. She shuffled through the orders on her desk in search of the right ones to send out. "I can't talk right now. The store's been crazy all morning. Everybody wants to shop the day before Christmas."

"Of course they do. I know you're busy, particularly today. I just want to know if we're still on for lunch this afternoon, or do you want to do it another time?"

"No way. I need to get out of here for sanity's sake. Lunch is definitely still on, but it'll have to be a quick one. I'll meet you in the restaurant in an hour."

Whitney agreed. "One more thing, I gather you haven't seen this morning's paper yet?"

"Haven't had time, why?" she said, and then moaned in exasperation when she realized that she and Michael might be in the newspapers again. "Don't tell me."

"You guessed it. Actually this article is a bit more interesting than the others. It seems you and Speed Hunter were seen leaving church last evening. The article implies that the two of you are talking marriage."

"Marriage?"

"You heard me. Grab the newspaper and check it out. I'll see you in an hour."

Whitney hung up. Prudence stood in the middle of her office barefoot and stunned.

Tanya popped her head into the office seconds later.

"It's here," she sang cheerfully. "I was just getting back from lunch and stopped by shipping. These just arrived." She waved the Houston store's annual buyers' meeting itinerary in the air.

"It's about time. I'm supposed to leave in three days."

"Umm," Tanya hummed happily. "Four days of hulking cowboys in tight leather chaps," she said wistfully, then shivered for effect. "My, my, my. Now, that is the life. I am so jealous."

"Don't be, every year it's the same thing, traveling Christmas night to be there first thing in the morning. Four days of meetings about the same old ideas, then lugging back dozens of boxes of samples. No, thank you, I'd rather just stay at home. Believe me, the annual buyers' meeting at the main office in Houston is not all it's cracked up to be."

"Yeah, but those Texas cowboys every night can more than make up for the boring days."

Prudence looked at Tanya and shook her head ruefully. "Do you ever think of anything else besides men, men, and more men?"

Tanya casually strutted to the desk. "Hardly ever," she said truthfully. "Come on now, even you've got to admit that you're looking forward to the annual buyers' meeting in Houston."

"I'll only admit that I'm looking forward to a warmer climate and no snow. Believe me, that's the only good thing about the meeting."

She was shuffling through the papers on her desk again when the phone rang. "Prudence Washington."

The slight pause immediately told her who was on the other end. "Merry Christmas, Prudy."

She sighed heavily. "I don't have time for this." She hung up abruptly.

Tanya watched Prudence's expression change to anger. "Was that another one of those calls?"

"Yeah, it's the third one today."

"Did you check the caller ID?"

"It still doesn't show the number. Here it is," she said as she finally found the orders she'd been looking for. "I have to get down to shipping and receiving." She picked up several packages and started around her desk but paused suddenly and looked around the office. "Oh yeah, did we get today's newspaper?"

"Yeah, I think I saw it on the counter this morning." They both walked over to the large counter and moved the merchandise and boxes. "Here it is," Tanya said.

Prudence took the paper, flipped to the style section, and handed the rest of the newspaper back to Tanya. She scanned the section thoroughly. There was no mention of anything related to her or Michael, so she turned to leave.

Tanya flipped through the rest of the newspaper. She turned several pages before her mouth dropped open. "I presume this is what you're looking for."

Prudence moved to Tanya's side as she neatly folded the paper into quarters and handed it to her.

The telephone rang again. Tanya reached down to pick it up, but Prudence stopped her. "Wait, I'll get it, no reason you have to deal with this idiot too."

"Do you want me to inform security, just in case?"

"No, I'm fine," Prudence said with determination as Tanya reluctantly left the office. On the fourth ring Prudence picked up the receiver and pushed the record button. "Prudence Washington."

"Don't you ever disrespect me like that again, woman."

The man's calm, icy tone angered her. "What do you want?"

"You're feeling rather daring today, I see."

"Actually I'm feeling rather hurried today. I have a lot to do, so get on with your childish games."

"This is no game."

"Crank calls, hiding behind a telephone, I call those childish games."

She looked down at the display on the caller ID. The panel read *no number available.*

"Feeling defiant as well, I see. I like it. It will make your taming that much sweeter."

"Lucky me."

"It is not my intention to harass you, Prudy."

"Don't call me that, you don't know me."

"That's where you're wrong, I do know you. I know you very well, and I'm closer to you than you think."

"Are you finished?"

"We haven't even started."

"You're pathetic. You make obscene phone calls and send trash packages like a typical trench-coat-wearing pervert. You're a bully and a thug who can only get off with threats of intimidation. You disgust me."

His outburst of joyous laughter prompted her to hang up the telephone. Angry and still trembling, she yanked opened the small machine and pulled out the tiny audiotape.

Enraged by the caller, Prudence picked up her four packages and left her office. She hurried past Tanya's desk.

"Was that him again?" Tanya asked.

"Yeah." Prudence smiled knowingly. "And I got him on tape this time." She held the small tape up between her fingers.

"I bet it was that first guy who stopped by a few days ago looking for you."

"What first guy?" Prudence asked.

"This strange-looking guy came by looking for you the day of Speed's birthday party. But you had already gone."

"Who was he?"

"He wouldn't say, but I had security follow him to check him out just in case."

"You said first guy. Was there someone else looking for me?"

"Yeah, Rick Renault, he didn't leave a message either. But he did mention a party."

"This whole thing is getting so ridiculous." Prudence wrapped her arms around herself and shivered slightly.

"Are you okay?"

Prudence nodded. "I'm fine."

"What did caller ID say?"

"No number available."

"Anything on the voice?"

"No. I'm taking this tape to the security office." Prudence began walking. "I want a copy."

"Oh, before you go to security, shipping and receiving called again, they're still waiting for you," Tanya called out as Prudence headed out of the department.

"Tell them I'm on my way," she said as she hurried to the store's main elevators. She stood there a few moments, then nervously looked around the secluded area. She hammered the glowing button several times and impatiently paced the floor.

When the elevator arrived she rushed onto the platform without looking and bumped right into a solid wall of muscle. She gasped loudly as the four packages she was carrying flew everywhere.

"My bad," the deep masculine voice boomed apologetically, and the man bent down to pick up the clutter.

"Excuse me," Prudence stammered, physically shaken by the solid impact of the man's body. Her first thought was his vague familiarity. He picked up the packages and handed them to her. Prudence finally looked up into his trimmed goatee and dangerously sexy eyes.

His boyish grin was genuinely warm and charming. "I wasn't watching where I was going," he confessed as he folded his cell phone in his hand. Then, holding out an overly folded piece of paper, he added, "I was on the phone and trying to decipher this shopping list. It's almost impossible to figure out what I wrote down."

His sparkling green eyes were mesmerizing. Prudence smiled in spite of herself. "No, really, it was my fault," she declared cautiously as the doors closed behind her and she moved to the opposite side of the elevator.

"What floor?" he asked, preparing to press the button.

"First floor please," she answered.

The festive holiday music seeped through the elevator speaker as the two passengers silently waited and watched the descending floor buttons light up.

"You're Prudence Washington, right?"

"Yes." She turned to him. "Do we know each other?" A hint of familiarity filled the air.

He beamed. "In a manner of speaking, yes, we do."

Prudence frowned as her heart began to race thunderously. The last thing the caller had said was that he was closer than she thought. Prudence instantly stepped back against the wall.

"We met a few weeks ago at the church the day before Thanksgiving." The tall stranger extended his hand. "I doubt you remember me. My name is Rick Renault. I play football with the Knights, with Speed Hunter."

"Yes, of course, Rick Renault. It's nice to see you again. How've you been?"

"Working hard," he confessed.

"Yes, so I hear, the team looks good. Are you ready for the play-offs to begin?"

"We're ready."

The elevator's bell rang as it came to the second-floor level. Several passengers boarded, heavily laden with shopping bags. Prudence stepped back and moved closer to Rick.

"By the way, I stopped by your office a few days back to invite you to Speed's birthday party. Apparently I just missed you. I spoke with your assistant."

"Oh, so you're the mysterious man who'd been looking for me. She just told me about you."

"She mentioned Speed's party, so I expected to see you there. Next time I'll make sure to leave a more detailed message."

"Your accent is very distinct."

"New Orleans."

Prudence nodded. "New Orleans is a beautiful city. I

went to the Thanksgiving festival a few years back. It was one of the most incredible events I'd seen in a long time."

"I don't get back home much."

"Looks like you're a last-minute holiday shopper," Prudence said, noticing the unfolded shopping list in his hand. "That list looks pretty healthy." She motioned to the paper still in his neatly manicured fingers.

"Guilty. Unfortunately, I'm not having much luck."

"Why not?" she asked.

"Other than not being able to read my own writing, I can't find half the things on the list, and when I do find them I can't decide."

Prudence smiled, as did the two women standing immediately in front of them. "That sounds about par for holiday shopping, particularly last-minute shopping. Why not enlist the services of a professional at the store's shopping concierge department?"

"The store has a concierge?"

"Yes, we have staff members that are professional shoppers and they're very good at what they do. They'd be delighted to help you spend your money. Give them your list, any ideas about the gifts' recipients, and voila, your holiday shopping is all done, gift wrapped and delivered to your door or to theirs, for a nice fee, of course."

"That sounds perfect," Rick said.

"Quite a few people take advantage of the service. It's easy, quick, and painless. All you have to do is supply a little information and a credit card number."

"One of those miracle workers wouldn't happen to be you, by any chance?" Rick asked hopefully.

Prudence smiled for the first time since getting on the elevator. "No. But I'd be happy to direct you to their office."

"I have a better idea. Why don't *you* give me a hand with this list?" The elevator beeped again as it arrived to the first-floor level. Everyone stepped out as others patiently waited to get on.

"I wish I could, but unfortunately I'm on my way to fix a major crisis in the shipping department," she said as she left the elevator and quickly headed to the forbidding double doors marked EMPLOYEES ONLY. "Take the next right, walk down the hall past customer service. The concierge is the last door on the left after the water fountain."

"Prudence," an older man exclaimed as he opened the double doors and nearly bumped into her. "I was just coming up to get you."

Prudence turned to him. "Here you go, I'll be right there."

He immediately took the four packages from her and hurried back through the doors.

She turned back to Rick and smiled. "It was nice seeing you again, Rick, happy holidays." They shook hands but he held on to hers longer than she expected.

"Maybe we can get together sometime, get to know each other better," Rick said, his insinuation obvious.

"Sounds great," Prudence said, loosening her hand from his grip. "Why don't you and Michael pick a day and time? I'll bring a friend for you."

Rick smiled broadly, understanding her completely.

"Take care," she said as she disappeared behind the swinging doors.

Rick's smile broadened wider and a chuckle was released as he watched the two swinging doors still. He could see why Speed was so fascinated with Prudence. She had an intensity and energy that registered as class and sophistication, and he found it interesting. She had an open, genuine sweetness that was oddly appealing, although definitely not his cup of tea. She wasn't his usual scantily dressed football groupie who'd hang on every word he uttered. There was something more substantial about her.

He looked in the direction she'd pointed out toward the store's concierge, then at the long list in his hand,

and finally to his Rolex diamond-faced watch. It was a no-brainer.

Over chicken salad on croissants and hot herbal tea, Prudence and Whitney sat across from each other at the lunch table laughing and joking about the photo and article announcing her upcoming nuptials. "I still think that you should have told a sistah. After all, I *am* your best friend."

"I didn't know myself," Prudence said sarcastically. "It's a good thing I have the style section to let me know what's going on in my own life." They laughed again as the conversation turned to her upcoming trip to Houston and then to the holiday season, gift-giving, and the store's outrageous last-minute shopping crowds.

"Have you gotten any more calls lately?" Whitney asked as the waitress placed the check on the table and poured more tea into their glasses.

"As a matter of fact I did. This morning and then again this afternoon."

"This is getting too ridiculous."

"Tell me about it. Every time the phone rings I get angry. Although I did manage to get his voice recorded on tape and the security department is making me a copy."

"I've been thinking about the timing of the calls," Whitney said, then paused and cleared her throat before sipping her tea.

Prudence looked at her curiously. "What do you mean, the timing of the calls?"

"Garrett's been in town, he has been on and off for the past few weeks. He's doing a segment for an upcoming network special."

Prudence sat up uncomfortably. The mention of Garrett's name had always made her tense. "And?" she prompted.

"And I just find it curious that your calls come each time he's in town."

"There is such a thing as long-distance phone calls. If he wanted to harass me, he could just as easily do it from New York or Chicago or wherever else he's based. Besides, what would Garrett have to gain from this?" Prudence asked.

"It's just a feeling I have," Whitney said, shaking her head and looking away. Having been the one to introduce them, Whitney had always half blamed herself for Garrett's unscrupulous behavior. Although she'd repeatedly warned Prudence of his reputation, she still felt responsible when the truth of his lies and deceit had been revealed and his actual intentions came to light.

"Whitney, you know Garrett, he does nothing unless it furthers his career. What would he have to gain from harassing me now?"

"I don't know. But I still have a gut feeling about all this. I don't trust him and I'd put nothing past him."

"I know, and I agree."

"I didn't tell you this before because you had so much on your plate with the Speed Hunter thing and the Thanksgiving dinner and of course your father's campaign."

Silence stilled the table as each woman reflected on the current conversation. "Is he coming back?" Prudence asked in almost a whisper.

"No, there was talk about him returning to the area, particularly since he had pissed off the wrong New York executive and was looking to change markets again, but it turned out to be nothing."

Prudence grinned shamefully at his misfortune. "He pissed off the wrong New York executive. That sounds about right." She chuckled. "So why exactly is he here?

"He's doing a piece on illegal gambling. Since he grew up in Camden, the grapevine says that he's centering it on Truman."

"Truman again. Whatever that man does, trouble follows."

"Yeah, his bio reads like a forty-page rap sheet. Rich kid bucks the system, turned rapper, turned real estate entrepreneur, turned man most wanted for questioning. He's been up on charges so many times he has his own courtroom entrance. They say that he knows the law better than most high-powered lawyers."

"Oh God, that's all we need, a thug with legalese."

"But I think that his arrogance will be his downfall."

"I sure hope so," Prudence said as they gathered their coats and purses and stood to leave the restaurant.

Once outside they paused and looked around. The cold air immediately gripped Prudence and she pulled the collar of her coat closer to her neck. "I'll be glad when spring gets here."

"Prudence, it's barely winter, you've got all of January, February, and March, not to mention that April can sometimes be just as brutal."

"Thanks for the winter weather recap. Maybe you should be doing the weather report instead of your usual morning talk show." Prudence chuckled.

Whitney smirked. "Funny, very funny. All right, girlfriend." They hugged. "Have a safe trip and call me when you get back." The two hugged again and went their separate ways.

That evening the tape played a third time, then ended. Keith shook his head. "I still can't figure out what that noise is in the background." He clicked down the stop and rewind buttons. "It's definitely muffled voices, but there's something else."

Drew added, "There's also music at the beginning, did you hear it?"

"Did anyone catch the accent?"

Everyone shook their heads no, then Marian added, "Prudence was right, it's definitely southern."

"Texas?" Keith asked. Jeremy and Drew looked at each other, then to Keith.

Jeremy began, "Texas, as in—"

Drew finished the thought. "San Antonio?" The three looked at each other, then to Prudence.

"Michael doesn't have anything to do with this," Prudence said soundly.

"Has he ever been around when the phone calls have come?" Keith asked.

Prudence shook her head no. "No, but you weren't there when the calls came either, and you certainly didn't make them. The same could be said for 99.9 percent of the male population of Philadelphia. And a southern accent certainly isn't indisputable evidence. It's not even circumstantial."

"You're beginning to sound more and more like an attorney," Drew said.

"Gee, thanks," Prudence said dryly.

"But still it is an interesting possibility," Keith said.

"He's not a suspect," Prudence said emphatically.

Blake spoke up finally. "I disagree. No one should be eliminated at this point."

Marian raised her brow and frowned. "I do believe Prudence is astute enough to recognize Michael's voice even if he did try to disguise it."

"True, but the phone calls did begin again just after the two of them met," Blake put in.

"So did the influx of newspaper photos and mass of reporters," Drew said. "I put my money on one of the reporters."

"That's a possibility," Blake said, "but what would the motive be?"

"There's always the question of increased circulation," Marian said.

The room went silent for a moment as everyone pondered the possibility that a reporter was behind the calls.

"Louisiana," Prudence said suddenly. Everyone turned as she stood and spoke. "After this last phone call I ran into one of Michael's teammates and I remember that he mentioned that he was from New Orleans."

"Where, at the store?"

"Yes, in the elevator. He was on his cell phone when I got on," she added curiously.

"Background sounds, people talking, elevator music, closer than you think, he was in the store."

"Who was it?"

"Rick Renault."

"Of course, Hunter took first string when he signed. Rick was kicked to second string. Motive, he could be trying to get back at Hunter through you."

"That makes absolutely no sense," Marian said. "You can't suspect someone just for being on an elevator, on the phone, with a southern accent. That's ridiculous. I'm sure his being there today was just a coincidence."

"I agree with Mother," Prudence said.

"But it makes perfect sense," Blake said.

"Why would anyone go that far?" Prudence asked.

"Professional jealousy, competitiveness, resentment, it makes perfect sense," Keith said.

"Speculation is one thing, playing amateur detective is another. There is no proof to any of this. We should leave the investigative practices up to the professionals," Marian insisted.

The discussion continued without her as she turned away and looked around sadly. This was Christmas Eve, a time to celebrate love and family togetherness. But instead, here she sat debating the identity of some idiot's voice on the phone.

She stood and walked over to the large bay window. The houses were all decorated with icicle lights, glistening trees, sparkling reindeer, and seasonal mangers. She smiled. At least Christmas was being celebrated somewhere.

"I don't want this public. So far few people outside this room know about this, and I'd like to keep it that way," Prudence said.

"Of course," Marian said. "The more public this is, the more chance of copycat calls."

"Exactly."

"So other than us," Drew asked, "who else knows about this?"

"Gene and Tanya at work, Michael, his coach, McGee, and the PR director, Luther Phillips."

"Fine, let's keep it that way." Everyone immediately agreed.

"I don't buy that a reporter is behind this," Keith injected, drawing Prudence's attention back to the conversation. "It's too personal. It's as if this nut has a special interest in Prudence. Case in point, the photos of the gift box and his attack on James Pruet. I can't see a reporter being that committed. It must be Renault. But my question is, what does Michael know about all this?"

"Maybe it's time we found out," Drew said.

Again the discussion escalated around her as Prudence sat quietly and utterly confused. She didn't know what to believe. Why would a reporter make the calls? Could Michael possibly be involved in any of this? She looked back out into the night, knowing that her answers were somewhere out there.

Chapter 19

The glittering San Antonio evening was the perfect backdrop to the annual Christmas party at Hunter's Lodge Retreat. The weather was crisp and every star in the heavens shone brightly. Michael sat out on the veranda alone. His tuxedo was his only protection from the cool evening breeze. He looked up at the night sky and smiled. He hoped that somewhere in Philadelphia Prudence would be looking up at the same night sky and thinking about him.

As if by magic Prudence had wound her way into his thoughts again. Still. There he was, standing in the center of a maelstrom of femininity, when a scent she'd worn the last time they were together wafted past his nose. He instantly searched the room for her. Of course she wasn't there, but that was the end of his evening. And to the annoyance of the women around him, it was the end of their night too.

He turned away from the inside lights and looked around into the empty darkness. Hunter's Lodge was his mother's pride and joy. It was a large estate inn situated on nearly fifty acres of land right next to a world-famous golf course on the outskirts of San Antonio. Four stories high, it had thirty-five full suites, complete amenities, and a private six-bedroom family-resident attachment next door. It was always filled to capacity with an envious waiting list; everybody who was anybody in Texas had stayed there at one time or another.

This was his home. He and his brothers grew up running, jumping, and playing here. The scenic mountain range on the horizon was his backyard and the prestigious golf course was his front yard. He was happy here, but lately there had been an emptiness in his heart. He'd thought that moving his contract to another city would fill the void, but it hadn't, at least not until he'd met Prudence.

"Michael?" a delicate voice asked as his mother approached. "What on earth are you doing out here?"

Michael smiled and looked down at his mother. Two strapping sons, both over six feet tall, from this tiny petite woman. She was remarkable. "Hi, beautiful," he said as he removed his jacket and draped it around her shoulders.

Accepting the jacket, she stretched her arms through, then wrapped it closer to her neck. "Don't tell me that the bright city lights of Philadelphia have you hooked already." She straightened his tie and adjusted his suspenders with motherly tenderness.

"No, of course not, San Antonio will always be my home in here." He motioned to his heart.

"So what is it then?" Elizabeth asked, then speculated, "Prudence?"

Michael flinched. "What makes you think it's Prudence?"

"Isn't it? Aren't you?"

"Thinking of Prudence?"

She nodded. Michael smiled and reached out to his mother. There was no way he could ever fool her. She could read his thoughts as well as she knew her own. She had called it her "mom antenna" when they were younger. She always knew when one of her sons needed an extra hug or an encouraging pat on the back. Apparently her antenna was still hard at work and doing just fine.

"Yeah, I guess I am."

"Tell me about her. What kind of woman is she? I've seen the pictures, naturally, but I'd like to know more."

"Prudence works as a fashion buyer at one of the largest department store chains in the area. It's the East Coast flagship store with its headquarters in Houston. She is very dedicated to her work and her family. Her mother and father are both attorneys, as well as her three brothers. Her father is the mayor of Philadelphia, her mother a district judge. She's a church girl and she . . ." Michael took a deep breath. "Drives me crazy most of the time." He paused, closed his eyes, lowered and shook his head, then chuckled silently.

When he raised his head seconds later he simply stated, "Prudence is impossible. She's the most exasperating woman I've ever met. She's headstrong, stubborn, and quick-tempered, particularly when she thinks she's right. She's like a cobra, always waiting to strike. Whenever she's around, you feel like you're at the base of a volcano and any second she's going to erupt."

Elizabeth Hunter laughed the entire time he spoke. Michael's description was exactly as she'd imagined. "Sounds like you really like her."

"I do, she's got a passion, a drive, a love of life, something. I can't explain it but it pulls you in. I admire that."

"And quite possibly more than just admire her, perhaps?"

His shoulders slumped and his head dropped again. "I keep asking myself why," he said, ardently. "Why her? She's nothing like the women I've dated in the past. But for some reason"—he stopped speaking and looked up at the stars—"I can't get enough of her." He looked back down into his mother's eyes. "Is that crazy?"

"No, of course not." Elizabeth reached up and stroked her son's jawline. She smiled. "This is the season of hope and love and wonderful gifts. Sometimes God gives us a special gift and we have no idea why. Cherish your gift, dear. Enjoy your time with Prudence. She sounds like a very special lady and I can't wait to meet her."

"No way." Michael shook his head repeatedly. "I don't want that hellfire erupting anywhere near you."

"Somehow I don't think the woman you've just described will be the same woman I meet."

Michael grimaced, confused.

"The two of you are so busy agitating each other because you don't want to admit that deep down inside there's something very special growing, a fondness, a tenderness, and yes, perhaps even love."

"Believe it or not, the last time we were together I told her that I loved her," he said.

Elizabeth nodded, suspecting as much.

"I can't believe I told her."

"Do you love her?"

Michael paused for a moment, then nodded slowly. "Yeah. Yes. I do love her." Elizabeth nodded again. "But you already knew that, didn't you?" He held his arm out to her. "Is that your mom antenna talking again?"

She nodded, smiled, and took his extended arm. "Perhaps. So, when can I expect to meet her?"

"She's not exactly just around the corner. She lives in Philadelphia. There's no way she's gonna just drive to San Antonio any time soon."

"Obviously, but doesn't she travel, perhaps on business?"

"Yes," he said, remembering that Prudence had mentioned that she'd be in Texas right after the holiday. "As a matter of fact I think that she's supposed to be in Houston for the next few days."

"Perfect, I'll expect her for dinner this weekend."

"She's traveling on business, a conference or meeting, I think. She may not have the time to drive a few hours to San Antonio for dinner."

"Of course she will," Elizabeth stated easily. "The last day of her meeting you'll drive down to Houston, pick her up, then come to dinner. She can just as easily leave from San Antonio airport as from Houston."

"She might already have plans."

Elizabeth reached up and patted her son's smooth

face. "Who could possibly turn you down?" Before he could reply with another excuse she continued. "Now let's get back inside before your father sends out a search party for us."

Together they slowly walked back to the gaiety and merriment of the Christmas party. Elizabeth's smile broadened. She knew now that this time, more than any other, she was absolutely correct in her suspicion, Michael was truly in love.

When they stepped inside Elizabeth removed the jacket and gave it back to her son. "I'm serious about meeting Prudence this weekend," she said, smiling the smile of an assured woman. "You'll find a way to arrange it."

The discussion was over as far as she was concerned. She walked over and greeted one of her many guests, leaving Michael bewildered and perplexed.

"How in the hell am I going to pull this off?" he mumbled to himself as he headed to the bar.

Early in the afternoon, exhausted and bone tired, Prudence slid the key card down the slim opening and waited for the tiny green light to blink. As soon as it did she turned the latch and walked zombielike into the hotel room.

She kicked off her shoes, moved to the nearest double bed, and collapsed in a heap, tired and weary. A few moments later she sat up, grabbed her briefcase, and began going through the loads of material she'd picked up earlier. She was shuffling through several pages of notes, looking over the designs she favored as she glanced up and noticed that the message light on the telephone was lit.

Prudence moaned inwardly, *what now?* In the two days since she had arrived, it seemed that everything that could have gone wrong had gone wrong. The very moment she stepped off the plane at the Bush Intercontinental Airport, to her surprise and horror, she had learned that her luggage went to Phoenix, Arizona. When that was finally straightened out, the Houston hotel lost her reservation and she had to get a room in a hotel twenty minutes away.

The weather was cold, wet, and miserable. It had rained both days. Today, her last day in town, was the first she'd seen the sun peeking through the persistent clouds. The meetings were scheduled to end the following afternoon, but she'd had enough of Texas and rescheduled her flight for nine o'clock that evening. She decided to spend the last few hours in the pool, spa, and bed. Not necessarily in that order.

She picked up the phone and pushed the message button. Seconds later she was connected to a voice-mail system. She listened as a familiar voice brought a smile to her face for the first time in two days. "I hope you don't mind, your assistant Tanya gave me your itinerary, after much cajoling on my part, I might add. I'll be downstairs in the hotel's café until two. Join me."

Prudence was stunned. Of all the people to hear from, Michael was the last person she expected. She checked her watch. It was twenty minutes after two. Her heart thundered as she grabbed her purse, jacket, and key card and headed for the elevators to the hotel lobby.

As soon as she arrived she looked around the open lobby until she spotted the small café across from the front desk. She walked over slowly, patiently. Knowing that she had gotten the message late, she realized that there was a real possibility that he wouldn't still be there, but she walked over anyway.

The café, a large green and yellow brightly lit room with buffet tables along one side of the wall and an open glass walkway on the other, was empty except for a small group of excited fans in the far corner. She knew instantly that he was still there.

A delightful smile warmed her face as she spotted him. He lit up the room with his cool casual charm and charisma as he sat in a corner booth surrounded on both sides by fans.

A woman with two children and a camera positioned each child beside Michael, then stepped back to take a photograph. Prudence smiled with a mischievous sparkle when next the woman ushered her older children away and placed a young screaming child on his lap for another photo.

The child, screaming wildly, didn't faze Michael's even-tempered calm in the least. He whispered something into the child's ear and the child instantly stopped crying long enough to look up and have his mother take the picture. The mother cheered, delighted at her success. Moments later, after she had placed the child back in the stroller, the screaming began all over again.

Prudence took her time walking over to his table. The sight of him was amazing. He was a true Texas cowboy through and through. Jeans, denim shirt, cowboy boots, a big silver belt buckle, and a cowboy hat sitting on the table told her that. You couldn't get any more cowboy than that.

She had had her misconceptions before with his perfectly tailored Armani suits, Calvin Klein casuals, and *GQ* attitude. But that vanished like the thick rain clouds on a sunny day with just one look at this brawny, rawhided man. He was vigorous and robust and 100 percent unadulterated Texas masculinity.

Heat flushed Prudence's face as her heart beat thunderously and her stomach dipped and fluttered. *I love you, Prudence Washington.* Those were his last words to her, words that she'd never forget as long as she lived, words that she longed to hear him say again.

Michael looked up, as if sensing her presence. He stood as she approached. She couldn't help but smile when their eyes met. How any woman could resist this man was unthinkable. Prudence bit at her lower lip as she considered the pleasurable possibilities of his hard body. The memory of their time together quickened the pace of her heart. She smiled as enticing thoughts penetrated picture-perfect images in her mind. She groaned a throaty, lustful sound, then chastised herself for her musings. "You're starting to sound just like Tanya," she muttered silently.

"Speed, Speed Hunter!" the shrill southern voice tweaked loudly as a perfumed priss dashed past Prudence, nearly knocking her down as she targeted Michael with bull's-eye precision.

"Remember me, Speed?" the woman continued. "We were in school together. Dinah-Lee Randolph, I was a cheerleader, remember?"

Michael shrugged and averted his eyes from Prudence to the western-clad woman with a huge mass of store-bought hair. As the woman reached him, he leaned back to ward off her overly familiar greeting. Prudence paused to observe the spectacle.

His dread was evident and his kindness admirable. The still peppy former cheerleader produced a pen and paper and told him exactly what she wanted him to write. He did dutifully, and then, with less ado than her arrival, she happily departed.

Prudence approached. "May I have your autograph?"

Michael, watching her steadily as she approached, excused himself and slid from the booth. He smiled seductively as he stood. "You can have anything you want." The gathering of fans looked at each other knowingly as he thanked those around him. He shook hands and waved as the crowd began to disperse.

When they were alone, standing at the table, Michael leaned over and kissed her slowly, tenderly. "Welcome to Texas."

"Thanks." She couldn't help smiling as soon as he spoke.

"Would you like something to eat or drink?"

"No, thank you."

"How was your holiday?"

"Great. Yours?"

"Good, a little lonely."

"Really?"

"Uh-huh."

"I just got your message."

"I noticed." He returned her bright smile.

They stood for a moment, just smiling at each other like a couple of teenagers standing at a locker between classes. "Don't take this the wrong way, but what are you doing here? I thought you were in San Antonio. Isn't that like . . ." She paused, having no idea where San Antonio actually was. "Some place else?"

"Yeah." He chuckled. "It's about three hours away from here."

"That's pretty far. You drove three hours just to stop by and say hi?"

"Actually, there's a little more to it. How's the conference going?" he asked, completely off the subject.

"There are meetings, and they're good, very informative."

He looked down, seeing her holding her purse. "Are you on your way some place?"

"No. As a matter of fact, I'm just getting in."

"So when are the meetings over?"

"Tomorrow afternoon."

"Is that when you leave for Philly?"

"No, I have a late flight this evening."

"This evening, you're leaving already? You just got here," he said, surprised.

"I got here two days ago."

"And you're leaving so soon? I hope Texas hasn't disappointed you."

Prudence decided not to go into all the drama she'd been going through since she arrived. "No, but it's been interesting," she said. "What exactly are you doing here?"

"I came to give you a ride."

"A ride to where?" she asked.

But before he could answer a young boy walked up and handed Michael a piece of paper and an ink pen. Michael signed his name and jokingly rubbed the boy's head. The boy smiled a toothless grin, then hurried back to his parents.

Michael leaned close to Prudence's ear. "Let's get out of here." He dropped a couple of large bills on the empty table, took her hand and intertwined it in his arm, then pointed her toward the café's street door. Bright sunlight greeted them as soon as they exited.

"A ride to where?" she repeated.

"San Antonio."

"Why would I be going to San Antonio?"

"You've been invited to dinner."

"Really, by whom?" she asked, already guessing the answer.

"My mother," he confessed.

"How did she know I was in Texas?"

"I might have mentioned it in passing."

"So you drove all the way here just to invite me to dinner?"

"Yes," he said matter-of-factly.

"Three hours there, dinner, and three hours back. I have a nine o'clock flight tonight. There's no way I'll be back in time."

"Don't worry, I'll take care of everything."

To her amazement, it took relatively little time for Michael to talk her into meeting and having dinner with his family that evening. She'd packed, checked out, changed her departure from Bush to San Antonio International Airport, and loaded his truck with her suitcase. In less than thirty minutes she was on the road traveling west on Interstate 10 headed to Hunter's Lodge Retreat in San Antonio, Texas, with Michael at her side.

The exhaustion of the past few days, the easy sway of the truck's movement, and the continuous hum of the muted engine gently rocked her to sleep. She awoke two hours later just outside San Antonio, Texas.

"How was your nap?"

"Great, I can't believe I fell asleep like that."

"You were apparently exhausted."

Prudence sat up and looked around. "Much further?"

"No, we'll be there in about twenty minutes."

She nodded nervously. Second thoughts had begun to tug at her. What was she doing? Admittedly, she was stunned and flattered to hear that he'd drive three hours just to get to her in Houston and bring her back to his home. But meeting his family was a major step that she wasn't sure she was ready for. Yes, he'd met her family, but that was an unusual occurrence and not a planned gathering.

"I can't believe I'm doing this. I can't believe I actually let you talk me into this," she said.

"It'll be over in a few hours and then I'll take you to the San Antonio International Airport and you'll be on your way back to Philadelphia on a nine o'clock flight as scheduled."

Prudence, more surprised with herself than with Michael, still couldn't believe how readily she'd agreed to accept his mother's invitation to dinner. Granted, she was curious and had secretly hoped to someday meet the woman responsible for him. What was wrong with her when it came to this man? All her common sense and levelheadedness went right out of the window as soon as he looked her way or opened his mouth.

Michael, speeding steadily, lost in his own thoughts, smiled at the outcome. Truthfully he wasn't sure Prudence would agree to his request, but she surprised him as usual. Then without much consideration he voiced a question that had burned in his memory since their first night together. "Tell me about him," he said.

"Tell you about who?" she asked.

"The man who broke your heart."

Prudence had forgotten all about the conversation they'd had so long ago. She sighed heavily and stalled. Suddenly it had gotten too close and very warm. She opened the top button of her shirt and tilted her head into the open-window breeze. She began fanning her face with her hands. "Is the weather always warm and humid this time of year?"

"Texas has a very even climate. Not too cold, not too hot."

"Nice." An awkward silence drifted between them as she continued to stall. "Congratulations on making the play-offs."

"Thank you."

"Don't you have practice or something?"

"It's wild-card weekend. We have the week off," he said, keeping his eyes on the road while waiting patiently for her to answer his question. But, instead, earsplitting silence surrounded them again.

Prudence relaxed back into the comfortable leather. Maybe, just maybe, if she finally talked about it, she could put the empty feelings to rest.

"Garrett Marshall."

"Garrett Marshall, the investigative reporter?"

"Yes, although he wasn't the huge personality he is now. When I knew him he worked at the local television station as a weekend anchor. He always had dreams of becoming bigger. I even encouraged him."

"So I assume you two dated for a while."

"Yes, for about six months. Unfortunately, I didn't know that the entire time he was using me to do a piece on my father and possible corruption in his office."

"You mean he was given the assignment because he was dating you?"

"No. There was no assignment. He came up with the whole idea on his own, then sold it to the network afterward. They okayed it only after he fabricated a report from the mayor's office concerning building improprieties and the exchange of personal gratuities. He told the network that he had firsthand knowledge and that he could back everything up with irrefutable proof, so they announced the segment as a special undercover investigative report on the mayor's office."

"I assume by this time you had dumped him."

"No, he swore to me that it was all a misunderstanding. I believed him until the media implied that I was in on it with him and had willingly sold out my family."

"No wonder you have a problem with the media."

"It gets better. Garrett had also presented the segment to the network's nationally televised news magazine. Getting to the network had always been his goal, and he didn't care how he got there."

"Sounds like a man with an ambitious ego."

"Garrett was offered a position at the network level. He took it and never looked back. When the segment was set to air, the truth prevailed. He couldn't back up any of his claims, so the network had to pull the story and cancel the segment after making a public apology to the mayor's office."

"Did the segment ever run?"

"Yes, Garrett's story was eventually watered down to nothing but speculations and innuendo. But even so, his accusations damaged my father's reputation and his political career."

"I see."

"No, you don't. I defended him in the beginning because I was sure that he could never use me like that. I stood against my family arguing that the man I adored was honest and scrupulous. I was wrong. Because of me and my stubborn blindness, the story nearly destroyed my family."

Michael reached over and took her hand, brought it to his lips, and kissed it. "I'm sorry." She nodded. "I guess since I met you in a swirl of publicity it brought back a lot of painful memories, kind of like once burned, forever scorned."

"Something like that."

"I hope you've changed your mind about me by now."

Prudence smiled broadly. "I haven't decided yet. You're still pretty arrogant."

"Thank you. I'll take that as a compliment."

"Okay, now it's your turn. Tell me about her."

"Her?"

"Yes, the *her* in your life."

Michael turned to her and smiled. "I would have thought that was obvious. You, Prudence, are the *her* in my life."

She blushed slightly. "Before me."

"I haven't had that much luck with women."

"I find that hard to believe. You're a professional football player—quarterback—extremely popular, handsome, and worth a fortune."

"Exactly, for all those reasons you just mentioned. I'm a bit gun-shy when it comes to swimming in the relationship pool. Women have a tendency to not exactly be themselves around me. Mostly they just cater to everything I say."

"That's sad."

"I completely agree and I think that's what instantly attracted me to you. You didn't exactly send out a welcoming committee to greet me."

"Actually there was a welcoming committee to greet you."

"Ah yes, but you were openly hostile and rude."

"I beg your pardon, I was not rude. I was justifiably annoyed."

"Yes, you were." He chuckled. "I loved seeing the fire spark in your eyes." He glanced over to her. "I still do, shows you have good taste."

Prudence shook her head at his renewed arrogance and smugness. There was no getting around it. He was impossible, incorrigible, and completing irresistible. And she loved every enticing inch of him. As the conversation subsided, she looked around at her surroundings. "How far are we from your parents' place now?" she asked, interrupting his reflective thoughts.

"Actually we've been on their property for the last ten minutes."

Surprised, Prudence continued to look around at the lush, verdant scenery. Everywhere she looked, in every direction, she saw flourishing, thriving shades of green.

Through dark sunglasses she squinted. The distant mountains that ran along the western terrain seemed to be watercolors painted against the rich, watery blue sky. Cattle grazed lazily along pastures dotted sporadically with barnlike structures. This was more like she thought Texas would look, not the monolithic cookie-cutter buildings in the city.

"We're here," he announced as he climbed the ridge and rounded a slight bend leading to the front entrance. He drove through open cast-iron gates with the name HUNTER'S LODGE RETREAT scripted in gold with an ornate lion's head emblem.

The building, a cross between a southern plantation and a huge modern hotel, was nothing like she had expected. With the name Hunter's Lodge Retreat, she had anticipated seeing rustic log cabins with smoke billowing out of chimneys and old wooden porches held up by aged tree trunks with creaky old rocking chairs padded with worn denim.

Instead, she saw what could have conceivably been a modern building in any city in the world, surrounded by lush greenery and manicured lawns. Prudence looked curiously at the crowded parking lot. There were dozens of cars and trucks parked in front. "Your parents live in a hotel?" she asked.

"An inn. But next to it is more accurate, and technically, it's a lodge," he said. "It was my mother's idea back when we were kids. She was tired of staying home alone when my father traveled with the team, so they purchased the adjoining property, and built a hotel and golf course and called it Hunter's Lodge Retreat."

Prudence looked up at the building's less than rustic exterior. It hovered against the radiant horizon like a floating mirage. The brilliantly smooth sheen of the multicolored natural stone contrasted with the caramel sunset and reflected the purple hue of the far-off mountains. It was breathtaking. It resembled an old-fashioned southern plantation, complete with two-story columns and twelve-foot windows and shutters all around.

Michael circled the driveway entrance, then found a parking space along the side of the building's secondary structure. As he shut off the ignition he reached over and grasped her hand. "Ready?"

Prudence smiled. "As I'll ever be."

"Let's do it."

After exiting the car, the two walked up the curved stone path that led toward a rose-laden trellis. The beauty of the perfectly formed roses that lined both sides of the walk resembled an artist's palette. Prudence inhaled deeply as she walked beneath the aromatic canopy. The scent, sweet and full-bodied, was like heaven. "The smell of roses always reminds me of home," Michael said as he took Prudence's hand.

A few yards farther down, the path split in two. One led toward the front entrance of the lodge and the other led to the side of the secondary structure. Prudence began walking toward the lodge's main entrance until Michael led her away. He pointed to the side. "This way. It's the family entrance." They followed the path around to the side of the building, then walked up the stone steps leading to a small porch and double oak-screened doors.

Two large bright red, gold, and green hot chili-pepper wreaths hung on each stained-glass inset. Prudence smiled to herself. She never would have thought to hang chili peppers with large green ribbons on a door, but somehow in this setting it worked perfectly.

Michael walked slightly ahead of her to get the door, but it opened before he even touched the knob. "Well, well, well. Looks like little brother finally did good." The man's infectious smile was a carbon copy of Michael's.

"Hey," Michael said as he reached out to the man. "I didn't know you were gonna be here."

"And pass up this opportunity? No way. I just arrived." The two men shook hands, then hugged briefly. But as soon as the older brother noticed Prudence he turned his full attention toward her with a brilliant smile. She smiled back.

"Perfect timing, I'd say," he purred. "Hello, pretty lady." He beamed adoringly and reached out to take Prudence's hand.

"Prudence," Michael began, "this is my brother Gabriel."

"*The* Prudence Washington." Gabriel smiled. "It's a pleasure to finally meet you. I've read quite a bit about you." He lifted her hand to his lips and kissed the back. "And my brother of course."

Prudence blushed in spite of herself. "Don't believe everything you read."

"I never do, particularly when it's about myself."

Prudence had recognized Gabriel "G-Man" Hunter as soon as he appeared at the door. He had been a basketball phenom for years. His exploits on the court were overshadowed only by his reputation as a ladies' man off the court.

"It's a pleasure to meet you," Prudence said.

"Funny," Gabriel said. "You don't look like the little spitfire they make you out to be. But tell me, did you really poke Michael in the chest and tell him to get out of your face?"

Prudence opened her mouth to explain their first meeting, but stopped when she was interrupted.

"All right, all right, that's enough. Out of the way," a sweet, warm voice said firmly, and the two brothers, standing side by side, parted immediately. Prudence smiled as a petite woman appeared between the twin towers. Her face lit up as soon as she saw Prudence.

Michael bent down to kiss her cheek. "Hi, Mom," he said, lovingly.

"Hello, dear," she said to Michael as she turned her attention back to Prudence standing across from her.

"Mom, this is Prudence Washington. Prudence, this is my mother, Elizabeth Hunter."

"Prudence." Elizabeth smiled as she took both of her hands and held them tightly. "You're exactly as I imagined you'd be."

"It's a pleasure to meet you, Mrs. Hunter."

"Call me Elizabeth, please." Prudence nodded. "Well, let's not stand in the doorway all evening, come on into the parlor and get comfortable." Elizabeth locked her arm with Prudence's and led her down the short hallway toward a bright sunny room at the end. As they entered she stopped and turned to Michael and Gabriel, who were talking and joking as they followed the two women.

"Dinner will be ready shortly. Why don't you go down to the stables and get your father?" On cue, both Michael and Gabriel reached into a pocket and pulled out a cell phone. "In person," she suggested firmly.

Gabriel turned to leave, Michael reluctantly following. As soon as they left Elizabeth turned to Prudence and smiled warmly. She beckoned for Prudence to sit at the small table already set with a pitcher of iced tea, glasses, and tea cookies. "I've been looking forward to meeting you for some time."

"Me, really?" Prudence said, somewhat surprised by Elizabeth's frankness. "Any particular reason?"

"Of course," Elizabeth said as she poured and handed Prudence a glass of tea. "It appears that my son is smitten with you, or is that just the media's perception?"

"Our local media have a tendency to exaggerate."

"And have they in this case?"

"You might want to speak with Michael about this," she said, uncomfortably evasive.

"I already have."

Prudence remembered Michael telling her once that he told his mother everything. The curiosity bit at her. What exactly did he tell his mother about them?

"Come," Elizabeth said, changing the subject. "Let me show you the lodge."

"I'd like that," Prudence said as she stood and followed. Together the two women slowly strolled through the house to the connecting doorway into the lodge. Elizabeth showed her the various rooms, the great room, the dining room, and the many common rooms. When they finally returned to the screened parlor of the family's private residence, Elizabeth and Prudence had become well acquainted.

"So, has your family met Michael yet?" Elizabeth asked.

Prudence smiled and laughed at Elizabeth's inquisitive glance and raised brow. Her finding humor in such a simple question seemed odd to Elizabeth. But after Prudence explained their initial meeting, she laughed so hard tears streamed down her bronzed cheeks. "I suppose asking what your parents thought of him would be a moot point."

"Actually that first meeting was a bit shaky, to say the least. But since then, everything's been pretty much fist-free."

"I'm glad to hear that," she said gratefully. "What does your mother think?"

"Truthfully?" Prudence asked.

Elizabeth nodded. "Please."

"When the news reports first started putting us together, my mom wasn't exactly pleased. She was very concerned about Michael's reputation. And, of course, since I am her only daughter . . ."

Elizabeth nodded her head in agreement. "Say no more, I understand completely. I realize that my sons aren't exactly the archangels they're named for. But both Gabriel and Michael are decent, respectful, and honorable men."

"My mother has always been overly protective, even more so than my father and brothers. She'll come around."

Elizabeth nodded again. "Of course she will. Michael has a tendency to endear himself quickly."

Prudence looked out the window across the back. Three riders on horses were moving in the distance.

"Elizabeth followed her line of vision. She smiled at

seeing the Hunter men approaching. "They'll be here shortly. We'd better go check on dinner."

Ten minutes later, loud talking, laughter, and good-humored joking erupted as three strapping men walked into the house. Prudence noticed that Michael and Gabriel had changed clothing. The third figure, a stately man with slightly graying temples, walked over and kissed Elizabeth lovingly. Then he looked over at Prudence and smiled. "Prudence Washington, I presume."

Chapter 20

Prudence snuggled deep within the warmth of Michael's Philadelphia Knights jacket. The spicy scent of his cologne enveloped her as she closed her eyes and smiled in the darkness. She couldn't believe that she'd so completely lost track of time. But she had such a wonderful evening enjoying the antics of the Hunter family men that it was well worth it.

When Michael told her that she had just an hour and a half to get to the airport thirty-five miles away, she said hasty good-byes, promising to keep in touch with Elizabeth, and then they hurried out.

"I had a really good time tonight," she said.

"I'm glad. I think my family really liked you."

"They're sweet, I felt right at home as soon as I walked in. Gabriel reminds me of my brother Drew."

Michael smiled and nodded as he took a brief second to look in her direction. "So what did you and my mom talk about while Gabriel and I were out?"

"Nothing much. This and that. You know, girl talk."

"Uh-huh," he grunted and looked back at the road.

Prudence chuckled at Michael's concerned look. "Don't worry, she didn't tell me any of your little boy secrets or show me pictures of you lying on a bearskin rug in the buff."

"That's good to hear. I certainly wouldn't want that."

Prudence smiled at his facetious remark. "So it's just the two of you, you and Gabriel, no sisters."

"Yep, it's just the two of us, although we do have quite a few cousins. But it's basically just Gabriel and me."

"And he's the oldest?" she asked.

"Barely, he's only older than me by eleven months. But he still, even now, insists on calling me his little brother."

"Believe me, I know that feeling. Being the youngest isn't all it's cracked up to be. At times, it's downright frustrating."

"It must have been for you. Three brothers, Keith, Drew, and Jeremy, I bet they really teased you."

"Actually, not so much, I learned at a young age how to stick up for and defend myself. They're more over-protective of me than anything, especially Keith, being the oldest. But I guess you kind of know that already."

"Yeah, they can punch pretty well too. I walked away with quite a few bruises that night, not to mention spending the next morning in the whirlpool."

"I would have thought that you had shaken that off."

"Believe me, when three angry men, brothers, attack, protecting their younger sister, you don't come away un-scathed and just shake it off."

"I imagine not." Prudence smiled, thinking of her brothers' love and protectiveness. They had always been there for her no matter what. She didn't always see or understand their reasoning at times, but she always loved that she felt safe because of it. "I had no idea that G-Man was your brother. I have at least a dozen friends who'd love to meet Gabriel."

Michael smiled and nodded. "He gets that a lot."

"I bet. Tall, dark, and handsome, kind, sweet, talented, and funny. He's every woman's idea of the perfect man."

"What about your idea of the perfect man?" He looked at her.

She looked over at him and smiled evasively.

"Do you and your brother still live at the lodge?" she asked as they traveled down the dark highway headed to-ward the San Antonio International Airport.

"No, Gabriel lives in Houston and my house is in that direction, just outside of Austin." He pointed and glanced toward a mass of twinkling lights on the horizon.

Prudence followed his line of vision, looking in the general direction that he pointed. All she saw was darkness. She bit her lower lip mischievously as an idea sparked. "How far is it?" Her voice was low and husky.

"Not too far. A few miles, thirty minutes, give or take," he said, looking over at her. "Why?"

"Just curious."

He nodded with interest. "Would you like to see it?" he asked.

She looked at him as he kept his eyes purposely focused on the dark road ahead. "Yes," she said boldly. "Yes, I think I would like to see it."

"You'll miss your flight again," he warned as he glanced in the rearview mirror, then maneuvered the truck into a different lane.

"There'll be another one later."

"Probably not tonight."

She shrugged. "Then I guess I'll catch a flight in the morning, if, of course, you don't mind company tonight."

Michael smiled, embracing the idea of Prudence in his home. "Not at all."

She smiled in the darkness. "Don't worry. I'll give you a minute or two to clean up before I go inside."

"I'm not worried. I have a cleaning service and they do a very thorough job."

"That's not the kind of cleaning up I was referring to."

"What kind . . ." he began, then paused. "Oh, you're talking about lingerie and curlers, right?"

"Yeah, among other things."

"I assure you, the house is clean."

"We'll see," she said slyly.

Michael chuckled softly at her green-eyed curiosity.

They drove in silence until Michael turned off the main highway and down several dark streets leading away from the twinkling lights. "So tell me about growing up in Texas."

"What do you want to know?"

"I don't know, anything. Tell me about your home. What was it like growing up at Hunter's Lodge?"

Michael chuckled. "Not much different from growing up in any other place. I guess the only difference was that there was always something to do after school and on weekends—swimming, horseback riding, amusement parks, fishing, cultural activities, and historical sites. I'd go to the Alamo and other places regularly because of the lodge's daily trips. Sometimes we'd go skiing up in the mountains and hiking out in the desert. Then, of course, there were always the basketball and tennis courts and local football fields."

Prudence smirked. "Of course, but what about the people? How different was it having a lot of people, strangers, around all the time?"

"The majority of the staff has been with us since I was a kid. So they're like part of the family. Most of the time the guests come and go so quickly you never really see them much. They're like a blur. They come for the golf or the shopping or just to sit back and relax. So they just do their thing and go home."

"So the family is pretty much separate from the guests?"

"Yes and no. Some of the guests have been coming to Hunter's for years, so they're more like old friends of the family than visitors."

"I guess that the family residence is completely restricted."

"Yes, most of the time the family home is strictly off-limits to guests. But sometimes my mother invites special guests over for dinner or a visit. It's rare but she's done it before."

"Did you work in the lodge as you were growing up?"

"Oh yeah, I was a busboy, a bellhop, a caddy, a life-guard, front desk clerk. You name it, I've done it."

"I bet you really know the hotel business."

"You'd win that bet."

"You said that the residence was off-limits. How separate is it?"

"Mostly everything, separate entrance, kitchen, pool, fenced-in grounds. It's just a house attached to a lodge."

"I saw you and Gabriel riding earlier. You look like a real cowboy out there."

"I just about grew up on a horse."

"What's your horse's name?"

"I have several. But Casper is the one I ride most often."

Prudence chuckled. "Casper, as in the white, friendly ghost?"

"Actually, Casper is a jet-black stallion. He's a breeder."

"A breeder?"

"I hire him out to breed with certain mares."

She chuckled in the darkness. "Does that make you a panderer, procurer, or pimp?"

"I prefer businessman."

"So, you have horses, what else?"

"It's not a farm. We don't have cows, pigs, and goats."

"I saw cattle when we first got to the lodge."

"Cattle?" he questioned.

"Yeah, cattle, you know, like roping out on the open range or something like that. Cattle drives and cowboys."

"There're only a few dozen head out by the fenced meadow, nothing serious. We just keep them around." Michael smiled at her western preconceptions. "So, we have a golf course, not cattle. And FYI, not all Texans have cattle or oil wells."

"You said earlier that your parents built the lodge while your father was still on the road. What did he do?"

"He was a professional basketball player."

"And now?"

"He's a general manager."

"And your brother plays basketball too?"

"Yes."

"Why didn't you play basketball?"

"I do, sometimes, but I'm better at football."

Ten minutes later, as the conversation continued, Michael drove through an open gate and circled around back. He pulled up in front of a multicar garage and stopped the truck. He pushed a button on the dashboard to open the first garage door, and then drove inside. Michael turned off the engine and removed the key. He looked over to Prudence. She looked at him. "Shall we?"

They got out and walked. "It's really dark out here. I can't see a thing," Prudence said.

Michael looked around, completely used to the midnight-dark surroundings of his home. "It's beautiful. I'll show you around tomorrow. You're gonna love it."

They walked from the garage around to the front door. The narrow path of landscape lightly glowed as she looked up at the large structure.

To her surprise, Michael's home was not at all as she expected. The modern classic building she had imagined turned out to be a huge, rustic log cabin. As soon as she entered she was greeted by waxed stone floors, Persian carpets, and a thirty-foot stone chimney fireplace flanked by bookcases that spanned the width of a single living room wall. Big overstuffed sofas, chairs, and ottomans were comfortably situated around for easy conversation. Masculine to the point of burly, it wasn't exactly how she thought he lived.

Michael watched her expression. "You look surprised."

"I am. It isn't at all what I expected."

"What did you expect?"

"I don't really know. Something modern and grand, I guess. Maybe something more like your house in Philadelphia."

"That's leased for the season. It's not really home for me, this is. Texas will always be my home."

In the corner of the living room she saw a baby grand piano. She walked over and pulled the cover up. The polished black and white keys gleemed like new money. She struck a few keys, then sat down comfortably on the padded bench. Michael watched as she aligned her fingers on the proper keys and gently played a few chords that led into a Bach minuet. He walked over to stand behind her. "Do you play?" he asked, reaching down to place his hands on her shoulders.

"I was forced to take lessons when I was a child. I was seven or eight at the time and I hated them. I wanted to play the drums, but my mother refused to buy me a drum set. So I joined the school band in the percussion section." Prudence smiled at the memory of her rebellion. "My mother found out and had a fit." She chuckled. "So, to answer your question, I don't play well." She continued to tinker with the keys, finding her memory of playing lacking more than she realized. "Do you?" she asked.

Michael came around to her side and sat down as she scooted over to make room for him. He placed his hands on the keys and began to play *Fur Elise*, a sweet lullaby familiar from her childhood.

"Ah, that's nice," she said sweetly.

Michael immediately began playing Beethoven's Fifth Symphony in E minor. Then he segued into "Moon River," followed by a stirring rendition of "Amazing Grace," into "Stand by Me," and finished with the old Motown classics "You Can't Hurry Love" and "Ain't No Mountain High Enough."

"Show off," she sneered jokingly.

The quick, precise movement of his fingers floated across the keys with ease and agility. Prudence, amazed by the performance, laughed at his display of bravado. His remarkable talent was diminished only by the magnificence of the music he played.

"You're good. When did you learn?"

"A very, very long time ago."

He continued showing her which chords to play to add to the lilting sound of the ivory keys. Prudence stumbled awkwardly, laughing wildly as Michael finally stilled her hands and the atrocious sounds she was making. "I see we'd better get you back to taking lessons again as soon as possible."

"I beg your pardon." She playfully slapped his arm, then began concentrated two-finger playing. "How dare you? I'll have you know I am quite good when I actually put my mind to it."

Michael instantly picked up the melody, filling the room with the familiar tune "Chopsticks." Every so often Prudence would watch his hands gently traverse the keys, adding a jazzy rhythm to the basic beat. Several times she lost her place, focusing not on what she was doing, but on Michael and his proficiency on the piano.

"Enough," she finally called out after completely messing up and losing her place one last time. "I give up." She placed her hands on top of his to stop their performance. She stood and looked around the living room again. "How long have you been here?"

"A while."

She nodded. "I like it. It's you somehow. But not the classy, suave, confident playboy . . ."—Michael began laughing at the exaggerated description—". . . but the quiet piano-playing cowboy with the horse, a black stallion named Casper, and a thing for gingerbread cookies."

Michael burst out laughing openly. "You saw that, huh?"

Prudence sucked her teeth and shook her head knowingly. "I think I just found out the chink in the armor. Samson had his hair. Achilles had his heel. Superman had kryptonite. And you"—she pointed as he crossed the room to her—"you have gingerbread man cookies with raisin eyes and frosted icing vests and pants."

He took the finger that she held pointing in his direction and placed it on his heart. "Now, you wouldn't tell anybody about that, would you?"

"I don't know." He smiled and lit up her face. "I might."

"Because news like that could seriously damage my reputation."

"What's it worth to you to keep my silence?" She giggled and he circled around her and wrapped his arms around her waist, tickling her neck and ear with tiny kisses.

"What do you want?"

"I'll tell you what. I'll keep your secret for now, but one day I'm gonna call on you, and I'm gonna want a favor." She did her best Godfather Don Corleone imitation.

Michael shook his head and laughed again. "That was so bad."

Prudence feigned hurt and rolled her eyes childishly. Michael pulled her back into his arms.

"Come on, show me the kitchen. You can tell a lot about a man from his kitchen," she said.

Still laughing wildly, they walked into the kitchen. Michael turned on the lights. After a second or two, the room came to life with subdued brightness. A hammered copper chandelier hung in the breakfast nook above the table while recessed lighting lit the rest of the area. Michael went to the refrigerator and pulled out a bottle of Cristal champagne, then grabbed two glasses. Prudence continued to walk around the kitchen looking at everything. "This is really nice," she said, admiring the beauty of his kitchen.

Michael looked up proudly. "This is my play area. I love to cook."

She stopped at the counter and watched him admiringly. "Really, sometimes you truly surprise me."

He looked at her as he undid the foil from the bottle's cork. "How so?" he asked as he twisted the cork slowly. The deliberate action caused Prudence to flinch, knowing that the cork could pop at any second. It did, giving her a sudden start. But Michael caught it before it flew across the room.

"The cowboy boots, the hat, the four-wheel-drive truck, the big silver belt buckle, and then there's your home. It's pure vintage Texas rustic. To tell you the truth I imagined you in a penthouse suite on top of a hotel in the center of the city. And here you are in the middle of nowhere, in a log cabin of all things. Doesn't exactly go with the *GQ* image of you wheeling around Philadelphia in a late-model Mercedes-Benz sedan, does it?"

"I'm a man of many talents." He filled the glasses.

"Really?" She tilted her head curiously and moved by his side. "Care to elaborate?"

He smiled seductively. "In time."

"Something to look forward to?" she asked, prompting further.

"Oh yeah," he promised as he moved closer and handed her a glass. He gently touched his glass to hers. "To many talents."

She smiled. "To many talents," she repeated as she sipped her champagne, then set the glass down on the counter. She moved closer to him. "Michael."

"Prudence."

"The last time we were together, at my apartment, you said . . ." She paused to sip from her glass again.

"Yes, I said . . ." He took her glass from her hand. ". . . that I love you, Prudence Washington."

Prudence took a deep breath and looked up at him. The certainty of his feelings was reflected in his eyes, and it burned into her heart. But she couldn't say it, not yet. With her heart filled she opened her mouth to speak, but nothing came out.

Michael smiled. "In time, remember. You lead, I'll follow."

She nodded. He would always be her heart.

Chapter 21

"Kiss me," she said. In an instant Michael swept her into his arms and kissed her passionately. She melted there, molding her body to his in complete submission. She closed her eyes dreamingly and was swept away in the fantasy of his kiss and the reality of his love. The strength of his embrace overwhelmed her as his desire consumed her. It was a kiss that was meant to last a lifetime, a kiss that washed away all her fears and left her knowing that she was truly loved.

His hands drifted to her breasts as his mouth relished her neck and shoulders. Weak-kneed, she leaned back, allowing him to sandwich her between himself and the counter. She instantly felt how much he wanted her. Her body yielded. The power she wielded over him was intoxicating.

She circled her arms around his neck as he lifted her to perch on top of the marble counter. She wrapped her legs around him and collapsed her body against his, crushing her needful breasts into him. The kiss broke with exaggerated protests as they sealed their embrace with promises of passion.

Michael buried his face in the crook of her neck, then opened his mouth to taste the sweetness of her lips mingled with the sparkling champagne. Like a man parched by desert dryness, he devoured her mouth, drinking in the intoxicating mix of rapture and ecstasy.

"Are you gonna show me the rest of the house?" she muttered, rasping breathlessly.

"Sure," he replied, still kissing her neck. "Where would you like to begin?"

"Show me your bedroom," she gasped from swollen lips between stolen kisses. Breathless and weak from the embrace, she slid down from the counter into his arms. He held her there tight, collapsing his body against hers in a life-affirming hug.

Prudence felt his heart racing against his chest as they stood there in silence. "I want you so badly," he muttered in her ear.

She leaned away, drawing his eyes to hers. She slid her hand into his. "Show me your bedroom."

Michael took her hand and led her back through the living room, then up the wide circular staircase to large double doors at the end of the hall. He opened one side for her to enter. As soon as Prudence stepped inside she felt at home. This was where she belonged.

She walked over to the large bed and lay down in the center on the fluffy lamb's-wool comforter. It was like floating on a cloud. She closed her eyes and savored the rich soft feeling of the fantasy beneath her. A few minutes later she looked to where he still stood in the doorway. She sat up and peeked around the bedpost. She smiled, her head tilted seductively around the wooden beam. "I believe you were telling me about a talent you had?"

Michael walked over as she tucked her legs beneath her and kneeled up on the bed. They faced each other at the perfect height, eye to eye, mouth to mouth. Michael smiled and whispered, "Close your eyes."

Playfully she crooked her finger, daring him to come to her. He did. She smiled openly, then closed her eyes, sensing that he would kiss her. He didn't. Not then. Instead, she felt the gentle touch of his fingers on her face. Her eyes opened automatically.

"Shh. No, keep your eyes closed," he whispered. He

drew his finger over her lips, her eyes, down the side of her face, and across her brow. The sensual feel of his hands on her sent an electric tingle surging to every nerve.

The erogenous pleasure of something as simple and basic as his touch on her face was more arousing and stirring than she could ever have imagined. Sensual and divinely satisfying, his hand played her sensitive skin just as he had played the piano earlier. Expertly tuned to his touch, her body responded with heart-pounding, knee-weakening desire.

Her eyelashes fluttered when he stroked the gentle curve of her neck and the softness beneath the curl of her chin. Her labored breath came in gasps of delight as her mouth opened to speak. But only silence drifted between them. He leaned in, nuzzling her neck, then kissing her parted lips gently, chastely. She began to open her eyes. "Closed," he whispered, again.

Holding on to his shirt, she muttered inaudible words as she pulled him closer, but he backed away. She frowned, and then softened when she felt his fingers on her face again.

She rolled her neck back and his finger drew a line down her neck and between her breasts. Slowly each button was released and his finger continued to draw intricate designs on the lace of her bra. First, a series of swirls circled around her nipples, and then paisleylike touches twirled and looped, rounding the fleshy orbs of her breasts until her taut nipples hardened in yielding protest. Prudence raked her lower lip with her teeth. It felt so good. He felt so good.

The sensation of his touch drew a gasp of weakness as she grabbed and held on to his shoulders for support.

"Lie back," he beckoned. She did, with awkward ease and strained control. She felt his hands at her side pulling the zipper of her pants. Then a slight tug released her leather pants down her legs. She reached out for him, but he stilled her hands at her sides. His fingers continued drawing enticing designs all over her body, pausing briefly at her bra and panties. A tiny moan escaped.

Michael smiled. Delicate and desirable, she was his ultimate perfection. The fantasy of Prudence lying on his bed gave him a sense of euphoria and contentment. His life was complete. Leaning over her, he felt his heart swelling at the sweet calmness of her expression. She trusted him and he vowed never to cause her a moment's distress about his worthiness.

She, Prudence Washington, was his perfect match on every level, his equal in intellect, in spirit, in ambition, and in passion. He could never walk away from her again.

Sensing his stillness, Prudence opened her eyes and smiled in lazy contentment. Michael returned her smile, reached down, and stroked the side of her face. "I love you," he whispered gently.

She sat up to kneel, then smiled down at him as she pushed him back onto the bed, reversing their positions. "I love you too."

She fingered the top button on his denim shirt. It slipped through the open hole easily. Seductively, she drew her nail over his lips and down to the open button. With ease and confidence she released the remaining buttons and pulled his shirt from his broad shoulders. Her mouth watered at the exposed strength and power. His chest was firm and toned with muscles etched with shadowed scars and discolored bruises.

She fingered the largest bruise. "Does it still hurt?"

He looked down to see what she was referring to. "No."

She leaned in and gently stroked, then kissed the indigo mark on his chest. He moaned, enjoying the sensation of her mouth on his chest. Boldly she continued by tasting his nipple, then kissing her way across his chest. A throaty groan escaped his lips as he leaned up. She purposefully pushed him back onto the lamb's-wool coverlet.

"Shh, my turn, close your eyes." He did, and unlike

the piano, she played with his body like a virtuoso, sending him closer and closer to the edge of his resistance.

The power she wielded was exhilarating. She unfastened his belt and slowly pulled it from the loops. After tossing it over her shoulder and onto the floor, she unsnapped his jeans and pulled them down.

She climbed back onto the bed and inched up to straddle his hips. He opened his eyes. The smile she gave him said everything. Michael sat up and wrapped his arms around her body, holding her close. He rested his cheek on her breasts and closed his eyes, at perfect peace. He dipped his nose to the swell of her bosom and bit at the bra's clasp. It unsnapped easily, freeing the hindrance.

The treasure he uncovered visibly pleased him as he delighted in the weighted fullness of her breasts. Round and smooth, they beckoned to him. He covered them, feeling the softness in the palms of his hands. The tide of arousal continued to pull, drawing him closer, increasing the hardness of his desire.

The intense need that he felt for her was all-consuming. His heart thundered and his pulse quickened. He reached over to the side table and pulled a packet from the drawer. He covered himself, protecting them, then holding her tightly he slowly rolled her over and hovered above, pressing her body firmly into the coverlet.

He raised her leg to rest on his shoulder, then slowly eased into her. His thick, sweet fullness filled her body, inducing a gasp of pleasure from her lips as he plunged deeper. Then with deliberate motion he rocked forward, drawing sighs and gasps and sending her into a whirlwind of pleasure. "Oh, Michael," she moaned as she clenched the fur beneath her.

He delved deeper, then pulled back just enough to stimulate the sensitive nip of her desire. She arched her back as his body paced their arousal. Moving with steady strokes, Michael leaned in and buried kisses along her face, neck, and shoulders. An awakening storm brewed inside her, building a tumultuous crest powered by each thrust. She held her breath, feeling the power of each spasm as he quickened and increased the pace and hastened their pleasure.

Prudence held tight to his body riding the wave as it rose to crest on the arch of desire. The pulsating rhythm of her body writhed beneath his power as she matched his thrusts.

Then, in a stunning blast of release, she soared to her climax with him at her side. A rage of passion blinded them, sending them over the edge. Tensed and strained, he gripped her in his protective arms and held her there until their return to sanity.

Moments later they lay in each other's arms. The weight of his body pressed her into the soft covers, but she hardly felt it as her breathing finally began to relax and return to normal.

In her sated state Prudence opened her eyes and lazily looked up at the bedroom's ceiling. Through the skylights above the bed, the moon shone down brilliantly and the surrounding stars twinkled against the darkness, too tranquil and blissful. The only thing she could do was smile. "You, sir, are very talented."

Michael chuckled as he rose up and rolled to the side, bringing her with him. He lay there looking up at the sky as well. "Funny, I was just about to say the same thing about you. Woman, you literally take my breath away." He gathered her closer.

Silence fell as they lay together, both in their own thoughts, each staring up at the heavens and thanking God for bringing the other into their lives. The miracle that brought them together and the miracle that kept them together were now bonded by their enduring love.

Prudence closed her eyes first and slept wrapped in the safe, comforting arms of the man she loved. Her life had turned around, and Michael was the reason why. For the first time in a long while she rested with ease. The bad times were behind her, and, thanks to Michael, happily ever after might be more than just a fairy-tale ending.

Eventually the calm ease of her breathing lulled Michael to sleep as well. His thoughts were simple and profound: There was no way he ever wanted to be without this woman in his arms, in his bed, and by his side. From the moment he laid eyes on her, he was smitten by the fire burning in her eyes. Now, lying here, he was smitten by the fire of love burning deep inside his heart.

A few hours later Michael awoke alone to a cold bed and an indented pillow. He looked around the bedroom. Prudence was gone. He got up and went downstairs. He found her outside, dressed in a jersey she'd found in his bedroom, standing at the wooden rail overlooking the sprawling meadow behind his house. He took a moment to relax against the terrace door and observe her watching a fawn sip water from the small creek that ran through his property.

She was even more beautiful than she was last night. Seeing her standing there, branded with his numbered jersey, sent a thrill of possession through him. He wanted Prudence in his life permanently. "Good morning," he said.

Prudence turned and smiled. Seeing him completely naked, she smiled even more broadly. "Good morning." She looked him up and down. "I see you dressed for the occasion."

He held his arms out matter-of-factly. "Nothing too formal."

She smiled, openly observing his abundance. "Perfect."

"I missed you." He walked to her side and pulled her against his body. Tall and muscular, his body completely overshadowed her as he wrapped his arms around her. She immediately felt how much he'd missed her and turned into his embrace. "Come back to bed," he whispered in her ear as he kissed her neck. She leaned back to see his face.

"We've been in bed all morning. If you're gonna show me around here, we'd better get dressed and get started."

"We have plenty of time, come back to bed," he moaned in her ear again as he dribbled kisses down her neck.

"It's late. I'm missing another flight." A tingling sensation of passion rippled through her as she reached her arms upward and around his neck, drawing the jersey up to her bare bottom. "I don't think the plane will just sit and wait for me."

Michael, feeling the tender firmness of her buttocks, instantly hardened for her. "I'll buy you a plane." He gently massaged the firm tightness as he pressed her buttocks to his groin, then moaned loudly. "Come back to bed." His voice was husky with desire. He kissed her shoulder, down her arm, to her hands and fingers.

"There isn't another flight . . ." she began, then gasped as his hand found the tight curls beneath the front of the jersey.

"Miss it," he pleaded in earnest.

". . . for three hours." She continued her thought, desperately trying to focus on the conversation.

"Three hours. No, not enough time, miss it." He turned and walked her backward into the living room. "I need you for at least another sixty years."

Prudence giggled as he tried to pick her up and she blocked each attempt. "Michael," she said, batting his hands away, "I have to leave Texas sometime."

"No, you don't." He continued walking, gently coaxing her up the stairs to the bedroom. He led, she followed.

"Yes, I do."

"No, you don't." They entered the bedroom and crossed to the bed. Michael lay back, pulling Prudence down, spread-eagled, on top of him.

"I have a career, and a condo, and my family—"

"Get a new job down here, live with me, be my family."

"Michael." She sat looking down at him as his hands traveled beneath the jersey and tested the strength of her resistance.

"Prudence," he answered, caught up in his own mission. He grabbed another packet from the nightstand, impatiently opened and tossed the wrapper, then eased it on to cover his throbbing hardness.

He pulled the jersey up and over her head. It flew across the room as she tumbled forward giving him full access as she hovered above him, her hands planted firmly on his shoulders.

His mouth instantly opened, drawing her breast into the warmth therein. Her breath caught, held by the quickness of the physical intimacy. She shivered with delight. His tongue licked and savored the sweetness drawn by her passion. Her hips began to move and her hands roamed freely over his chest. They delved deep into the abyss of their desire. Surging and riding the swell of their passion, he sucked, kissed, and caressed her, sending a shock wave of nerve endings dancing on edge.

She leaned back and looked into his eyes as she angled down to center herself above him. A knowing smile spread wide across her face as his eyes filled with a desire that matched her own. Then slowly, she lowered herself onto his throbbing hardness. A gasp of pleasure instantly escaped her lips as Michael held her waist in place. They stayed like that for an instant, letting the feel of her body surround him and the depth of his passion engulf her.

Then, kissing wildly in a mass of unbridled passion, they writhed with pleasure as she rode hard and he bucked with controlled rhythm. Power surged through their bodies, giving them more pleasure than they ever thought imaginable. Gone was the slow, tender lovemaking, replaced with a fierce powerful struggle of wanton passion. Erotic in its basic need, the climax they sought was equaled only by the passion they expended.

Then, as if communicated silently, the pace slowed.

Michael held her waist in place as she breathlessly leaned over to balance herself on top of him. She kissed his neck, then gripped his earlobe and lovingly raked it between her teeth. He groaned with pleasure and hissed with delightful ecstasy. When she finished, she kissed and licked the tender lobe, then repeated the action on the other ear.

Then, with slow, deliberate movements, they rocked up and down, in and out, back and forth, letting the tempo of their lustful dance beat a rhythmic cadence into their hearts. Panting with breathless purpose, they quickened the pace again, allowing passion to dictate. The plunging force of her body drew gasps of rapture as she savored the feel of him inside her. This was how it was meant to be. This was where she was meant to be.

A blinding light of ecstasy exploded before her eyes as she drew her breath and slowly exhaled. She smiled with pleasure as she collapsed onto him. He embraced her firmly, holding her body in place on top of his. They lay there in each other's arms.

"That was seriously a new chapter for the Kamasutra," she muttered.

"I don't think I'll ever get enough of you," Michael professed in her ear as he pulled her closer.

"You'll never have to," Prudence promised as she closed her eyes and sighed. His body formed a perfect pillow and she relaxed on top of him with comfort.

Michael drew her even tighter, wrapping his arms protectively around her. "Only you, Prudence, only you."

With that said they slept in sated bliss for the next few hours with the knowledge that there would always be another flight, another time.

Chapter 22

Four hours later Prudence looked at Michael as if he'd lost his mind. "If you think that I'm getting on that, you are sorely mistaken."

Michael continued to hold his hand down to her. "You said that you trusted me."

"I do trust you," she stated assuredly. "It's him I don't trust."

"Casper is as docile and tame as a puppy."

"Uh-huh, okay. But I'm still not getting on him. In case you didn't know, I'm a city girl. There aren't a lot of horses in Philadelphia."

"I happen to know that there are plenty of horses in Philadelphia." Prudence continued to shake her head no. "You wanted to see the grounds, how else am I supposed to show you around?"

"Drive the truck."

"It's better this way."

"No way, not gonna happen."

"Come on, trust me." The sugar-sweet glistening of pure honesty in his eyes weakened her resolve. She stopped shaking her head and looked at the massive neck of the beast standing in front of her. The jet-black mane glistened in the bright sunlight. The horse turned to her as if to impatiently show its annoyance at her apprehension.

"Okay, but if I fall off and break my neck, I'm gonna haunt you for the rest of your life."

"I wouldn't have it any other way." Without warning

Michael reached down, grabbed her around the waist, then hoisted her to his side. She instinctively threw her leg across to straddle the horse's body. As soon as she was sitting comfortably in front of him, he nuzzled in her ear. "You're gonna love this ride."

"We'll see," she said skeptically, then shrieked as Michael clicked his tongue twice and Casper moved forward. She leaned back into the curve of Michael's chest fearfully. Michael, steady and in complete control, wrapped his arm across her firmly while he also held the reins and directed the horse.

Skepticism slowly melted away ten minutes after they began. Prudence, initially panicky, then felt at ease and relaxed. Slowly she began enjoying the freedom of the experience.

First Michael prompted Casper along the creek with the fawn that Prudence had seen earlier. Then in gentle slow motion Casper ascended a winding path and veered westward away from the main road. "I want you to see this," Michael said. As they neared the top of a small hill, Michael urged Casper to a smooth, steady trot. At the top of the hill they stopped.

"Oh, Michael, it's beautiful," she uttered in wonder.

"Welcome to my Texas." The expanse of his property was a staggering vineyard lined with rows upon rows of neatly grown grapevines. Several newly constructed buildings dotted the distant landscape and an old farmhouse, barn, and windmill sat at the bottom of the hill.

"This is incredible. I never imagined."

Michael clicked his tongue again and spurred Casper toward a narrow path leading down to the old farmhouse. When they got to the house he guided Casper through an open pen, then got down and held the reins loosely and walked toward the barn.

Still looking around, Prudence didn't realize that she was actually riding on Casper alone and being led through the pen's doors. Michael tied Casper to a post near a water trough and a bale of hay, then reached his arms up to Prudence.

She leaned down and clumsily fell into him, knocking them both down to the ground. Laughing wildly at her less than graceful dismount, Prudence and Michael lay there on the dirt path beneath the shade of a century-old oak and enjoyed the moment. Eventually Michael sat up, bringing her with him.

"Are you okay?" she asked, realizing that she had fallen squarely on top of him.

"Never been better," he said, chuckling, as he stood up and helped her to her feet.

Prudence dusted the dry dirt from her jeans as she looked around. "This is kind of cool in a rustic, *Little House on the Prairie* kind of way. Who does this belong to?"

"Me," he said, looking at her oddly. "Who else?"

"Of course, so you have a huge modern home over that hill and this old run-down log cabin on this side. Do you have a split personality that I don't know about?"

"Actually I guess I do in a manner of speaking." He looked around in thoughtful consideration as they began walking toward the front of the cabin. "I don't come here that often. It's kind of my place of solitude and reflection." He slowed his pace, then stopped walking completely and just stood looking around. "The truth is, this old house is the reason I bought this land in the first place."

"Really, this place?" Prudence asked as she turned and looked up at the small A-frame structure. It wasn't particularly different from any other structure she'd seen. Constructed of thick logs and natural stone, it was small with narrow windows and no particular redeeming qualities.

"Yes. This whole area was originally set aside for the Native Americans sometime around the mid-1800s. They in turn gave property to some buffalo soldiers who had been helpful to them in their struggle."

"Buffalo soldiers?" she asked. "As in *the* buffalo soldiers who helped settle the West?"

"One and the same. The Native Americans gave the soldiers that name because they honored and respected their valor and courage. Jonah Blackwell was one of those soldiers. He was deeded this land sometime in the late 1870s. The records are pretty sketchy, but he was a former slave who had fought in the Civil War in 1864. He moved west and became a member of the Tenth Cavalry Regiment, known as the buffalo soldiers, in 1866. A few years later he received this land, married, and started a family. Then after serving in the Spanish-American War in 1898, he made this land his permanent home."

"Wow," Prudence said in bright-eyed amazement. They began walking again, a slow easy stroll around to the front side of the building. When they reached the entrance Michael stopped again.

"Jonah lived here all his life, raised a family, and watched them grow. But as I said, the records were pretty sketchy; the land's ownership came into question just after the turn of the century. After he died the ownership was contested. Given the times, the dispute lasted only a few weeks. The land was sequestered and held in probate. It was eventually awarded to Pete Hemmer, the neighboring landholder, for a tenth of its worth."

"He just stole the land, just like that?" she said quietly as she and Michael entered. They looked around the single empty room. Dusty and stuffy, it was exactly as she expected.

"Those were the times when, if someone wanted something that belonged to an African-American or a Native American back then, all they had to do was question legal ownership in court. The law was usually on their side. There were no African-American attorneys, so they got it, oftentimes without major consequences . . ."

"Damn," Prudence muttered, feeling the truth of historical suffering and injustice sting her eyes. "I guess I now have a newfound respect for my family's law degrees."

"Ah, but the story continues. As I said, *oftentimes without major consequences*. When Jonah's family moved north, folks said that his wife cursed the land and vowed that her people would one day take the land back and that the landowner would never be at peace living here."

"Good for her."

"Pete Hemmer started the winery over there. But the grapevines he planted died and every grape died on the vine. So he planted more, and more, and more. He tried to get too big, too fast, and wound up in financial ruin. After a while the taxes were so astronomical he couldn't afford to pay them."

"The curse." Prudence smiled.

"Hemmer was so angry that he decided to burn out this part of the land, starting here at Jonah's old house." Michael pointed at the singed bricks around the front door as they exited. "But it started raining and the flames were instantly extinguished. Instead, lightning struck his house and destroyed it." Michael smiled to himself at the irony. "By this time he was pretty much scared out of his wits. He tried to contact Jonah's widow to lift the curse, but he died of a heart attack before he could. His family filed for bankruptcy and left the area. The property passed from person to person until I eventually bought it a few years ago."

"That was a great story." She smiled happily. "I guess local history is just another one of your many talents."

"You could say that," he said, pulling her into his arms.

She reached up and kissed him passionately, then smiled mischievously. "This is very enlightening, Michael Hunter. You're a local historian, you play the piano like a virtuoso, you cook like a four-star chef, you give an incredible massage, and . . . you . . . make . . . love . . . like . . ." she drew out temptingly, then stopped, biting her lower lip seductively.

"Yes, like what?" he probed with added curiosity.

Prudence tilted her head in thoughtful consideration, then frowned. "Funny, I can't seem to remember."

She looked around and spotted the huge barn across the path. "Maybe," she said as she began pulling him toward the barn, "you'd better remind me."

Michael smiled, laughed, and agreed readily. "Maybe I'd better." As soon as they entered the barn, Prudence pulled him over to the haystack against the wall. She pushed him down on the hay and landed on top of him while laughing wildly. "Now," she began, "tell me more about your many talents."

Truman watched James as he entered his office. The saunter in his step and the absolute glee on his face were nauseating. For the first time in months he had actually won a substantial amount of money. At seven to one, Jimmy's Back on Top had won by a nose and it was time to pay out, a detestable and unfortunate obligation, but a necessity. Truman arched his fingers beneath his chin, his smugness exuding confidence.

"Not exactly the outcome I had in mind, but a win is a win, and almost only counts when playing horseshoes. Here's your take." Truman tossed a small rubber-band-wrapped bundle of cash to James.

He caught it clumsily, then quickly flipped through the bills and smiled. It wasn't as much as he expected, but something was better than nothing. It had been a long time since he'd had a payoff of any kind. Maybe, just maybe his string of bad luck was turning around thanks to Jimmy's Back on Top.

"Thanks," James said as he placed the cash in his jacket pocket and turned to leave.

Truman cleared his throat and turned to ask a question. "My friend wants to know when he can expect something."

"Yeah, about that, I think Blake's suspicious of me."

Truman looked him up and down. "Do you blame him? Look at yourself." Truman frowned as James looked down at himself, not seeing anything particularly wrong. Constantly nervous and edgy, James was anything but cool and reserved. ". . . Blake's a politician. He's suspicious of everybody, that's how the game is played."

"Still, getting anything from his office is impossible."

"Why?"

"Blake's moved the main focus of his campaign to his home office. Everything of importance is there. That includes the papers on his negotiation with McGee. Everything's on his laptop."

"So, go to his house and get the laptop."

"I can't just walk into his home, break into his office, steal his laptop, and then just walk out with it."

"Make copies."

"He doesn't have a copy machine hooked up to the laptop."

"Make copies on discs."

"The laptop's disc drive is sealed."

Truman jotted down his personal e-mail address and handed the paper to James. "Call me when you have the files. I'll download them. Just make sure you're careful. I don't want information flowing both ways. My files aren't exactly public knowledge, and there are quite a few people who would like to get their hands on my data." He laughed at the absurdity and impossibility of that idea.

Years ago he had safeguarded every conceivable attempt to infiltrate his computer files. It had cost him a fortune but it had been worth it. Rarely did he open his personal system up. The vulnerability of his business was at stake, but this was a sure thing as far as he was concerned. All James had to do was download the files and he'd end the link and resecure his system.

"I still can't do it. Blake and Marian are usually at home in the evening."

"So do it some other time. He's at the office all day; she's on the bench all day. What's your problem, afraid to go out in the daytime? Just do it."

The snap in Truman's tone startled James. Then it dawned on him. It hadn't occurred to him to go to the Washington home during the day. He was racking his brain trying to figure a way of gaining an invitation in the evening, then getting into Blake's office and taking the files.

James looked at his watch. It was late, but if he hurried he could get to the Washington home before they got home. "Okay, I'll get you what you need in the next few days."

James left, assured of his mission. He knew that he needed to get Truman something that he could use, and there was only one way to get it. He drove directly to the Washington home and hoped that no one was there.

As soon as he drove up, he spotted Blake's car in the rearview mirror pulling up behind him in the driveway. *Damn, just my luck.* He was certain that Blake had a political engagement this evening and that Marian was also scheduled to attend. He grabbed the file he'd been compiling for Prudence and decided to use it as his cover.

"James, what are you doing here?" Blake asked as he approached James's car. It was obvious by his expression that Blake was beginning to get suspicious. James needed to do damage control and show his good intentions. And the best way to do that was to be the knight in shining armor. If he could discredit Michael, he'd get attention off himself, plus hopefully cement his relationship with Prudence and the family.

"Blake, Mr. Mayor, we need to talk," James said in his most seriously concerned tone.

"Yes, we do," Blake said, equally determined.

Ten minutes later he had laid out his argument with assurance and self-confidence. "Blake, Marian, this whole thing can be settled before Prudence even comes back from Texas," James insisted. "But we need to act now if we're going to take care of this. We have the evidence, it's right here in black and white. Mr. Mayor, all you need to do is make the call. I'll take care of everything else."

"I disagree. This isn't evidence," Blake said as he

dropped the package on his desk. "This isn't even mitigating circumstances."

"The phrase that comes to my mind is 'entrapment,'" Marian said, adding her opinion.

"It's at least enough for a search warrant," James said.

"The whole thing's ridiculous. With this evidence you might as well arrest or search half the city," Marian said. "It's not even enough to bring anyone in for questioning. Then of course, there's the method of acquiring this alleged evidence."

"Something has to be done," James insisted firmly as he looked at Marian with annoyance. He'd gone through a lot of trouble and a lot of expense to gather this information. "Prudence is in danger and nobody is doing anything."

"James—" Marian began in complete exasperation; her calming voice did little to dissuade his intentions.

". . . Mrs. Washington, Mr. Mayor, you need evidence. Here it is in black and white. The facts are indisputable. What more do you need?"

Blake, sitting behind his desk with his laptop in front of him, drew James's eyes.

"This proves nothing," Marian insisted, as she dropped the blurred photo and the receipt on the desk along with the other material.

James gathered and picked them up, then looked again at the expertly posed photo. It showed just enough without divulging too much detail. Grainy to the point of being barely recognizable, the video still should have been all they needed to pull Michael Hunter in. Once that was done and he and Prudence split apart, he'd easily take care of the rest. But unfortunately, to his annoyance, Blake and Marian didn't agree with his logic.

James closed his eyes and shook his head in disgust. This wasn't going at all as he had anticipated. He had assumed that as soon as he walked in with the photo and receipt, Blake and Marian would fall to his feet with thanks and instantly have Hunter hauled in for questioning. And that would be the beginning of both of their downfalls.

"A man fitting Michael's description, with a Philadelphia Knights jacket and cap, was seen purchasing those exact items. The sales clerk will even testify that she remembers him being in the store that day," James maintained as he handed over the notarized affidavit.

Marian quickly read through the affidavit, then handed it to Blake. "The sales clerk remembers a tall man in a Knights jacket and cap, that's all. Any judge would laugh at this so-called evidence if this was all the police had for a warrant. And any first-year law student worth his salt would shoot this down before it even gets to the courtroom. It's not enough for a warrant, questioning, let alone a conviction, and you know it."

"I'm not going for a conviction," James said. "Prudence needs to back off and stay away from Hunter until this thing is cleared up and the election over. And the best way to do that is to get Hunter out of the way."

Both Blake and Marian looked at James questioningly. His loose morals stuck out like the Goodyear Blimp in a minivan. Marian looked at Blake. Although neither spoke, they had the identical expression. *How did we not see this before?*

"James, exactly when did Prudence tell you about what was going on?"

"When she stopped by the office a while ago."

"Funny, she didn't mention anything like that to me," Marian said.

"It probably slipped her mind," he said as he smiled and sat watching the couple's interaction with added interest. He knew that he needed something big, and if Mayor Blake Washington had Michael Hunter arrested, that would certainly sway the voters. He needed Blake to lose the election, and Blake's blinding love for and devotion to his family were the perfect solution. The Garrett Marshall incident had proved that.

"Where exactly did you get this, James?" Blake picked

up the photo and stared at the grainy black-and-white image.

James spoke up, more confident. "Actually, Blake, I have a friend that works in the Galleria security office. I told him what I was looking for and he remembered seeing Hunter at the mall that afternoon."

"That's awfully convenient." Marian looked at James suspiciously. "And where did he get it?"

"Does it really matter where he got it? What matters is that Prudence has to stay away from Speed Hunter."

"Yes, it most certainly does matter where it came from," Marian insisted.

James frowned; he hadn't expected to be questioned on the photo and receipts.

"The validity of this information is critical. If you're going to accuse someone like Michael Hunter, or anyone else for that matter, you'd better have more than a blurred photo of a man in a jacket and hat and a cash receipt. Not only will his family lawyers have a field day, but the team lawyers and press will massacre Blake in the media. We have an election to win, or have you forgotten that?"

"Prudence's well-being is more important," James stated firmly, but in actuality he was more concerned about his own well-being. He had promised Truman something big, and now he needed to deliver.

"I agree, but *if* Michael has allegedly sent those items and has been calling her, then *yes*, we go after him full force. But if we're wrong, not only do we jeopardize the election, but Blake will be the laughingstock of the city, and worse yet, Prudence will never forgive us."

James stood and nearly shouted, "He did it. He's the one."

Blake and Marian turned to stare at James again, questioningly. His outburst, unwavering certainty, and predatory interest continued to summon a myriad of questions.

"Sorry about that," he said, then paused to regain his composure. "It's just that I have a gut instinct about this. I know I'm right. Listen." He spared one last look at the laptop on Blake's desk. "I'm gonna go. I know you have that thing this evening. "I'll let myself out. But, if nothing else, just think about what I've said."

James hurried out of the office. He walked through the living room, but instead of leaving, he detoured to the side dining room and unlocked the window. Afterward he continued to the front door. Smiling as he left, he hurried to his car. At least that worked perfectly. All he had to do now was slip back in and upload any interesting files he found on Blake's computer.

"There's something else, isn't there?" Marian said as she watched James through the office window. Blake went into his briefcase and pulled out a file and handed it to his wife.

"What's this?" she asked.

"Read it."

She did. "This is legit?"

"Word for word. I have the original tape." He pulled it out of the briefcase and dropped it into his microrecorder. They were silent as they listened. Blake looked at Marian as she came around behind his desk and looked down at the photos again.

"What exactly does James stand to gain from all of this?" she asked.

"Other than his continued employment here, I'd say that was a good question. I think it's about time we found out. Keith and Drew are meeting us at the function this evening. They might know something."

"Good idea."

Three hours later, after dry chicken and several even dryer political speeches, Blake, Marian, Keith, and Drew sat in the Washington family den discussing Blake's and Marian's earlier conversation with James. The conversation lasted well into the night.

"I think we need to take him outside and knock some sense into him," Keith said angrily.

"No," Marian said firmly.

"Fire him, then charge him with theft and stupidity," Drew said.

"No, too much publicity, too close to the election, and not enough evidence," Blake added.

"Set him up," Keith said smoothly, then smiled.

"Set him up," Drew repeated, nodding his head agreeably. "That might not be a bad idea."

"What do you have in mind?" Blake asked of Keith and Drew.

"Why don't we give James exactly what he wants, political information?" Keith said.

"Are you kidding?" Marian said. "No way. No one's going to sacrifice your father's career for this."

"No, wait a minute, let me finish. I said that we should give James political information, I never mentioned what kind."

"No," Marian said. "I'm uncomfortable with this idea. He's still my friend's son. He has a weakness, gambling, he needs help."

"Help, are you kidding?" Keith asked. "James is a money-grubbing, two-faced ingrate who's not only stealing information from the mayor's office and most probably selling it to our opponent, which I might add is a federal offense, but is also quite possibly, for all we know, the idiot harassing Prudence in order to draw attention away from his illicit activities."

Prudence had mentioned earlier that she once thought it was him.

"I understand that," Marian said, "but as I see it, Truman is the puppet master. James is only a pawn. He's nothing compared to the real threat."

"True," Blake said.

"So we need to get Truman," Drew said.

"Do you know how many law enforcement agencies have been trying to do just that? The Philadelphia police, the Camden police, the DEA, the FBI, you name it. He's nearly untouchable," Keith said.

"Ah, but he does have one weakness," Drew said.

"What's that?" Marian asked.

"He loves to manipulate," Keith said.

"Manipulating a football game I can see. Everyone knows he's at the center of illegal gambling in Camden, but why would he want to manipulate James?"

"Maybe it's not just James he's manipulating," Drew said.

"Of course, my opponent," Blake stated. "Truman is openly supporting him."

"You're right, he is," Marian agreed.

"This has been a particularly nasty campaign. I wouldn't be at all surprised if he didn't have his hand in this too. My opponent's smear tactics regarding my association with McGee and the Knights' stadium have been a major issue."

"Good point. So if Truman is indeed manipulating both your opponent and James, to what end?"

No one answered right away. Then Marian spoke. "The stadium." Everyone turned to her. "The stadium will be built, that's a given. The only question is where. Your opponent wants it on the Camden waterfront. You proposed it here in the Philadelphia area. What if Truman, a noted real estate entrepreneur, has more than a vested interest in the mayor's office and the stadium being built in Camden?"

"So, why don't we give them both exactly what they want? We can even have James deliver the package for us," Keith said.

"You mean send in a Trojan horse?" Drew said.

"Misinformation?" Blake corrected.

"Exactly," Keith said.

"He'll get caught with his pants down."

"And just maybe more than that."

"I like it. But what kind of misinformation?"

"That's the easy part. Ever since Garrett's promised

expos, and your opponent's allegations, the integrity of my administration has been called into question. I suggest something on that line. Given his track record, Truman won't be able to resist blackmailing Blake."

"Good idea, but what information?"

"Leave that to me," Marian said, smiling at Blake. "I'll get you something scandalously titillating. Truman won't be able to resist. He'll think he's got the mayor's election locked up.

"Okay, we have the bait. What about the hook?" Drew asked.

"James knows that for security reasons you keep the bulk of your personal correspondence on your laptop, which is always here in your home office. If he's looking for something, chances are he's going to have to look here," Marian said.

"Fine," Blake said.

"I'll input the data," Drew said.

"How's that going to do anything but prove that he's a thief? I thought the whole idea was to go after Truman," Keith said.

"I'll also encrypt a trace and retrieval program. Not only does the Trojan trace the files to the destination computer, but it also retrieves all data from that computer and forwards it to a third designated system, even if the trace is interrupted," Drew said.

"That's brilliant," Keith said.

"I don't know, this smells an awful lot like entrapment and coercion," Marian cautioned.

"No, not necessarily," Keith expounded. "If James opens or goes through the contents of the laptop, then it's of his free will. And if he uploads data it's a lock."

"Then what? Truman's not going to just roll over and thank James. He's going to be out for blood."

"Then James will have to testify so he'll be protected."

Chapter 23

Prudence yawned deeply and dropped her chin into the palms of her hands as she leaned on her desk. She closed her eyes and smiled uncontrollably. The unconscious dreamy expression had been a permanent fixture on her face since she arrived back in Philadelphia late last night. Sleep was impossible. Every time she closed her eyes pretending to sleep, Michael's face appeared and she found herself fantasizing about being back on the ranch with him. There was no denying it, she had fallen head over heels in love with him.

After a few stressful days in Houston, she had spent three glorious days and two wondrous nights in Austin with Michael and she had been in heaven every minute. They had gone horseback riding, fishing in the pond behind his house, and had just hung out and enjoyed each other's company at the ranch.

But the most memorable times were the evenings, just after Michael prepared their dinner, when they sat out by the pool and watched the sun set behind the distant mountains as each evening a purple-red haze backlit the horizon, setting the whole sky on fire. It was breathtaking and wondrous and spectacular, and the most exciting time of her life.

"Well, well, well, welcome back, stranger," Tanya said when she peeked into Prudence's office and found her sitting at her desk staring and smiling into space.

Prudence jumped, startled by the interruption. She

instantly sat up straight at her desk and cleared her throat. "Hi," she barely croaked out, somehow feeling guilty for being caught daydreaming like a schoolgirl.

"So, how was the buyers' meeting and Texas?"

Prudence looked up as Tanya entered her office with a knowing smile. "Great," she said innocently.

"Uh-huh." Tanya smirked knowingly.

"It was a very productive trip," she continued. "It was extremely informative and enlightening. I have some files for us to update our computer system and, uh . . . uh . . . I shipped back several boxes of samples. They should be arriving soon."

"Got 'em, they arrived yesterday."

"Good, we can go through them next week, after the holidays are over."

"Fine," Tanya said, still smiling at Prudence.

Self-conscious, Prudence looked away. She dug through the files on her desk, then shuffled the garments and samples.

"What?" Prudence asked when Tanya didn't move. She looked back up at Tanya, who smiled, patiently waiting for more. "Okay," she said, surrendering, too exhausted to be evasive anymore, "Texas was unbelievably fantastic."

"It must have been. You're two days late," Tanya taunted.

Prudence smiled guiltily. "I decided to use a little vacation time. You know, see some of the local sights, and check out what the Lone Star state had to offer."

"Good idea," Tanya said as she neared the desk. "And what exactly did the Lone Star have to offer?"

Prudence picked up on her added inflection on the term *Lone Star.* "Are you ready for the new year?" she asked, ending the conversation and hoping to distract Tanya from the subject of Texas.

"You know it. I have tickets to a serious off-the-hook party downtown. I'm gonna count down to the new year, then lip-lock the first unattached man I see."

"Sounds great."

"What are your plans?"

"I'm looking forward to a nice quiet evening at home."

"With a certain Texas quarterback, I presume? The news last night mentioned that Speed was supposed to be back in town a few days ago. I hear he even got a few-thousand-dollar fine for skipping the last two practices." The shock registered on Prudence's face was all the confirmation Tanya needed. "But I'm sure he feels that his extra time in Texas was well worth every penny. Don't you?"

Prudence smirked at Tanya. "I wouldn't know."

"Prudence, all joking aside, I'm so happy for you, really. After everything you've gone through in the past few months, it's about time good things came your way." Tanya understood that the past few months had been particularly stressful for Prudence, so for her to just kick back, relax, and simply enjoy the moment was just what the doctor ordered. And spending quality time with Michael at his home in Texas was a dream come true for her. And she was truly happy for her friend.

Prudence nodded. "Yeah, I'm kinda happy for me too." They paused and smiled knowingly. "Okay," Prudence began, "I have to get back to work. Being away for a few extra days has thrown me back a week."

"I'll be on the floor setting up the new displays," Tanya said as she grabbed the last few items she needed and walked out of the office.

As Prudence expected, the first day back from Texas was insufferably hectic. Stock was depleted. There were several sales meetings she had to attend and she had six boxes in shipping waiting for her approval to send out.

Rushing into her office between meetings, she picked up the ringing phone as soon as she reached her desk. She grabbed the files she needed as she answered. "Prudence Washington."

"You were supposed to be back in Philly three days ago."

"I beg your pardon? Hello, Keith, I'm fine, thanks for asking. Texas, my trip? Oh, it was wonderful. I got my work done, then took some vacation time to check out some local sights," she said sarcastically.

"I get your point, small talk. How was Texas?"

"Great. Busy. Swamped," she said with less enthusiasm than she felt. "Listen, I'm running late for a meeting. I'll call you later."

Tanya popped her head into her office and pointed to her watch. "We need to talk, Prudence. I stopped by the house the other day. Drew and I had an interesting discussion with Mom and Dad."

"About what?" Prudence nodded to Tanya and held her index finger up, asking for a few more minutes.

"Office leaks."

"Again?"

"No, but a certain person definitely has been trying to get inside information."

"You know who it is?"

"Yeah, we just found out. Dad left his recorder on and James took a call in his office."

"Let me guess, it's James Pruet, someone who's already inside," she surmised.

"You knew?"

"I've had my suspicions. What's Dad going to do about it?"

"It's already taken care of." Keith told her in detail what had been planned.

Tanya popped in again. Prudence mouthed silently that she would be off in a few minutes as Keith finished. "Although there's no guarantee James will go for it."

"If I know James, and it's a gamble, he'll take the bait. Greed is his weakness. He'll do it, but why at home and not at the office?"

"That would be too much like entrapment, and we

can't take a chance of actually having what's in the computer come out."

"What exactly did you use?"

"Dad's affair with a married woman."

"What?"

"Apparently Mom and Dad have conversations over
the Internet."

"So, then it's just two married people."

"She doesn't use her name."

"Oh." She started laughing until she saw Tanya glance
in again. "I gotta go."

"One more thing, about Hunter. I think—"

"I know what you think and I can't get into this with you
right now, Keith. I'm on my way to a meeting and I'm already late. If you have a problem with Michael, get over it."

"Prudence, this isn't only about Hunter—" he began
again.

"I really have to go. I'll call you tomorrow." She hung
up and hurried to her meeting.

Hours later, the panic and rush of the workday had
slowed to a near snail's pace. As the day drew to a close,
the ridiculous notion of actually getting work done on
the eve of the new year was absurd. Still Prudence was
determined to give it her best shot.

The remainder of the day was filled with last-minute
shipping arrangements for merchandise returned and
advance orders for the upcoming seasons. Strenuous
and demanding, it left little in the way of focused
thought and wistful thinking. Yet Prudence's thoughts
slipped away from time to time to stray memories of the
moments on a ranch in Austin so far away.

She stared at the computer screen and tried again to
focus on the detailed description listed for the spring
season, but it was useless. It was New Year's Eve, an hour
before the store's early closing, and she and Michael had
planned to spend the evening together. She sat back and
rested her head on the back of the chair. Her mind wandered back to her hot Texas nights.

Michael's appetite was insatiable. For food, for fun, for love, he was ravenous, and she loved every minute of it. A shiver of excitement sparked through her as the thought of making love to him again made her blush. For three days and two nights they'd made love with equal parts fervor and passion.

"This just came for you," Tanya said as she placed an overnight package on her desk. "I'm on my way out now, happy New Year."

"You too. Enjoy your party," Prudence said.

"I will, see you next year," Tanya said as she hurried out.

Prudence saved her file and closed the screen, promising herself that she'd focus better after the new year. She reached over and grabbed the overnight package and, without thinking, opened it. As soon as she tilted the package, she paused, holding the gift-wrapped oblong box in her hand. Her heart thumped wildly and her hands began to tremble. "Not again," she muttered.

She picked up the mailing package and read the return address. The package was sent from New York, shipped next-day overnight express from a boutique she'd never heard of. She picked up the box again and gingerly pulled the ribbon apart. Holding her breath, she lifted the box's lid.

The phone rang. She jumped and instantly reached for it.

"Prudence Washington." She breathed cautiously, expecting the worst.

"Hey, beautiful."

A sigh of relief washed over her at hearing Michael's voice.

"Hey there." Her smile beamed over the phone. "Are you here yet?"

"Yep, I just got in. As a matter of fact I'm still at the airport."

"Are we still on for tonight?" she asked.

"Of course. But one change, how about if we grab a quick dinner and then go back to my place?"

"Fine."

"Perfect, I'll see you tonight," he said.

"Okay."

"Oh, before I forget, I sent you a little something special for you to wear for tonight. But I forgot to include the card."

Prudence smiled as relief washed over her. "I just got it. Should I open it now?"

"No, no, wait until tonight. I want to put it on you myself."

"Okay. I'll see you tonight."

Tempted or not, when Prudence hung up the phone she neatly rewrapped the box with the ribbon, then placed it back in the mailing package and put it in her briefcase. She turned the computer back on and began dutifully confirming her orders. The last hour flew by in a flash. She was just about to clear her desk when a slight rapping on her office door got her attention. She looked up. "James?"

"Hello, Prudence."

Stunned by the unexpected guest, she paused a moment. "What are you doing here?"

"We need to talk."

"Talk about what?" she asked, continuing to gather files.

She looked at her watch. "It's late, James, can't this wait?"

"No, it can't," he said as he looked around her crowded office, then walked over to her desk and placed a manila envelope in front of her.

"What's this?" she asked.

"Open it."

"All right." She did. Two minutes later she placed the file and receipts back on the desk in front of her.

"Is this supposed to mean something?"

"Don't be naïve."

"I can't believe you're doing this," she said.

"I'm trying to protect you."

"From who, Michael?"

"You need to end this thing with Hunter now, today."

"My relationship with Michael is none of your business, James."

"It is when it jeopardizes the mayor's office and my job; then I make it my business."

"Since when is the campaign in jeopardy? The last I heard, the publicity of our seeing each other was only adding to my father's poll numbers. He's still way ahead. What happened to my seeing Michael being a boost in the polls?"

"Polls change," he said.

"So do political assistants," she snapped back in warning. Her meaning was clear and he understood perfectly. She had no intention of being bullied into anything by him.

"How can you defend him after I've shown you this proof?"

"A cash receipt and a blurred photo of someone in a Knights cap and jacket are hardly what I'd consider proof. As a matter of fact this man, whoever he is, doesn't even look like Michael. His build is all wrong."

James snatched the photos. "And you would know that from intimate knowledge, I assume," he sniped.

Prudence gave him a warning look, then smiled tightly. "That's none of your business. This whole conversation is ridiculous. You can't build a case from a blurred photograph and some smudged receipts. This could be anyone. As a matter of fact it looks more like Michael's teammate Rick Renault than Michael. It makes more sense that it would be him. He at least was at the store just after one of the calls came in."

"Rick Renault or Speed Hunter. Either way, they're both going down."

"Listen to yourself, you sound paranoid. No, make that crazy."

"I assure you I am very sane. Face it, he's another Garrett Marshall and you're feeding right into it all over again.

How can you be so blind again? The lies, the deceit. He can't be trusted."

"Can you?"

The sting of her words cut through him like a knife. He wasn't sure exactly what she implied, but he questioned what she thought she knew.

"Look . . ." James paused, deciding to change his approach. "Everyone's concerned about this relationship, Prudence, your parents, your brothers, me." He reached across her desk and placed his hand on hers. "Your safety and happiness are all I'm concerned about right now."

"Oh, please," she said as she stood and walked away, her temper precariously teetering on the edge of a meltdown.

"I'm warning you, Prudence."

"You're what?" she asked, hearing exactly what he said.

"You heard me, I'm warning you."

"Warning me?" she asked, still not believing her ears.

"Yes." He stood to face her angrily. "I'm sure you don't want another Garrett Marshall fiasco on your hands, not right in the middle of your father's reelection campaign." Prudence's mouth dropped open in shock. "I cleaned up for you and your family once before. I don't intend making it a habit."

"That's low, even for you. I think you know where the door is."

"Look, Prudy," he began, using her family's pet name for her, "I don't mean to be callous or nasty. I know what that whole Garrett thing did to you. I just don't want to see you like that again. Michael Hunter is dirty. McGee is using him to get a four-hundred-million-dollar stadium tax-free."

"You don't know anything about Michael."

"I know he's not what you think he is. I know that the whole meeting was planned. I know that as soon as your relationship became public your father's numbers began to climb. I know that he's using you just like Garrett, McGee, and Blake."

"What?"

"That's right."

"My father is using me?" she scoffed.

"Yes, to further his career, of course he is. Who do you think set this whole thing up? Blake needs McGee to build that stadium on this side of the river or his credibility as a politician is shot."

"The stadium has nothing to do with me."

"Of course it does. You were the bait. Keeping Speed happy would keep McGee happy, would keep the Knights in the city. Blake needed them here. It's all about revenue, money, dollars. He made promises, he had to keep them."

"What happened to you?" she asked calmly, surprising even herself. "You used to be—"

". . . A pushover, taken advantage of, walked all over . . ."

"No, I was going to say a nice guy. But apparently things change."

"I learned from the best."

"Perhaps your association with your *Mr. Truman* has tainted your judgment."

"Truman?" he questioned with mock innocence, surprised at her mentioning the name. "You don't know what you're talking about."

"I think I do," she said, realizing the cause for his paranoia. "You're gambling again, aren't you? That's why you sold your home and that's why you're working with . . ." She stopped suddenly.

"What I do in my personal life is none of your business."

"Funny, I believe that I just said the same thing to you."

They stood glaring at each other a moment until he finally responded. "You don't know anything about me or my associates."

"You mean Truman," she ventured. "I know he's a maggot who crawled out of the sewer and is infesting this city like a plague. And apparently he's got a hell of a hold on you."

Prudence walked to the door. She opened and held it for him. "Good night, James."

He understood her obvious invitation to leave. He took his time walking to the door. When he reached her side he stopped and reached out to take her hand. She leaned back, avoiding his touch.

"What happened to us, Prudence?"

"Us? James, what us?" She nearly laughed in his face. "We went out on two dates and decided to be friends."

"You decided to be friends."

"Whatever."

"Whatever?" he repeated with added earnestness.

She chuckled and shook her head at the ridiculous remark. "Yeah, whatever," she said, with no intention of listening to another word from him.

"Happy New Year, Prudence." He leaned in to kiss her. She backed away. "It's like that, huh?"

She nodded while staring directly in his eyes. "Yeah, it's like that."

"Fine, I'll take care of this myself. I'm on my way to Keith's house. I'm sure he'll listen to reason."

"If you're referring to *your* reasoning, don't bet on it."

James glared at her one last time, then walked out without another word. His eyes burned with hate. Hatred of Michael for everything he should have had, hatred of Prudence for choosing Michael over him, and hatred of the Washingtons for their holier-than-thou, above-the-scandal attitude. He was definitely going to enjoy watching Truman and his friends bring them down.

James walked to his car. His mind raced with ideas. He'd promised Truman that Hunter would be shaving points or Blake would be out of the race by now. Either way the ultimate goal was the stadium's location. Neither had happened and the last thing he needed was to have Truman on his back again. He unconsciously rubbed his ribs, remembering the last time he'd failed to deliver a promise to Truman.

There was only one thing left to do, but first he needed to make a quick stop. He got into his car and drove. Twenty minutes later he arrived.

Keith was the only member of the Washington family that he felt he actually had something in common with. Keith was ambitious, indomitable, and stood by his convictions. If anyone would get the ball rolling against Speed, he would.

"Keith, man, I'm glad I caught you in."

"What do you want, James?" he said coldly.

"We need to talk. It's important, it's about Prudence," he said, ignoring the chill from Keith.

Keith paused and looked at James standing in his doorway. He had to play this out. Of the very few people he actually trusted, James Pruet was nowhere near that list. James's weakness for gambling and living the good life had caused major problems over the years. But his latest debacle would be his undoing. He was just about to close the door, but the mention of Prudence's name made him relent.

"What about Prudence?" Keith asked tightly.

"She's in trouble," James said hastily.

Keith stepped back and allowed James to enter. As soon as Keith closed the door behind them James began. "It was Hunter all along. He's probably using Prudence to get to your father, just like Garrett Marshall. I bet McGee put him up to it. They'll do anything to get that new stadium built."

"What does this have to do with Prudence being in trouble?"

"Here," James said as he handed the manila envelope he'd been carrying to Keith. Keith took it and unclasped the seal, then pulled out the file. James waited patiently for Keith to read the label on the file's cover.

"What are you talking about, James, what's this?" Keith asked.

"Read it."

Keith opened the file and read through the first page of the file. "This report was confidential. Where did you get this?"

"A friend of mine works in records. I pulled some

strings. Apparently Hunter and his family paid quite a bit to have the report buried. There was never any publicity on it. The whole thing was handled completely under the table. His attorneys were very thorough but not thorough enough."

Keith continued to scan the file. "The allegation was withdrawn and the charges dropped." Keith closed the file and handed it back to James.

James, obviously refusing to take it, persisted. "Don't you see. It's right there in black and white. Hunter paid her off."

"It's inadmissible, not to mention illegal. I shouldn't even be looking at this."

James finally took the file from Keith. "But it goes to intent and predisposition. If he did it once he'd do it again."

"James—"

"He has a history of harassing women. It's all right there in the report."

"We can't use this. The case was dropped."

"What if we get the woman to refile?"

"Statute of limitations. Double indemnity. There's no case, drop it." Keith turned to walk back over to the front door.

"Wait, what about this? Everything's right here in black and white. You have to listen to reason. I can make this happen. Hunter will go down."

Keith took the photos and receipts and glanced over them quietly. "Yeah, I heard about these. My suggestion to you, leave it alone, James. There's nothing there."

"Look, Keith, yes, I've already spoken to your mother and father. They're on the fence at this point, that's why I wanted to talk to you myself. You're a man of principle and action. If we work together we can make this thing happen. I'll have a friend of mine—"

Keith continued walking to the front door. As he opened it James hurried to get in front of him. "I'll have a friend of mine dig for more dirt. We'll find something."

James stepped back as Keith moved forward. "What kind of friend digs for dirt for a living?"

"He's an associate really."

Keith nodded. "This associate wouldn't happen to work for the opponent as well, would he? I mean if he'd go as far as getting information on Michael Hunter, then getting information on Blake Washington would be a piece of cake."

"It's not like that," James insisted.

"Then tell me what it's like. Tell me about the information leak in the mayor's office. Tell me about messages being left for you by Truman." Keith waited patiently.

James was speechless as Keith's piercing eyes burned into him. "Look, I'm trying to help here. Obviously you'd rather I stay out of it. Fine, it's on you," he huffed angrily, turned, and marched down the steps.

Prudence called her parents' home. Something had to be done about James. As far as she was concerned he had lost his mind and needed serious help. When the store bell rang for closing, she was the first person out of the building. She drove directly to her parents' home through a horde of preholiday traffic.

"So you already know about this?" she asked.

"Yes," Marian said. "We've suspected James for some time. We just weren't sure how deeply involved he was and with whom."

"Truman." Prudence elaborated on the conversation she'd had with James earlier and the one she'd had with him in her father's office weeks ago, including Truman's call.

"This is more troubling than we even expected," Blake said. "If indeed James is with Truman, there may not be a way of getting him the help he needs. I'm afraid he's in too deep."

"Keith called and told me about your plans. Do you think it will work?"

"Once Truman gets the download from James, the possibility that he might manipulate Blake would be too tempting. It's the only foreseeable solution."

"What will happen to James afterward?"

"Keith has a friend in the FBI. If he agrees to testify, he'll be protected."

Prudence left, feeling solemn, anxious, and apprehensive. She pitied James but was also furious with him. His gambling and stupidity had sunk to a new low, even for him. But with him backed into a corner, she couldn't even conceive of what he'd do next.

James crept around the corner and spotted the car. He snuck up beside it, looked around, then took the hammer and smashed the taillights and removed the license plate. When he was done he looked around again and smiled. One down.

Twenty minutes later he repeated the actions with a second car. Afterward he tossed the second license into his backseat and drove away.

The evening had been perfect. They dined on the waterfront, eating lobster and drinking champagne. The hired limo drove them back to Michael's home off City Avenue. As soon as the driver turned into the driveway she smiled, remembering the first time she'd been there.

They got out of the car. She was dressed in an elegant evening gown, and he in an Armani tuxedo. They were the perfect pair, straight from the fashion pages of Milan, Paris, and New York. Prudence waited as Michael unlocked the door and held it open for her. She entered expecting to find a reasonable facsimile of Michael's Austin home, but instead found a classic-styled home with antiques and traditional furniture.

"You are a man of many surprises, Michael Hunter:

dinner, dancing, the limo, everything was absolutely perfect."

"I'm delighted that you enjoyed yourself. Although I can't take full credit for the limo. That was Luther's doing. Someone smashed and broke my taillights, then stole my license plate. Had we taken my car tonight we'd have been pulled over."

"Kids," Prudence said, knowing the pranks of teenagers.

"No problem, I'll take care of it tomorrow. But for tonight that limo seemed perfect."

Just then a cat circled his legs, then jumped into his arms purring for attention. Michael caught her easily, stroked her fur a few seconds before she leaped from his arms.

Prudence watched as the cinnamon-colored tabby slowly, purposefully swished away. "And who was that?"

"That was Spice, although she has yet to answer to that, or any other name for that matter. She adopted me a few years ago. She just showed up on my doorstep in Austin one day and has been by my side ever since. She stays with my neighbor's kids when I'm away. They spoil her rotten."

Prudence nodded and raised her brow with interest. She slowly moved to circle, then stand in front of him. She looked up into his soft brown eyes. "Is there any other female in your life that I should know about?"

Michael instantly wrapped his arms around her waist. "Well, there's this woman in Texas that I'm rather fond of, and another in New Mexico, oh, and one more in Arizona, then there's California, Nevada, Massachusetts, and—"

Prudence spun around to walk away, but Michael caught her arm as she turned away and pulled her back into his arms.

"Wait, I'm not finished yet. And finally there's a beautiful, exciting, sexy, hot-tempered woman in Pennsylvania"—he leaned in and kissed her neck—"who has captured my heart." He continued to nibble her neck.

"Really?" she said, giggling at his ticklish nibbles.

He reached up and gently stroked the smooth plane of her face. "Really," he assured her. "You are so special to me."

"I bet you say that to all the girls," she joked.

Michael tipped her face up to his. His eyes sparkled with the brightness of new love. "Only you, Prudence, only you."

Overwhelmed with happiness, Prudence reached out to him, rendered speechless by his honesty. She kissed him gently, lovingly, with all the passion she felt inside.

Tenderly he wrapped his arms around her body and pulled her closer. "I've waited a lifetime for you."

"I don't know what to say."

"Yes, you do."

"Yes, I do. I love you, Michael."

He smiled, loving the sound of those words. "Thank you. I've been waiting for you to say those words. I love you too, Prudence Washington."

The telephone rang just as he leaned in to kiss her again. Michael looked at his watch. It was well past two in the morning. "It's probably my parents calling to say happy New Year. I'll be right back. Remember where we were." He kissed her again briefly.

Prudence nodded happily as he walked into the living room and picked up the phone. She heard him talking calmly, and then his voice rose slightly. She walked to the living room doorway just as he hung up. He turned to her, his face visibly shaken. She looked at Michael questioningly. "Is everything okay in Texas?"

"That was Luther. Rick was stopped for a traffic violation, then detained."

"Detained, detained for what, what did he do?" she asked half jokingly, knowing of Rick's reputation all too well, particularly after the birthday party he had sponsored for Michael.

"I don't know yet. Luther just said that apparently he was detained by the police on unrelated charges."

Prudence's heart skipped a beat. Surely James hadn't

done anything without consulting her first. "Unrelated charges, what does that mean?" she asked cautiously.

Michael picked up the phone and began dialing. "I don't know, but I intend to find out."

"Who are you calling?" she asked.

"Rick."

Prudence nodded. "I'm gonna get something to drink. Where's the kitchen?" she asked. Michael pointed to the rear of the house. She nodded and disappeared around the corner and down the hall. Prudence turned the kitchen lights on and walked to the refrigerator. But instead of getting something to drink she just stood at the double doors and held on to the handles. There was no way anyone would do anything without talking to her first, right?

That's how Michael found her when he walked into the kitchen. "Why didn't you tell me about your friend?"

Prudence took a deep breath and turned to him. She saw an expression on his face that she didn't recognize. He was furious. "What?"

"Your friend, why didn't you tell me about your friend?"

"What are you talking about? What friend?"

"You know exactly what I'm talking about, your friend, your father's assistant, the one that was mugged a few weeks ago."

"James, what about him?" she asked curiously.

"Rick was stopped on a traffic violation apparently because someone had broken his taillights and stolen his license plate."

"What?" The shock of the coincidence registered on her face. "Why?"

"Good question. I don't even know the man. Apparently afterward Rick was detained and questioned regarding harassing phone calls to you. Apparently someone, on your behalf, accused him of being your harasser. James Pruet's name came up. Luther also mentioned an attorney by the name of Keith Washington."

"What!" she said, then remembered her earlier conversation with James and the accusations he had made. "Michael, it's a misunderstanding. My brother had nothing to do with Rick Renault."

"Did you tell Pruet that you suspected Rick and have your brother go after him?"

Prudence looked away. "No, no, of course not. The only thing I did was mention to James that Rick was at the store right after one of the calls came in, that's all."

"So were a few thousand other people. Apparently, that was enough for him. Why Rick?"

"The caller has a southern accent."

"So does half the country, so do I when I want to." He paused and stepped back away from the counter. "Do you think that I have something to do with this also? Is that why my car was trashed also?"

"No, of course not. I didn't say that."

"But it's a possibility for you, isn't it?"

"Michael." She reached out to him, but he pulled away.

"No, tell me, honestly, it's a possibility, isn't it?" he asked.

"This is ridiculous, what am I supposed to believe?"

"Exactly, what am I supposed to believe, Prudence?"

An uncomfortable silence surrounded them as Spice came into the kitchen. She snubbed Prudence, then curled herself between Michael's legs, purred several times, and walked out again.

"Come on, I'll take you home." He walked away silently.

Prudence stayed in the kitchen until she heard the front door open. She slowly walked to the foyer.

"Michael," she said, seeing him about to leave.

"I thought you knew that I could never hurt you," he said as he turned to her.

"I do. I do know."

"Then why?"

"Michael. I didn't do anything."

"Neither did Rick."

"How can you be so sure? How well do you really know

him? You know that he's after your job. How can you trust him?"

"How can you not trust me? Prudence, half the college football players in the country are after my job. That means nothing to me."

"It should."

"I can't believe you're actually saying this. I've known Rick for over ten years. He may be a player, and he's had his share of troubles, but he'd never stoop this low. He never professed to be anything other than what he is. He's certainly no saint, but then again neither am I. I have a past. We all do. This isn't Rick."

"But how do you know that?"

"Because I do, I know him, I trust him."

"I don't."

"Do you trust me?"

Prudence brushed by him and began walking toward the car. Speed repeated the question as he followed. "Do you trust me, Prudence?" She continued walking without a word. "Answer me. Do you trust me?"

She didn't answer, she couldn't for the flow of tears streaming down her face. She was too hurt.

Michael reached her before she got to the limo, and spun her around. Tears glistened in her eyes. "What are you running away from, the question or the answer?" She looked at him, then looked away. "I think I just got my answer, didn't I?"

He opened the door and she got in. They drove in silence.

Twenty minutes later Prudence watched Michael get back into his limo from her living room window. She looked down as he glanced up. Their eyes held a few seconds before he turned to get back into the limo. She watched as his red taillights disappeared from view. "Good luck on Sunday," she whispered.

Chapter 24

The breakup was harder on her than she had imagined, even harder than her breakup with Garrett. Unlike him, Michael had touched a part of her and reawakened the trust and love she had hidden away. Now, to question his integrity, she was no better than James with his deceit and lies.

As Prudence steered her car off the exit she spotted a small speeding blur cross the intersection in front of her. She recognized the flash of red and the license tag instantly. "What's he doing here?" She continued driving to her parents' home. Then she spotted James's car again.

It was parked two blocks from her parents' house. Prudence parked her car a few cars behind his. She got out and watched as James unfolded his long legs and got out of his red sports car. Dressed in a Knights leather jacket, sunglasses, and a baseball cap turned backward. "Why is he dressed like that?" Then it occurred to her. The blurred photo was of a man wearing the exact outfit.

She got out of her car and followed James the two blocks to her parents' home. She watched him look around, then open the side window and crawl into the house. As soon as he entered he went directly to her father's office. James was in there sitting in front of her father's laptop computer uploading information and speaking to someone on his cell phone. "Are you ready? Good, I'm sending the files now." He smiled, hung up, and pressed a key on the keyboard.

"It was you all along. You're the one taking information from the mayor's office. You slime, how could you?"

James looked up at Prudence, then back down as he completed a file upload and prepared for another. "Oh, please, don't be so dramatic. To answer your question, it was easy." He chuckled. "Blake is so trusting, I'm surprised everyone hasn't done it. And childish name-calling is so beneath you."

"Slime is the kindest name I could think of, considering what I could have said. You've worked with my father for over five years and now you decide to sell him out just like that?"

"You can say that I got a better offer. You have no idea what it's like not getting the respect due me. It was me, I put Blake in the mayor's office, I made him what he is today. All he did was stand around smiling and kissing babies. I did everything. He was nothing before me."

"You arrogant jerk. I suppose his thirty-five years as an attorney was nothing. His twenty years as the city's prosecutor, ten as the city's district attorney, meant nothing. His spotless reputation with every political person on the East Coast, his personal relationship with the president, all were because of you? You seriously need to get a grip."

"Nothing in the last five years was done without me."

"What exactly did you do? He gave you a job when no one else would because of your gambling, and this is how you repay his generosity?"

"You should talk. You're right in the middle of this, so don't do that innocent thing. I don't buy it."

"Me? Don't you dare turn this around on me."

"McGee was actually leaning toward Camden before Blake put you and Speed together."

"What are you talking about? My father didn't put us together. Michael and I met by accident."

"There's no point in playing stupid. Grow up, Prudence, everything is political. You were the bait and Stud Speed latched on, hook, line, and sinker. And just like that"—he snapped his finger—"minds changed."

"What are you talking about?"

"A stadium."

"A stadium, what about the stadium?"

"As I said, McGee was leaning toward Camden for the location of the new Knights stadium. Everything was almost set, and then Speed met you." He highlighted and uploaded another set of files.

"What does my relationship with Michael have to do with where a stadium is located?"

"You keep Michael happy, Michael keeps McGee happy, and Blake pulls the strings and makes everyone happy. That's why it was imperative for you and Speed to part ways as soon as possible." He smiled broadly. "I tried everything. Any other woman would have been suspicious of the phone calls, but not you."

"It was you."

"Of course it was me. You finally got the hint and got that idiot Garrett out of your life. Then just as you and I are ready to get back together, you dump me again for some football player. First Garrett, now Speed. I am sick of being dumped."

"You are truly psychotic."

"And you are truly naïve," he said calmly. "Tell Blake to consider this my resignation. He's finished in this town anyway after this comes out."

"What are you talking about?"

"Your father's affair with a married woman," he said pointedly.

Prudence started laughing. He'd taken the bait. "His affair," she said, rather than asked.

"Yes," James said, arrogantly gleeful. "The holier-than-thou Mayor Blake Washington is having an affair. As a matter of fact I just read the last e-mail entry. He's taken his married lover to the shore for New Year's." He smiled and chuckled buoyantly. "Truman's gonna love this as soon as he opens it."

"You are such an idiot."

"Good, that's right, keep calling names. How about adulterer?" James laughed openly.

"I have a better one, how about Nairam?" she said as James stopped laughing. "Yes, that's right, I already know about Nairam, my father's lover. He's been with her for years."

James smiled and shrugged. "Now everybody's gonna know about her."

"They already do, idiot. Nairam is Marian, his wife, my mother, Marian Washington."

The color instantly drained from his face. "You're lying to protect him. Marian is—"

"Nairam spelled backward. They've been writing letters to each other for years. Now they write to each other online."

Suddenly his attention was distracted as the laptop beeped twice. James looked down at the laptop's screen. It was completely blank. "What the—" he muttered as he pushed the Escape key, then the Control, Alt, Delete keys. "What's going on? What did you do?" He immediately tried to retrieve the files he had just sent to Truman. Frustration raged and his brow sweated as his eyes looked panicked. It was too late, the files were locked in cyberspace on their way to Truman's personal computer.

"What was that?" he stuttered nervously. "What happened?"

She smiled happily, delighted to finally hand him his comeuppance. "The files you just uploaded to your friend, Truman, are now uploading his entire system of files to an office in Washington, D.C. I don't think your friend is going to be very happy with you when he realizes that the files you sent him self-destructed but not before forwarding everything on the receiver system to the FBI."

"Oh my God. Do you have any idea what you just did?" He began pushing buttons desperately.

"I didn't do anything. You did."

"You set me up," James yelled.

"You set yourself up."

"Truman . . ." James muttered, shaking his head at the thought of Truman's anger upon receiving the files and watching his computer crash.

". . . Is going to be very upset with you, I'd imagine," Prudence said. "If I were you I'd talk to my brother. Keith has a friend at the FBI. They might be very interested in what you know about Truman in exchange for their protection."

She watched as James hurried out.

The satisfaction of retribution for his harassing phone calls, obnoxious gifts, and cowardly stupidity was even more satisfying and thrilling than she had anticipated. But unfortunately after everything James had done, it was her own suspicions and mistrust that hurt her most.

Chapter 25

Prudence, Valerie, and Whitney sat in Prudence's living room watching television and munching on donuts, Danishes, bagels and cream cheese, and assorted fruits while sipping mimosas and banana daiquiris. There was nothing like girlfriends when it came to commiserating a broken love affair. So as soon as Prudence broke the bad news to Valerie and Whitney, they planned an immediate eat-in.

Having told her friends everything that had transpired, including her unexpected visit from James and his new troubles, she sat with the two of them, discussing the recent events.

"Drew and a few of his DEA friends doctored some of my Dad's e-mails and embedded a nasty little virus. Whoever downloads will get a nasty little surprise. Besides a tracking device, there's also a nice little encryption program that deciphers and forwards everything on the host system to a third terminal, in this case in Washington, D.C."

"I don't believe that Truman's finally gonna be indicted," Valerie said.

"I can't believe James is hanging with Truman again," Whitney said. "What was he thinking?"

"I still don't get it. Other than jealousy, why would James go after Michael and Rick? He doesn't even know them," Prudence said. "They have absolutely nothing in common."

"Sure they do—football," Valerie said as both Whitney

and Prudence followed her lead and turned to the television. Michael's picture covered the screen. "It's obvious, the answer is football. Both Michael and Rick play football, Truman's a bookie, and James is a gambler."

Still furious, Prudence hadn't spoken to Michael since the day before. So, why she'd decided to watch him on television now was completely beyond her. All she knew was that she needed to see him, even if it meant on the playing field on a twenty-seven-inch screen.

Whitney shook her head as she watched the replay. Michael threw the ball onto the sidelines, then went down like a ton of bricks beneath three linebackers. "Ouch," Valerie said, seeing the replay again, this time in slow motion. "He needs to scramble out of that pocket; they're killing him out there."

"You're right, Truman's a bookie and gamblers flock to him like bees to honey, particularly during the play-offs," Whitney said, wincing after the slow-motion replay.

"That would explain James's connection, but what about Rick and Michael?" Prudence said.

"Throwing a game?" Valerie asked.

"No," Prudence said with certainty. "Not Rick and definitely not Michael; they love the game too much."

"I agree," Whitney said.

"Maybe James wanted to manipulate the odds," Valerie said as Whitney and Prudence looked at her, confused. "If James bet on football, and he had a way of indirectly manipulating the odds in his favor by throwing suspicion on Michael or Rick and getting them distracted, that would definitely improve his chances of winning, right?" All three women nodded in agreement.

"So by distracting Michael and Rick, the quarterbacks, he would actually affect their performance on the field and nobody would really know except for him," Prudence said.

"Makes sense, and I can definitely see James doing it.

He can be pretty desperate when it comes to his gambling," Whitney reasoned.

"But what about Truman, what's his deal?" Valerie asked.

"Maybe he was putting James up to it," Prudence said.

The three women turned back to the television as Prudence shut the mute off. Boisterous cheering from the stadium crowd blasted through the speakers as Michael huddled with the other players and the sports announcers began their commentary. As the huddle broke, Prudence focused in on Michael watching his every movement.

Michael yelled out a few numbers and seconds later men scrambled around the field, while others ran nonstop toward the end zone. He motioned for a man to cut to the left, but shook his head and looked to the opposite side. He scrambled as men fell at his feet all around him. Prudence held her breath as soon as she saw the wayward beast run through the scattered linemen. His target was certain. "Michael," she whispered as if he could hear her.

Prudence sat up as he went down. The *crack* of the helmet sent an icy chill down her spine. A collective "ah" arose from the packed stadium as spectators stood on their feet. He remained down. "That looked really bad," Whitney said as she and Valerie glanced at each other, then to their friend.

"He's down for too long," Prudence muttered as she watched several team members gathering around while the cameraman focused in on Rick Renault warming up his arm. The medical team hurried onto the field as Michael lay completely still. Valerie and Whitney inched closer to Prudence's side and held her gently.

The pain of the slow-motion-replayed hit sent her heart tumbling in a free fall. The air around her stilled and her breathing became labored. This wasn't happening. The three woman sat on the sofa, their eyes glued to the television screen, each heartbroken by the sight of Michael still lying on the field.

The announcers detailed the hit and surmised that it was just a tragic incident. After yet another slow-motion replay they showed Michael's stats from the day's game. Surprisingly, he had been relatively free from serious injury since he started playing the game over ten years ago.

The broadcasters announced a commercial break and the three relaxed for just a moment. Silence surrounded them, and then suddenly they jumped at the unexpected sound that sent Prudence scrambling for the ringing phone. "Hello?" she said anxiously.

"Prudence, did you—" Keith asked.

"Yeah, I saw it."

"Are you okay?"

"No."

"I'm on my way."

Keith opened his front door to leave just as James raised his hand to ring the doorbell. Keith continued through the doorway, pulling the door closed behind him. "I'm going out, James; whatever it is will have to wait."

"Keith, I need your help." The worried, wide-eyed fear in his eyes instantly got Keith's attention.

"I guess you uploaded a few files from my father's computer."

James didn't speak. He just looked away. Of course, Keith knew about it. What else did he expect? Keith reached into his wallet, pulled out a business card, and handed it to James. "My friend in Washington is expecting your call."

"I'm sorry, man," James said. Keith closed his door and kept going, leaving him standing on the porch.

Chapter 26

Prudence's hostility was bluntly evident. "If you've come to gloat or say I told you so, make it quick. I'm not in the mood for any of your extended, drawn-out, two-hour-long closing statements. Just get to the point and go." Her eyes burned with the sting of hurt, and she definitely wasn't in any mood to hear her brother's crap.

She and her two friends had tried for an hour to get information on Michael's condition, but to no avail. Apparently everyone in the city wanted to know what was going on, and the team's doctors weren't talking. The not knowing made it worse as speculation about his injury escalated from a temporary concussion to permanent paralysis.

After Rick took over in the last quarter and the team easily won, the city went wild for the win and panicked for information. The team closed ranks and not even a whisper was leaked to the press. It was a waiting game of patience and endurance, one that Prudence never played well. Worry had eaten away what little patience she had. But she tried desperately to hold on.

Keith had barely gotten through the door when she opened up on him. He smiled as he closed the door behind him and followed her into the living room. "That's not why I'm here."

She plopped down on the sofa, slammed her feet up on the coffee table, and waited for the lecture she knew was coming.

I told you so had been Keith's favorite song of delight since as far back as she could remember. Keith, the oldest, the perfect, the righteous, was always right about everyone, about everything, and every time. It never failed that he knew the outcome of nearly every situation days before anyone else.

She remembered the first time she had brought Garrett to meet him. Keith nearly bit his head off. He immediately told her to dump Garrett and save herself a lot of bitter pain and anguish. But no, she didn't listen, she did the exact opposite, and look where that got her—bitter pain and anguish and nearly bringing the entire family down in the process.

So now here he was again, and this time she intended to listen. She loved Michael with all her heart, but she couldn't hurt her family again. She knew Keith detested Michael; the fight in her living room proved that much. So, if he went as far as to physically object, she needed to at least listen to him and not her heart.

"I know why you're here, and you're too late. Michael and I had a fight on New Year's Day and the relationship's over. Happy?" she added sarcastically.

She grabbed the muted remote control she'd been flipping through when he knocked on the door and continued her search for sports news on Michael's injury.

"Everybody pays for what they do in life, good or bad, right or wrong, it doesn't matter. Rick Renault and Michael Hunter aren't choirboys, by any means. But then again, neither am I. As to whether they're the ones behind harassing you, I doubt it seriously."

"It was James. He was jealous."

"I figured as much. He just stopped by. I gave him my FBI friend's card."

Prudence looked up at Keith for the first time since he had arrived. "So what are you saying, you approve of me being with Michael?"

"I never disapproved."

"You nearly killed each other about a month ago."

"The fight wasn't because I disapproved of him. I assumed that there was someone in here that didn't belong. If I disapproved of him, there'd be no question of it, you'd know."

"Like with Garrett."

"Exactly like with Garrett."

"So why did you and James have Rick detained by the police?"

"The whole thing never made sense to me. I got a visit from James two days ago. He seemed incredibly anxious to bring Michael and Rick down."

"So he was the one that had Rick detained by the police."

"Yes."

"And you had him released."

"Yes."

Keith's cell phone rang, interrupting their conversation. He opened it and answered. Prudence listened to his side of the conversation and gathered that it was someone he knew and that it was important. A few moments later he hung up. "Let's go."

"Where?"

"To the hospital."

"Michael?" she questioned.

"Yeah. That was Rick. Michael's conscious and asking for you."

Prudence hurriedly gathered her coat and purse. On the way out she locked her door, then turned to Keith as the oddity of the last few minutes dawned on her. "Wait a minute, Rick Renault has your cell number? How?"

"I did say that neither he nor I were choirboys."

"You want to elaborate on that remark?"

"He and I have friends in common. We've bumped into each other from time to time."

"I bet," she said.

The drive to the hospital was quick with Keith at the wheel. They arrived in less than fifteen minutes. Keith went to the front desk and asked to see a particular doctor. The receptionist sent them to the fifth-floor office.

As soon as the elevator doors opened, Prudence noticed an abundance of overly huge men walking around on the floor. It occurred to her suddenly that they weren't going to any doctor's office, they were going to Michael's hospital room.

Several men she recognized greeted her as they passed. She saw McGee, the owner, and Coach Hawkins standing at the desk, each talking on the phone facing opposite directions. Luther appeared out of nowhere as usual. "Prudence," he called out as they approached the information desk. "Prudence. We were expecting you earlier." He softened his tone as he continued. "I was just about to make an announcement to the public. Would you like to come along?"

Prudence opened her mouth to speak, but when she spotted Rick down the hall coming toward them, her voice left her.

"She'll pass," Keith said, sending Luther hurrying in the opposite direction. Rick addressed Keith first. The two men shook hands and spoke easily. "Hello, Prudence," Rick said finally.

"Hi, Rick. I'm sorry about the trouble."

He nodded. "Michael's down the hall. He's waiting for you."

"Thanks." She looked at Keith.

He nodded. "I'll wait for you here."

Prudence nodded, turned, and walked down the hall to the room she saw Rick come out. She knocked quietly, opened the door, then entered.

Michael was sitting up in bed talking on the phone. He looked up on seeing her enter. "I'll call you back." He hung up and smiled as she approached.

"Is this your way of getting my attention?" Prudence asked.

"It's all I could think of. Did it work?"

"Yeah, you got my attention."

"Good."

"How are you feeling?" she asked, looking at the two hanging plastic IV bags and the tube attached to a vein in his arm.

"Other than the army of sledgehammers in my head, the aches and pains, and the concussion, I'm feeling great."

"Concussion?"

"Don't worry, it's only temporary. I've had one before. Unfortunately it comes with my chosen profession. I get hit once in a while."

"Yeah, I saw." She smiled anxiously. "Over and over again, then several times more, then in slow motion with the commentator's illustrated diagrams and even backward."

"I hear it was the hit of the day," he joked. "You gotta love those replay guys."

Prudence didn't smile, she just nodded. "There was a yellow flag on the play, late hit."

Michael smiled and nodded at her newfound insight into football.

"Maybe you need to consider scrambling out of the pocket more."

Taken off guard by her sudden football familiarity, Michael laughed, then winced. "Okay, thanks, I'll have to consider that next time." Being the league's leader in scrambling yardage, he just smiled and nodded agreeably.

"Good," she said as she crossed the room, coming closer to the side of the bed. She took his hand as he reached up to her. "You really had me worried," she said in all seriousness.

"I'm fine."

"Michael," she began. "I know you're probably still angry about what happened with Rick, and I'm sorry about that. I had no idea anything like that was going to happen. Keith told me that James—"

"I don't want to talk about that," he said.

"We need to talk about it, it's important."

"Rick's fine," he said.

"I know. He's out in the hall talking to my brother." She half laughed at the odd coupling.

"You sound surprised."

"I am. Apparently they know each other well."

"Rick told me that Keith took care of everything."

"Not everything. You invited me into your heart, and all I gave you was pain in return, because I'm too afraid to let go of my hurt and mistrust. But when I saw you go down like that, I thought I was going to die. I couldn't breathe."

"Prudence, love isn't something you turn on and off. It's something that you work at every day. It's hard sometimes, but I hear it gets better."

"I hope so."

"I missed you," he said softly.

"I missed you too."

They embraced, letting the emotions of the last few days wash over them like water on sand.

Prudence leaned back. "Okay, when you get out of this bed, we have some making up to do."

"Come here." He beckoned for her to move closer. She did. "Closer," he said. She moved even closer. They kissed as she lay by his side.

Epilogue

Anticipation swelled as seconds ticked from the clock, eroding the hopes and dreams of nearly three hundred million people as they watched with bated breath from all parts of the world. Like a spinning rocket, the football had sailed nearly sixty yards and had been plucked from the air and planted on the three-yard line.

The huddle broke, the cadence calls were made, and the play began. As if in slow motion, the line of scrimmage surged forward, sending numerous players in scramble mode. Michael tucked the ball beneath his arm and in tunnel-eyed vision ran directly forward, then leaped into the air, propelling his body the length needed to cross the invisible line separating the field from the end zone. A collective gasp was heard as he stretched his body flat and sailed.

Prudence, deciding at the last minute to attend, placed her hand over her mouth and waited eagerly for the signal. Seconds later it came. *Touchdown.* The euphoric moment that millions of people had waited for had come. The Philadelphia Knights had won the Super Bowl.

Michael, now at the bottom of the pile, had managed to free himself as the crowd went wild and poured down onto the field. Security did their best to stave off the rampaged onslaught of fans, but their efforts were futile. The Knights had won the Super Bowl and everyone wanted to celebrate.

In full running mode and chased by a detail of reporters and fans, Michael headed straight for the fifty-yard line. As he approached, Luther hurried to his side. Taking his helmet off, Michael tossed it to Luther, who in turn handed him a team cap. Getting a running start, Michael jumped up into the stadium seats, finding Prudence in the front row. He scrambled over the barricade to stand by Prudence's side.

In vibrant brilliance cameras clicked and flashed, nearly blinding him as he knelt down and took her hand. Prudence, teary from the spectacular game ending, opened her mouth as he took a small velvet box from a pocket within the cap and opened it to her. Deafened by the onslaught of fans and reporters, she barely heard his question.

"Will you marry me?" he mouthed a second time. In hushed silence the crowd waited for her answer.

Prudence looked around anxiously. The most private of moments was about to be witnessed by millions of people. She looked down at Michael, still on bended knee. The smile in his eyes gave her the peace she had so desperately sought all her life.

Suddenly she didn't care that the world was watching. All she cared about was that Michael was at her side and would be for the rest of her life. "Yes, I will," she agreed, nodding her head animatedly.

Michael stood and wrapped his arms around her, spinning her around several times. The dizzying spell of being wrapped in his love was exhilarating like no other. As he stopped and held her close they looked up to the massive screens at either end of the field. They waved at the fans in unison. A rousing cheer of acceptance shook the stadium.

It was a glorious day.

Dear Reader,

Something new and different is always thrilling, so I hope you enjoyed reading the wild and wonderfully exciting romance of Prudence Washington and Michael "Speed" Hunter. I had a great time researching and writing this book, and I hope it shows on each page. It's a very different type of story with very different characters. Some say that writing a romance novel with sports is taboo. But I think anything can be written and enjoyed as long as the romance is engaging and the characters are strong. So I hope you'll agree that Prudence and Speed are perfect together and their love will last a lifetime.

Now, for those Mamma Lou fans and those making bets along with the Evans/Gates characters, look for *The Art of Love* coming your way soon. It's Kennedy Evans's story and it's filled with dozens of surprises, a touch of suspense and enough romance to singe you fingers. Believe me when I say you ain't seen nothing yet. Also, for those of you who wrote me letters and sent e-mails (over a hundred and counting) regarding Roberto Santos's story from *Reflections of You*, I heard you loud and clear. Yes, Roberto's story is also coming very soon.

Lastly and most importantly, I am incredibly thankful for your continued support, well wishes, and dedication to my work. Since my very first BET novel, *Priceless Gift*, in March 2002, I have been blessed with so many wonderful new friends. Reading your heartfelt letters and e-mails gives me the encouragement to try new things and test new limits. I am genuinely touched by your comments. And each book helps raise my writing level, giving you more excitement, suspense, intrigue, and, of course, romance. I try my best to answer each and every letter as soon as possible. So please feel free to write and let me know what you think. I always enjoy hearing from readers. Please send your comments to conorfleet@aol.com or Celeste O. Norfleet, P.O. Box 7346, Woodbridge, VA 22195-7346. Don't forget to check out my website at http://www.celesteonorfleet.com.

Best wishes,

Celeste O. Norfleet